VISE MANOR

VISE MANOR

DANIEL VERASTIQUI

CHANNEL 8 PRESS
Austin, Texas

Second Edition, April 2025

ISBN: 978-1-967847-12-9

danielverastiqui.com

Cover design by RavenFire Studios

"To build without understanding is not invention
—it is revolution by accident."

- From The Reflections of Noetica, Volume VII

GUEST LIST

Adelai Vaught
ADELAI ASSOCIATES

Carter Price
DYALOGUED

Elias Shaw
CORTICAL LUX

Lucas Cotton
MESH FOUNDATION

Reno Cardenas
PLOMO PESADO

Robert Hargreaves
HARGREAVES GROUP

Stanton Blumenfield
FUTUROLOGIST

Wade Vunak
NIXLE CHRONOS

ONE

The doorman brought the mail up a little after 3:00 p.m.

Adelai heard the elevator ding from the leather couch in the living room. She'd been there for the last hour, staring at the tall windows, watching a world turned beige by the thin blinds. The last of the birds were migrating through the city; they stopped to rest on the many perches the high buildings provided. Adelai knew the feeling. She too had sought out warmth and safety in her penthouse perch high above the city streets.

The stereo in the corner played classical music at an ambient volume; only during the swell of some passionate symphony could she hear the individual strings and horns. They mixed nicely with the crackling of the fireplace, providing just enough white noise to keep the dead silence at bay, but not so much that she couldn't hear the conversation happening down the hall in the foyer.

"Afternoon, ma'am."

Though a small army of doormen worked in Eames Tower, only a handful were authorized to come up to the penthouse. It was either Hector, Raymond, or Harold—three men with impeccable records who, each in their own time, had been personally interviewed by Adelai.

"Good afternoon, Harold. How are you today?"

The silky voice that greeted the doorman belonged to Simone, and Adelai imagined her standing primly with her hands folded and smile beaming.

"It's quite the haul today, Mrs. Vaught. An entire box of mail and half a dozen packages. All on the small side, thankfully."

"Oh, yes. I hope it wasn't too much trouble carrying them up here."

Adelai smiled as she fingered the rim of her wine glass. She had no intention of getting up and was more than happy to sit and listen to Simone speak. It was one of her wife's better qualities, the way the words flowed from her mouth like a swarm of butterflies—dazzling the eyes with their colors and comforting the soul with the sound of their gentle flapping.

"No trouble at all, ma'am. Happy to do it. I'll just stack them here on the table."

"That'd be great, thank you. How're the grandchildren? Have they picked out their Halloween costumes yet?"

So polite. So genuinely charismatic.

Harold was ostensibly their employee, and yet Simone went out of her way to be interested in him—and not just to *pretend* to be interested, but to actually remember that he had six grandchildren from both a son and a daughter. If pressed, Simone could probably even rattle off their names.

Adelai got up and nudged aside the red heels she'd kicked off earlier. She padded along the thin carpet to the tall windows and spied a massive, winged creature on a ledge across the street. It was the color of wet evercrete and looked like a gargoyle had come to life.

Maybe it was the wine.

"…a ghost, and Maya wants to be a caterpillar this year."

Simone's effortless laughter sounded like kisses bubbling up from a pool of love.

Adelai chuckled at herself and looked down at her glass. She didn't count her drinks—a real woman never did—but if she had to guess, the number that came to mind was four, maybe five. And really, she didn't know why she'd had so much. It was just a cheap cabernet she'd picked up at a bodega a block over. Hand to God, the label said it was bottled in 2020. She had shampoo that had been around longer.

"That sounds delightful. You'll have to show me pictures."

She wasn't just blowing smoke. Even if Halloween came and went and Harold forgot, Simone would seek him out and make him show her his phone. Regardless of how cute the children were, she would offer glowing praise. Harold, in turn, would feel better about himself, and somewhere in the back of his mind, a synapse would solidify into a single thought: *I feel better about myself when I'm around Simone.*

Such was Simone's gift.

The Eames Tower swayed. It did that sometimes. It certainly wasn't Adelai feeling the effects of the alcohol. After all, she'd only had three, maybe four drinks, and really it was uncouth to count.

"Is there anything else I can do for you two?"

"No, thank you though." Perhaps Simone cast a glance down the hallway to see if Adelai was in view. "Adelai is tied up with work at the moment, but we'll stop by and visit when we head out for dinner later."

"I will look forward to it."

Adelai groaned and put a hand on the cold glass. It was true they had dinner reservations at some cramped restaurant nearby, one of those trendy places where the plates were small and the portions were smaller, but she had no desire to go. She'd left work early eager to come home and crawl into a bottle of wine and had done so without considering what the rest of the evening might bring. Perhaps Simone was simply keeping up appearances with Harold. She likely knew that after a few drinks, Adelai wouldn't feel like going anywhere except to bed.

They traded farewells.

A button chimed.

The elevator dinged.

Soon, the clacking of Simone's Jimmy Choo heels echoed down the long hallway.

She always wore her dress shoes when she was working, even if she were doing so from home. She entered the room untucking a white blouse from her red skirt. They had celebrated her sixtieth birthday over the summer, but to Adelai, she didn't look a day over thirty-five. Simone had a youthful face with clear skin and only the smallest of wrinkles around her eyes. Small rubies hung like suspended drops of rain from her ears, and she wore her hair in a high and tight ponytail.

She looked the very picture of business casual, as ready to meet Harold the doorman as Harold the President.

Adelai, on the other hand, wasn't even wearing underwear under her silk robe.

Simone sat down on the couch and placed a rectangular black box on the table.

"What…" Some foul noise escaped Adelai's mouth. She cleared her throat and tried again. "What is that?"

"No idea," said Simone, folding her hands, "but it's addressed to you. Want me to open it?"

"Was it hand-delivered? It doesn't look like a shipping box." She narrowed her eyes, observed the discreet lid and blood-red ribbon wrapped around it. The bow on top would never have made it through the mail intact.

"I don't see any stamps," said Simone.

Adelai waved a hand. "Go ahead. Maybe it's another bottle of wine." She gave a slight groan and fell into a plush side chair, crossing one leg over the other.

Simone appraised the box as if examining an ancient artifact. She ran her fingers over the edges, and having felt the material, brought them to her nose.

"A little like crushed roses," she remarked.

"How very posh." Adelai leaned her head back on the chair and let her eyes take the ceiling out of focus. The faux wood blurred into a grayish fog. She closed her eyes and listened to the sounds of a ribbon coming free, a lid lifting, and a box sucking in air. Something soft touched the coffee table.

"Mother-fuck-me."

Adelai laughed and sat up. Simone's eyes were wide; pale brown dots sat alone in seas of white. The rim of the box obscured its contents, and when she asked what was in it, Simone simply pushed the box across the coffee table with an outstretched finger.

Adelai blinked. Blinked again.

It was a hand—a woman's hand, by the shape of it—with long slender fingers ending in sculpted but unpainted nails. The forearm to which it was attached extended for several inches before ending abruptly in a clean—both in smoothness and lack of gore—cut. The limb sat on a bed of black velvet, and if Adelai hadn't seen Simone place the box on the table, she would have sworn someone was beneath the glass sticking their hand up through a hole in the bottom.

The skin was pure alabaster.

Adelai reached for her wine glass and drained it.

"Is this for my vagina or yours?"

Simone shook her head. "What?"

"It's obviously one of those fisting hands you see online all the time, so I want to know whether you bought it for me or yourself."

"I didn't order this," said Simone. "And I really don't think it's a sex toy, Addy."

"Maybe I'm wrong. I've had a couple glasses."

Simone scooted closer on the couch. "If it were meant to go inside you, it'd be made of some kind of plastic. This looks too realistic."

"Maybe it's a real human hand."

"Yeah, sure. Look, you can see little hairs on the forearm."

Adelai squinted but saw nothing.

"I'm going to touch it."

"You will not," said Adelai.

Simone reached her hand out anyway and stroked the top of the limb. Pale fingers stirred at her touch.

Adelai yelped.

Somehow, the detached limb had sensed her.

"Calm down." Simone rotated the box until the hand was facing her. She slipped her own fingers underneath, as if she were going to bring the back of the hand to her lips for a kiss. In response, the limb moved again, curling around Simone's fingers with all the care of a lifelong lover. When Simone removed her hand, she was holding a small slip of paper the size of a business card.

"What does it feel like?"

Simone looked up from the card as if she hadn't heard the question.

"It's… soft… and warm. It feels as real as your hand." Her eyes drifted back to the card. "This is an invitation."

"Read it."

"*You are cordially invited to dinner and a demonstration at the home of Winston Vise, founder of Vise Robotics, on the night of October 22, 2021. Cocktails at 5:00 p.m. Dinner at 8:00 p.m. Please RSVP at your earliest convenience.* There's a phone number and an address upstate at the bottom." She turned the card over in her hand. On the back was another message scribbled in pen. Simone read, "*If this is what her hand is like, imagine the rest of her. Let's discuss. WV.*"

"Vise Robotics," repeated Adelai. "That means this is a synthetic hand."

"Looks like it. And far more realistic than anything we've seen at trade shows. But I've never heard of Winston Vise or his company before, have you?"

Adelai shook her head and drummed her fingers on the coffee table. She gasped when Simone grabbed her hand and placed it on the severed limb.

"See? Nothing spooky about it."

"Marvelous." It was the only word that came to mind. The hand felt *marvelously* real, so much like a human's that if Adelai drank enough wine and closed her eyes, she wouldn't be able to tell the difference. The fingers were delicately textured and radiated a subtle warmth. Adelai took hold of them as she had seen Simone do, and when the hand grasped hers, she sighed.

An effective demonstration.

An even better invitation.

Adelai looked up to find Simone smiling back at her.

"Falling in love over there?"

"It's not just holding my hand, Momo. It's… it's like it's caressing my fingers."

"You're *not* putting it in your vagina," Simone warned.

Adelai shrugged. A sudden chill ran up her spine, and she let go of the hand. "I'm getting more wine." She stood and retreated to the kitchen, leaving the hand and the memory of its touch behind. From the nearly empty wine fridge near the pantry, she pulled the other bottle of cabernet she'd bought at the bodega.

She couldn't get it open fast enough.

"What do you think about going?"

"I'm guessing *you* want to?"

Simone stood and joined Adelai in the kitchen. She leaned against a stool by the massive granite-topped island. "Yes, but how do you feel about it?"

"How do I feel? Hmm." Adelai put her palm to her chin and pressed for a moment. "Look, I know you're going to say it's the wine, but I…" She waved the cork in the direction of the living room. "Having that thing hold my hand made me feel something. It uh…" She took a quick sip. "I got a tingle."

"A tingle?"

"Not that kind of tingle, but… I don't know how to explain it. All I know is that it was like touching a real person. I've never felt that at a trade show with any of those plastic sex dolls."

"So we're going then?" Simone's teeth shone through her smile.

"I don't know. It's really short notice. Don't we already have plans for this Friday?"

"We'll cancel them," said Simone. She tilted her head. "Please?"

Adelai nodded. "Fine, but let's make sure Rayburn looks into Winston Vise. If he signs off, we'll go."

Simone gave her a quick hug. "I'm so excited." She turned and put her hands on the kitchen island, looked back at the living room where the black box lay open on the table. "And what about that thing?"

Adelai took a long sip. "Let's see what else it can do."

TWO

The air conditioner in the truck went out somewhere along the flyover to 610 South.

Robert Hargreaves had sensed something was wrong for a couple of weeks. Even though it was late October and the daily highs in Houston were no longer in the triple digits, his aging Dodge Ram had been struggling to keep the cab cool. It was especially noticeable after the glossy black truck had been sitting in the sun all day, baking as Robert practiced his pitching at Red's Indoor Driving Range. He'd had every intention of taking it into the shop, but with the year waning and the temperatures dropping, he'd decided to let it slide. Now, as the climate inside the Ram turned Saharan, he wished he'd paid more attention.

"Are you still there, Bob?"

The digitized voice of Frank Kagan rumbled through the truck's many speakers. Robert had forgotten his whisperer at home, and with the city's strict hands-free driving ordinances, he had no choice but to take his calls in surround sound.

"Yeah, I'm still here. I just…" He rapped his knuckle against the environmental panel, as if that had ever helped. "Looks like my AC just went out."

Kagan's laugh filled the cab.

"But I heard you," continued Robert, "and I guess I'm not sure what the *Vitra* in *Vitra Systems* is supposed to mean. Where'd you come up with that name?"

"I didn't. I hired one of those Zoomer marketing firms to workshop some names for me. That was the winner."

"And so what, it would be an umbrella company?"

"Yeah," said Kagan. "Just like how Vinestead International has a bunch of subsidiaries—Vinestead Pharma, Vinestead Synthetics—we'll do the same. Between the two of us, we've got a lot of little companies that could be combined into something bigger, something that could compete on an international scale."

Robert slowed to allow a speeding Audi supercar to cross in front of him into the HOV lane.

"Yeah, I don't know," he said. "It'd be a big shift."

"The world turns on big shifts."

"Is that what it does?"

A notification flashed on the dashboard—an incoming text message from Laura. She was probably wondering what was taking him so long to get home.

"Well, you think about it, Bob. We can talk more on the course tomorrow."

"Sounds good. I gotta get home and see Laura. She said we got some kind of mysterious package and she's scared to open it."

Kagan chuckled. "I can't imagine that woman's scared of anything."

"You're damn right. See you tomorrow, Frank."

"Goodbye."

Frank Kagan's photo cleared from the main display; an album cover featuring Randy Travis replaced it. The first bars of *Is It Still Over* began to play.

Robert tapped the voice control button on the steering wheel and asked his phone to read his last text message.

Message from Laura Hargreaves. Wide-eye emoji. Hurry up.

He considered replying that there was no such thing as *hurrying* in Houston traffic, but she knew that already. She was just excited about the package they'd received—a *mysterious* package, as she'd called it.

It made Robert think of a gift he'd been given a few years back. A week before his birthday, a handwritten letter had arrived in his mailbox. It told of a young boy who had gone missing in the late eighties and how the local police force in Wherever, USA had been unable to solve the mystery. The letter's author implored Robert to help, and a few days later, a box of clues arrived.

Of course, the whole thing was just a game, a mystery box service thought up by an entrepreneurial Agatha Christie descendent. But there had been a moment when Robert was unsure what was real and what was not. Those few seconds had made his heart race.

Now another box had come to their home, and though it wasn't anywhere near his birthday, it was only a week or two out from Halloween, which was cause enough for suspicion. Laura was always looking for new activities for them to share, new ways to fill the empty hours of retirement. He wouldn't have put it past her to order some kind of service, another mystery box for them to solve late at night with the lights dimmed low and the wine flowing.

Perhaps it was a Ouija board. Or a monkey's paw. Robert had never seen a monkey's paw in person. He imagined it smelled horrible.

The traffic held all the way down 610. Exiting was a nightmare, as he had to cross three lanes on the feeder road to take a right. The farther he got from the highway, the worse the roads became. He had to keep the truck under thirty-five miles per hour to keep the strain on the suspension to a minimum.

Robert could feel the sweat pooling under his arms as he pulled into the driveway. The large, wrought-iron gate swung forward at an agonizingly slow pace, until finally there was enough room to bring the Ram under the carport. He didn't waste any time getting inside, pausing only slightly to bask in the mercifully cool air drifting down from the ceiling. He dropped his wallet and keys on the side table near the door and walked into the kitchen.

"Laura?" Her name echoed in the quiet house.

"Upstairs!"

He followed her voice to the staircase at the front of the house and trudged up the wooden steps two at a time. On the second floor, he found Laura sitting on the long white couch that backed up to the rear windows. She wore frayed blue jeans, a fitted Houston Texans jersey, and a mischievous smile Robert hadn't seen in a long time.

"What's the fuss, babe?"

She pointed emphatically to the coffee table. Four oak pillars supported a heavy slab of polished evercrete that had been cleared of its usual picture books and coasters. Now it held only a rectangular black box, too small for boots and too big for shoes.

"This came for you earlier."

"What is it?"

"You have to open it."

Robert cocked his head. "You already opened it, didn't you?"

She shrugged. "Just come on." She patted the cushion next to her.

Suspicious but nonetheless curious, he sat down next to her on the couch and slid the box closer. He lifted the lid to find fine velvet cloth. Unwrapping the layers slowly, he revealed a perfect replica of a human hand.

For a moment, he simply stared at it.

"I… love it?"

Laura nudged him with her shoulder. "It's not from me. It came in the mail today, addressed specifically to *you*." She handed him a black business card. "This was under the hand."

"You touched the hand?"

"Yes, I handled the hand."

Robert took the card and muttered, "Well aren't you handy." He read the card twice. "Winston Vise sent this."

"Do you know him?"

"No, but I think Frank does. I might have traded cards with him a few years back. One of those east coast trust fund tech guys, if I remember correctly. I wasn't aware he'd started a synthetics company, but I'm not surprised. Someone would have to be almost recklessly confident and a little stupid to go up against Perion and Vinestead."

"Yes, but look…" Laura lifted the hand from its tiny coffin. "Hold out your arm." When he did, she laid the hand gently on his forearm.

He felt slender fingers press into his skin. There was warmth too, and at some level, he almost detected a pulse—synthetic blood racing through plastic veins.

Though he expected to be repulsed by a disembodied hand gripping his arm, he felt only comfort.

"Okay, that's pretty impressive."

"Now try this." Laura couldn't contain her giddiness. She gripped the arm with both hands, lifting it and replacing it against his cheek.

Again, the fingers readjusted to his body, conforming to the curve of his jaw. The thumb, he felt, rested just below his eye. It moved back and forth in tiny movements, as soft as the velvet it had arrived in, as warm as any touch Laura had ever given him.

Robert closed his eyes and enjoyed the sensation.

"How did you know it could do this?" he asked.

"What do you mean?"

He opened his eyes, smiled at her. "You weren't surprised at all when it held my arm. I feel like you were doing some experimentation before I got home, weren't you?"

"Well, I told you to hurry."

He pushed the hand away. Laura set it back down in the box.

"I'm surprised it doesn't creep you out." He leaned back in the sofa and crossed one leg over his knee. "I mean, who sends a severed limb through the mail like this?"

"Someone who wants to get your attention." She curled up next to him, drawing her legs onto the cushion. "I mean, think about it. *Dinner and a demonstration.* It's gotta be some kind of sales pitch. We wouldn't even be talking about it if he'd just sent you an email. Or if he just dropped a meeting invite on your calendar."

"I would've blocked him so fast."

Laura nodded. "Whoever this Winston Vise is, he knows how to get his foot in the door. He's like one of those old school traveling vacuum salesmen who throw dirt on your carpet the second you answer the door."

"More like a drug dealer."

"How so?"

"First one's free." Robert gestured to the box. "He sends a taste of what he has to offer and hopes whoever opens it gets hooked."

"Are you?"

He shrugged. "I don't think it matters. Investing in a synthetics company when the market space is dominated by two huge players doesn't make a lot of sense. Who cares if it can rub my cheek? Vinestead is turning out synthetics who can run prisons and fight wars. Perion's imprinting human minds in synthetic bodies. This is… a hand."

Laura tapped the card he was still holding. "Did you see there's a message written on the back?"

Robert turned the card over.

Written in white ink was the message *Count the numbers 1-2-3, knock three times, and then you'll see. -WV.*

"Knock three times? Where?"

Laura nodded at the hand.

"Have you tried this already?"

"I was waiting for you."

"Are you lying to me?"

"I would *never*."

Robert sat up and leaned over the coffee table. He cleared his throat.

"One, two, three." He still wasn't sure where he was supposed to knock, so he rapped his knuckles on the back of the hand three times.

On the third knock, the hand sprang to life, bolting upright like Thing Addams. Fingers became articulated legs; they jerked like a spider testing its web. Though the hand had no eyes or face, it turned to Robert and appraised him. Then, without warning, it leapt from the table.

Laura screamed as Robert pushed her out of the way. They were both up and off the couch before the hand could reorient itself. Once it was standing on the cushion again, it looked back and forth between them, as if deciding which human to kill first.

"Was it trying to attack you?"

Robert shook his head. "I don't know, but… maybe we just back away slowly."

Laura took a step. The hand focused on her.

"Stop," he told her. He waved an arm to get the hand's attention. "Okay, we're in a *Jurassic Park* scenario. It senses motion, so I'm gonna lead it away. When I do, you run down and get a trash bag. We just have to hope it can't tear its way out of it."

The hand crouched as if ready to pounce.

"Go!" Robert turned and ran back to the stairs. He heard the pattering of synthetic digits on the floor behind him. He was halfway down the stairs when he heard Laura scream, heard her heavy footsteps moving across the landing. Turning around, he saw he was no longer being followed.

Laura screamed again.

He scrambled back up the steps and caught a glimpse of her disappearing around the corner with the hand sprinting along the floor behind her. Then came a sudden thud, like the sound of a grown woman hitting the carpet in the game room.

"Robert!"

Her desperate protests sent his heart rate into the red, even as they died out and returned as laughter. He ran, rounded the corner, and found her doubled over on the floor, bent into a fetal position with her head thrown back. There were already tears in her eyes, and her laughter was broken by short, punctuated gasps for air.

"Babe… what…"

"It's *tickling* me!" She sounded angry and happy at the same time. "Make it stop!"

He went down to a knee and fished into the small space between Laura's legs and stomach. The hand was bouncing around, fingers flailing, trying to draw laughter from its prey. Finally, he was able to grab onto the forearm and draw it out. He knocked three times on the back of the hand and tossed it across the room.

Thankfully, the fingers slowed, relaxed. Somewhere beneath the smooth unbroken flesh came a tinny, clown-like giggle. He thought of the last line on the card.

And then you'll see.

Vise Robotics wasn't just about creating lifelike synthetics. They had intelligence too—enough to chase after someone and tickle them, which in a lot of ways, was more difficult than just killing them outright. It took finesse.

Robert found himself wondering what Vise's full synthetics could do, and he chuckled. Winston Vise had done it. He'd come into his home and sprinkled dirt all over his fine carpet. Now he had no choice but to see a full demonstration.

Laura quieted after a minute.

"Are you alright?"

She wiped tears from her cheeks. "I peed."

He laughed and offered his hand to help her up.

THREE

The house was quiet at night; the ghosts who roamed the empty rooms did so with light steps and hushed voices.

Carter Price heard them sometimes, little clicks and clacks running in the hallways, echoes of whispers uttered decades before he was born. As manors went—which was how the listing had described the house, as a *manor*—it wasn't the largest he'd ever stepped foot in, especially in the last couple of years. Even so, of the fifteen thousand square feet of usable living space in the single-story home, only about a thousand of it was in use. Coming from his parents' three-bedroom townhome in Jersey had left a majority of the rooms empty, with nothing in them except the dust that had been accumulating since the previous owner died or moved out.

His bedroom was furnished, of course, though the high ceilings absolutely dwarfed his queen-sized bed. His IKEA furniture looked out of place as well, just thrown against the wall and haphazardly decorated. The attached bathroom was itself larger than his old room, with a locker room style shower that had more nozzles than he had body parts. His clothes barely filled a quarter of the walk-in closet, and though the built-in tie rack by the door had space for thirty, it held only five.

The only other room Carter used was a converted garage at the back of the house. There, the ground sloped away into a valley, leaving the first floor overhanging into empty air. The previous owner had dug out and closed in the space. Steep stairs now connected the former garage to the hallway just outside the kitchen. From the photos in the listing, Carter knew the garage had once held golf carts and wall-to-wall clubs.

The simple drywall had a more modern, familiar feel than the rest of the house, which must have been built in a previous century, whether the 1900s or 1800s, Carter didn't know. He'd left the massive garage door intact, a single, sprawling metal slab that required three motors to lift it. When up, the missing wall provided him a wide view of the countryside, with no roads or visible lights save for his neighbor a few miles away.

He'd christened the room with a new couch that faced the door, then added a desk, a workbench, a wall-to-wall vidscreen, and finally, a dedicated virtual reality immersion chair. Most days, he walked from his bedroom to the garage and back, with occasional stops in the kitchen or bathroom. He often took his meals at the two-top just outside the garage on the edge of an evercrete porch that dropped off into a thicket of thorny bushes.

Tonight, he was at his workbench, peering at a mechanical marvel through a large magnifying lamp while the ghosts roamed the house above his head. He would have heard them moaning and rattling their chains had it not been for the vidscreen blaring some 80s horror movie he didn't know the name of, some *Friday the 13th* rip-off no doubt. He'd left it on a random broadcast channel, and this close to Halloween, the offerings so far had all been the so-called *scary movies*.

But how scary was a homicidal killer anyway?

People snapped every day. That one might reach the breaking point and kill everyone around them shouldn't have surprised most people. Jason Voorhees, after all, was just a man.

Ghosts on the other hand, unexplained phenomena—that was the real terror. As much as he liked to tell people his house was haunted, he knew the creaks and moans were byproducts of the house expanding and contracting with the heating of the day. Every mysterious sound he heard at night—if he heard anything over the subtle roar of his white noise machine—had an explanation.

Even if something appeared supernatural or magical—for example, the synthetic hand that had been delivered to his home earlier that day and that now sat inert in his workbench's clamp—had a logical reasoning behind it. Carter had never heard of Vise Robotics, but he was pretty sure Winston Vise wasn't cutting off the forearms of dead women and using voodoo to breathe life back into the limbs.

So the hand could mimic human movements.

So it could count.

So it could tap out messages in Morse code.

It was all just engineering and programming. Opening the hand with a scalpel and spreaders had been the first step to proving the hand's mechanical origins, and Carter had been unsurprised to find synthetic tendons and glowing green sinew and other fleshy but demonstrably inorganic components that had not come from the other side but rather a production plant in China.

He was poking around the tendons, tugging on the thin metal strands to move the fingers, when his palette lit up and gave a little chirp.

A photo of Braxton Price appeared on the screen, neatly contained in a bordered circle in the center. Two large buttons of green and red read *Answer* and *Reject*, respectively.

Carter mounted the palette in the grasp of an articulating arm and hit the glowing *Answer* button.

A portal opened to Sacramento, and beyond the broad shoulders of his older brother, Carter could see the last slivers of the sun disappearing behind tall Redwood trees. Braxton was three hours behind New York, but based on his bright orange Under Armour shirt and damp hair, he was already off work and had just completed his evening workout.

Braxton narrowed his eyes. "You've got red shit on your face." He waved his fingers vaguely at the camera. "Just because you're worth half a billion doesn't mean you don't have to wipe your mouth anymore."

He'd been making the same joke since Carter sold his startup, Dyalogued, to Vinestead International in 2018. Too rich to wipe his face. Too rich to comb his hair. Too rich to live in Jersey like a normal person.

Carter reached for the paper towel he'd slipped under a paper plate of pizza rolls. As he wiped his mouth, he checked his reflection in the palette video.

"I have a woman who comes in three times a day to wipe my face, but I gave her the night off. Because I'm a good person."

"You're a man-child who still eats pizza rolls and Cap'n Crunch."

Braxton was Carter's only sibling, and a half-one at that. Thirteen years older, he'd been born during their dad's first marriage, with Carter showing up during the second. As a teenager, Braxton hadn't wanted anything to do with his baby brother, but as the years went on, as he settled into a lucrative career and family life, his feelings had changed. His mentorship had been crucial in the sale to Vinestead, and yet when Carter had offered him a portion of the windfall, he'd refused.

"That's just what brothers do," he'd said at the time.

"I'll be eating pizza rolls until the day I die." Carter picked up a half-exploded specimen and popped it in his mouth. The crust was leathery and cold.

"Uh huh." Braxton nodded to someone off camera. He was seated at the kitchen table; Katie and their two little girls would be running around somewhere. "What did you need from me that couldn't go in a text?" He lifted his phone and started scrolling.

Carter turned off the magnifying lamp and pushed the arm away. "I wanted your opinion on something. My neighbor invited me to a dinner party and I'm not sure if it's expected that I bring a guest. The RSVP card has a spot for my date's name though."

"You're asking if you can go stag?"

"Well…"

"Of course you can go by yourself. Why wouldn't you be able to? You know, that's generally how people meet other people, Carter. What kind of dinner party is it? And how well do you know your neighbor?"

"I've never met him." He glanced out the open garage door at the twinkling light in the distance. "His name is Winston Vise."

"Should I know that name?"

"He's got a robotics company, but according to the net, it's pretty new." His gaze drifted to the disembodied hand on the workbench. "He's legit though. He sent me a hand that tapped out *Hello World* in Morse code."

Braxton put his phone down. "A hand?"

"Yeah, you want to see it?" Carter swiveled the arm to point the palette's camera at the hand.

"Ha! Of course you opened it up. Dad was always on your ass about taking things apart when you were a kid."

"I had to see what makes it tick." Carter swung the palette around again. "So yeah, it can communicate using Morse code, which I had to download an app for. That means it can translate dots and dashes into linguistic data, similar to what I was doing at Dyalogued. But I've been digging into this thing for a couple hours now and I can't identify a single CPU or ROM chip. Everything is hidden under this kind of glowing green goo. I mean, I'm sure it's in there, but seriously Braxton, this is next-level tech."

Braxton nodded slowly. "Ah, so that's what you're worried about. You think Vise invited you because he's done something better than you and wants to gloat about it."

"No, I'm worried he invited other people like me. Engineers. People in tech that I should know. Bigwigs. What will people like that say if they think I can't scrounge up a date to a little dinner party? A force in the boardroom but a bore in the bedroom?"

"Literally no one has ever said those words." Braxton waved them away with a dismissive hand. "Anyway, it shouldn't be too hard to get a date. Just drive back to the city, find a group of people, and whip out that robot hand for the first woman who shows an interest in you."

"I can get a date. I already have someone in mind."

Braxton's smile faded. He crossed his arms. "Tell me you're not thinking of inviting *her*."

"Why not? I like her."

"She's not real, Carter." He leaned into the camera and whispered conspiratorially, "She's a prostitute, man. She's paid to make you like her. That's not love; that's codependency."

Carter rolled a utility knife on his workbench, watched the light glint off the blade. "I know what it is. I know it's not real. But it's just like VR, you know? When it's happening, when I'm in the moment, it does feel kinda real, even though I know it's going to end. Either way, I'd rather bring her than show up alone."

"They're gonna know." Braxton waved an accusatory finger. "They're gonna know she's an Associate the second she walks in and when little miss… miss…"

"Jane."

"…when little miss Jane is out of earshot, they're going to whisper and snicker, and it'll be just loud enough for you to hear."

"I can handle that."

Braxton shook his head. "Then there's no talking to you." He brought a water bottle in from off camera and took a long pull. "Well, if you're looking for my approval, you won't get it."

"No, I just need to know how I'm supposed to introduce her."

"What's wrong with *this is Jane, my sex slave for the evening?*"

Carter felt the heat rise in his cheeks. "You know what I mean. Do I say *this is my friend* or *this is my girlfriend* or what? I just imagine introducing her as my girlfriend and them thinking *what is this guy like fifteen?*"

"God…" Braxton rubbed his thick beard.

"Come on. You're a politician. You know about these high society types."

"High society!" He laughed for a while, more than Carter appreciated. When he finally settled down, he spoke through a wide smile. "Okay, okay, fine. Look, you're my little brother, so I'm gonna help you out. You're probably right about this Vise guy inviting other tech people, so that's not high society, which by the way doesn't even exist anymore. They're called the *wealthy elite* now, but anyway. Tech people are actual people, other nerds like you. They're not gonna give a handful of fucks about who you bring to this thing. And since you're a wunderkind hacker who sold his company to the biggest conglomerate on the planet, you don't have to give a handful of fucks about what they think anyway. You put Jane on your arm, walk in there like you're God's gift to tech, and say, *this is my girlfriend. I pay money to put my wiener in her.*"

Carter huffed, looked away.

"I'm not kidding, bro. I've been to hundreds of these things. I've seen grown-ass men in their fifties introduce some perky coed as their girlfriend. They don't give a damn. You just tell it like it is. Friend, girlfriend, partner, fiancé, wife… whatever. Don't worry about what other people think."

"I literally say that? This is my girlfriend Jane?"

"Better than prostitute."

"Don't talk about the future Mrs. Carter Price like that. You may have to give a toast at our wedding someday."

Braxton rolled his eyes. "I'll have my assistant start working on a speech right away." He motioned to the side, as if he were trying to swipe the video to the left. "Show me the hand again. I've never seen inside a synthetic before."

Carter hesitated, but then turned the palette around to face his bench. He took a small hook tool from the stand and used it to pull one of the tendons. The ring finger on the hand twitched.

Braxton chuckled. "That's wild. But why is it green inside? It looks radioactive."

"I don't know, maybe it's Vulcan," said Carter. Truthfully, he hadn't given it much thought since green blood had oozed from the first incision.

"Nerd. Show me some more. I've got a few minutes before dinner."

Carter obliged, and as he was clearing space around a metallic ulna, a dulcet tone sounded in his ear. His whisperer, dormant for most of the night, crackled to life. The voice of his digital assistant, Champion, which he had programmed to sound like Dr. Frankenstein's assistant Igor, spoke in a raspy tone.

Master, message from No Reply Daemon at Adelai Associates. Your request has been received. A representative will be in touch within twenty-four hours to confirm final details. Would you like to reply?

Carter muttered a soft *no* and dug deeper into the synthetic arm until Braxton was finally pulled out of frame by his girls.

FOUR

On the subjects of dedication and professionalism, Rakesh Singh always complained that no one was willing to put in the hard work necessary to get a job done, least of all Americans.

"If you do a job for someone, you don't just do it well. You do it better than anyone has ever done it before."

The longer Diya Singh worked as a personal assistant, first for Joanne Cedillo, director of the Dahlstrom Academy advisory board, and more recently, for Winston Vise, founder of Vise Robotics, the more she tended to agree with her father. Diya's main responsibility was to manage Winston's life outside of work, which meant interfacing with vendors and various companies with which he did business. Sometimes, he called on her to act as a full-fledged event coordinator, as he had with the dinner party he was planning to host at the end of the week.

For two months, Diya had worked to line up food, entertainment, decorations, and a surprising number of other small items. Despite the short guest list, she had spent almost every day battling contractors and vendors to get the right stuff delivered at the right time.

None of them wanted to put in the work, even when they were being paid well.

She had even called her father a few times to vent about it. He always listened, let her get it out, and then remarked on the dark skies behind her, asking why she was working so late. She didn't want to tell him there was too much work and too little of her. That would have sounded lazy.

"Just promise me you will get some rest," he'd said, after she'd told him she was just finishing up and would be heading home soon.

Monday was another late night. Diya was sure everyone else at the office had gone home, but she still had emails to write and last-minute checks to perform. The dinner was on Friday at Winston's home in the countryside, and the first of the trucks would be arriving Wednesday morning to set up. She would have to be there, of course, and since the dinner was her only concern, she'd made plans to stay a few days in what Winston had named *Vise Manor*, as if it were some stately mansion in the English countryside.

Winston himself was out of the country and wouldn't be back until Friday evening, so it was just going to be Diya alone in the large house with only the assets to keep her company.

She was in the middle of writing a follow-up email to the flower company that was doing the table centerpieces when one of her gofers, Bradley Hollinger, knocked softly on her office door. He was younger than Diya and looked almost skeletal in his thinness. He hadn't yet grown into his tall frame, which made his white Oxford billow around his chest like the sail of a ship. As usual, he had his sleeves rolled up on his skinny forearms.

Diya liked that look on men. Formal but hardworking—a far cry from the meme t-shirts and flip-flops most of the software engineers wore around the building.

"Got a minute?" he asked.

"Sure." She minimized the email window and pushed back slightly from the desk.

"I printed out those delivery confirmations you asked for, and I also sent digital copies to your inbox. It looks like all of them were delivered except one. It was marked *Return to Sender* for some reason. I don't know if we want to try again or what."

She beckoned him into the office and pointed to a chair on the other side of her desk. "No, Winston wasn't expecting everyone to come." When he dropped the papers on her desk, she picked them up and began leafing through them. "We're overbooked by two couples, so we need at least that many to decline. All I see are addresses here."

"I have the names on my palette, hold on." Bradley sat down in the chair and pulled a palette from his breast pocket. His dirty blond hair fell around his face in little curls. "Want to go down the list?"

"Sure." They might as well. Rakesh Singh wasn't going to fault her for doing a thorough job, not when someone else might have succumbed to fatigue and simply gone home.

Bradley traced a finger down his palette. His eyes narrowed, eliciting a single age line near his left eyebrow. "Alright, so the RTS we got was from Wade Vunak in Austin, Texas." He looked up. "He's the founder of Nixle Chronos. They do augmented reality, nothing public at the moment, but they've got a satellite office in Umbra where they do demos, and people say it's pretty impressive tech."

"You did your homework."

"Of course." He smiled. "I learned from the best."

Having her own team of assistants was one of the perks of the job and part of the reason she'd left Dahlstrom Academy. There was something about the prospect of educating someone else in the teachings of Rakesh Singh that intrigued her.

"So did I," she said, nodding to his palette. "Continue."

"We got delivery confirmations and digital signatures for the other seven packages. Robert Hargreaves in Houston, Texas. Elias Shaw in Sacramento, California. Lucas Cotton, Los Angeles. Adelai Vaught, New York City. Carter Price—he's the neighbor. And last but not least, Reno Cardenas, Ciudad de MX." He read the last part in a poor Spanish accent.

"Tell me about the MX national."

Bradley tapped a few times. "Not much on the net about him. Some conflicting stories that he was either cartel or military, but in the last few years, he's been making noise with synthetic soldiers—*Máquinas*, they call them. That's Spanish for *machine*. Nobody's really sure what's going on down there, but it looks like Mr. Cardenas got a leg up from somewhere, and he's probably looking to make another leap forward. It makes sense Mr. Vise would want him there."

The mention of synthetic soldiers set Diya's arms itching. She rubbed them with both hands. "How do you feel about that?"

"About what?"

"Selling the assets to an international arms dealer. I mean, that's essentially what Cardenas is, right? Who exactly do you think his Máquinas are fighting?"

"American soldiers?"

Diya nodded.

"Fine, it's a moral gray area," he admitted. "I don't know if we're paid to worry about that sort of thing."

On this point, Rakesh Singh was uncharacteristically silent.

She dropped the papers on her desk and folded her arms. "Okay, so of the remaining seven, which do you think we'll get RSVPs from? I've already got nameplates printed and everything, but it'd be good to know as soon as possible if we're overbooked."

Bradley furrowed his brow again. "Well, I think Carter Price is a lock. It'd probably be rude of him not to accept. Adelai Vaught is probably ninety percent; what New Yorker wouldn't want an excuse to get out of the city for the weekend?"

"Naturally."

"I don't know about the rest. Robert Hargreaves runs a stable of businesses under the Hargreaves Group, so he might be interested in checking out a potential acquisition. Elias Shaw owns the only stateside manufacturer of cortical implants. I think I read even Perion Synthetics uses them sometimes when there's unrest overseas. Lucas Cotton strikes me as the wildcard. He's more of an engineer than a businessman, so you're looking at professional curiosity more than anything. Reno Cardenas will be interested in the assets for obvious reasons, so I think that only leaves Stanton Blumenfield."

Diya nodded. She eyed the open dossiers on her computer screen. Nobody had asked either of them to do deep dives on Winston's invited guests, and yet they had both done so on their own.

"Stanton Blumenfield," she said. "Not a businessman. Not an engineer. Just a moderately decorated writer."

"Futurologist, according to his Wiki page."

"Futurologist. He's probably not in any position to purchase the company or even one of the assets. So just like Lucas Cotton, it would be pure curiosity that brings him to the house. I don't know if there's enough there, even with Winston's unusual invitation."

Bradley shrugged. "Have you read any of his books?"

"I read the summaries."

"So then you know, he's big on synthetic transcendence. I read the first few pages of *The Soul of the Mechanical Man*, and I think Mr. Vise invited him simply to show off, like a pride thing. He wants to be seen by an artist so he himself can feel like one. That's my theory anyway."

Diya hadn't considered that. Maybe Winston was just looking for validation. "Go on."

Bradley hugged his palette. "Someone like Blumenfield, he would be asking himself the same kinds of questions. Why the invite? What does Winston Vise want with someone like me?" He chewed his lip for a moment, then smiled. "He'd see right through it. He'd know his presence would only be to serve Mr. Vise's ego, so he'd refuse."

"So that's your pick then?"

"Yeah, I guess so." He blinked. "You don't agree?"

"I don't *not* agree… I just think Winston overestimates his drawing power sometimes. Wade Vunak's a great example. He didn't just respond *with regrets*; he straight up refused the package. I don't think he likes Winston, at all. And if you go back through the records for the State of the Net conferences in Umbra over the last ten years, you'll find Vunak has spoken at every one of them. And who else do you think sat on the same panel with him every single one of those years?"

Bradley scanned his palette again. "Lucas Cotton?"

"That's the one. You see them on the feeds together all the time, so if anyone else isn't going to respond, I bet twenty bucks it's Cotton. He may keep the invitation, but I doubt he ever walks through the doors of Vise Manor."

"I'll go for twenty," said Bradley. He leaned forward to offer his hand. "I still say it's Blumenfield."

"Then it's a bet."

"What if neither of us win?"

Diya shrugged. "Then, my friend, we'll have to give up our dream of opening our own detective agency. Singh and Associate, Private Detectives."

"Fine. I'll just change my last name to *Associate* and tell people it's French."

"Well, Monsieur…" She typed rapidly into a translator app on her computer. "…*Associe*, I think we've had enough fun for one night. You should get out of here while you can."

"You sure you don't need me… to stay?"

She smiled, turned back to her computer. "No, I don't *need* you, Mr. Hollinger. You're wonderfully helpful, but I could get by just as easily without you." She started typing gibberish into the translator to give the appearance she was working.

"Okay then." He stood to leave, paused at the door. The low light cast dark shadows over his cheeks. "You know, I was thinking about you heading out to Mr. Vise's place on Wednesday. You're gonna be there alone for a couple of nights. You sure you don't want some company? I know he doesn't want me there the night of, but I could hang out for a day or two, help with the setup. I'm sure he's got spare rooms already lined up for the guests, so…"

Diya leaned over her desk and supported her chin with her hand.

"You just couldn't resist, could you?"

"Resist what?" Half of his mouth rose in a smile.

"You've fallen in love with me."

"What?" He chuckled nervously, adjusted his tie.

Diya pushed her purely decorative glasses up her nose and returned her attention to the screen. "My father tried to warn me about American boys." She lowered her voice, affected a weak Indian accent. "You be careful, Diya. American boys are only interested in one thing, and it's disgusting."

"I didn't mean it like that."

"Are you sure?" She refused to look away from her screen. "Because either you're in love with me, which I understand, of course, or you're implying I can't handle a couple of nights alone in a big scary house because I'm just a little girl and I need a big burly man to protect me from the empty halls and creaking floors." She pulled her glasses down quickly and shot him a glare while doing her best to hold back a smile. "Which is it, *Brad?* Are you trying to dip your pen in company ink or are you just a misogynist?"

He stared back at her for several seconds and didn't relax until the edges of her lips began to tremble. He tapped his palette against the doorjamb twice.

"Goodnight, Ms. Singh. Go home and get some beauty sleep." He turned to leave and muttered under his breath, "You need it."

Diya let out the laughter she'd been holding in. She called after him as he disappeared down the hall.

"You can't run from your feelings forever, Bradley!"

FIVE

There was a tall stack of papers on Adelai's desk when she returned to work the next day.

Just the sight of the bland manila folders, each with its own pink paperclip holding a photo to the inside flap, made her heart sink. The pool of applicants had been growing since mid-summer, but the quality of those applicants had been declining so quickly that Adelai couldn't remember the last time she'd encountered a girl she liked. If there weren't anyone in the stack on her desk worth bringing into the program, that would make fifty-nine candidates rejected since July—a record for her.

Adelai put her purse down on the credenza by the door and slid into the large leather chair behind her desk. Outside, the cold and dreary afternoon had streaked the windows with rain, causing the city to deform behind a thin sheet of water. Not that there was much to see. The Adelai Associates offices in the Brandt Building were only on the fifteenth floor, which meant her view was mostly other windows, other professionals carrying on with their day, doing their best to pretend they were enjoying their work.

She imagined there might be someone out there who was doing something they loved, but Adelai couldn't give that person a face or a name or a reason for living. Everyone had their own nearly invisible glass desks to sit behind, their own stacks of folders to go through. Maybe they were all disappointed in the crop of girls the summer and early fall had produced. Maybe they were all worried they wouldn't have any new talent to trot out in the spring when everyone came back from winter vacation.

Adelai placed her hand on the folders, considered picking them up. It was just going to be more of the same: fresh-faced girls who thought they wanted a life they knew nothing about. Even if all five were ideal candidates and were accepted into the program, history said only one would come out the other end as a viable asset.

It was too much work, and though she offloaded most of it to Simone, the final say was hers alone, which meant she had to be involved, had to be the gate, and had to be the one who sat the girls down and told them what they would be doing in their new roles—and who they would be doing it to.

None of them came to her naïve, but their young imaginations often had rarely conceived the breadth of the job's responsibilities. Some panicked, some tried to fake it until they eventually burned out, and a precious few made it to the end, finding some way to kill that piece inside of themselves that said *this is wrong*.

Adelai pushed the folders away and sat back in her chair. She asked the stereo on the credenza for some smooth jazz, which always sounded melancholy in her ear, even if the song was upbeat and energetic. Perhaps it was the trumpet, always the loudest in the ensemble, always standing a head above everyone else, exposed and lonely.

That was the way she felt most days, and the only way to feel safe was to curl up on the couch with a bottle of wine in her hand and a warm blanket against her naked skin.

Are you busy?

Adelai perked up, looked around for Simone before realizing her voice was coming from the whisperer in her ear. She activated the whisperer's microphone with a soft tap of her finger.

"No, what do you need?"

Your sign-off on something. Didn't want to interrupt.

Adelai turned her chair to the door. "Please interrupt."

A minute later, the double doors at the end of Adelai's office opened, and Simone stepped through. She carried in her hands a single folder, though thankfully not one of the drab manila variety. This one was bright red, which meant it was the file of a girl who had already been through training and was now a regular. The red signified they were paying special attention to her.

Adelai tried and failed to slip into her professional persona. All she wanted to do was melt into the leather chair and never take the form of a woman again.

Her gaze drifted to the window as she asked, "What do you have for me?"

Simone waved the folder. "We've had an engagement request come in for a probationary case—Jane Moretz. You said you wanted to approve her personally."

"Still?"

"Two years," said Simone, pretending to check her watch. "Still a couple of months to go." She opened the folder and placed it on Adelai's desk. There was a red arrow sticker at the bottom of a long page listing Jane's previous engagements.

Adelai examined the list. She counted sixteen versions of her signature.

"Did we vet the client?" she asked.

"No need. He's a repeat. Four-timer, third with Jane."

"Someone's falling in love." She grabbed a pen from the holder next to her monitor and signed her name with a flourish. "Seems to be a pattern with this one." When she looked up, Simone was smiling down at her, a sparkle in her eyes. "What?"

Her eyebrows danced. "Don't you want to check out the engagement rider?"

"Do I need to?"

"Oh, it's all vetted." Simone spread her hands. "You should still look though."

Adelai flipped to the next page and ran a finger down the rider. She looked for anything out of the ordinary but saw nothing amiss.

"This looks like a standard Meet Cute to me. Carter Michael Price, fourth engagement, two nights with the option to extend. What am I missing, Momo?"

Simone walked back to the door and closed it softly. When she returned, she came around the desk and bent over to point to the paper. Her light floral perfume wafted down from her perfect neck.

"Look at the itinerary," she said. "Initial delivery here, second waypoint at the client's residence, and then…"

Adelai followed her finger and read the text beneath it. The address in the New York countryside wasn't familiar, but it was followed by a name in parentheses.

"Vise Manor? Vise Manor!" She read it again. "Are you serious? Same night?"

Simone nodded and clucked her tongue. "Looks like we weren't the only ones to get an invite to this exclusive event. We're going to be dining with an employee and a client at the same time. Now *that's* a dinner party I want to go to."

"No," said Adelai, shaking her head. "We can't possibly go, Momo. It would be too inappropriate, wouldn't it?"

It wasn't really a question. Associates held the same level of confidentiality as psychiatrists—they would never reveal their nature or an existing relationship outside of an engagement. If Jane randomly passed Carter on the street, she would pretend not to know him. And if that's how Jane was supposed to behave, then it went double for the people who employed her. Carter likely wouldn't introduce Jane as a hired woman at the dinner party, and neither Jane nor Simone nor Adelai herself would reveal it, but their mere presence provided the opportunity to let something slip.

It would be a bad experience, and that's not what the client was paying $7,000 a night for.

"Why would it be inappropriate?" Simone straightened and put a hand on her hip. "It's not like we're going to see Jane and make some joke about just seeing her at the office."

"But just us being there is dangerous."

"I disagree. We know him. He doesn't know us." She put her hand on Adelai's shoulder. "We just won't talk about the business. If people ask, we'll just say we're wealthy spinsters. We could get some costume jewelry and little clutches from a vintage clothing store. We'll pretend we escaped from a nursing home and…"

Adelai smiled weakly.

"You know, as I'm saying it, I don't like it." Simone leaned against the desk; the hem of her skirt rose on her thighs, revealing more of her black hose and its intricate stitching. "Maybe we just go as ourselves. If anyone asks about work, I'll pretend to faint so you can run away."

"I imagine that will be a lot of fainting."

Simone shrugged. "It's worth it. I'd love to get away this weekend. I want to go to a fancy dinner party and be fed roasted quail and delicate bone marrow." She lifted a leg and placed her foot on Adelai's chair. "I want to watch men fawn over you like they always do at these things. And at the end of the night, I want to take you back to whatever extravagant room they put us in and make love to you on expensive sheets. I want to make you scream loud enough for all those men to hear."

"Is that so?"

Simone leaned in, put her mouth next to Adelai's ear. "She cried *Mo, Mo, Mo…*"

Adelai whispered, "It's still inappropriate."

"By the end of the night, decorum will be the last thing on your mind."

"I don't deserve you." She patted Simone's leg. "But I don't get out of bed for the promise of a little vacation sex. Did you reach out to Rayburn about this Winston Vise?"

Simone put her foot down and stood. "I was going to forward you the rundown he sent me. Evidently, we're saying his name wrong. It's Vise as in *ice*, not like *wise*."

Adelai spun a finger in the air.

"Rayburn says he's just another forty-something businessman who's been hopping from one startup to the next for most of his life. He's called himself CEO of a dozen companies, nothing I've ever heard of, but this Vise Robotics appears to be the most significant of the bunch. Privately held, incorporated in Delaware, not much on paper except several rounds of VC funding."

"Anyone we know?"

"Seraphim Capital. That's Charles Berkman, a Diamond Club member."

"Give him a call and get his take."

"And if he signs off, we can go?"

There was so much hope in her eyes, or maybe it was just the natural glisten she got when something excited her.

Adelai played with her hands in her lap. "What's in it for me again? Besides the vacation sex and bone marrow?"

"You really want to know?"

"I'm all ears."

Simone nodded and drifted away to the window. There, she crossed her hands behind her back. "Come over here. I want to show you something."

Adelai joined her at the window, tried to follow her gaze, but Simone wasn't looking at anything in particular. "What are we looking at?"

"Outside." The playfulness left her voice. She was no longer coy and flirty Simone. "You need to get out of this office, and not just for a weekend in the country. We need a longer break, weeks, maybe a month, however long it takes for the stress of the job to leave your body. We can hire someone to vet the girls in your place or we can just let them stack up until we get back." She slipped an arm around Adelai's waist. "I have loved you for half of my life, in every form of you, even as a borderline alcoholic who sits around the house all day wearing nothing but a robe. I don't mind that last part, actually."

Adelai looked away but allowed herself to be hugged.

"And I'd let that go on forever if you weren't so unhappy."

"I'm not—"

"You can't lie to me, Addy. I see it and I feel it. It breaks my heart to see you like this, and most of the time I just feel so helpless to do anything about it." She slipped between Adelai and the window. "But I'm your wife, and I'm not letting depression take you. I vowed to take care of you, and that's what I'm going to do, even if it means burning this company to the ground to make you happy again."

Adelai put her forehead on Simone's shoulder. "You're obsessed with burning things to the ground. Besides, I started this company, and you helped me build it into what it is today. You're probably right that I need a long break. We've got a good stable of girls, don't we? We could shut down recruitment for the rest of the year, pick up in January. I don't think that would put us too far behind."

A hand appeared on the back of her neck. Adelai sighed. Simone's touch was and would always be a hundred times more real than any synthetic's.

"It's whatever you want, Addy. Let's just go. We'll call it our Winter Adventure. First, we'll go to a fancy dinner in the country and check out some one-armed robots. Then we'll jet overseas to Paris and see where that takes us. We can monitor the business from the road if we have to, but otherwise we're waking up in villas and sipping drinks on stony beaches."

"I'd like that." She hugged Simone, breathed in her perfume again. Beneath the hint of peony and citron, she could smell the woman she'd also spent half of her life with. "Okay, fine. Never mind about Berkman. We'll go. But if we lose the Price account, that's on you."

"If he walks, I'll get you three more just like him when we get back from Europe."

"Deal. I guess you can go ahead and send the RSVP."

Simone wrapped her arms around Adelai's, pinning them to her side.

She whispered, "I already did."

Adelai tried to wiggle out but couldn't.

She replied, "Of course."

SIX

The morning fog was still lingering around the clubhouse when Robert arrived at the Pebble Beach golf course. It was his third time to visit Carmel, and usually he liked to come in the summer when the daily temperature was in the balmy 70s. Now, in late October, it was cold enough for long sleeves and a jacket, at least for a lifelong Texan. The wind coming off the rolling ocean carried with it the sounds of lapping waves and the salty aroma of the Pacific.

The California shore was so unlike the beaches in Galveston or South Padre, rockier and less welcoming. Laura hadn't wanted to come at all, even when he reminded her about the spa at the golf course and all the touristy spots in the multi-hyphenated *Carmel-by-the-Sea*. She'd opted to stay behind, but only after making him put the synthetic hand in the large gun safe upstairs. She wasn't jazzed about being alone in the house with *that thing*, but locking it behind several inches of American steel was an acceptable compromise.

Robert had messaged her shortly after his plane touched down to ask if the hand had escaped and tickled her to death. She replied with a photo of a Glock 41 resting on a side table with the safe out of focus in the background.

"Everything's fine... for now," she'd replied.

He checked his phone again before stepping out of the clubhouse, but there weren't any other updates. Outside, in the gloomy air, he felt a sudden pang for home, for the traffic he lamented and the heat he constantly complained about. He pushed the feeling down when he saw Frank Kagan standing near the first tee, club already in hand, loosening up with some light stretches. Nearby his custom golf cart with its pearlescent blue paint job stood dully just off the path. Some things just weren't as pretty without the sun to light them.

When Kagan saw Robert approaching, he lifted a white gloved hand in greeting. The color matched his shirt, his pants, and his shoes. Of the many things Frank Kagan claimed to be, a fashion icon was not one of them. Robert wondered if the man was trying to distract from his hair, which, although gray, was several shades darker than his clothes. Clean-shaven with pale blue eyes, Kagan had a grandfatherly air to him, though Robert knew that was just a façade. There were few people he'd met as ruthless as Frank Kagan.

"You made it. Thanks for coming out, Bob."

Robert shook the man's hand when he got close enough. "Hey, you send a plane to my city and I'm gonna get on it. That's just how I was raised."

"Glad to hear it." Kagan smiled, nodded to the tee. "Why don't we get started? Normally I'd say guests first, but I'm already limber so why don't I kick things off?"

"It's your course, boss." Robert stepped off the tee and carried his bag to the waiting golf cart.

It always felt strange to be deferential to Kagan, even though the term *boss* didn't carry much weight back home among his peers. After all, Kagan was only a few years older, and though the Kagan Group held twice the number of companies as Robert's, their market valuations were more or less the same. They had made similar moves independently for years without realizing it, and only by chance did they meet at a fundraiser for some upstart politico who had disappeared after losing a primary to a reality television star.

Kagan was quiet as they made their way down the course. Everyone who knew him was aware of how focused he could be, and how nothing would get in the way of the *thing* he wanted. He'd invited Robert to play golf, and that meant they were going to play golf. Nothing else would happen until that minimum requirement was met.

It was a harmless quirk and a small price to pay for personal access to a man with his expansive network of connections.

Robert focused on his own game, eager to test his improved driving skills at the course that had hosted the U.S. Open just a couple of years ago. The course was over a hundred years old and yet it still felt new, and at times, otherworldly. Between the weather, the rugged coastline, and the enormity of the Pacific Ocean, Robert felt transported.

The fog stayed with them until they reached Arrowhead Point, at which time the air cleared almost instantaneously. The sun, now directly overhead, glinted on gentle waves.

"Not a bad view, eh?"

Robert nodded. "Nothing like this back home. Sandy beaches and pretty sunrises, but nothing like this."

"Same in L.A., I look out my window at home and all I see are mountains. I've got a condo in Santa Monica, but I don't get down there much. Never enough time."

"I know what you mean. We're supposed to be retired. Now I feel like I work harder than ever."

Kagan slotted his putter in his bag. "How about we take a break? Let's walk to the edge of the point there. They put in a seating area before the Open in '19." He started walking without waiting for an answer.

"What about the cart?" It was parked just off the putting green. "Won't we hold up—"

"There's that Texas hospitality," said Kagan, the wind blowing his voice back to Robert. "Always worried about getting in other people's way. I bought the course out until four. No one's going to bother us today."

Robert shrugged and followed his host toward the rocks. As promised, a small arrangement of benches had been set up facing the water. Kagan sat down on the center bench, and Robert joined him.

Evidently, the golf quota had been met.

"Seven holes, Bob. When I was younger, I could do seven holes standing on my head with a club in one hand and a John Daly in the other. Now I'm winded before the turn."

Robert gave the man a once-over. There was no flush in his cheeks, nor did he appear to be out of breath.

"I know," said Kagan, noticing his stare. "It's the Angel in my neck. You can't hear her, but she's been pestering me since the fourth hole, telling me to slow down and drink some water." He huffed. "Technology was supposed to set us free, but really, it's made us all slaves."

"What's wrong with a little assistive tech? Laura and I both have Guardian Angels too, and I'm pretty sure mine headed off a stroke a few years ago."

"I'm not saying that's not a great thing, but I miss the old days. It used to be simple. You go to the doctor, doctor says your heart is bad, tells you to take it easy, not exert yourself. And what do you do? You ignore him. You keep playing golf. You keep popping little blue pills. And then when you have a heart attack, you tell your doctor with a straight face that you *were* trying to take it easy, and he pretends to believe you when you say you have no idea how coke *and* speed got into your bloodstream."

A group of small birds flew past, murmuring beneath the edge of the cliffs.

Kagan chuckled, continued, "Now I've got this thing in the back of my neck and it's watching my heart rate and oxygen levels and everything else. When it sees something it doesn't like, it rats me out to my doctor, and then I get this little voice in my ear telling me to slow down." He turned to Robert, frowned a little. "I don't like that. I'm not even seventy and they're telling me to *slow down*? And if I turn it off, there goes my life insurance and a little spending money for junior."

"How is your son?"

"Disappointing." Kagan groaned. "But what else is new? I thought college would straighten him up, give him something to focus on, but every weekend he was back in L.A. partying with all his trust fund friends whose parents don't care whether their kids make something of themselves. He dropped out last year." A sigh. "I bought him a house in Burbank so I wouldn't have to see him at home."

Robert nudged the artificial grass under his feet. "I'm sorry to hear that, Frank."

"Never have children, Bob. They're just going to let you down."

"My companies are my babies, and speaking of which, I think I have a new prospect, a new bun in the oven, so to speak."

"Oh yeah? Who's that?"

"Vise Robotics."

"Vise Robotics?" Kagan cocked his head. "That's Winston Vise's latest venture, isn't it? I heard he's been telling everyone he's made the next great leap forward in synthetic humans."

"Really? From who? You're the first person I've talked to who knows anything about him."

Kagan waved an uncertain hand. "Well, you know what they say about keeping your enemies close, don't you? You meet a lot of interesting people in our line of work, Bob. Some good, some not so good, and some rotten pieces of cat turd who give capitalism a bad name. Winston Vise is a bona fide cat turd who needs to be scooped out of the litter box and left in a flaming paper bag on someone's porch."

"That bad, huh?" Robert crossed one leg over the other. His decision to RSVP seemed hasty now.

"He's an asshole. And I should know; I'm raising one."

"Huh." Robert tapped his foot a few times. "Well, I've only met him briefly, so I don't know much about him, but evidently he knows me. We got an invitation yesterday to come up to his place in New York for some kind of demonstration."

"Of what? Synthetics?"

"I think so. He sent a synthetic hand as an amuse-bouche. It was actually kind of impressive until it tried to tickle Laura to death."

Kagan coughed, put his hand to his chest for a moment. "Well, I can't speak to the technology. There's talk he's onto something new, but I can't imagine he's got anything that can go toe-to-toe with James Perion." He wasn't one to brag often, but even Kagan couldn't resist leaning over and nudging Robert with his elbow. "I've met him, you know."

"No shit?"

"Yeah, both of him. I met the real James Perion before he died and then later the synthetic who took his place. Bit of a difference in perspective between the two, but he was more or less the same person. Still brilliant. Lots of good ideas. If Perion Synthetics weren't worth five hundred times my stable of companies, I would have bought Perion City outright." He softened his voice, as if providing a voiceover for a commercial. "*Perion Synthetics, part of the Kagan Group*. It has a nice ring to it. I just hope I live long enough that he or that son of his agrees to license the technology. Imprinting human minds on synthetic bodies is the way of the future, Bob. I can't wait. The *check engine* light on this meat suit has been flashing for way too long."

The fantasy washed over Robert like waves over the rocks. He saw himself and Laura restored to their youthful bodies, his hair a lustrous dirty blond, his biceps bulging through his sleeves. It was a cruel joke that they should have the financial freedom to go anywhere and do anything long after their bodies were willing and capable.

"Do you think it'll happen in our lifetimes? The whole imprinting thing, I mean."

"That's what I'm hoping Vitra Synth will be—a path forward."

A minute went by as the men listened to the ocean. The wind whipped at the seventh hole flag.

"Do you think it's worth it?" asked Robert. "Going up to see Vise?"

"As much as I hate to admit it, yes, I think so. *Demonstration* is just another way of saying *sales pitch*. He's got something he wants you to buy, but if he's selling synthetics, then there has to be some intelligence behind them. Now, if he's inviting you all the way up there just to demo some procedural code, any of that *machine learning* or *deep learning* bullshit, then he's not only an asshole but a dumbass to boot." Kagan rubbed his chin. "My guess is he's got some kind of artificial intelligence, which means he either grew one from scratch or he's playing Perion's imprinting game better than Perion. Honestly, neither of those sound likely."

Robert laughed.

"What's funny there, Bob?"

"I don't like being manipulated." He shook his head. "What Vise is promising sounds too good to be true, which means it has to be bullshit. And yet…"

"And yet the clock keeps ticking," said Kagan. "And yet we still search for immortality at the bottom of our graves."

Robert leaned forward, tried to arrange the pieces in his mind.

"If it's true artificial intelligence, that doesn't do you or me any good. Game over. We die from the coke and…"

"Speed. It's called a Fizzball."

"…speed and—what? No it's not, is it?"

Kagan laughed. "No, but it should be."

"Alright, we die from Fizzballs. The devil gets his souls. *But,* if it's synthetic transcendence, copying a human mind into a mechanical body, *and* it's ready to go to market before Perion's, then that would be a very useful company for one of us to own."

"Very useful," said Kagan, nodding.

Again, the silence crept in. Robert felt as if he were floating above the world, seeing the larger game playing out beneath his feet. He imagined the presentation Winston Vise would give, playing it out in fast forward, skipping over the sound and fury to focus on the moment of truth.

Robert cleared his throat. "He could highball."

"He could highball," said Kagan.

"Maybe higher than I could go."

"True."

"Maybe higher than you could go."

"Not likely."

Robert took a breath. "But probably not higher than we could go."

"Joint venture?" asked Kagan.

"Joint venture."

"Fifty-fifty?"

"Split down the middle."

"Gentlemen's agreement."

"Bought and paid for."

Robert put out his hand and Kagan shook it.

"But if it works, I get to go first."

"Of course." Robert patted him on the back and stood up. "You can work out all the kinks for me."

A thin smile stretched on Kagan's face. His eyes narrowed into thin slits.

"In that case, maybe I'll ask my son if he wants to be a robot."

SEVEN

Carter stayed at the workbench until he started to nod off.

He didn't bother to ask Champion for the time; he knew it was late. The long walk upstairs to his bedroom wasn't as scary as usual, perhaps because he was just too tired to entertain the idea of ghosts watching him from around corners. He stumbled into his room, stripped down to his briefs at the edge of the bed, and climbed beneath the covers. In the shallow dreams that came like distant lightning out of the clouds, he saw an underground factory churning out hands by the thousands—not synthetic bodies, just the hands. The factory ran without human intervention; long assembly lines rumbled in the darkness while thick, robotic arms placed a tendon here, a fingernail there. The deep thrumming of the motors and the tempo of the drills created a symphony that made Carter's chest feel tight. It was a relentless, expanding sound, growing ever larger in his ears, until the *thump-thump-thump* was all he could hear.

At the far end of the factory, hands fell off the ends of conveyor belts into an abandoned quarry, a stark white multi-level pit that burrowed deep into the earth. And yet, the pile of hands grew taller, reaching ever upward.

Carter awoke to the sound of the heavy curtains retracting. They were set to open every morning at 8:00 a.m. He braced for the sunlight they would allow into the room, but it never came. He saw through blurry eyes that the windows were streaked with rain, that low clouds rested on the rolling hills behind the house, obscuring the sun. Runoff from the roof tapped steadily on the tiled balcony outside, pooling in the grouted canyons.

It was a good day to lie in bed and drift in and out of sleep. Carter let the fantasy wash over him as he pulled the covers tighter around his body, but when he closed his eyes, he saw the factory again.

He was back at the workbench thirty minutes later, his face washed and teeth brushed. The plate of congealed pizza rolls was waiting for him when he arrived; he pushed it aside and put his half-eaten breakfast bar and Blue Rain in its place. The dissected hand lay inert in the clamp, its flesh pulled back and most of the inner workings removed. Carter had been searching the sinew and glowing green sludge for some kind of control board, a centralized place where the hand's intelligence was kept.

Now, in the dreary light of morning, he couldn't remember where he'd left off. He kept looking for a control board, but there wasn't one. Instead, he found what looked like a translucent box for a deck of playing cards. Inside, half a dozen small crystalline squares floated in a neon-green sludge several shades brighter than the synthetic blood around it. There were no connections between the squares that he could see.

Carter touched his ear to make sure his whisperer was there.

"Champion, play back my notes from last night."

Yes, Master.

He carried his Blue Rain over to the garage door and opened it while he listened to his own tired voice play in his ear.

…substantive dermal reinforcement…

…filaments… that's how they…

…white guys who call each other 'brotha'…

Outside, the rain fell steadily in a calm breeze, though there was little danger of water encroaching on the garage floor. Carter stood for several minutes until the can was empty. He crushed it and tossed it into a blue bin in the corner of the garage.

…maybe a plumbus…

…but how do they talk?

…should ask the P…

"That's what I did," he said aloud. The last dreamy hour of the previous night came back to him.

There was no control board in the synthetic hand, at least not in any form he had seen before. Every piece of electronics he had ever owned had the same basic components: a central processing unit, random access memory, and usually, a place to store data. With those three elements, the modern machine could do pretty much anything. In specialized applications, those elements were combined into a single unit called a System on Module or SOM. Even if there wasn't a large circuit board like in the computers of old, the hand should still have some version of a SOM, even if it were miniaturized.

And yet, dissection of the hand had yielded no such thing, only what he assumed were tiny microchips floating in the suspension fluid. Carter remembered the moment he finally thought to look at the chips under the microscope and found they were all pinless with no visible physical interface. That had sent him down a rabbit hole into near-field communications and eventually to a frequency on which the small chips were talking. He couldn't actually query them directly, but they weren't as tightly locked down as they should have been.

The proper response to an unknown query was silence, but like many poorly secured servers on the net, the chip instead shot back a communications preamble, an advanced version of the simple SYN/ACK exchange used in a TCP/IP connection. The last thing Carter recalled doing before heading to bed was copying the preamble into a chat with Pyrosius, a friend from high school who'd gone down a less legitimate path in the tech world. Together with a few friends, they maintained a private chat room hosted in a Philippines-based darknet. Pyrosius had been the only one online and talking the night before, so Carter had given him the preamble and asked him to look into it.

There was no way Pyrosius was awake so early in the morning, but there was a chance he'd left a message in the chat.

Carter rolled his chair from the workbench over to his desk. He tapped the spacebar on the keyboard as he sat down, bringing the large vidscreen crackling to life, almost blinding him with a desktop background depicting a tall, well-endowed blonde dressed only in red stockings against the snow-covered mountains of an expensive ski resort in the French Alps. The woman's name was Elena; Carter had met her in the lodge following an afternoon of skiing, as he'd requested in his engagement rider with Adelai Associates. He remembered the headache from that morning—his punishment for a long night of drinking and revels. And yet, they'd managed to pull themselves out of bed at sunrise to take a photo on the pristine snow. Elena had fallen shortly after the camera snapped. They'd laughed loud enough to wake neighboring cabins as they stumbled back to their room.

Now, when he saw the picture, he couldn't help but smile. His life had changed so much in such a short time. He could hardly believe that just a few years ago, he was still living in his parents' basement and spending every dollar just trying to get Dyalogued off the ground. Selling the company and its intellectual property to Vinestead International had made him a multi-millionaire overnight, and he'd done the only reasonable thing in response: he fled the country.

A month in the Alps had been a fitting celebration. The wine, the women, the wasting of money: all of it convinced him of one thing—he didn't want to go back to work, at least not in the way Vinestead wanted him to. A year after the sale, he'd exited Dyalogued, handing over control to a new CEO Vinestead appointed to the role. Since then, he'd been free to explore his own interests, content to walk the path from his bedroom to his workbench over and over until the next great idea occurred to him.

As it turned out, it was his neighbor who had the next great idea.

When the chat window loaded, Carter found a single message waiting for him: *Sent you a DM.*

He clicked over to the private chat with Pyrosius. A video message filled the screen.

Pyrosius was a thin guy, but in the glow of his computer vidscreen against the dark of his room, he looked absolutely ghostly. He was clean-shaven, had thin eyebrows, and wore a ponytail on the very top of his head like his ancestors. At least, that's what he told people. Carter knew the truth was that they'd seen that hairstyle in a video game when they were fourteen, and Pyrosius had decided then to grow his hair long and wear it like an ancient Chinese warrior.

His face was frozen in withered fatigue until Carter clicked the *play* button.

"Hey, asshole. Thanks for dumping this on me and then just disappearing. It's not like I have a match tomorrow or some ATM to hack across state lines. No, it's far more important that Mr. Corporate sends me on a snipe hunt while he sleeps like a baby in his mansion."

Pyrosius reached out for the lower corner of his vidscreen. A black window appeared, along with a snippet of code that scrolled to a final *endif* statement.

"This is my mockup of the preamble. It's nothing special, just an alphanumeric string, about the length of a standard root certificate. I ran it against every repository I know, and nothing came back. No partial matches, no common bits—nothing." He rubbed his face. Glossy black fingernails reflected the white glare of the vidscreen. "And that's weird, because even with proprietary code, you'd expect to see some traces, some lifts from an open-source project or something, but yeah. This must have been black boxed until it went into production, or it's so new that no one has broken the seal on it yet. I looked at the zero-day boards and anonymous drops, but again, dead halls and blue balls."

Carter checked the length of the video. Twelve minutes. For a guy who hadn't found anything, he'd certainly spent a long time yapping about it.

"I was about to give up, but then I got a hit. Not a direct hit, but like…" He looked down, shook his head. "An echo? I guess? It was the same preamble, but transposed, as if someone was trying to mask where the code had come from. And you know what? That makes sense… because I found the match in the Fall of Brigham."

"No fucking way," said Carter.

The Fall of Brigham, or Fall of Brigham Plaza, had made news a couple years back as one of the biggest data breaches in Vinestead International history. A hacker named Danny Guns Montreal had broken into a protected construct in VNet and laid its contents bare for the world to see. Major revelations came to light as a result, including transcripts from air traffic controllers that seemed to exonerate Kaili Zabora for Calle Cinco de Mayo. But for every major news story to come out of the Fall, there were hundreds of other small archives, code stolen from every major software and electronics company in the world. Decades of software development went from proprietary to de facto open source overnight.

If the preamble existed—in some form or another—in the Fall of Brigham, it meant Vinestead had either stolen the code from Vise Robotics, or Vise Robotics was using code stolen by Vinestead from some other entity. The latter seemed unlikely. Why would a startup robotics company take a chance on duplicating someone else's intellectual property?

Carter scratched his chin.

"There's no way to tell where the data originally came from, but my guess is Vinestead was into Vise Robotics before the breach." Pyrosius took a pull from a can of Pabst Blue Ribbon. "They probably got their hands on some code, decided to stash it away for a rainy day, and Vise was forced to make some changes."

Carter nodded, relieved to have come to the same conclusion as Pyrosius.

"Then again, is it enough? Did they make enough changes that Vinestead couldn't hack it once they go into production? Or did Vise just get lazy? From what I can tell, Winston Vise has no professional connections with anyone Vinestead, besides living next door to one, I guess."

Pyrosius put his hands up as Carter muttered, "Hey!"

"And you can deny it all you want, but if you take Vinestead money, you're Vinestead. Doesn't mean we can't still be friends, just that I'm not sharing any of my passwords with you." He sat back in his chair, rubbed his eyes. "So that's it, I guess. Vise Robotics is using compromised code. Vinestead had it, and now the world has it. Someone should probably bring that up to the boss man."

Yeah, thought Carter. *That'll make great dinner conversation.*

"I mean, if he doesn't know Vinestead broke into his network, then maybe he'll give you a reward. And since I helped you figure it out, maybe you throw a little my way. Segmented Reality has a new immersion rig out this month. Five large, fully loaded. I could quick-scope like a motherfucker with one of those." He drummed on his desk. "Hit me up if you need anything else. I mean I guess I work for you now, not that I'm calling you Master like Champion or anything."

The video cut out, froze on a frame of Pyrosius leaning to the side and rolling his eyes in his sockets. It was as if he had no irises at all.

Carter closed the chat program.

"Champion…" A double tone sounded in his ear. "Remind me to send the P a new Segmented immersion rig."

Yes, Master. You have a large transaction to review on your American Express.

"Really? How much?"

Seven thousand U.S. dollars, Master.

"From who?"

Adelai Associates, LLC. Do you approve of the transaction?

Carter smirked, remembering the spiel he'd been given over the phone the first time he'd made a reservation for himself. First night's charge due at contract signing. Remainder due on first day of engagement.

The charge meant Jane was coming with him to Vise Manor.

"Approved."

Thank you, Master.

EIGHT

Barinson Services, which had been dodging Diya's phone calls all day Monday, finally sent over a revised contract and invoice at 1:57 p.m. on Tuesday.

Diya immediately forwarded the message to Bradley, looked over the contract twice, checked in again with Bradley for his sign-off, and then added her digital signature to the file. As it left her outbox, she allowed herself a small moment to breathe. There was still so much work to do, but after finally wrangling all the vendors and signing all the contracts, she felt as if she'd just free-soloed El Capitan in Yosemite. Now, standing at the top of the mountain, she caught her breath and tried not to think about the long descent.

Something could still go wrong. The vendors could flake or deliver the wrong items—or deliver the right items in the wrong way.

But that was a tomorrow problem.

She was on the road thirty minutes later, and by the time she crossed the bridge heading out of Manhattan, the threat of rush hour slowing her down was well behind her. The city may have been descending into gridlock, but she was free, zooming along the highway at a brisk seventy-five miles per hour in her little silver Mazda. For the first hour of the drive, she listened to music, a peppy mix of Top Hits and New Rap. When the landscape flattened and the buildings that normally towered over her faded into the rearview mirror, she started to feel lonely, something that was almost impossible in the city, where there was hardly enough space to exist. There was always someone nearby, and if she couldn't see them, she could usually hear or smell them.

Diya used her whisperer to dial up a sampling of the day's trending podcasts. A woman's voice filled her ear. The timbre was old and raspy, and her words were not so much spoken as extruded. She was in the middle of a story about a little boy who used to stand at the end of her bed every night. Being unmarried and childless, the boy's presence was in itself startling, but what made the encounter utterly terrifying was her complete paralysis. The woman was awake, she could move her eyes, but her body wouldn't respond to any commands.

The boy stared at her.

She stared at the boy.

Background music swelled as the woman reached the climax of her story.

"Until one night," she said, leaving a pause as wide as the Hudson River, "the little boy opened his mouth like he was going to speak. He had no teeth, no tongue, but there was a sound there, low and rumbling. It grew, like a kettle starting to boil, and I realized it was a scream. But it was more than that. It was a shriek, a primal sound so full of fear that it touched me at the lowest level of my being. I almost felt pity for the boy... almost... until I realized..."

Diya turned her head as if to hear her whisperer better.

"...it was *my* scream. The boy was screaming *my* scream."

Her phone buzzed in its mount, rattling the air conditioning vents. Diya jumped, but the soft burble in her ear that followed told her it was no ghost trying to scare her—it was just an incoming phone call.

Diya eyed the phone. Its screen had come alive and showed a heavily filtered photo of her friend Millie at Ventura Beach, her eyes and teeth sparkling unnaturally. Below it, a microphone icon pulsed.

"Answer." The phone's screen refreshed into a keypad. "Hey, Millie."

"Hey, where are you?" She was practically yelling. In the background, traffic noise threatened to drown her out.

"I'm on the road, headed out to the country. Why, where are you?"

Millie grunted. "I'm at your building, lady. I wanted to see you before you went home for the day."

Outside, the trees were a hundred shades of orange, and many of them had already started to shed their leaves. If she had to be away from home, the country wasn't a bad option. It was so much more alive than the city, so much more nature than man. Diya did long for home, but not her apartment in the city. She wanted to be back in Pennsylvania, back in the small, one-story house she grew up in on the outskirts of Pittsburgh. Though, her parents had recently moved into the city proper, and now her childhood home was a place she could only visit in her memory.

"I decided to leave early." Diya blinked a few times to clear her head of the woman's story. "We're hosting that dinner party I've been telling you about on Friday, but I've got two days of long nights ahead of me. And you know what my dad says about working long nights."

"*Get a good night's sleep and start fresh first thing in the morning.* I remember." She gave a mock cry. "But ugh, I forgot that was this week. I thought it was the Friday before Halloween."

"I think most people would want to spend that weekend with their family."

"Whatever," said Millie. "You were talking about it being all fancy; I just thought it was going to be one of those things where everyone wears a mask and a cloak and then there's an orgy and then it's just holes and poles all night."

"Holes and poles?"

"Ugh, I heard that from my boss today. He's in his fifties, but he talks like he's twelve. Honestly, I don't know why I work for these Harvard Law Chads. It's like I can feel hands going up my skirt every time I walk into the office."

The Mazda's navigation system indicated an upcoming exit. Diya guided the car off the highway and onto a smaller two-lane road.

"You should dress up as one of those *Mad Men* this year," said Diya. "Slick your hair back and walk around the office calling all the men *sweetcheeks* and *dollface*, see how they like it."

"Right. They'll probably think it's an invitation to bend me over the copier. No, I'm going as the Lady in White this year, which you would have known, if you'd seen my latest Pattrn story."

"You know how I feel about social media." Rakesh Singh had never been a fan of handing over his personal details and activity to some faceless company, and Diya had followed suit.

"Like you'd have time anyway. All you do is work." She huffed. "I don't understand the point of having a job if you can't go out and live your life."

"No one wants to work in this country."

"You can't be daddy's girl forever, D. Eventually you're going to have to jump out of the nest and flap-flap your wings."

"I flap," protested Diya. "I flapped when I got my first tattoo. And I totally flapped when I lost my virginity in Isaac Tomky's basement my sophomore year. I've done a lot of things Rakesh Singh wouldn't approve of."

"The fact that you call him Rakesh Singh instead of *dad* says everything about how much you *flap*, lady. You could be coming to a pre-Halloween party with me this weekend, but instead you're going to be cleaning up after some East Coast elites."

"That's different, Millie. That's my job."

"Yeah, I know." She sounded wistful. The background noise had cleared, and Diya imagined she'd ducked inside a building. "I just… I guess I feel like we're wasting the best years of our lives working for people who don't appreciate us. I know you say your boss treats you well, but you've only been working there since what, last spring? You've busted your ass for him every day for six months and now he's got you hosting dinner parties at his home on the weekend? Whatever he's paying you, it isn't enough."

Diya shrugged; she'd never told Millie exactly how much Winston was paying, but it was more than clerking at a law firm.

"It's not that bad," said Diya. "Now's the right time to be doing this type of work. When I'm older and chasing Isaac Tomky's rug rats around our two-story brownstone in the suburbs, I won't be able to dedicate this kind of time to work. I'm pretty sure that's why Winston hires people in their early twenties as assistants. We're the only age group with no life to distract us from work."

"I'm sure that's exactly why he hires twenty-year-old girls to be his assistant. Nothing to do with all those fresh faces and tight bods walking around the office."

Diya wagged a finger at the phone. "His previous assistant was named Lawrence, and he still had acne. Smart guy though. Shitty handwriting. Thank god he kept most of his notes on the computer."

Asphalt rumbled under the Mazda's tires. Diya kept turning onto smaller and smaller roads, until finally she had slowed to thirty-five miles per hour on a path made dark by a thick canopy of overgrown trees.

Her headlights came on automatically.

The navigation screen showed the remaining travel time.

7 miles. 16 minutes.

"Well…"

"I can't believe I have to go to this party alone," said Millie.

"I'll be there with you in spirit."

"Not good enough."

Diya gripped the steering wheel with both hands. "I'm really sorry, but I don't think I'm getting out of there until Sunday afternoon. I have to make sure all the vendors get loaded out. You wouldn't believe all the stuff we're bringing in for *one* night."

"Must be trying to impress his guests."

"Or maybe he's just trying to show respect. I get the sense these aren't the kind of people you feed fast food to. Can you imagine? Fancy dinner table, satin placemats, ruby chargers… and just edge-to-edge Big Macs and McNuggets still in their cardboard containers. Fries piled in porcelain tureens. And Winston just standing there on the other side of the table, arms spread wide, shit-eating grin on his face, like he's King Ronald himself feeding his loyal subjects."

Millie chuckled. "At least you wouldn't have to worry which side your salad fork is supposed to go on."

"No salad forks. Just a plastic spork. Really wouldn't matter which side of your paper placemat you put it on, so long as it doesn't cover up the word search."

Low static.

Silence.

Diya enjoyed the quiet moments with Millie. Those kinds of pauses were unheard of at work, whether that was Winston or Bradley or any of the dozens of companies and vendors she spoke to during her week. There was always business to be done with those people, but it was never about just *being* with them. In the days before full-time jobs, Diya and Millie had spent many nights hanging out in some private spot on the Syracuse campus just leafing through websites on palettes or window shopping a magazine they'd picked up at a bodega. And though they never ran out of things to talk about, they spent a lot of time in silence, just being with each other.

That too was home to Diya, and unlike the house in Pittsburgh, she could go there whenever she wanted, wherever she was, even on the road.

"Well, I guess I should let you go. You really shouldn't be talking and driving at the same time."

"You sound like Ra—my dad."

"I just want you to make it home safe, unlike you, who doesn't care if I go to a party by myself, drink way too much, and end up leaving my costume on the floor of some seedy New Jersey hotel room."

The canopy covering the road ended abruptly, and Diya squinted at the sudden brightness. She slowed at a junction where a sign stood pointing both left and right. Over the arrows were the numbers *1* and *3*. Embossed letters at the top read *Dark Hallow Road*.

Diya turned left toward Vise Manor, casting a glance in the other direction to where Carter Price lived.

"I'm almost at the house now," she said. "I'll let you know when I'm headed back to the city. Maybe we can get dinner Sunday night. There's a new pho place I've been wanting to try."

"Fine. I guess I can wait for you."

"Go home before it gets dark. Nothing good happens in the city after sunset."

"Right away, Mr. Singh." She laughed. "Love you, D. Text me some photos of the orgy if you can."

"I will. Love you too."

The connection dropped, and the podcast resumed with an ear-splitting wail. Diya tapped her whisperer to stop the audio. For a brief, horrifying moment, she had seen the little boy from the woman's story, had seen him plain as the road in front of her, standing at the end of her bed. Only now, his face was brighter, and his chubby cheeks and brown bowl cut reminded her of Isaac Tomky.

She was still laughing at herself when she pulled up to a guard shack next to a tall wrought-iron gate with black braided bars. The house wasn't even in view yet; the GPS showed another two miles to go.

A guard approached her door as she rolled her window down.

"Hi, I'm Diya Singh, Mr. Vise's personal assistant."

"I know who you are, Ms. Singh." His massive jaw barely moved when he spoke. "We weren't expecting you until tomorrow morning."

"Well, it's like my dad says, *don't put off until tomorrow what you can do today.*"

"I believe that was Benjamin Franklin."

"Are you sure?"

He nodded, smiled. "Pretty sure, ma'am." He motioned with a gloved hand to the gate. "Just follow the driveway and mind the gravel. I'd keep it under thirty if you don't want to ding your car."

"Thank you, sir."

He touched the brim of a black hat embroidered with the word *SECURITY* on its face. He stepped back as the wrought-iron gate broke apart in the center and swung inward.

"Welcome to Vise Manor, ma'am."

NINE

The bed was damp and cold.

With sweat beading on her chest, Adelai wanted nothing more than to wrap herself up in a warm comforter and sink several inches into the soft mattress. Except, there was no comforter nearby, nor were there any pillows that she might drape across her body. She could feel something soft and cushiony under her hips and vaguely remembered a pillow being thrust there earlier in the night. Not that she wanted anything to do with it now; it was covered in sweat and who knew what else.

The silver blades of the ceiling fan caught the faint light from outside as it trickled in through the drawn blinds. She watched the blur and shivered.

"Are you cold?"

Adelai turned to look at the shadow sitting at the foot of the bed. Shoulders heaved in the darkness; a head hung low in exhaustion.

"A little."

Colin Rayburn groaned as he stood up and came around to her side of the bed. As he got closer, Adelai could see the sweat still clinging to his cheeks and chest. Thick arms tugged at the sheets around her feet, and once loosened, he pulled them up to her neck.

"The blanket fell on the floor. Let me get you a new one."

"It's okay," she told him, wringing every last bit of warmth out of the thin sheet. "I should get going soon."

He nodded. "Still. Might as well be comfortable while you're here." Rayburn disappeared into a closet and shut the door behind him before he turned on the light.

Adelai closed her eyes and listened to the rain falling against the windows. Somewhere on the other side of the room, a stereo played soft jazz, though the current song was somewhat aggressive, building repeatedly to a peak only to suddenly relent to almost nothing. The tempo matched the cadence of Adelai's mental command to throw back the sheet and get up. Her body didn't listen. It just wanted to rest.

She hadn't moved by the time she felt Rayburn return. He draped a thicker blanket over her and patted her shoulder.

"Thank you."

"Of course." He retreated to the foot of the bed again and sat down on a small bench. His breath was still ragged.

"Are you alright?"

"Yeah, I'm fine. Just need a minute. The synth has a weird taper."

Rayburn always seemed to have issues with synthetic drugs. He was forty-five years old and didn't have a single augment in his body, nothing to help with his stamina or blood flow or arousal. He was as natural a man as could be found in the city, and if he had the choice between synth and a nice glass of wine, he would choose the wine nine times out of ten.

Tonight had been different though. Adelai had walked through the door with a code card in hand and hadn't given him a choice. She'd wanted to ascend to a higher level of existence, and she'd wanted him to come with her.

"Do you know what time it is?" Her watch and whisperer were both on the dresser in the little glass jewelry dish he kept for her.

"A little after ten. Why?"

"Just wondering how much longer I can lie here."

"Is Simone expecting you?"

Adelai sighed, turned her head to the window. Hazy yellow squares on the building across the street stared back at her.

"Sooner or later," she replied. "She had a spin class at eight and then I think she was going for a massage. She's probably on her way home now to do some packing."

"Is she going on a trip?"

"We're heading overseas for a couple months. Our flight leaves Sunday, after we get back from that overnight at Winston Vise's place. Simone keeps saying it's the unofficial start of our winter vacation, so I guess that's something to look forward to."

"I didn't think you were going to that."

"Why not?"

Rayburn stood and walked to the dresser. He grabbed one of the water bottles he'd placed there earlier and twisted the top off.

"I thought after my report, you wouldn't think it was worth your time."

"What do you mean? Simone said you didn't find anything wrong there."

"Nothing wrong as in nothing dangerous," he said, pulling fresh boxers from the dresser. "But did you read the section on former and current personnel?"

She hadn't read any of it, she realized.

"I only know what Simone told me. Mostly financial stuff."

Rayburn came to sit in a chair on Adelai's side of the bed. "The financials are solid enough. There's money and lots of it. I did a deep dive on Vise and didn't turn up anything overly suspicious. But if he weren't a successful businessman, he'd be one of those eternally poor schlubs who keeps losing all their money on get-rich-quick schemes. I wrote in there, it's not *what* business he's in that bothers me, it's *how* he runs it."

Adelai slipped a hand over her eyes. "I should have known Simone would hold out on me."

"Maybe she just didn't see what I saw."

"And what did you see, Colin?" She rolled onto her side to face him. When he noticed her head hanging awkwardly, he pulled the throw pillow out from behind his back and helped her slide it into place.

"Cracks," he replied. "Fuzzy edges. It happens all the time when I'm vetting people. You start going in on them, and you collect all these puzzle pieces, but they don't really fit together. Every mismatched edge is a red flag. Vise's pieces all go together, but just barely. I guess it was a gut feeling."

Rayburn had overseen Adelai Associates' background checks for over a decade. In all that time, he'd never made a decision based on a gut feeling. There was always supporting evidence when he recommended approving or passing on a potential client.

"What did you find?"

He sighed, took another drink. "Everything kept coming up clean, so I went deeper." He made his hand into a blade and sliced at the air. "And I got down to the employees. All of them checked out. Recent grads, some lifers, but all with work histories and references. I thought I'd hit another dead end until I read one of his employee's resumes, a software engineer named Jon Maruska. Nothing really special about him. Twenty-eight, graduated from Maryland in 2016, Computer Science."

"Sounds like a child to me."

"And a bit of a fuck-up too, at least according to his resume. He's been out of college five years, and he's held positions at seven different companies. Vise Robotics is his longest gig at eleven months. Once I saw that, it got me thinking about the other employees, and some of them are just as bad as Maruska. In fact, no one working at Vise Robotics, besides Winston Vise himself, has been there more than two years. They have so much churn, they've never in the history of the company paid health insurance for every currently employed head. They've always got new people coming in to replace the older ones going out."

Adelai pulled the blanket tighter. "Sounds like a shitty way to save a buck."

"That's just it. Vise doesn't need to save a buck. They're flush with capital. So really, the question is, if they're turning over employees every year to year and a half, saving money on benefits, and mostly hiring entry level people, then where is all that money going?"

"Synthetic humans." As the words left her mouth, she wished she could have them back. After Rayburn didn't reply, she continued, "He sent a sample to the house on Monday. It was a hand, a synthetic hand. Beautifully crafted. Colin, it was just like touching Simone."

"Just a hand?"

"Mm-hmm." Her eyelids dipped; the bed was growing warm again. "I can't imagine he'd want to send the entire synthetic unsolicited like that. He didn't ask for the hand back, so now it's just sitting in its box in the living room." She chuckled to herself. "Honest to God I thought it was a sex toy."

Rayburn huffed. "You think that's why he invited you out to his house? To sell you a synthetic?"

"I guess it doesn't really matter." Adelai shrugged beneath the blanket. "Momo wants to go, enough to withhold information from me, evidently. I get the feeling she's been cooped up too long here in the city. I look at this like one of those tacky timeshare presentations. We go, she gets to dress up and feel sexy, we eat Vise's food and drink his alcohol, and all it costs us is the time we spend sitting through his little slideshow. Besides, Colin… what use would I have for a synthetic?"

"Maybe not you, but the company?"

She shook her head. "If people want to fuck an inanimate piece of rubber, they go to Companion Dynamics. If they want the real thing, they come to me."

"I hear that." He raised his bottle.

"Come here," she said, scooting back toward the middle of the bed. He obliged, and once he was reclining in the space she'd vacated, Adelai laid her head against his chest, felt the fine hair against her cheek.

She loved how he smelled, how different it was from Simone.

He stroked her hair for several minutes.

"Sometimes I don't know what I'm doing."

Rayburn made an agreeing sound that made his chest rumble. He moved his hand to her back and said, "Tell me."

"I just… thinking about this weekend and this trip. Simone's excited, and I feel like I should be excited too, but I'm not. When I hear her talk about it, I think to myself, *oh, well, that's just one more thing.* One more thing to get through, to get past. It's like everything in my life is an obligation that I don't want." He pinched her lightly on her butt. "Okay, not *everything*, but you know what I mean. I could lie here and complain about work and the sun would be coming up before I ran out of things that bother me."

"You should try that sometime. I'm happy to listen."

"I know you are, but I couldn't do that to you."

"And you don't want to tell Simone?"

"I couldn't do that to her. And beyond you two, no one else really cares. I'm a wealthy, white, female business-owner. They don't make violins small enough to play my sad song." She buried her face in his stomach. "I should just shut up."

Rayburn didn't respond, and after a few minutes, Adelai assumed he'd fallen asleep. Instead, he inhaled sharply and said, "I remember when Donald was born, I was only nineteen. Lots of people who have kids when they're young say they weren't ready to be parents. I was. I was ready to change diapers and wipe noses and love that kid with everything I had. He pissed me off, but I loved him, still love him. If there was anything I wasn't ready for though, it was *time*. From day one, that little bastard has been just one massive time suck."

He laughed; Adelai felt the vibrations in her cheek.

"I remember thinking *I just want to sleep* or *I just want to watch the game*. And you know what? That kind of thinking poisoned every moment with him. Holding my son started to feel like a chore. Reading to him at night felt like something to just *get through* so I could go watch TV or open a beer. That was the hardest part: appreciating what I had, and not obsessing over all the other stuff I wanted to do."

He squeezed her shoulder again.

"But that was me. My obligation was an actual obligation to a helpless, innocent baby. Besides the company, which you could easily hand off to any number of capable CEOs, you don't have any real obligations. But maybe you see them that way because you'd rather be doing something else. Maybe the job just doesn't interest you anymore."

"Maybe."

"If you could do anything starting tomorrow, what would it be?"

"Oh God…" The longer she thought about it, the less certain Adelai became that she'd ever find a good answer. Her imagination produced nothing but a familiar scene of her sitting on the couch with a bottle of wine in hand. "I just want to sit. Sit and do nothing. I don't want to have to participate anymore."

"You could do that, if you really wanted to."

"It's a nice dream." She patted him on the stomach. "And maybe for a man, it's easy to imagine taking your foot off the gas for a few seconds. But that's not my life. I have to hustle every day for the things I want."

"And what do you want right now? More than anything?"

She breathed in his scent again. "I want to fall asleep right here with you."

"Then stay. Stay and sleep. Put everything else off 'til tomorrow."

"That's a nice dream too, but that's all it is."

She closed her eyes.

Darkness fell.

Across the room, her phone chirped and rattled in the shallow jewelry dish.

TEN

A light rain fell on the gently sloping backyard of the ranch house Robert and Laura had rented for the night.

Great sheets of misty air billowed over the green, slightly overgrown grass, like ghostly waves running down a beach, trying to get back to the sea. None of it touched them on the covered porch; the chair swing was set far back enough that all they felt was the cool, rain-soaked air, which Robert imagined wouldn't bother a local but had them bundled up in their jackets and cowering under a flannel blanket they'd stolen from the couch.

Robert enjoyed the warmth the blanket created, as well as the feel of Laura's legs draped over his. Though they often spent their evenings out on the patio at the house in Houston, it was never like this. The ever-present heat—as if the devil himself lived in H-Town—wouldn't allow it.

They sat in silence for a long time, swinging gently, listening to the patter. The house was half a mile from the main road, and there were no engines or horns or sirens to intrude upon the stillness. Every now and then, Laura would sigh contentedly. Robert wondered what she was thinking about, even as his mind drifted back to his conversation with Frank Kagan. After finishing their round at Pebble Beach, they'd had a surf and turf lunch at the clubhouse. Robert had never known Kagan to be wistful in any sense of the word, but the shrewd California businessman had allowed himself to dream about a synthetic future, if only for a little while. He hadn't drunk enough John Dalys to come right out and say he was afraid of death, but Robert had easily read between the lines.

Frank Kagan was worried about his legacy—something Robert had given up caring about long ago. While Kagan lamented his rudderless offspring, the only heir to the family fortune, Robert enjoyed the buttery lobster and medium-rare steak, content in the knowledge that when he died, things would be pretty straightforward.

If he went before Laura, her instructions were to dissolve the Hargreaves Group and pocket the proceeds. She might be sad at his passing, but she would have enough money to be comfortable for several lifetimes. If she died before him, and he passed later, their money would go to various charities and the children of distant relatives who never phoned or visited. It was neat and tidy, a simple closing of the book on Robert Hargreaves.

Even the specter of his own mortality could hold no space in his mind. He thought instead of the steak, of how each bite melted in his mouth, and whether a synthetic tongue could make it taste the same way.

"Should we order a—"

"Maybe we shouldn't go tomorrow." Laura lifted her head from his shoulder and smiled. "Sorry. You go."

"No, I was just going to suggest we order a pizza or something. I don't think there's any food in the kitchen."

"That sounds fine." She put her head down, sighed again.

"But what'd you say? You don't want to go tomorrow?"

She shrugged. "I don't know. It's just so nice here. I think about all the work involved in getting dressed up and mingling with all those people... it's just exhausting. Why do that when we could just sit here another night, just you and me?"

"I'm sure we'd get tired of this in no time." He patted her head gently. "It's not hard to grow greener grass. The problem is *where* you grow it. We've got our own little patch back home, and when the mood strikes, we can walk to a dozen different restaurants. I don't even know if there's a pizza place that'll deliver out here. And if they do, it's going to be some Mom and Pop like Maple Leaf Pizza or Gino's Pies. That's the kind of trade-off you make in this type of acquisition."

"I'd trade Central Houston for this. Hell, I'd trade the walk to the Galleria for this. I can get everything I need at the Wal-Mart in town. Couple of sundresses, a coat for the winter, and I'd be good."

"It sounds nice, I'll give you that."

He wasn't going to argue with her. Laura had a habit of romanticizing the places they went, always saying they should put down roots in San Francisco or New York or Naples or Normandy. The location didn't really matter, so long as it was away from Houston where she had been born in heat and raised on sizzling evercrete. Robert sensed her desire to run away, to leave behind decades of life that had transpired before he met her. And though he took her on dozens of trips each year, they were never enough.

"I don't know. Maybe I'm just bored. Ever since we retired, I haven't had anything to do except take care of the house. And if that's all my life is going to be, then it doesn't matter where that house is. It could be here. I wouldn't mind a life with fewer modern comforts. No electronic billboards. No self-driving cars trying to run me off the road. No disembodied hands trying to tickle me."

Robert laughed, remembering how terrified she'd been of that little hand.

"Maybe you're just hungry," he suggested.

She looked up at him, narrowed her eyes, but said nothing.

For a time, the swing moved back and forth at the whim of the wind.

"Frank Kagan thinks there might be some real potential here." The words weren't really meant for Laura. "It's the old saying that competition breeds innovation. Right now, you've only got two players in the synthetic human space. A third player like Winston Vise could upset the balance and force Perion and Vinestead to respond. That could speed things up. Imagine synthetics living and working alongside us. Imagine us becoming them and living forever. Imagine—"

"Why are you telling me this?"

"Just talking out loud. There's a good reason for me to go tomorrow night and see just how competitive Vise Robotics actually is." He felt her sink against him, resigned. "But there's no reason it has to be at a dinner party. I don't know who else we're going to meet at this thing, but it sounds like Vise is putting on a spectacle, and if that's not your thing, then it's not my thing either. I have a feeling our presence is going to give Vise validation that real, serious people are interested in his products. Just by being there, we're helping him sell to the others. You know how I feel about that kind of thing."

Laura pulled her legs off his and sat up. The blanket fell into her lap.

"You don't like being used." She gave him a quick glance. "And I don't like being used either. Maybe the rain will hold until tomorrow. We could open the windows and lie in bed and watch TV all day. I feel so far away from everything here." Her hand fell on his leg. "It's nice, you know? Not having obligations."

A crack of thunder sounded from the other side of the house.

"Then that settles it. We won't go."

She smirked at him. "You'd do anything for me, wouldn't you?"

"That's my job. That's what I do."

"So original." She tossed her side of the blanket at his chest and stood up. The swing tried to follow her as she stepped closer to the edge of the porch.

Robert admired how much at home she looked standing with one shoulder against a tall post, one hip slightly raised, her faded skinny jeans stretched over her legs.

She folded her arms in her cardigan and spoke over her shoulder. "What if I asked you to go skinny dipping in that lake? Would you do it?"

He eyed the small pier in the distance, shorter than his driveway back home. It was hard to imagine himself running naked to the end of it and launching into the air. It was raining, cold, and his back was still sore from the eighteen rounds in Carmel.

"Of course," he replied. He stood and started unzipping his jacket.

She waved him away. "No, don't. I was just asking. Besides, the Lady of the Lake would probably take you down to the bottom and keep you as a sex slave. Then I'd have to fly back home alone."

"What lady?"

Laura shrugged as if the answer were obvious. "Every lake in the countryside has a Lady. Think of how long people have lived on this land and tell me none of them ever walked into the water without any intention of coming out."

"Wouldn't that mean every body of water on the planet is haunted?"

"Well, not sewers and whatnot. Just natural lakes and ponds like these." She gestured into the rain. "Probably the house too. Think about it, Robert. Old house, sprawling land, miles from civilization. If I were a ghost, this is where I'd hang out."

"Ghosts do take their privacy seriously, I'll give you that."

She raised an eyebrow at him. "Are you mocking me, Mr. Hargreaves?"

"With love," he assured her.

"Oh, as if that excuses it. *But honey, I cheated on you with love.*"

"I would never—"

"*But officer, I suffocated him in his sleep with love... and a pillow... but mostly love.*"

Robert pointed to the back door. "I'm going inside to order us some dinner *with love.* Then I thought maybe I'd start a fire with love. Would you like to join me... with love?"

She shrugged, smiled. "If I *have* to."

As expected, there was only one place in the nearby town of Jensen that served pizza, and Robert had to promise them an extra twenty bucks for delivery out to the ranch house. Luckily, Bambino Italy was also a full-fledged Italian restaurant, so he was able to order two bottles of cabernet along with the large pizza— pepperoni with added mushrooms on one side.

An hour later, with a hot pizza steaming in a box on the coffee table, they sat together on a furry white rug in front of the fireplace. The rain had picked up, and what little sunlight remained couldn't keep the large windows from becoming shadowy mirrors. Robert watched the reflections out of the corner of his eye while Laura expanded on her theory about haunted lakes. At one point, she suggested they watch a scary movie, but there were no televisions in the house, despite its large footprint and many rooms. Of the doors open to them, there wasn't much more than a bathroom, a game room with a pool table upholstered in blue felt, and a small library.

"The library's probably haunted too," said Laura, in between sips of wine. "I bet when we're not looking, books float off the shelves and flutter around the room like little butterflies."

Her theories on the supernatural became more outlandish as the night wore on and the wine flowed. An ornate German cuckoo clock above the fireplace ticked the minutes away. Soon, Laura was lying with her head on Robert's lap. He stroked her hair absently until she started to snore softly.

A light touch on her neck woke her up.

"Hmm?"

"Want to go to bed?"

"No…" Her voice was heavy with sleep. "The bedroom is haunted."

He chuckled. "Come on, let's go. If there're any ghosts in the bed, I'll chase them away." He helped her to her feet, then watched as she stumbled down the narrow hallway like a toddler fighting sleep. "Are your PJs still in the suitcase?"

She touched his nose with the tip of a shaky finger. "You know I sleep in the nude… in the buff… in my birthday suit."

"No, you're thinking of me."

"Well maybe I will tonight. Give the ghosts a show." She raised her voice to make an announcement. "Fifty-five-year-old woman about to get naked. Everyone gather 'round."

Robert turned on the bedside lamp; a soft yellow glow filled the room, just enough to see the buttons on Laura's jeans. He helped her undress, taking care not to snag her shirt on her hexagonal earrings. He stood back as she removed her bra and pushed her underwear down her legs past pink wool socks.

"Everyone getting a good look?" She turned her attention to the corner of the room near a dresser as if someone were standing there. "All me," she said, lifting and dropping her left breast in demonstration.

"Yes, we're all very impressed." Robert laughed as he took her by the shoulders and guided her down to the bed. When she was laid out, he pulled the sheets up to her neck.

"Now you," she said, her eyes drooping. "Drop your britches, mister…" She yawned. "…Hargreaves."

He ignored her and retrieved his sleep shorts from the suitcase. When he finally crawled into bed with her, he expected her to be fast asleep. Instead, she rolled over and put a hand on his chest.

"Good night, I love you," she said.

"'Night, sweetie. Get some rest. We've got a long day of lying in bed together ahead of us."

"No. We'll go to the dinner."

"Really? Are you sure?"

She slipped her hand beneath his undershirt and teased the fine hair on his stomach. "Yeah, I can tell it's important to you, so it's important to me. I don't know why I said we should skip it. We came all this way."

"It's like I said: you were hungry."

Her eyes opened a little. "No. I still don't want to go, but I'd do anything for you. Anything at all."

"With love?"

"Always with love."

Robert reached over her to turn out the light.

ELEVEN

There wasn't much to do in the nearby town of Jensen, but Carter had run out of every manner of frozen pizza, and a week of isolation had left him craving the sounds of living people.

He drove in a light but steady rain, careful to observe the many stop signs once he got into the town proper. The main drag was quiet; the resident teenagers were likely taking shelter at the small rec center near the fire station. Everyone else was either at home or at one of the half-dozen restaurants with their bright, rain-streaked windows. Blackburn Street reminded Carter of a food court at the mall; there were basically six places to eat, each offering a different cuisine, but none matching the authenticity of what could be found in the city.

The exception was Bambino Italy, who made a carbonara that rivaled anything Carter had found anywhere else. It had a quaint atmosphere, with a dozen tables set close together in the main dining room. Black and white photos on the wall gave diners something to gaze at while they ate their pasta and drank their wine. Laminated menus on the tables listed the restaurant's offerings, while on the back, a short paragraph described how the current owner's grandparents had come over from Brindisi, Italy in the 50s and set up shop in Jensen.

It was a classic American Dream story, full of hard work, perseverance, and of course, the best Italian food this side of the Atlantic. Carter wasn't sure whether any of it were true, but it didn't matter. Bambino Italy provided the closest thing to a home-cooked meal that Carter could get without driving back to Jersey to see his mom and her new boyfriend.

When Carter arrived a little after 7:00 p.m., the dinner rush was in full swing. Most of the tables in the dining room were occupied, and the sounds from the bar area on the left side of the building were raucous and jovial. The hostess was a young girl named Dana, with dark brown hair and bangs that hung slightly over her eyes. She was one of the owner's many daughters, one of five females in the latest generation. She was listening to a young man in a Bambino Italy polo complain about having to make a delivery outside of their normal routes when she noticed him approach.

"Welcome, Mr. Price," she said, with just a hint of a lingering Italian accent in her voice. "There's plenty of space at the bar if you don't want to wait."

Carter thanked her and headed left through the saloon-style doors into what looked like a speakeasy from a hundred years ago. A large, oval-shaped bar cut down the middle of the space. Various townsfolk dressed in their fall flannels sat around the polished wood drinking from tall glasses of amber beer. Flanking the bar, set against the walls, were high-top tables that fit only two people. A small wooden partition separated the two back-to-back chairs; on its faces were histories of Italy's largest families written in calligraphy on aged parchment.

The bartender, a thick-jawed man with piercing gray eyes named Antonio, who was the brother of Claudio, the owner, nodded to Carter as he came around the bar. There was an open table halfway down the room, about as close to the jukebox as Carter liked to get. He sat on the chair facing the rec area in the back where a pool table, dart boards, and a long shuffleboard provided entertainment for Bambino Italy's loyal customers. A group of men were playing pool, leaning on their cues while they sipped from bottles, occasionally ogling the young woman at the dart board near the glowing emergency exit sign.

Camilla brought him his usual—a healthy pour of a malbec, nothing too fancy, but not the common swill they would serve to a drunk person who wouldn't know the difference. Carter had never been a wine person until a couple of years ago when Jane had introduced him to it, cementing in his mind the idea that classy, upscale people drank wine, not hard liquor. He liked the way he looked with a glass in his hand. The alternative was sitting at the bar nursing a small tumbler of whiskey, which he thought made him look old.

Wine, on the other hand, communicated to those around him that he was a happy person looking to be just a little bit happier.

"Anything to eat tonight?" Camilla slipped an abbreviated menu onto the table in front of him.

Carter didn't even glance at it. "Just the flatbread. Pepperoni. The smaller one."

"Sure thing, Mr. Price."

Another of Claudio's daughters, Camilla shared the same features with Dana, enough that it was hard to tell which of them was the eldest. Carter had met all of the family members, and had even seen them around town, but they were a long way from being friends or even acquaintances. At Bambino Italy, they treated him like an honored guest, as they treated everyone who walked through their doors. They were deferential, always called him *Mr. Price*, but there was no doubt in Carter's mind that all of it was just part and parcel of *the service*.

Hospitality was a business transaction—nothing more.

Only Camilla said it with anything more than practiced formality. The way her eyes lingered on him, the way she hurried whenever he raised his hand to get her attention, spoke to an interest Carter found difficult to ignore. She was a few years younger than him, pretty in a way he could learn to love, but for some reason, he had no real interest in her. The same went for everyone else in Jensen; they were the townsfolk, and he was an outsider. There could be no crossover, not in a place Carter didn't believe he belonged.

He sipped the wine as he waited for the pizza, content to watch the people around him, how they moved and spoke. He thought of the multitude of conversations happening at the same time and how the software he'd written at Dyalogued could parse it all with almost perfect accuracy. A couple at the bar were talking about their weekend plans. A group of friends were discussing the latest superhero movie. The former high school football stars at the pool table were trying and failing to flirt with the woman playing darts. She ignored their advances, seemingly in her own world, one that stretched from a high table to the dart board and back.

The pizza didn't take long, and Carter ate it while checking his phone for messages. Pyrosius was still dumping text into the chat, mostly resource locators for places of interest in VNet. He kept tabs on the woman's attempt to fend off the circling sharks, to the point that he found himself thinking about her faux black turtleneck and how its sleeves couldn't decide whether they were short or long. A couple of times, he caught eyes with her and looked away quickly.

"Everything tasting good?" Camilla rubbed her shoulder against his.

He used the opportunity to lean into her ear. "That woman playing darts. Do you know her?"

"Why? Do you like her?"

"I haven't seen her around before."

Camilla glanced over her shoulder. "She's probably just passing through."

"What's she drinking?"

"Soda. Diet Dr. Pepper." She scrunched up her nose.

Carter held up his malbec. "Could you send her a glass of this?"

Camilla sighed. "Fine, but I think the lady just wants to play darts."

"She can still play darts with a glass of wine sitting on her table."

"Right away, Mr. Price."

Carter watched Antonio pour a new glass at the bar before handing it to Camilla to deliver to the woman's table. When she motioned to Carter, he lifted his glass slightly. The woman took her glass, mirrored his toast, and smiled. As Camilla walked away, Carter noticed her rolling her eyes.

Maybe she was right. Maybe the woman was only there to relax and play some darts. But then why had she looked over at Carter so many times? Why the glances and the occasional smile? She wasn't doing the same to the pool jocks.

His phone emitted a soft, rising chime. He opened the chat app and saw Pyrosius had posted an animated image of Bugs Bunny slamming his face repeatedly into a keyboard.

Been awake too long, read an accompanying message. *Jacking out.*

Carter scrolled back through the chat to see what Pyrosius had been working on. Most of it was fragmented, just bits of text interspersed with monospace CLI pastes, which under closer inspection, were results of a *diff* command on two blocks of code. He'd been staring at the messages for several minutes before he felt someone standing next to him.

It was the woman. She was taller than he expected, and when she looked down at him in his seat, her chestnut hair fell alongside her face in loose curls. She wore a deep shade of red lipstick that drew his eyes to her mouth.

"Hi."

"Hi," he repeated, happy to get the word out without stammering.

She tapped her wine glass with unpainted fingernails. "I just wanted to say thanks for the drink. How did you know malbec was my favorite?"

He shrugged, touched the stem of his glass. "It should be everyone's favorite. Cabernet's a close second, but nothing beats an oaky malbec. And they usually have a good vintage here…" He let out a chuckle. "I'm sorry. I don't know anything about wine. Someone much classier than me introduced me to malbec, and I just haven't tried anything else yet."

She smiled. "Wow, honest. Embarrassing, but honest. Well, I'll admit I'm not much of a wine drinker myself. It's more of an occasion drink, I'd say. It needs to be a nice dinner or maybe celebrating a promotion. Or when you have to drive and don't want to get too wasted." She sighed and looked toward the exit.

Carter followed her gaze. Beyond the swinging doors, lightning bathed the front windows of Bambino Italy.

"I didn't think you were a local. You don't have that country look about you."

"NYU," she replied, tugging at a bracelet on her wrist. There, three gold charms spelled out the initials of the college. "I'm going home to visit my parents for the weekend, thought I'd take the scenic route. I got a late start and forgot to eat before I left, so here I am." She gestured to the bar.

"Well, you picked a good place. They make a killer carbonara here. Do you… do you want to join me?"

She eyed the empty chair across from him. "I would, but I had something when I got here." She said it more like a question. "And I wouldn't want to interrupt your dinner. I really just came by to say thank you."

"You're not interrupting. I'm done anyway."

"No, I couldn't."

"I insist."

She took a step back from the table. "Really, I feel like I've been sitting all day. Do you maybe want to play some darts?"

"I'm not great at it," he admitted.

"Me neither, but I've been obsessed with it lately. I even got a board for my apartment." She looked down, laughed at herself. "I had to put some plywood underneath it because I kept missing the board." Her eyes came up again—enameled blue, like the tiling in one of his house's many half-baths. "Would you like to join me?"

Carter pushed the half-eaten pizza to the side and slid off his chair. "Sure, I'd love to." He grabbed his drink and followed her back to the dart board.

The guys at the pool table mumbled under their breath; one even managed a sneer.

Once they were settled at the table, Carter turned to the woman and held out his hand. "My name is Carter, by the way."

She shook his hand but said nothing.

"And you are?"

"Win a game and I'll tell you."

It was easier said than done. He'd played darts a few times when he was younger at Pyrosius' house, but they were both far more interested in computers than standing around throwing metal sticks at a board. Darts had always seemed like one of those games that would require constant practice to get good and stay good. With everything else going on in his life, Carter hadn't had the time to commit, not to darts, or golf, or even consistent exercise. Though, had he known one day his dart skills would stand between him and learning a beautiful woman's name, he probably would have purchased a board for the garage.

An hour went by. Then another.

Each round moved slowly into the next as they stopped to chat, order more wine, and share a plate of crispy calamari. With each drink, Carter felt his hand-eye coordination slipping away, and he became convinced the woman would soon be on her way with nothing left behind but the curve of her jeans lingering in his memory. She had a way of half-jumping whenever she landed a dart in the right place, and those startling blue eyes seemed to twinkle to the point Carter thought they might be augmented.

Camilla stopped offering them more wine after a while, but it wasn't until Antonio came by to tell them they were closing soon that Carter realized most of the other patrons had left. The pool guys who had been so loud and annoying before were gone, and the balls had been left neatly stacked in the triangular rack.

"What do you say?" The woman handed Carter a trio of darts. "One last game? Closest to bullseye wins?"

"Yes, yes… once more around the bend." He approached the throwing line and tried to find his balance. He'd known for a while that he wouldn't be driving himself home, so he'd gone heavy on the wine. He thought how stained his mouth must be and sucked in his lips.

The woman giggled. "The pucker-fish gambit. You don't see that often."

The first dart fell well short of the board, but the second hit just a few inches from the bullseye. Buoyed by unearned confidence, Carter threw the final dart only to see it ping off the edge of the board and fall to the floor.

He hung his head in defeat as he slunk back to his stool.

The woman tried to comfort him, touching his leg as she passed. "Don't beat yourself up. Maybe you'll get lucky."

Carter heard the words and caught her gaze. She didn't look away, not when she threw the first dart, or the second, or the third. When she was done, only one dart was even on the board—his.

The woman held out her hand.

He took it, felt the warm fingers slide over his, felt the electrical charge sizzle between their palms.

"Hi," she said, pulling herself close to him. Their lips touched briefly, and he felt her breath on his cheek as she whispered, "Nice to meet you. My name is Jane."

TWELVE

Diya dialed off the hot water with an outstretched foot.

Her apartment in Brooklyn didn't even have a bathtub, let alone a shower she could spread her arms in. Her suite in Vise Manor, on the other hand, was mostly bathroom. The sleeping area was large enough to hold a king size bed, a small desk, and a dresser over which hung a vidscreen, but it was the attached bath with its heated, tiled floor that took Diya's breath away. From one wall to the other, it was bigger than her entire apartment and so well-appointed that she imagined Winston had simply stolen the design from a spa in the city. Every surface held some kind of individually wrapped toiletry, from toothbrushes to small Q-tips to an assortment of tampons and pads in nondescript white wrappers.

The tub was long and deep, with a contoured floor that held her body in repose. As she lay back with her head supported by a rolled towel, she watched her breasts break the surface of the soapy water as she drew in each breath. She enjoyed the feeling of the cooler air on her skin before she exhaled and sunk below the water again.

The first night in the house, she'd enjoyed the tub as a novelty, a rare occasion in which she could enjoy the same comforts rich people probably took for granted. With soft classical music playing from her phone by the sink, she'd let her hands wander over her body, eventually settling into a rhythm as she moved her hips against her fingers.

Forty-eight hours later, just thinking about the energy involved in masturbating made Diya groan. She was tired in a way she had rarely experienced before. Being a personal assistant wasn't for the faint of heart or weak of back, but the last two days had pushed her to the absolute limit. Vendors had come and gone from Vise Manor like a chain of tropical storms hitting a Caribbean island one after another. They arrived on each other's heels, dropping their torrents of wind and rain before disappearing without so much as an acknowledgement of the destruction they had caused. Each time Diya thought she might be able to take stock of the aftermath, another one arrived.

She hadn't even bathed on Wednesday night. The last truck didn't leave until after midnight, and by the time she got the last boxes squared away and the house locked up, it was already two in the morning. She managed to get her skirt off before collapsing into the large bed, but that was it. She awoke four hours later, splashed some water on her face, and started the process over again.

Energy drinks helped until they didn't.

Synthetic drugs got her the rest of the way.

When her biochip unloaded *Andiamo* at the end of the day, Diya felt as if someone had dropped a hundred-pound weighted vest onto her shoulders. It took everything she had to run the bath, remove her clothes, and lift her legs one at a time over the edge of the tub. Now, with the almost scalding water increasing blood flow in her muscles, she felt as if she could relax, or failing that, could at least remember what relaxation was. She'd forgotten to turn on some music before she got in, so the only sound in her ears was the random drip of water from the faucet.

Vise Manor was silent and still.

Winston himself wasn't getting back from his trip until the following evening, a couple hours after dinner was to be served. The grounds did have a security detail, but they stayed outside, mostly on the perimeter. Diya was alone in the house, and yet she didn't feel as anxious as she had expected. The security system was no joke; during lockdown, there was literally no way in or out of the house. All the windows were shatterproof, and every door was reinforced. Before heading up to her room, Diya had put the house under partial lock, with entrance and exit only available at the front door. On the other side of that door stood an armed guard with some kind of machine gun slung over his shoulder.

I'm alone in a strange house, she thought, *and nothing can touch me. I can lie in this bath all night if I want to. I could sleep here until I turn into a prune,* something Rakesh Singh had warned her about on several occasions.

Diya shut her eyes and let her mind drift in the darkness. Imagined flashes of light coalesced into moving trucks followed by white vans with sliding doors followed by men in beige jumpers either pushing or pulling dollies loaded with plastic tubs. When she tried to direct her mind's eye somewhere else, she saw the never-ending checklist on her palette, so pristine just a few days ago but now marred with notes and checkmarks. Even though she knew the list was finished, that every Thursday task had been completed, the items nonetheless continued to scroll on her imaginary palette. The text slowed and accelerated as if an invisible finger were paging down, struggling to reach the end.

She groaned, tried to turn the palette into something else. She imagined Millie holding it, then remembered the party she was going to alone. A vision of Millie walking into the party dressed scantily as a whorish secretary from the 60s filled her head. A party followed in hazy detail, with laughter bubbling up all around her.

Diya awoke sometime later in a tub of tepid water. The heater was still on, and there was sweat beading on her face. She sank beneath the surface for a moment, wetting her hair for the first time. When she emerged, she used the towel she'd been resting on to dry her eyes, and then began the arduous task of getting out of the tub. Her legs were sore, and even the encouragement from her biochip couldn't get them to move without shaking. The last thing she wanted was to slip and hit her head on the tile, so she took things slowly, listening to her own groans and creaks.

Finally, she sat on the edge of the tub, dripping onto the towel she'd laid at her feet. She stared for a moment at the birthmark above her left knee, thought about how ashamed she had been of it since early childhood. Now she hardly noticed it, except when it was missing, as it almost always was in her dreams. Its presence now confirmed she was awake, that she wasn't still dozing in the tub.

Wouldn't that be something? If I—

A distant thud broke her train of thought. Thinking it might be thunder, she turned and looked at the high window above the tub. Though there was a hint of lightning, there was no accompanying rumble, just a light fall of rain on the glass. After a full minute of silence, Diya stood and grabbed a fresh towel from the warming rack by the sink.

She was drying her legs when she heard the far-off booming again. It seemed to be coming from below her, on the first floor. Though she was tired and wanted nothing more than to climb into bed, she knew she had to investigate. There was no way she would be able to sleep with strange sounds popping off in the house, and more importantly, it was her job to make sure everything was ready for the next day.

Diya pulled a white robe from the back of the bathroom door. It was fluffier and warmer than what she would have expected out of even the nicest hotel, and it had a blood red *V* emblazoned on the breast. She tied the sash, stepped into soft slippers, and opened the door. It was colder in the bedroom, but the robe hung at her shins and kept the drafts out. She hadn't bothered emptying her suitcase into the drawers the day she arrived, so it took her a moment to fish out a pair of underwear.

She didn't need Rakesh Singh to tell her not to go investigating strange sounds in a big scary house with her bare ass hanging out.

In the hall, Diya padded softly to the landing at the top of a large staircase that ran along the perimeter of the foyer. She stood at the railing for a moment, listening. Whatever was making the sound didn't keep her in suspense for long. The thud came again, twice in quick succession. It didn't have the sharpness of someone knocking, nor was it deep enough to evoke images of a person throwing their shoulder against a door. Instead, it sounded more like a fist on the wall, the butt of a closed hand striking and resting.

The staircase made three right turns before finally depositing Diya on the ground floor. There, her slippers sounded flatter on the hard tile. To the left, she could see the darkened dining room where the guests would gather the next evening. Tucked under the stairs to the right were two open sliding doors that led into the parlor. Leather chairs gleamed in the low light from the bookcases that bordered the room.

Diya stood for a moment and listened.

When the pounding rumbled through the floor, she tracked it to the hallway in front of her. Small LED plates in the wall barely gave off any light, but as she approached, they ramped up, illuminating the walls and the frames hung there. Diya had seen them all before, covers from a dozen tech and business magazines, all of them featuring sensational headlines over a professional headshot of Winston. An unsuspecting visitor might think Winston was the most influential figure in the tech world, ever. Diya, on the other hand, had noted one of the magazines was *Beyond 2000* and identified her boss as the owner of Vise Robotics. Unfortunately, that magazine had gone out business pre-millennium, long before Vise Robotics was ever incorporated. The other covers were similarly fabricated, but Diya didn't think Winston vain. Even Millie owned one of those mirrors with the *TIME Person of the Year* text superimposed over the glass.

At the end of the hallway, with the pounding growing louder, Diya walked down three steps to a sunken area no bigger than her office at work. The framed magazines wrapped around the wall and met on either side of a massive black door, the surface of which was made with a special material that not only reflected no light but actively absorbed it. It had the appearance of an empty square in space, as if someone had forgotten to draw this particular piece of reality.

The word *abyss* came to mind.

The door sat in a metal frame with a gap just wide enough for Diya to insert her finger—not that she had any intention of doing so.

Another thud, this one close enough to feel in her chest.

Diya examined the gap and saw cylindrical metal bars extending from the door into the frame. Further to the right, a small keypad glowed a steady ominous red.

The door was locked up tighter than a bank vault, and yet, Diya's mind didn't ease. If anything, the heavy security made her wonder what the locks were protecting from her—or what they were protecting her from. Winston hadn't mentioned anything about the door, but he also hadn't given her access to open it, so the message of *keep out* was pretty clear. Still, she couldn't help but reach out and place her hand on its cold face.

Thud.

She recoiled.

"Hello?" Her voice echoed down the empty hallway, but she had no clue whether it could penetrate the thick door. "Is someone there?"

There was no response. A minute passed, then another. The warmth of the bathroom began to fade, and the chilled air made its way into her robe.

Then, ever so faintly, enough to make her turn her ear to the door, she heard a different sound, like a tapping or shuffling.

She listened until it disappeared completely, and only then did she realize what she had heard.

Footsteps.

Footsteps departing with the casual speed of someone walking to the kitchen for a midnight snack.

Diya lingered at the door until finally the fatigue in her legs and lower back became too much for her. She inspected the locks once more, made sure the keypad was still glowing red, and then retreated quickly back up the staircase. In her room, she closed the door and engaged both the deadbolt and the chain. She sat on the edge of the bed for a while before climbing under the covers.

She watched the door with drooping eyes.

In the dream that followed, she saw her bedroom door, but now a little boy, shrouded in darkness, stood before it, his back to her, his fist raised above his head. The small hand fell against the wood, again and again, creating an impossibly loud sound.

Thud, thud, thud.

THIRTEEN

Winston Vise had offered to send a car, but Adelai didn't trust anyone except her drivers to ferry her and Simone out to the country.

When Felipe buzzed from the lobby just before noon, both Adelai and Simone were still stuck on separate calls, despite their best efforts to tie up all the loose ends at work the day before. They'd staged their luggage with Harold earlier that morning, so all they had to do was transition from the apartment to the back of the town car where they sat as far apart from each other as the spacious back seat would allow.

Adelai took questions from the legal department about how they were to conduct business while she was away, and when the call finally ended, she was surprised to find they were already in the country, well past the highways that connected the two. Now it was just winding roads barely wide enough for two cars to pass.

The sun was still high, suggesting it might be warm outside the car. Adelai knew that to be false, as evidenced by Simone's insistence they turn up the heat in the back. The environmental controls showed the heater set at seventy-six degrees. It made Adelai groggy, and the gentle vibration from the car didn't help either. She watched the trees pass outside, only vaguely aware of Simone talking, until finally she heard her own name.

She turned. Simone was looking at her, her head cocked.

"What?"

"I asked if everything's okay," said Simone. "You look miles away. What were you thinking about?"

"Nothing." And it was true. Her mind was empty, as if it couldn't summon the energy to form more thoughts beyond what was absolutely necessary.

"I feel like I haven't seen you in days." Simone placed her hand on Adelai's leg.

Adelai rolled her eyes. "Don't be silly. I saw you this morning, and last night, and the morning before."

"But not the night before." She traced a finger up her thigh. "I had to sleep alone Wednesday night, and then yesterday was so hectic trying to get everything done, and today too. This is the first time we've been able to slow down in a while."

"Did you miss me?" asked Adelai, struggling to keep the sarcasm out of her voice. Simone's needy side always put her off; she expected more from a woman who at all times presented herself as strong and independent.

"Always."

"Look, I'm sorry about Wednesday night. I meant to come home, but I was just so exhausted. You didn't need to worry though."

"I didn't. Not too much." She touched one of her spiky gold earrings. "When you didn't respond to my texts, I looked up your location and saw you were at Rayburn's. If you had told me ahead of time, I wouldn't have bothered you."

Adelai shrugged, looked back to the window. "It was a spur of the moment thing. You were gone at spin class, and I really needed something to just... I don't know... fuck me out of this funk I'm in. I didn't want to take you to this thing and be a downer."

The car slowed to make a right turn. A stop sign rolled past.

"And did he?"

"Did he what?"

"You know... fuck the funk out of you?"

"Don't be vulgar," she replied, pausing for a moment. "But no, I think I just made it worse by going there. That's probably why I didn't come home. The disappointment on top of everything else was just too much."

"Well—"

"But that doesn't mean I'm not going to turn it on for you. I'm here, Momo. And I promise you, we're going to have a good time."

Simone stared back as if she were trying to read the truth in Adelai's face. When nothing was revealed, she smiled and reached for the small bar in front of her where a pre-corked bottle of champagne and two glasses sat waiting for them. She filled each flute halfway and handed one to Adelai.

"What are we toasting?"

Simone lifted her glass. "To random sex toys showing up in the mail."

"I was thinking more like *date night* but okay."

"To never trusting a man to do a woman's job." She squeezed Adelai's leg with her free hand.

"To listening to my wife more."

Their glasses clinked, and they drank.

Simone leaned in and kissed Adelai on the cheek, then the lips.

The intercom buzzed, and the driver's digitized voice filled the cabin.

"We're five minutes out, ma'am."

"Thank you, Felipe." She turned back to Simone. "Well, our adventure is about to begin. Any last words before we step into the abyss?"

Simone downed the rest of her champagne in one gulp. She placed her manicured nails to her lips as she let out a small burp.

"Just a reminder that we don't acknowledge Jane no matter what."

Adelai nodded. "The lawyers already reminded me."

"Never hurts to hear it again."

The smooth asphalt gave way to gravel. Through Simone's window, Adelai saw a guard shack slide by, complete with a black-clad figure holding an assault rifle. The gate they passed through was high and made of thick wrought-iron tines that ended in sharp arrows. Even in its open position, the gate looked formidable, like the jaws of a snake getting ready to bite. The driveway seemed to go on forever, climbing the long, gentle slope of a grassy hill as it curved around a large pond. About a hundred yards from the house, they slowed to a stop in front of a young woman with her hand outstretched.

Adelai rolled down her window as the woman approached with a palette cradled in her arms. She was dressed in typical hospitality garb—black pants and a black button-up with a golden name tag pinned to her chest—and though her makeup was perfect and her hair was pulled back into an immaculate ponytail, she wore the strangest rose-tinted sunglasses straight out of the 1960s.

"Good afternoon. Mrs. Vaught, I presume?"

"Yes."

"My name is Amber." She touched her nametag. Written in smaller script under her name were the words *Barinson Hospitality*. "I'm going to ask you to wait here while we settle the guest before you. As soon as they are inside, we will bring you up and have you meet with Ms. Diya Singh, your hostess for the evening. She will acquaint you with the grounds and go over the welcome packet we've assembled for you."

"Why do we have to wait for them to go in first?" asked Simone.

Amber bent lower to address Simone directly. "For privacy, ma'am. Both yours and theirs. We're asking all guests to remain in their rooms until cocktail hour, at which time the communications blackout will begin. Mr. Vise would like his guest list to remain private for as long as possible due to the nature of the event."

Adelai leaned toward the window but couldn't see the front door of the wide, two-story manor. Tall gables full of black shingles reached to the sky, creating a fitting cap to the moss-stained stone of the house itself. Massive windows along the front were orange and opaque under the glare of the sun.

"Is it the Queen?"

"The Queen, ma'am?"

"You know, the Queen of England." Adelai put out a flat hand. "Little old lady, wears a crown."

Amber smiled—a bit too much for such a silly joke—and said, "No, Mrs. Vaught. The Queen was unable to attend due to previous commitments." Her eyes jerked to the right as a voice spoke into her ear. "Alright, Ms. Singh is ready for you. Please proceed to the front door and have a wonderful evening."

The car began to roll again, and over the crackling of the gravel, Simone said, "We should have asked Rayburn to find out who else was coming. I didn't even think about it."

"We already know two other people who are coming."

"Yes, but we have to act surprised when we see them." Simone crossed her arms.

The door locks clicked as they pulled up in front of an Indian woman with thin eyebrows and a single lock of loose hair hanging on the left side of her face. Two valets in red vests approached each door and opened them, offering a hand to help Adelai and Simone out of their respective sides. Once Adelai was out, she turned and waited for Simone to join her before acknowledging the woman standing nearby.

"Mrs. Vaught, Mrs. Vaught," she said, without a hint of an accent, "I'm Diya Singh. Allow me to welcome you to Vise Manor."

"Thank you, Ms. Singh. We're excited to be here." Adelai felt a hand slide inside her arm and squeeze.

"Thomas and Frederick will take your bags to your room. You are in the Red Room, which is the second door on the right coming off the stairs. It will be the only open door."

"Because of the secrecy," whispered Simone.

"Yes, ma'am. We appreciate you playing along with us tonight." Ms. Singh gave a weak shrug. "I'm sure you're familiar with Mr. Vise's reputation as a bit of a showman. At any rate, I promise the inconvenience will be worth it. You'll find your suite well-appointed, with refreshments and snacks to tide you over until cocktail hour. If you need anything else, you can reach the concierge via the vidscreen panel in your room until 4:00 p.m."

"What happens at four?" asked Simone.

"The support staff leaves at that time, ma'am. I will be the only team member staying behind to make sure things keep running smoothly. Otherwise, it will only be you, Mr. Vise, and the other invited guests."

"He must have the cure for aging in there."

Adelai nudged Simone.

"What?" she asked. "I'm serious. I can understand theatrics, but this is a bit much, don't you think? Like I'm going to run to Pattrn and post pictures of the other guests with the caption *you'll never guess who is here shopping robotic sex dolls.*"

"Momo," said Adelai, feeling the warmth rise in her cheeks.

"Mr. Vise appreciates your indulgence, Mrs. Vaught. Now, also in your room, I've placed a printed itinerary on the desk. I've highlighted the 5:00 p.m. communications blackout. If you need to place any calls or post anything to Pattrn, please do so prior to the blackout. If I may offer a suggestion for tonight: leave your phones and palettes in your room. I promise you will find the evening and assembled company more than entertaining."

"Not as entertaining as the Queen of England," said Simone.

"No," said Ms. Singh, smiling again, "but then who is?"

Adelai heard the trunk slam and looked over her shoulder to see Felipe tipping his hat at her. The valets—and their luggage—were already gone. Farther down the driveway, another car had come through the gate. Amber, distant and a little blurry, was flagging them down.

"Now, before you head inside, I have these for you." Ms. Singh produced two small cloth bags from her pocket. From the first, she produced a loop of silver chain with a red glass charm in the shape of a *V*. She undid the clasp and gestured for Adelai's arm.

Adelai held out her hand.

"Vise Manor is not a hotel," said Ms. Singh, "so we don't have keycards for the rooms. This bracelet is coded to open the Red Room. I hope silver doesn't clash with the jewelry you chose for tonight."

She closed the loop around Adelai's wrist.

"It's fine," said Adelai. "If everyone will be wearing one, then I'll blend in."

Simone held out her wrist.

"And one for you." She closed the bracelet and slipped the empty bags back into her pocket. After a few quick taps on her palette, she stepped to the side. "This way please. The stairs are on your right. They open onto a single hallway on the second floor, then it's the second door on your right."

"Thank you, Ms. Singh."

"Please call me Diya, Mrs. Vaught. Enjoy your evening."

Simone squeezed Adelai's arm again and pulled her toward the door.

Inside, the foyer gave way to a cavernous atrium that stretched to the very top of the house where exposed beams crisscrossed the space. Every door in sight was closed, but Adelai could hear people moving and talking behind them. The message was clear: don't stop, keep moving, nothing to see here.

Simone climbed the staircase quickly, and as Adelai tried to keep pace, she couldn't help but be infected by Simone's enthusiasm. She was happy in a way Adelai didn't see very often anymore. Tonight would be good for her and for their relationship, Adelai decided. They needed more nights together doing something new and adventurous instead of just collapsing on the couch after a long day at work.

Adelai followed Simone into the Red Room where the two valets were waiting near twin luggage racks. Their suitcases had already been placed on the racks with their zippers facing out. Adelai reached into her purse for some cash, but one of the valets stopped her.

"That's not necessary, ma'am. We just wanted to make sure you found the room. The itinerary Ms. Singh mentioned is there on the desk." He pointed to a long white table that looked like it had been built into the wall. "And the concierge is available via the communications panel." He walked to the door and tapped the small vidscreen on the wall. It flashed a black *V* on a stark white background before loading a menu.

"Thank you," said Adelai.

"Welcome to Vise Manor," said Thomas. He and the other valet hurried out of the room, shutting the door behind them. Automatic locks clicked into place.

Adelai stared after them. Everything had moved so fast that for a moment, she didn't understand where she was. The room was new to her, but familiar in the way all hotels were—furnished with all the necessities but lacking in personal touches. The bed was large and littered with pillows. The two side-by-side windows on the far wall looked out over the back of the property, which meant she wouldn't be able to spy on the next guest that pulled up in front.

"Five o'clock, cocktails," said Simone. She stood by the desk holding a thin sheet of paper. "Dinner is at eight followed by *Presentation by Winston Vise* at nine-thirty." She flipped the paper over and read the back. "Tomorrow just lists a single event: private conversation with Winston Vise, at one o'clock."

"If we stay that long," said Adelai.

"If we're even awake by then."

"You're not going to overdrink, are you?"

Simone tossed the itinerary aside as if someone had just handed her a flyer on the street. "I am out of the house on a Friday night with what I'm almost certain is an open bar at my disposal. If you want to stay sober and listen to some suit talk about rubber vaginas and synthetic cocks all night, then have at it. But I'm going to Buzztown, population me."

"So long as you don't embarrass me."

"I can't make any promises." She drifted to the bathroom door and stuck her head in. Her whistle echoed back.

"What about making me cry *Mo, Mo, Mo?*"

Simone rolled her watch into view. The dainty silver chain with its red charm sparkled. "Maybe we can move it up in the schedule? This bathtub looks like it could fit three people. Meet me there in five?"

Adelai made a show of stroking her own cheek. "I'll *try* to wait that long." She watched Simone disappear into the bathroom. When she heard the water in the tub turn on, Adelai reached again for her purse and felt around for the smooth edges of the code card Rayburn had given her the day before last.

She remembered lingering in his darkened foyer just before sunrise, one hand on the door, ready to head back home where she belonged. Rayburn stood there naked, little more than a shadow, and reached for her hand.

"Sure you don't want one for the road?"

"Some other time."

He squeezed her hand and placed something thin and hard in it—a code card.

"Then how about this? They call it *Center Line*. It's not an upper or a downer. It just… brings you back to center."

Adelai smiled, slipped the card into her pocket.

"It's kind of you to think of me."

He reached past her to open the door, hid himself behind it as soft amber light poured into the foyer.

"I was actually thinking of Simone."

"Of course you were," said Adelai, speaking to the Rayburn of her memory. She pulled the code card from her purse and broke the perforated tab on the end. Before she could change her mind, she placed the card on the back of her neck and winced as her biochip latched onto the signal. What came next felt like reality sieved through pristine muslin. A rosy tint fell over the room, as if she had slipped on Amber's vintage sunglasses.

Somewhere on the air was the scent of Wisteria.

Simone called from the bathroom, bright and tremulous.

"Addy, are you gonna come?"

FOURTEEN

A small red dot appeared on Robert's face as he pulled the razor over his chin.

He wiped the blood away with the back of his hand, and then ran both his hand and the razor under the open faucet. Shaving cream swirled in the wide glass basin and disappeared into a copper grate. As he resumed his work, he saw the shower door open behind him in the mirror.

Laura stepped out wearing nothing but a pink shower cap and a glisten that made her pale skin look like it could have been carved from marble. The sudden change in temperature brought out goosebumps on her small breasts. She pulled a plush white towel from the hook by the shower and wrapped herself in it.

"You're ogling me," she said.

"Yes."

"Like a teenager."

Robert shrugged. "I see nipples standing at attention and I look. I'm too old to change my ways now."

"Well cut it out." She closed the glass door, looked at him. "Are you going to take a shower?"

He shook his head, dragged the razor down his cheek again. "Nope. Cameras." He made a show of glancing at the ceiling.

"I doubt Winston Vise put cameras in the bathrooms, Robert."

"No way to know for sure. The accommodations are nice, but this is someone's home. How do I know how this guy spends his weekends?"

Laura pulled a padded bench out from under the vanity and sat down. She patted her arms with a separate towel. "If you really thought there were cameras in here, you wouldn't have let me take a shower."

He turned slightly in her direction and shrugged again.

"Robert!"

He smiled, rinsed the razor a final time. "I showered this morning before you got up, so all I need is a little shave and a dab of cologne."

"After all these years," said Laura, pulling the shower cap from her head, "you still think you can grow a beard." A mass of wavy blonde hair fell onto her shoulders. She was a natural brunette, but it had been years since Robert had seen more than a hint of her original color. "Not that I mind. I don't care for beards."

She opened a zippered pouch and revealed a toolkit that rivaled a traveling doctor's.

Robert watched her begin her makeup routine. Her mouth set in steely concentration as she applied powders, drew lines under her eyes, and painted her lips with a soft pink color. As she lifted each brush or pencil, a thin silver bracelet shimmered on her arm. Robert looked at the matching bracelet on his own wrist. It was not the kind of jewelry he would ever wear, but as the hostess Diya had explained, it was like his access badge while in the house. The small gray *V* charm hanging from the clasp had some kind of NFC chip in it that unlocked the door to the Gray Room where they were staying for the duration.

"What do you think about these things?" he asked, waving his bracelet at her.

Her mouth was open so she could apply liner; her lips didn't move at all as she replied, "They remind me of the wristbands we get at ACL."

Robert grunted agreeably. They made the two-hour drive to the Austin City Limits music festival in the Capitol City every year, and though the styles and colors had evolved, they always had to wear a wristband to get into Zilker Park and to make purchases at the overpriced concession stands. Of course, those wristbands were cloth or plastic and nowhere near as fancy as the expensive silver they now wore.

"I guess that tells us something about how Winston Vise does business." Robert splashed warm water on his face to clear the remaining shaving cream. "You think about the difference in cost between these bracelets and a simple keycard… or just a key."

Laura grinned. "Are you doing that thing where you evaluate a company's founder so you know whether to invest in them?"

Ignoring her question, Robert patted his face with a towel. "Well, the way I see it, Vise is trying to sell the sizzle and not the steak. If he's going through this much trouble just to make us feel special, then that says a lot about the synthetics he brought us here to see. Are they not impressive enough to stand on their own? Does he really need all this?" He gestured at the opulent bathroom around them.

"He hired a good interior decorator," said Laura, shrugging. "What's the problem?" She capped her lipstick and slipped it into the carrying case. "Besides, that hand was pretty impressive all by itself. Scared the hell out of me, but then I've never seen anything like that before. I'm no Robert Hargreaves, but even I can see the potential there."

Robert waved his finger at her. "First, I'm glad you're not Robert Hargreaves because that would change the whole tone of birthday sex."

Laura shook her head. "You're just a horny teenager wrapped up in a middle-aged man's body, aren't you?"

"And second, that's what has me wondering about all this. *If* he's got a product worth investing in, *if* it stands on its own, then why all the extra showmanship?"

"Why does anyone do anything?" Laura tilted her head back and placed her hand on her chest. "Ego, darling."

Robert caught his reflection in the mirror. Though he rarely dwelled on his own appearance, he couldn't help but notice how old he looked, or rather, how thin. Men in their sixties like him, especially those who lived within driving distance of Texas barbecue, enjoyed a certain plumpness in their later years. Robert's cheekbones and chin were much more prominent than just a decade earlier, almost jutting, and the medium undershirt that had fit so snugly before now hung loosely from sharp shoulders.

Though the doctors said he was healthier than most men his age, Robert felt as if he were wasting away, losing a little bit of himself with each passing day. He remembered the conversation with Kagan, the promise of a future where humans could copy their minds into synthetic bodies and essentially live forever.

He flexed his arms; it didn't take much effort to bring the muscles to the surface.

Though he had no desire to look like a twenty-five-year-old Hollywood heartthrob, he had to admit it would be nice not to worry about moving too quickly down a flight of stairs or wonder which swing of his driver on the golf course would be his last. Even three days removed from his round at Pebble Beach, he felt the lingering aches and soreness in his lower back.

Transitioning to a synthetic body would be worth it just to stop the creaks, never mind the extra years he would get to spend with Laura. They had met so late in life, had done so much before they found each other. He just wanted more time.

He turned away from the mirror to look at her directly.

The towel was around her waist now; she patted her chest with an oblong pad, applying some kind of powder to her skin.

"You're wearing that red dress?" he asked. "The one with the…" He mimed the dress' plunging neckline with his hands.

"Yes, and I packed you a tie that matches."

"I like that dress." He nodded to himself as he left the bathroom.

The Gray Room was much larger than a standard hotel room, and the massive windows on the north wall made Robert feel like he was standing outside, as much a part of the landscape as the trees and rolling hills. The room had been bright and airy when they'd arrived, but now, low clouds were moving in from the north, and like a light with an unstable power source, the sun's brightness was going in and out.

Robert tapped the whisperer in his ear. When it chimed, he asked, "Is it going to rain today?"

There was silence before a despondent tone answered him. He checked the clock on the wall and saw the time was already past 5:00 p.m. The communications blackout had begun.

"Guess I won't be needing you," he said to the whisperer, pulling it out and placing it on the dresser next to his phone.

He dressed by the window, slipping on a gray suit that matched the accent color on the otherwise white floral wallpaper. His white button-down was still in its protective sleeve from the dry cleaner, and when he pulled it out, his nose crinkled at the overwhelming odor of starch. He slipped the shirt on and watched the clouds swallow the sun as he worked the buttons. In addition to the tie, Laura had packed his Hargreaves Group cufflinks; he pressed his cuffs together and threaded the small metal links.

"I think it's going to rain," he called.

"Why does it rain so much up here?" asked Laura, her voice distant.

"Maybe because New York is so close to the coast."

"*We* live fifty miles from the coast, Robert."

He slung the red tie around his neck, adjusted the length. "Not *this* coast, *Laura*."

She didn't reply, and Robert finished dressing to the sounds of muted conversation in the hallway. Cocktail hour had officially begun, and the other guests were making their way downstairs. Evidently nobody believed in being fashionably late anymore. As the time approached 5:20 p.m., he grew restless. In his younger years, he might have asked Laura how much longer she would be, but age and experience had made him wiser.

He poked his head into the bathroom. Laura was standing at the sink with her naked back to him.

"I'm going to step out into the hall for a moment," he said. There was a large bay window at the end of the hallway that he wanted to investigate.

"Alright, I'm almost ready. Just need to slip on my dress."

He eyed her backside. "No underwear?"

"The dress won't allow it."

"Oh, the *dress* won't allow it?"

She eyed him in the mirror. "*You* are more than welcome to wear my panties if you're so adamant."

Robert clucked his tongue. "I'll think about it." He tapped the door jamb with an open palm. "Meet me in the hall, Mrs. Hargreaves."

"Ten minutes."

The deadbolt in the door rolled back in its housing, and Robert stepped out into a hallway at least ten degrees cooler than his room. There was no one else in the hall, but he spotted two heads descending the staircase to his left. He turned and walked to the bay window, aware of how long it had been since he'd worn these particular dress shoes. They were now too loose, and his thin socks slipped in them with each step.

Long swaths of shadow lay across the western grounds of Vise Manor. The last patches of sunlight had disappeared, leaving a gray, gloomy atmosphere more in line with the temperature. From his vantage point on the second floor, Robert could see a sprawling garden stretching away from the house. Every bush and flower appeared meticulously well-kept, as if a team of gardeners descended on the house every morning to care for the plants. Such a verdant display would have never worked in Texas where the rain only fell occasionally, and when it did, it often flooded the city and killed a few Houstonians for good measure.

"Quite impressive, don't you think?"

Robert turned at the sound of a low voice and found an older man with sparse white hair standing next to him. He was dressed not in formal attire as the invitation had instructed, but rather in a thick brown sweater over a checkered red and white button-up. The end of the sweater hung over gray slacks. It took a moment for Robert to surmise this was no tech baron as he'd expected.

"Yes," he said, long after his response was due. "I was just thinking to myself how we could never pull something like this off back home. Too hot." He pulled gently at his collar.

"And where is home, might I ask?"

"Houston. Texas." He smiled and held out his hand. "Robert Hargreaves, of the Hargreaves Group."

The older man shook his hand. "Pleasure to meet you, Robert. I'm Stanton Blumenfield. I have no group to speak of."

"What business are you in, Mr. Blumenfield?"

Stanton turned his gaze to the garden. "I'm a writer. Mostly non-fiction, one or two silly space novels in my early years. Primarily, I do this." He gestured to the windows. "I stand at a window and think."

His accent sounded German or maybe Austrian. Wherever the gravelly affectation had originated from, it had a soothing effect on Robert. He felt himself caught up in the low rumble of each word Stanton spoke.

"What do you think about?"

"My cats. Sometimes the future. Sometimes nothing. It depends on my mood. The day has turned gloomy, wouldn't you agree?"

A door clicked behind them, and Robert turned to see Laura coming out of their room. The blood red dress held tightly to her body, enhancing the curve of her hips and the tapering of her legs. The deep neckline revealed the bones of her sternum and a hint of her breasts.

"It has its bright spots," said Robert.

Laura smiled and walked over, placing one white heel in front of the other. Robert took her hand when she arrived at his side.

"Sweetie, this is Mr. Blumenfield. Mr. Blumenfield, this is my wife, Laura."

"Please, call me Stanton." He took Laura's hand with both of his.

"Mr. Blumenfield is a writer," said Robert.

"It's a pleasure… Stanton."

He extended his elbow. "May I escort you downstairs? I'm afraid I'm here alone tonight, and I rarely have the occasion to walk into a room of strangers with a beautiful young woman on my arm."

Laura raised an eyebrow at Robert and laughed through her smile.

Robert grinned back and nodded slightly.

"I would be honored." She slipped her hand into his elbow.

Robert followed them to the landing at the end of the hall where the sounds of clinking glasses and polite laughter drifted up to meet them.

FIFTEEN

Carter watched Jane make the rounds from the safety of the bar.

Though he hadn't formed any kind of expectation about who else might be in attendance, it was clear he and Jane were the youngest of the group. The others appeared to be well into middle age or older; some of them even had silver or white hair. They all seemed comfortable in a formal setting, which only made Carter all the more uncomfortable. Several people were already milling around in the parlor when they walked in, and though all had politely acknowledged his arrival, none had come over to engage him.

It was Jane who suggested she ingratiate herself. She made it sound like some kind of secret mission, like she was a spy who needed to uncover the personal histories of everyone present. Carter watched her and her little black dress float from one couple or group to the next. How she had the courage to simply walk up and introduce herself was a mystery, but Carter figured it had something to do with how attractive she was.

Who in their right mind would pass up a chance to talk to her?

Jane was near the door when an older man arrived with a tall blonde on his arm. She was dressed in a floor-length red dress that didn't mesh with the frumpily dressed man beside her. Jane shook hands with both of them, laughed politely while playing with her hair, and then returned to Carter. Several pairs of eyes followed her back to the bar.

Carter sipped the whiskey and Coke he'd assembled from the self-serve bar, opting to spend more time on a mixed drink than simply pouring himself a glass of wine. Though he'd been expecting a bartender, he remembered what the hostess Diya had said about the support staff leaving at 4:00 p.m. On any other night, he imagined Winston Vise would have had a couple of bartenders serving drinks while waiters mingled in the crowd with hors d'oeuvres. Between that, the communications blackout, and the secrecy involved when they arrived, he figured tonight was no ordinary night.

Vise had something big planned. The question was *what*, along with *how much of it was based on compromised code?*

"Oh, thank you," said Jane, picking up his drink. She sipped daintily at the gold rim. "I usually take mine with a couple of cherries."

"Noted." Her eyes didn't drift away. She was comfortable having her back to the crowd. "You looked like you were having fun out there."

She touched a napkin to her lower lip. "I'm studying public relations at NYU. The core classes aren't very exciting, but once in a while, an elective will go deep on a subject you wouldn't think had any depth at all, like etiquette. *Business etiquette*, to be exact. So many rules, and so many of them deferential to men." She slid the drink into his hand, let her fingers linger on his. "Did you know there are multiple schools of thought on the correct order to introduce someone?"

Carter recalled the conversation he'd had with Braxton. "I… yeah, I did."

"Well, this crowd is well-versed in all of them. Not a stammer or misstep among them." She touched her index finger to her thumb. "Primo upper crust here tonight."

"What can you tell me about them?"

"Why don't we just go talk to them?"

"We will, after I've finished this." He took a drink. "In the meantime, what were you able to find out?"

"Alright, I'll tell you, but it's going to cost you." Before he could ask what it would cost, she began speaking in a low voice. "The old codger over there is Stanton Blumenfield. He's some kind of writer, mostly tech stuff, future of robotics, that kind of thing. The long-haired blonde is Laura Hargreaves, wife to Robert Hargreaves, the gaunt fellow in the red tie. He introduced himself as part of the Hargreaves Group, but I have no idea what that's supposed to mean. I wanted to tell him I'm Jane Martin of the Martin Group, but that would have been rude."

Carter realized she hadn't said her full name to him since meeting at Bambino's the night before. *Martin* sounded a lot like *Maxwell*, the name she'd used during their first awkward engagement at St. Regis Hotel years ago. He hoped he wouldn't get them confused.

"The squirrely looking white guy with the messy hair by the fireplace is Lucas Cotton. He's got a SoCal accent, I think."

"And is that his daughter?"

"Who? The Black girl? No, she works with Cotton. I mean, I guess she could be adopted or something, but I didn't think to ask. She mentioned she was a programmer, and… what?"

He realized he'd been staring at her. There was something about the way her eyes sparkled when she spoke, as if every accented syllable made her irises flare. She'd been wearing minimal makeup the night before, but for the dinner, she'd gone all out. The edges of her eyes were dark; smoky lines came to a point on either side. Hair that had once hung loose and wild was now braided behind her head, hanging like the decorative sheath of a thin sword.

"Sorry, nothing," said Carter. "You caught me staring. You're just so…"

"Just so what?"

"Is gorgeous too strong a word?"

"You're just saying that because you're anxious. You're taking that nervous energy and turning it into sexual energy. In class, we learned that misplaced tension is the reason there's so much misogyny in business. Men start to compete, and they drag women into it. You're focusing on me because of what I represent about you to them."

"Maybe you're just pretty."

She shrugged, took the glass back from him. "Maybe."

Near the fireplace, an older woman with short platinum hair sat in a tall chair upholstered in green velvet. She held hands with a woman who looked like she was wearing gold daggers for earrings.

"What about them?" he asked. "The lesbian power couple."

"Addy and Simone. Not sure about them. They were polite but tight-lipped."

Carter raised an eyebrow.

"You have a dirty, dirty mind, and I don't have to stand here and listen to your vulgarities." She placed a hand on his chest as if she might push him away.

He leaned closer to her ear. "Thanks for coming with me. I don't know if I could have done this alone."

"Are you kidding me?" she whispered back. "I should be thanking you. I never get invited to swanky parties in the countryside. Right now I'd probably be sitting in the living room watching the real estate channel with my dad instead of mingling with all these interesting people. This is like an adventure for me. It's exciting."

"Really? You're into robotics?"

Jane shook her head. "I'm into people, how they interact—that kind of stuff. That's why I talked to you last night. I like meeting new people, finding out what makes them tick. And these people… it's like getting a glimpse into another world."

The conversation around them dropped off to nothing. All eyes had turned to the door where a bearded man stood dressed all in black except for his white shirt and a hint of a dark blue vest. His slicked-back hair gleamed under the flickering sconces on the parlor walls. The man scanned the assembled group, locked eyes with Carter, and approached.

"Behind you," he warned Jane.

She turned just in time to greet the man.

"Hi, I'm Jane."

The man considered her for a moment before tentatively shaking her hand. "Reno," he grunted, rolling the *R* in his name.

"Nice to meet you, Reno. This is my lover, Carter Price."

Carter started to lift his hand but changed his mind. There was something off about Reno, something altogether unfriendly. Compared to the other guests, he didn't look like he wanted to be there, let alone belong there.

"Whiskey," said Reno.

Carter felt a surge of adrenaline. "I'm not the bartender, man."

"I'll make it for you," offered Jane. She filled the space between them, causing Reno to back away a little. She glanced at Carter and smiled. Once the drink was made, she slid it down the bar.

Reno picked up the glass and mumbled his thanks in Spanish.

"You're welcome. Where are you from, Reno? I love your accent—" Jane didn't even get to finish her question before the man turned and walked away. He settled in front of a vertical vidscreen and sipped his drink while a slideshow of blue and white diagrams faded between images.

"Well," she said, turning back to Carter, "he's a salty one, isn't he?"

"Bit of a tit if you ask me."

"Don't let him get to you. I don't think he's American. This might be his first visit to the Land of the Free."

Carter groaned. "They don't have manners where he comes from?"

"Hey, what did I just say?" She put a hand on his arm, and just like countless times before, as other versions of Jane, the gesture calmed him. "Do you remember those guys playing pool last night? Do you think I let them spoil my good time?"

"Sorry," he said, draining the last of his drink.

Jane tapped the rim of the glass. "How about you make us another one and I'll go see if anyone knows anything about our rude friend over there?"

"You do realize you introduced me as your lover, right?"

Jane frowned and shook her head. "Oh, my sweet man, I've been telling everyone you're my lover. I'm halfway to convincing them your neighbor invited *me* and you're just my plus one." She trailed her hand on his arm as she walked away.

He watched her until she joined the little bubble with the writer and the Hargreaves couple. Turning his attention back to the bar, Carter opened the bottle of whiskey again and fished a small can of Coke from a trough of ice. After mixing the two, he plucked two bright red cherries from a dish and dropped them into the fizzing drink.

"Did you get roped into bartending?"

Carter smiled at the young woman Lucas Cotton had brought with him. She had a nervous air about her, and her hand kept drifting to the side of her head where short black curls tapered into smooth skin. He wondered if she suffered the same kind of social anxiety he did.

"Jane and I are splitting duties."

"Oh, yeah. You're Carter, her lover, right?"

"Cute," he replied, trying not to stare too long at her long, curling eyelashes. "Can I make you something, Miss…?"

"Don't make it weird. Call me Roma. And I'd love a vodka soda, please."

"Vodka soda it is." He pulled a bottle of Grey Goose from the rack. "Jane tells me you're a programmer. What kind of work do you do?"

"Peer-to-peer communications." Roma settled onto a nearby stool and placed her clutch in her lap. "I work with Lucas at the MESH Foundation."

"I've heard of that. Distributed networking, fault-tolerant routing, that kind of stuff, right?"

"You got it. We're trying to make the world less reliant on VNet. The first step is to make it so people can communicate directly with each other without going through Vinestead's servers."

"Ah…" He placed a black napkin under the glass and handed it to Roma.

"And you? Jane didn't mention your occupation except as her personal sex slave."

Carter coughed. "I'm between projects at the moment, but most recently I was working for Vinestead."

The smile on Roma's face dried up in an instant. She sipped her drink.

"Well, not officially for Vinestead," he clarified. "I had a software company called Dyalogued that Vinestead purchased a few years ago. I stayed on for a little while, but as you know, you take heat working for the 'Stead. Now I'm independent and looking for the next big thing."

"Is that what brought you here tonight?"

"Not really. I'm Winston Vise's neighbor. I'm pretty sure he invited me out of obligation." He shrugged. "Not that I mind the free booze. So, tell me more about your work. What programming language are you working in? Phalanx? Coral?"

"Oh, nothing like that." She cast a glance at Lucas Cotton. "We had to come up with our own language, actually. None of the others were efficient enough to handle the throughput… I mean, we're talking exabytes of, you know, data."

"Not efficient enough? What does that—"

A hand landed on his shoulder. Jane had somehow gained a glass of champagne in her absence.

"Roma," she said. "What do you think of my friend Carter here? Nice catch, huh?"

"He's alright." She hid her smile behind her glass. "If you go in for that young and handsome sort of thing."

"I know, right?" Jane touched his face. "Look at these cheekbones. You could sharpen a knife on these babies."

"Thank you for the drink, Carter." Roma raised her glass and retreated.

"I leave you alone for five minutes and you start flirting with other women? What's your game, Carter Michael Price?"

"I…" He leaned his head to the side. "I never told you my middle name."

"Sure you did."

"No. I didn't."

Something flashed in Jane's eyes. For the first time since the night before, she seemed unsure of herself, as if a crack had formed in her shiny exterior.

"Lucky guess then. You look like your middle name should be Michael."

"Ladies and gentlemen, can I have your attention?" Diya Singh stood in the parlor doorway with her hands folded in front of her. She waited as the room quieted. "If you would kindly adjourn to the dining room, dinner will be served shortly."

A swell of excited chatter went up from the guests as they rose from their chairs.

"Are we okay?" asked Jane.

"Yeah, sure," said Carter. He placed his half-empty glass down on the bar.

Jane slipped her hand into his, but he didn't look at her as they exited the parlor. The truth was, he *had* told Jane his middle name, but that was during their last engagement, when she was a different version of herself. Now she was supposed to be just some girl he picked up in a bar and took to a party and plied with booze and fancy food until she went to bed with him.

He knew that as a person, she couldn't help but remember things about him from their previous meetings. But all of that was supposed to be erased. She was supposed to be a professional.

That was what he was paying for.

With a long night ahead of them, he wondered what else Jane might let slip.

SIXTEEN

Diya waited just inside the empty dining room as the guests descended from the second floor and gathered in the parlor.

The many cameras in the foyer captured every angle of their individual arrivals, from the regal side-by-side of Adelai and Simone Vaught, to the whispering schoolgirls Lucas Cotton and Roma Owens, and somewhat amusingly, the steal-your-girl Stanton Blumenfield escorting Laura Hargreaves while her husband Robert trailed behind them. Out of habit, Diya had marked on her guest list the order of arrival, despite it having little bearing on how the evening would play out. It was something Rakesh Singh would have appreciated, an attention to detail that would set his daughter apart from the rest of the crowd.

Carter Price had been the first to arrive in the parlor, accompanied by his plus-one, a social butterfly he introduced only as Jane. It was the MX arms dealer, Reno Cardenas, who came last, waiting until well after 6:30 p.m. to even come out of his room. Diya watched him on her palette, shifting camera angles as he came to the landing at the top of the stairs and looked around at the house as if he were considering buying it. He had a brutish, standoffish quality that made Diya feel small, and she was somewhat relieved he had stayed in his room for the majority of cocktail hour.

The other guests appeared to be getting along well, chatting and drinking like functioning members of polite society. Reno Cardenas would have been a wet blanket on a roaring fire. Fortunately, he didn't try to engage with anyone. Jane made him a drink and he took up a position next to a promotional vidscreen with his back to the crowd. None of the guests could see that Reno wasn't paying any attention to the vidscreen, but through the camera at the top of the frame, Diya noticed he was keeping tabs on the people behind him.

Diya watched for a while, glancing occasionally at the clock in the corner of her palette, waiting for it to hit the next checkpoint. Behind the video window, her list of instructions for the evening was slowly growing smaller. At any normal dinner party, there would be an army of hospitality workers scurrying around behind the scenes, prepping plates and making sure all of the guests were well-lubricated. And though Diya had hired a team of professional chefs to prepare the meals, they were now long gone, as were the porters who would have moved the dome-covered plates from the kitchen to the dining room.

That job, Winston had told her, was for the assets, and as with everything else, was simply part of the show.

Shortly after 7:00 p.m., Diya left the dining room and made her way nto the foyer. Her beige pencil skirt held tightly to her legs and made her long, natural stride impossible. She examined her itinerary as her heels clacked on the smooth tile.

7:10 p.m. – Begin moving guests to the dining room.

Diya stood at the entrance to the parlor and addressed her guests.

"Ladies and gentlemen, can I have your attention? If you would like to adjourn to the dining room, dinner will be served shortly."

She stepped back to allow the couples to pass by. They all seemed to be in good spirits, some already well into their fourth or fifth drink of the evening. Most passed with a small smile and nod of their heads. Reno looked past her as if she were mere decoration. Jane, a few steps ahead of Carter, slowed to admire Diya's outfit, which was a little more formal than the slacks she had worn earlier.

"You'll find nameplates at each setting," said Diya, as she followed the group into the dining room. She took her position at the head of the table, as her itinerary instructed, and waited for everyone to find their seats.

A small amount of unspoken uncertainty passed between the couples in the group, and Diya wondered if her research into proper dinner party seating had steered her wrong. Although it was normal for a husband to want to sit with his wife, the articles Diya had read said couples should never be seated together, but rather, should be placed across the table from each other.

After some brief hesitation, Robert helped Laura into her chair and then walked around the table to stand behind his own. He didn't sit down until all the other women at the table were seated.

On Diya's left, a smirking Adelai Vaught looked up and asked, "Will our host be joining us for dinner?"

"No, ma'am, but he is on his way."

"Is that some kind of power move?" asked Lucas, to Jane, the woman on his right.

"Maybe he prefers to eat out," she replied, trying to catch Carter's eye across the table, but he seemed more preoccupied with making sure his cutlery was straight.

Diya chuckled politely, then cleared her throat. She waited until she had everyone's attention.

"On behalf of Winston Vise and myself, I want to thank everyone for attending this evening." At the sound of her voice, the whisperer in her ear ramped up, feeding her the next few words of the speech she and Winston had worked on the week before. "As you may have noticed, Mr. Vise is not in attendance at the moment. I received word that his jet touched down a few minutes ago, and he will be here just as we are finishing dinner." She spread her hands to indicate the long table. "While Mr. Vise apologizes for not being here to greet you personally, he wanted to make sure you were well taken care of and in good spirits for the night ahead. He has a series of wonders and surprises in store for you, none of them dangerous, I assure you, but all of them fascinating and hopefully, well worth your time and expense in coming here."

"I would've come just for the open bar," said Lucas.

At the far end of the dining room, lightning lashed against the tall, rounded window. The accompanying thunder drowned out the muted laughter at Lucas' remark.

"Tonight," continued Diya, "Mr. Vise would like you to share in his vision of the future. *You*, in particular. The support staff have all been sent home, a security team is walking the perimeter of the grounds some two miles away, and all of us, right here, represent the only organic element in this house. Everyone else you will meet tonight, with the exception of Mr. Vise, of course, will be a synthetic… a robot… a machine. And with that said, we would like you to meet your servers for the evening."

She tapped on the check mark on her itinerary next to *Deliver Opening Dinner Address* and scrolled to the next line. There, Winston had placed a call to a computer script. Diya didn't know exactly what it did, but having used similar scripts throughout the day, she knew whatever it did was what Winston wanted. She didn't hesitate to tap the red *execute* button.

Thud.

The sound landed like a sledgehammer at the small of her back.

All night, the distant pounding had intruded on her dreams. She was reasonably sure the sound had stopped after her initial investigation, but through the night, she kept imagining it, drawing herself out of a restless slumber wherein she saw only the door, the blacker-than-black square that might have contained millions of universes for all she knew. All day, she had avoided the hallway that led to the door, and when she did look at it, there was always relief to see the access panel glowing red.

Thud.

Diya took a step backwards into the hall. She cheated her gaze to the left. Opposite the dining room door, she could see the length of the hallway that led to the mysterious black door. And just like something out of a nightmare, the access panel was now flashing green. The *thuds* she heard were those of heavy metal cylinders retracting into the wall. The sounds came faster, dozens by the end, until finally a hiss filled the hallway, and the door began to swing forward.

She had seen too many movies to expect anything less than the demons of hell to come rushing through the door—large, slimy beasts full of teeth and sharp nails. They would spill out and consume her before ripping the assembled dinner party to shreds. Hell would be unleashed, and the world would never be the same.

Something in the shadows beyond the door shimmered.

Diya held her breath until she saw a figure emerge—a thin, feminine form, not overly tall, with a hip-swinging gait no monster would be caught dead sporting. As the LEDs in the hallway lit up the figure, Diya saw it was indeed a woman and she was dressed in a classic black French maid outfit, complete with massive breasts spilling over white ruffles. Tall, black stilettos stabbed at the floor as she walked, creating a syncopated clicking that echoed throughout the house.

She was followed by another French maid, dressed and formed almost identically. There were eight in all, and at first, Diya thought they all might be the same synthetic printed multiple times, but as they passed her on the way into the dining room, she saw their faces were distinct. All had their hair pulled back and secured with a loop of white lace, but the color varied from dirty blonde to full black. There were round faces and sharp chins, narrow eyes and full eyebrows.

The variations reminded Diya of the dolls Lamshka Singh had bought her when she was very young. Like the synthetics taking their positions on the perimeter of the dining room, her dolls too had had interchangeable bodies—the heads were unique, but the same base body mold had been used for all of them.

Lucas let out a whistle. Farther down the table, Robert and Laura shared a laugh between them.

When the maids were settled in their positions, standing tall with hands folded in front of their abbreviated aprons, the crackling of an old-style record filled the room, followed by the opening salvo of a string quartet. As the music ramped up, the maids approached the table, standing in the gaps between the five guests on each side.

Simultaneously, such that the question seemed to come from everywhere at once, the maids spoke.

"Steak, fish, or vegetarian?" All in the exact same voice, same tone, same inflection.

A murmur of surprise went up from the table, followed by nervous laughter. As the orders were put in, Diya pulled the dining room doors closed. The foyer seemed to dim, though she attributed the sensation to being cut off from the rest of the group. The music drifted out, as did the growing sound of jumbled conversations, but Diya still felt alone. She took her palette to the center of the foyer and examined the itinerary. There wasn't much else to do until Vise arrived, unless she wanted to sneak into the kitchen and see what her boss kept in the fridge.

She minimized the itinerary on her palette, revealing the security camera feeds behind them. In one window, she could see the dining room. The guests were placing napkins over their laps and trading amusing anecdotes. In the kitchen, the maids were assembling plates from a bank of warming trays that had been brought in for the occasion. The difference in demeanor was not lost on Diya. Where the guests chatted and interacted like social creatures, the maids did not speak or even acknowledge each other's existence. And yet, they moved about the kitchen with such coordination that Diya wondered if some puppet master were controlling them all. Otherwise, how were they able to anticipate each other's movements?

If they were communicating, it wasn't through speech.

In the window below the kitchen, Diya saw herself standing in the center of the foyer. The camera was in the ceiling behind her, several feet above the front door. For a moment, she felt as if she were watching a movie. The character on the screen did not move, despite the swelling music indicating some kind of imminent threat. Diya kept waiting for something to enter the screen but—

Thud.

The character on the screen turned suddenly to the left.

The door at the far end of the hallway was still open, and all of the locks were retracted. What Diya had heard had come from somewhere deeper. Part of her wanted to investigate, to find out what other surprises Winston was hiding in what must have been some kind of basement. He hadn't mentioned anything about a basement in any of their meetings, and Diya hadn't imagined a house as old as Vise Manor would even have one.

Do I go look?

Should I tell someone first?

She looked up at the camera above the door. Would that be enough to inform the detective who would ultimately investigate her untimely death that she'd heard a sound and foolishly went to check it out?

A round of laughter erupted from the dining room.

Diya walked quickly to the parlor and slid the doors closed behind her. She used the panel on the wall to dim the lights until the fireplace was the brightest spot in the room. She sat in a chair near the bar where the shadows were the deepest and hugged her palette to her chest. As long as she stayed quiet and out of sight, she figured, whatever was in the basement would be drawn to the dining room first. Between the guests and the synthetics, the monsters would be plenty occupied while she made her escape.

If it came to that.

She swiped to another window on her palette.

Winston was still more than an hour away.

SEVENTEEN

Center Line was the synth drug Adelai had been waiting for all her life.

She'd tried all the popular treatments for her depression—yoga, acupuncture, therapists, SSRIs—but none had come close to giving her the sense of balance that *Center Line* brought on. Chemical solutions like alcohol and pot had only dulled her connection to the world, while the synth seemed to make everything clearer, more pristine. It filtered out all the bad bits and left only pure momentary presence.

Adelai hadn't felt anything like it in such a long time. For the first hour, all she had wanted to do was sit in a chair by the fireplace and soak it all in—the conversation, the clothes, and the raw sensuality oozing from Simone, who had sat across from her in the parlor and now again at the dinner table. Though she was engaged in conversation with Lucas Cotton, she kept looking over, catching Adelai's eye through the long stems of wildflowers.

Seated on Adelai's left was a young woman who had introduced herself as Roma. She had pretty skin and the most delightful constellation of petite diamonds running along her earlobe. Adelai wanted to talk to her, but she seemed more interested in Carter Price, who was seated on the other side of her. Joining their conversation wasn't an option, so she sat alone for several minutes, sipping at her wine, watching Simone casually flirt with Lucas, all without feeling the slightest hint of anxiety or awkwardness thanks to the synth coating her biochip.

To pass the time, she surveyed the framed portraits on the walls—relatives of Winston Vise, she assumed. She had noticed along with Simone the gold plaque next to the front door that read *Vise Manor, Est 1862*. The house had no doubt been in his family for a long time, and as her eyes drifted to the high, cathedral-like ceiling with its crisscrossing beams, she wondered if the dining room had at one time been a chapel. It wasn't far-fetched to assume the original window had been made of stained glass and merely updated when the latest Vise took ownership. Perhaps he wasn't the man of God his forebearers were.

It wasn't until the maids returned that she got to speak again. One of them placed a plate on the charger in front of her; the aroma of freshly grilled salmon and seasoned asparagus rose up to tickle her nose. As the maid was retreating, Adelai reached out and took her hand.

"I'm Adelai, and you are?"

The maid smiled but made no attempt to free herself. "I'm Catarine, if you need anything."

"And if I don't need anything?"

"I'm sorry, I don't understand."

"Who are you if I *don't* need anything?"

"I'm sorry, I don't understand."

Despite her words, there was no confusion on Catarine's face. Her eyes were slightly unfocused, as if bored. Thin eyebrows sat stoic in their default state.

"May I have a glass of Pinot Noir, please? Chilled."

"Right away, madam."

Adelai watched her disappear through the swinging door that led to the kitchen. Across the table, Simone had been following the entire exchange.

"Why are you teasing her?"

"I wasn't teasing. I just wanted to see how advanced they are."

"And?"

Adelai shrugged. "The salmon looks good."

Simone looked down at her plate and nodded. She'd ordered the same thing.

Once everyone was served, cutlery began to scrape against plates. Nobody said much of anything until the writer at the far end of the table addressed the group.

"Would anyone like to play a game?"

"What kind of game?" asked Robert.

Beside him, the scruffy man with the thick MX accent dug into his steak without looking up.

"A thought exercise." Stanton Blumenfield raised a finger as if he might conduct a symphony with it. "My wife and I used to play this at dinner parties before she passed."

"Oh, I'm so sorry," said Laura.

"Don't be, my dear. She lived a long and beautiful life. We should all be so lucky to go out on top."

Jane clinked her knife against an empty wine glass.

"It makes a fine icebreaker, I've found," continued Stanton, "because there is a fair amount of arguing involved. And what better way to get to know someone than to try to reach a common ground with them, am I right?"

"Absolutely not," said Lucas.

Stanton pointed to him. "That's the spirit. Now, the game begins with a simple question." He cleared his throat. "If you could have any superpower, what would it be?"

Adelai closed her eyes to keep them from rolling.

"Flight," said Laura.

Next to her, Carter answered, "Invisibility."

Jane followed quickly with, "Ability to speak all languages, even Dothraki."

Across the table, Simone mouthed, "Telepathy."

Stanton raised his hands to slow the barrage of answers. "Okay, yes, that is a good start. But here is where the game begins. The question is being asked by a rather lazy genie. They will grant any superpower we wish with the following stipulation: we all have to receive the same one, and the decision has to be unanimous. If we cannot agree, then we receive nothing. Shall we start at the far end of the table, with the young woman with the pointy earrings?"

"Who, me?" asked Simone.

Adelai clapped her hands softly.

"Well, I guess if we're just throwing out ideas… I'd probably like to read people's minds. I spend most of my day conducting interviews, so reading thoughts would really help me cut through a lot of bullshit. I'd want to be able to turn it on and off though. I don't want to be walking down Broadway and have to hear all the psychotic ramblings of every New Yorker I pass."

"How about you, Mr. Cotton?" asked Stanton.

Lucas stammered for a moment. "Uh, yeah." He gave Simone a puzzled look. "It's funny you picked telepathy, Mrs. Vaught. That's actually close to what we're trying to accomplish at the MESH Foundation. Not hearing the actual thoughts, but you know, being able to communicate without speaking, and maybe even feeling what the other person is feeling."

"Well, that's good," said Jane. "Now she can wish for something else."

"I'll have to think about it," said Simone. "Why don't you go, Mr. Cotton?"

"Okay, well, since we'll be able to read minds with technology soon, I'd have to say telekinesis. Since I was a little kid, I've wanted to be able to move things with my mind. As a man of science, I know that's impossible, what with conservation of energy and all."

"Or just physics in general," said Carter.

"Right, and that's the point. Telekinesis would be a giant middle finger to physics altogether. Plus, I'd love to be able to use it on the highway. Our offices are in San Francisco, but I live outside the city. You don't know how often I've wished for a giant crane to come down and lift a few hundred cars out of my way." He laughed. "How about you, Ms. Martin?"

Jane dabbed her lips with her napkin. "I like the idea of feeling what someone else is feeling, but also in the other direction. Like, if you wrong someone, and you say you're sorry, but you don't think they believe that you feel bad, you could just send that feeling over so they'd know for sure." She picked up her fork and put it down again. "I don't know. I guess it's a selfish power… to have your emotions experienced by someone else, to be truly seen by them."

"That's a great idea," said Lucas. "I hadn't thought of broadcasting in the other direction."

Carter huffed. "It's probably overkill. If you wrong someone and apologize, then it's on the other person to accept it and move on. If they want to hold a grudge about it, especially if it's something unimportant, then that's their problem." He sipped his drink. "People like that aren't even worth apologizing to."

Jane bowed her head to hide a smile. Adelai wondered what the hell had happened between them to elicit such a response.

"I believe the marker is to you, Mr. Hargreaves," said Stanton.

Robert had his hand closed in a fist around the stem of his wine glass. "Immortality. Bought and paid for."

"That's it?" asked Laura. "No explanation?"

"What's to explain? Living forever is the only reasonable answer. Mind-reading, telekinesis, and yes, even flying—those things only last until you die. Where are you going to fly when you're ninety years old? Whose minds are you going to read when you're a hundred? No, this is a once-in-a-lifetime opportunity people, and we need to get the biggest bang for our buck. That means a power that lasts *forever*. Wouldn't you agree, boss?"

The *boss* he was referring to was the MX national. He looked up from his plate to shake his head at Robert.

"Alright, since I've played this before, I'll skip my turn," said Stanton. "Please, Mrs. Hargreaves. What will you be doing while your husband is living forever?"

"I want to fly," she replied, tapping the table with her knuckles. "Bought and paid for. Case closed. Next game."

The table had a laugh at Robert's expense, which he accepted graciously with a lift of his wine glass.

"It's just that… nothing's meant to last forever," continued Laura. "I've always dreamed of flying, and even if I could only do it for five or ten years, I'd be so lucky to be able to just rise above it all, just fly up and let the world fall away. It'd be nice to have that kind of space just to relax for a moment."

Adelai nodded in agreement. She imagined herself floating high above New York City, the buildings like piles of rocks, the streets like ant trails scored in the dirt. Compared to reading people's thoughts, she'd take flying nine times out of ten.

"I'd just like to point out that with telekinesis, you could mentally lift yourself into the air." Lucas looked around for support. "So really, flight would just be a single silo version of my power. Essentially, the ability to lift just one thing. I mean, there's some common ground there."

Carter stepped in to fill the resulting silence. "I do like the idea of flight. Not having to drive or ride in planes. But I also wouldn't want to waste time traveling from one place to another. I vote for teleportation. You just think of somewhere you want to be and *bang*, you're there. Whatever you're carrying or touching goes with you." He nodded to Jane across the table. "So we could just pop out of here, watch the sun rise or set in Italy, and then be back for the big presentation. I'm sure it'd be great for awkward situations as well. Remember those Snickers commercials?"

"Like an ejector seat for life," said Jane.

"Exactly."

Stanton craned his neck. "What about you, Ms. Owens?"

"Well…" Roma had just bitten a stalk of asparagus and wasn't prepared to speak.

"Perhaps you'd like to pause time," suggested Adelai.

Roma nodded, then shook her head. "No, what I was going to say, is that no one is considering what happens after we walk out of here with our powers. I'm sorry to pick on you, Laura, but let's say we had the power of flight. How long would it be before someone saw us flying? I was reading an article about some mysterious jetpack person harassing planes at LAX. They want him because he's breaking the law; they'd want us because we have powers. It's your classic *X-Men* situation all over again. Whatever power we choose would make us targets for exploitation and experimentation. We'd have to keep our abilities hidden from the rest of the world."

"So what then, Roma?" asked Lucas.

"I know it might sound stupid, but ever since I was a little girl, I've always daydreamed about having a magic coin purse. Just a little one, black velvet, with a drawstring. And every time you reach into it, there's a twenty-dollar bill. And you could just keep pulling them out." She rubbed her cheek. "It wasn't until I was older that I started asking the tough questions like: are the serial numbers valid, where does the money come from, and does that mean a twenty is disappearing from someone else's pocket? It all became too much. I think all discussions about powers like that end in the same way—they're not worth the attention they'd bring."

"What happens if someone abdicates?" asked Robert.

Stanton turned his hand over. "Never happened before. We're certainly in uncharted territory now, friends."

Adelai didn't like the ominous words, especially when they were spoken in Stanton's gravelly German accent. She tried to get the game back on track.

"Mine is time," she said, not waiting to be prompted. "Time seems to be moving faster the older I get. I'd love to be able to slow it down, to relish in those moments when everything is perfect, or when someone asks me a question and I've just taken a bite of my food." She placed her hand on Roma's shoulder briefly. "And then there are nights like tonight, when I'm away from home, enjoying the company of relative strangers, but not wholly convinced the evening will be worth it." She gestured to the maids standing with their hands clasped behind their backs at the edge of the dining room. "I truly hope these well-endowed women are not the pinnacle of Winston Vise's synthetic prowess."

"They seem pretty impressive to me," said Lucas. "Like digital assistants made into people, no longer confined to our whisperers."

"I can imagine an entire restaurant staffed with synthetics," said Robert. "After the initial investment, you'd only have to pay for upkeep. Better yet, what if you outsourced your staff from a larger company that deals specifically in synthetic workers? A synthetic temp agency or contractor."

"No, I know what she means," said Simone. "Maybe this would be fine for a restaurant, but this isn't anything you couldn't already get now. I saw a synthetic barista at a trade show last year who could serve a variety of coffees. Couldn't speak like our maids here, but she had no problem placing cups on the counter. I guess we were hoping Mr. Vise had something more interesting to show us."

The maids appeared unconcerned with the conversation.

"Did everyone receive a hand?" asked Carter. "Or was that just me?"

Laura nodded. "Ours attacked me."

Across from her, Reno perked up.

"I mean, it started tickling me and wouldn't stop. Robert had to put it in our safe just to keep it contained."

"Ours wanted to hold hands," said Simone. "It was very gentle and sweet."

"Mine took dictation," said Stanton. "The note said to give it a pen, and once I did, it started writing out everything I was saying. No ears, no eyes, and yet the transcription was perfect."

"How was its penmanship?" asked Robert.

"Exquisite. Every letter the same every time."

"The maids don't have the same kind of hands as the ones we received," said Adelai. "Their skin is rubbery. If anything, they remind me of the sex dolls Companion Dynamics makes."

"No," said Carter. "These are nothing like a CD doll. They clearly have articulated—" He stopped short and picked up his glass. "Oh look, I'm empty. Another round please."

At the end of the table, Reno began to chuckle. "Te gustan las muñecas?"

"Ah, welcome to the party," said Stanton. "And what about you, friend? What did your hand do?"

Reno sat back in his chair as if debating whether to even answer. Finally, he reached up with one hand and pulled down the upturned collar of his jacket. There, beneath a dark, stubbly beard, were streaks of purple and black. He looked over at Laura and grinned.

"No pinche tickle."

EIGHTEEN

The powder room was tucked under the stairs just to the right of the parlor.

It had an ornate door of carved wood with circular waves rising and falling around the shapes of animals and stars. A frosted yellow window at eye level showed the lights burning on the other side, letting passersby know the room was currently occupied. Given its whimsical design and incongruity with the rest of the house, Robert assumed the door had come from somewhere else and that Vise had repurposed it for his powder room.

Laura had excused herself from the dinner table with the intention of going to the bathroom alone, but Robert had insisted on going with her, ostensibly to protect her from all the dangers of Vise Manor, but really just to get a small break from sitting next to Reno Cardenas. Not only was the MX national a conversational black hole, but he also smelled a bit like beer and gunpowder. Robert was happy to get out into the foyer for a little fresh air. Now, standing a respectful distance from the powder room door, he started to dread returning to the dining room.

Despite how airy and well-lit the foyer was, there seemed to be shadows everywhere, especially at the end of a hallway where a large door he hadn't noticed before now stood open. It reminded him of a bank vault or even the outer door at NORAD, just on a smaller scale and as dark as the inside of a crow's anus. Beyond the door, a single line of LEDs ran down a sloping ceiling, suggesting a basement beneath Vise Manor.

A tinkling of ice into a glass—a sound Robert could recognize across a crowded and noisy ballroom—came from the parlor. All the other guests were back in the dining room, so who was the mystery drinker? He stepped up to the doors and slid them apart slowly, fully expecting to see a sharply dressed Winston Vise standing at the bar with a whiskey rocks in his hand. Instead, he found the hostess, Diya, leaning against the bar on her forearms, lost in a private moment.

She noticed the movement of the doors and turned to him.

"Sorry," he said. "I didn't mean to disturb you. I heard a noise and thought our mysterious host had arrived."

Diya straightened up immediately, donning her hostess persona like someone slipping on a cloak. She abandoned her drink on the bar as if she had picked it up on accident.

"No worries, Mr. Hargreaves. I was just..." She gestured vaguely to the room.

"Taking a moment?"

"Yes." There was exhaustion on her face, a subtle dipping of her mouth before either synth or sheer force of will wrenched it back into a smile. "I know I shouldn't be drinking, but there's something about this house that puts me on edge. People weren't meant to live in a house this big."

Robert glanced up at the ceiling; thick beams of dark wood crisscrossed the room. "It is a bit much. Laura and I have a large home too, nothing like this of course, but big enough to hold what's important to us. Separate offices, a small gym, a couple of guest rooms—things like that. I wonder what it says about Mr. Vise that he has eight guest rooms, a parlor with enough books and booze for twenty people, plus a basement secured by one of the biggest doors I've ever seen."

Her mouth glitched again. "You... you didn't go down there, did you?"

Robert shook his head. "Laura needed to use the facilities. I just noticed it while I was waiting. What's down there?"

"I'm not quite sure. The door was closed when I arrived a few days ago and didn't open until those maids came sauntering out like a line of sexy ants. And now that it's open, I don't really want to look. It feels too much like going through someone else's drawers, know what I mean?"

"Drawers like underwear?"

Diya smiled wryly and shook her head.

"No," said Robert, "I know what you mean. And a door like that certainly says *don't look in here*. But now that you mention it, maybe he's keeping all of his little toys down there. The maids for sure, and whatever else he plans to show us."

Diya said nothing.

"You're not going to tell me, are you?"

"I'm sorry... it would ruin the surprise of the presentation, the *shock and awe*, as Winston put it."

Robert felt himself laugh a little too hard. He couldn't remember having any water in the last couple of hours, just glass after glass of the red stuff.

"But he *is* coming, right?"

"Who's coming?" Laura slipped an arm around Robert's waist and kissed him on the cheek. "Thanks for waiting, hon."

"I was just asking our delightful hostess if Winston Vise would be making an appearance."

"Why wouldn't he? He's the one who invited us, right?"

Diya shifted from one leg to the other before regaining her professional stoicism.

Robert continued, "I'm just saying it's strange for a host not to greet his guests when they arrive. He sends us a last-minute invitation to dinner and then doesn't even attend himself. I would at least speak directly to my guests before they moved into one of my rooms, drank my wine, ate my food, and—"

A small hand landed softly on his chest.

"Alright, Robert. Maybe it's time we mix in a water."

He raised an eyebrow at her. "I was *just* thinking that. Did you read my mind?"

"That was Simone's power. I just know you."

"I assure you, Mr. Hargreaves," said Diya. "Mr. Vise is on his way and should be here shortly."

"See, hon? She assures us."

"That's exactly what she would say if she were puppet-mastering this whole thing from behind the curtain." Robert knew he was being foolish, but he was too amused with himself to stop. "I predict that by the end of tonight, we find out Diya Singh is actually Diya Vise… oooh… Diyavise would be a great name for a perfume or some kind of clamp."

"Forgive my husband," said Laura. "He's a child when he's sober and worse when he drinks."

Diya folded her hands. "It's quite alright, but I do need to make some final preparations in the conservatory before the presentation. I'll come retrieve you from the dining room when it's time to begin."

"Thank you, Diya," said Laura. She tugged at Robert's arm. "Come on, it would be rude to be gone too long."

He grinned. "They probably think we snuck off to have sex."

She turned him around and led him away from the door. "It's bad enough when you do it to me, but now you put that image in that poor girl's mind. Shame on you."

Robert laughed and escorted Laura back to the dining room doors. Before opening them, he whispered, "She's nervous."

Laura glanced over her shoulder. "Who? The girl? Of course she is. This is probably a big night for her."

"No, I didn't mean nervous. Scared."

"Of what?"

Robert searched for an answer, even thought of pointing out the ominous vault door at the end of the hallway, but Laura wasn't scared of the same things he was. Her imagination didn't see monsters forming ranks in the shadows. She was only scared of real danger, of a hand crawling up her leg to tickle her stomach.

"Never mind," he said, and slid the doors open.

"It is clear our invitations were made custom for each of us." The table was transfixed on Stanton. The writer paused for a moment as Laura took the seat next to him. "This implies we were not chosen at random, and that once chosen, research was done to help predict what kind of behavior would most intrigue us. Mine could take dictation, yours could communicate in Morse code, as you said, Mr. Price."

Carter nodded.

"Could you tell us why that was so interesting to you? Has your neighbor ever asked you any leading questions in that regard?"

"Well…" Carter looked around the table, shrinking just a bit under the scrutiny. "*Neighbor* may not be the right word. I've never met Vise. But it's possible he did some research on me and found out I was into linguistical interfaces. I started a company in high school called Dyalogued that focused on human-machine language barriers. It would be the same kind of tech that allows a hand to communicate through dots and dashes, so yeah, I guess I found that interesting."

Robert didn't. His attention was focused on Laura, watching the way she held herself, shoulders back, curls dangling over her exposed clavicles. The smile on her face came and went, blooming when whomever was speaking happened to look in her direction. It was only after several minutes that she finally caught eyes with him, and though he wasn't sure what she saw on his face, her next move was to gesture to one of the maids and whisper something to her. The maid nodded and stepped back to resume her position on the wall.

For several seconds, nothing happened. Robert sat back in his chair and crossed his arms, enthralled by the scene unfolding in the background of this fancy dinner party. No one else seemed to notice the maids at all, nor had any of them remarked on how one was missing. He looked over his shoulder.

Four behind him.

Three in front of him.

Where was the eighth?

What the fuck is happening here?

Robert chuckled, took a sip of his drink, and waited. His buzz was so perfectly tuned that he hardly noticed the seconds ticking by.

Finally, some kind of timer must have expired, and the maid behind Laura left her post and headed into the kitchen. She returned less than a minute later with a tall glass of iced water in her hand.

"I sincerely apologize for the delay, sir," said the maid. She placed the water beside his glass of wine.

He thanked her out of habit, got no response, and gently raised the glass to Laura.

Stanton turned his attention to the smelly bearded man on Robert's right. "What about you, friend? Why would you be interested in a hand that tries to strangle you?"

"No te metas, güero," said Reno, which Robert translated to something like *leave it alone* but more aggressive.

"Are we supposed to say?" asked Laura. "I thought Mr. Vise was trying to keep us all in the dark about what we did for a living."

"Perhaps," said Stanton, "but most of you have been forthcoming with your places of work, with the exception of our friends at the end of the table, and of course, Mr. Reno."

It was Lucas who finally answered the challenge.

"His name is Reno Cardenas. He's one of the co-owners of Plomo Pesado in the MX." Lucas took a sip of his drink. "He's in the gun business."

Jane asked, "How do you know that?"

"I heard about him on the Lincoln Continental feed, maybe a year ago, when a couple of those synthetic soldados were trying to come across the border. *Five Biggest Arms Dealers in the MX: Number Four Will Shock You.* They were trying to figure out who was making the soldiers."

There was silence after Lucas finished speaking. It seemed no one wanted to press Reno on the charges. His apparent disinterest in the conversation might have been proof enough.

Even Stanton relented and instead focused on the couple at the end of the table. "Would you ladies be willing to share your places of employment?"

The silver-haired woman, Addy, started to speak, but her partner lifted a finger.

"I'd like to respond to the gentleman's question," said Simone, smoothing her napkin in her lap. "Respectfully, no."

That got a chuckle from Addy. The rest of the table looked to Lucas in the hopes he had heard stories about the women on the Lincoln Continental feed, but he raised his hands as if to say, *sorry, I have no clue.*

"Does it really matter either way?" asked Carter. "He did research on us. I'm sure everyone did research on him too. What's a little mutual cyber-stalking between potential business acquaintances?"

There were nods from around the table. Jane even laughed.

Stanton muttered, "Interesting."

"Well," said Simone, "if all of you had voted for my telepathy power earlier, we wouldn't be in this bind now. We'd know exactly what everyone was thinking. No secrets."

"Veto," said Jane.

"Seconded," said Roma.

Laura turned to Stanton. "You never told us what your power would be. Did any of us get it right?"

"There are no right or wrong answers, Laura dear. It's more of a social experiment, to see if we humans are ready to accept the coming future."

"And what future would that be?"

Stanton placed his hand on Laura's. "Immortality. Every time I've played this game, with people from all walks of life, the winning answer is invariably immortality."

Robert slapped the table with his palm. "I fucking knew it!"

"Yes, you're very smart, hon. Drink your water."

"Immortality," continued Stanton, "is the great equalizer. Telepathy, telekinesis, flight... technology will certainly fill those gaps sooner or later. Teleportation may take a little longer, and a credit card is more or less a magic endless coin purse, though the money isn't exactly free. Even time will cease to have meaning when we're immortal. Everything you could ever want is encompassed by the prospect of living forever.

"You all had wonderful suggestions, and each has its own merits, but as an old man who writes about the future, I am fully invested in the desire to see if I am *right*. When I think of all the technological progress that has occurred in my lifetime and try to imagine another hundred years of exponential growth... it makes this old man giddy, friends."

Laura turned to Robert and said perhaps a little too loudly, "I like this one."

"Should we put it to a vote then?" asked Jane, raising her hand. "I wouldn't mind living forever, so long as I get to choose my age."

"I vote yes, if I can be her age," said Addy, her eyes looking everywhere except at the person she was referencing.

Simone raised her hand. "'Til Armageddon do us part."

One by one, every person at the table raised their hand.

Reno looked up from his plate. He hadn't even touched the potatoes or asparagus.

"Nadie vive por siempre."

"Forgive me," said Stanton, "I don't speak Spanish."

Robert cleared his throat. "He said no one lives forever."

Across the table, Stanton chuckled, wiped his mouth with his napkin.

"Not yet, my rugged friend. Not yet."

NINETEEN

After the main course, the busty French maids served a small sampling of desserts to each guest. Carter ate some of his apple turnover, took a bite from the powdered beignet, but left the rest untouched.

He was starting to get a queasy feeling that usually came on when he was stepping over the border from buzzed into drunk. The large meal he'd eaten would help, but it was definitely past time to cut out the booze, at least for a little while. He asked one of the maids for a soda, and she brought him a fizzing glass without asking which brand he preferred. He sipped it slowly while the others finished their desserts.

Addy and Simone were the first to leave, with the former announcing she was chilly and wanted to sit by the fire. Lucas and Roma stood together near the doors for a while, examining one of the maids close up. The trio of Stanton, Laura, and Robert took up position by the window and continued their conversation about immortality. Jane gestured with her head to the group a few times before Carter relented and accompanied her to the large cathedral window.

Outside, strong winds heaved rain against the glass.

Carter only half-listened to their conversation. He smiled and nodded, taking his cues from Jane, as if they were both being held hostage and their only hope of escape was to play along. It wasn't that the others weren't interesting; they were just older, and from two completely different generations. Carter couldn't imagine what they would have in common besides a love of technology.

Luckily, it wasn't long before Diya reappeared and invited them to join Mr. Vise in the conservatory.

"I think I'll need a bio break," said Robert.

Stanton seized the opportunity to escort Laura out of the dining room.

Carter started to follow, but a hand on his arm held him back. Jane waited for the room to clear before speaking.

"Hey, I wanted to apologize for earlier. I'm really sorry. I didn't mean to ruin your evening." She put her hands on his hips. "It was kind of you to invite me. I should have been better."

Carter shook his head, uncomfortable with how sincere she sounded. "No, it wasn't your fault. I overreacted." He put his back against the glass; distant thunder made his shoulders tingle. "I'm…" He placed his hands delicately on her face and pulled her in for a kiss. She tasted of malbec and honey. "I'm sorry. I shouldn't have snapped at you. I just… I don't feel like I fit in with these people. It makes me nervous."

"I get it." Jane took his hand. "I feel that way sometimes too when I'm around strangers. But these people seem nice enough, right? I haven't heard any of them mention our age or call us *junior* or *sweetie.* I think they've been pretty accepting, except for the arms dealer, which by the way, what the fuck, right?"

He smirked. "That doesn't surprise me. I'm starting to think Vise isn't exactly a straight shooter. Selling tech to the MX may not even be the worst thing he's done."

Jane searched his eyes. "You know something, don't you?"

Carter nodded.

"Something the rest of them don't?"

The maids were all standing with their backs to the walls, but Carter couldn't shake the feeling they were paying attention to him. One even paused on her way into the kitchen, lingering in the doorway as if she'd forgotten something.

He lowered his voice.

"A couple of years ago, there was a big Vinestead data breach. People called it the Fall of Brigham Plaza."

She nodded as if hearing it for the first time, even though Carter and a different version of Jane had discussed it during their first engagement at St. Regis a few months after it happened.

"A hacker named Danny Guns Montreal accessed some data store in VNet and dumped the contents to the rest of the world. Just years and years of corporate secrets. Vinestead denied all of it, of course, but people have been connecting the dots between the leaked data and proprietary code owned by other companies."

Jane blinked a few times. "You lost me."

"It's no secret Vinestead steals from other companies. Guns exposed that, but to do so, he had to make all that code publicly available. Anyone could access it and use it." He pulled her closer as if they were dancing to a slow song. "I took apart the hand Vise sent me as an invitation. I looked at the components. Some of the code in the hand is the same as the stolen code from the Fall."

"And that's… bad, right?"

"If Vise is trying to sell us a product that uses stolen code, then yeah, that's real bad. No one is going to invest in that kind of legal liability."

"I see." She laid her head on his chest, took a few long breaths. "Are you going to say anything?"

"I don't know if I should. I mean, isn't that like going to a magic show and just pointing out how all the tricks are done?"

"When was the last time you went to a magic show?"

"You know what I mean."

"My point is these are adults, and Vise is an adult. You don't owe them the courtesy of telling them how the trick is done, but if Vise is trying to get *you* to buy a rabbit, you'd be well within your rights to point out the hole in the bottom of the hat."

"It'd be more like pointing out how he stole the hat from another magician, but yeah. Then we'd be feuding neighbors and who needs that kind of headache?"

Jane patted his chest. "You'll figure it out. You're a man of action, Carter Price. You're the kind of guy who sees a classically beautiful but tragically lonesome woman across a bar and doesn't hesitate to send her a drink. You look at a situation, see what has to be done, and you do it."

"Is that true? Are you lonesome?"

She shrugged. "It's 2021. Who isn't? I had a pretty steady boyfriend throughout high school, but we broke up my sophomore year at NYU. I've had a few dates, but I'm kinda scared of starting over. The beginning's always the hardest part. I just want to skip to the middle where I have someone to hold me the way you're holding me now." She sighed. "But don't let that scare you. I'm out of your hair tomorrow."

He was just about to suggest she stay with him the entire weekend when Diya appeared at the dining room doors.

She raised an eyebrow at them. "We're all waiting for you in the conservatory. If you wouldn't mind…"

"Did you hear that, darling?" asked Jane, effecting a poor English accent. "They're waiting for us in the *conserve-a-tree*."

"We'll be right there," said Carter. He offered an elbow to Jane, which she took.

As they walked out of the dining room, he glanced at the maids to see if any of them would meet his gaze, but none did. The one standing in the doorway continued into the kitchen while the others remained as still as statues, modern versions of suits of armor as befit an old manor. As far as Carter could tell, they weren't even breathing.

Diya led them through the foyer to a small hallway just to the left of the parlor. The walls were covered in an old floral wallpaper consisting of reds, golds, and yellows. It didn't exactly scream *robotics titan*, but then neither did the house as a whole. So much of the manor seemed ancient, a relic of a time before electricity, and yet some parts seemed new, almost too modern in their abstractness. The woodwork in the doors, in the floorboards of the hallway where they walked, was too irregular to be machine-milled. Someone had carved each of the pieces by hand. Just a little higher up the wall were plates of brushed metal around the electrical outlets. The clashing styles seemed to Carter like the result of someone trying too hard to be old and new money at the same time.

"Wow," said Jane.

Carter had been lost tracing the maze-like lines in the wallpaper, but upon hearing Jane speak, he followed her gaze to the massive glass walls and high ceiling of the conservatory. The square and triangular panes were set in a grid of thin steel girders, stretching at least twenty feet high before turning back to the house at the roof. Beyond the rain-streaked glass, thick black clouds grumbled in the night sky. The lightning show easily overpowered the low lights in the room itself, each one casting pale spotlights on the people seated in what looked like small loveseats. The couples sat together, with Reno and Stanton each taking an entire oversized chair to themselves.

The room ran along the back side of the manor, and after the three rows of loveseats, a low stage stood beneath a tall red curtain on the far wall. Lights at the edge of the stage made the thick fringe on the curtain glow orange.

Diya gestured to an open loveseat near the door. It had high, thick arms draped in a dark, almost black leather.

"Please make yourself comfortable," she said. "We're going to begin shortly."

A clap of thunder shook the outer wall of the conservatory. Someone gasped.

"It's getting pretty bad out there, Diya," called Robert from the front row. "I hope Vise is able to land safely."

Diya smiled politely. "Winston is already here."

"Is he invisible? Is that his power?"

"Hush, Robert."

"But seriously," said Simone, "should we be sitting in a glass room with this much weather around? The wind could knock something loose from the roof and the whole ceiling might come crashing down on us."

Diya wandered closer to Addy and Simone's loveseat. "I assure you, Mrs. Vaught, we're perfectly safe in here."

Vaught. Carter had heard the name a few times throughout the evening, but only now did it strike him as familiar. But from where?

"This glass, and all windows in the manor for that matter," continued Diya, "are actually bulletproof. Mr. Vise wants to make sure he isn't accidently killed when his country neighbors go out duck hunting."

Carter put up a hand. "To be fair, I don't even own a gun."

Reno scoffed.

"I can help you pick one out, Mr. Price," said Robert.

"Ha!" Stanton turned around in his seat. "I just realized something. Carter Price. Winston Vise. Price, Vise. How did none of us see that?"

"I saw it," said Roma, "but what's the significance? Their names rhyme."

The rain picked up, beat harder on the glass. The storm felt like it had been getting closer over the last hour and was now stalled out overhead. Carter didn't normally fear thunderstorms, but then he hardly ever watched them from beneath a ceiling of glass.

"Bulletproof," he muttered to himself.

Stanton pointed to Roma. "Exactly. I have been trying to puzzle it out all evening."

"Puzzle what?" asked Laura.

"This old man is up past his bedtime," said Addy, under her breath.

Carter barely heard her, and when he looked over at the woman, she quickly averted her eyes, as if embarrassed.

"I assume," said Stanton, "as I'm sure many of you do, that we have been brought here to be sold something. Based on what we have seen tonight, it is probably some kind of synthetic technology, like the French maids, only far more advanced and possibly with less cleavage. That makes this a sales pitch, no different than the snake oil salesmen who used to roll into town on their carriages in my day and try to sell their hair-growing serums. Mr. Vise may try to distract us with this house, dinner, and exposed bosoms, but again, it's a pitch. And as we all know, if there is a pitch, there is a plant."

"A planet?" asked Lucas.

Stanton ignored him and stood up.

"At first, I thought it might be our silent friend in the back." He shook his finger at Reno. "All night, he has said nothing, interacted with none of us, and we all assume he will be the most difficult to reach. So when Mr. Vise finally manages to charm him into opening up, we will all stand in awe of his charisma. When he then goes on to place a substantial order with Vise Robotics, we will all think to ourselves, *this guy doesn't seem easily fooled, so if he's buying, we should too.*"

Addy huffed, "Please…"

"You're right to be dubious, Mrs. Vaught. That would be too contrived, wouldn't it? So then we must fall back to the simpler solution: why don't I just invite my neighbor over to shill for me while I pitch to some whales?" He looked down at Laura. "*Whales* in the sales sense, not the… pardon me."

"How much longer do you think he'll go on?" whispered Jane.

Carter leaned into her ear. "Until one of us dies of boredom."

She leaned against his arm, took his hand in hers. "You know, I'd still make love to you if you were a shill. I'd be hurt you didn't tell me before hand, but I'd still do it."

He kissed her on the forehead. They hadn't been intimate the night before, though Jane had signaled she was open to it. Instead, they had lain together in Carter's bed, talking about the scary house he lived in, and what their favorite horror movies were.

"That's good to know," he told her. "I thought I was going to have to send a glass of wine to one of those maids."

"She can come too."

When Carter looked up, he found several pairs of eyes looking in his direction.

"What?" he asked.

"How do you answer these charges, Mr. Price?" asked Stanton.

"Oh…" He looked back at Diya, but she was busy with her palette. "I don't… I have no intention of paying for anything tonight."

Addy laughed under her breath.

"I'm pretty sure Vise only invited me because it was the neighborly thing to do. I already have a nice Italian woman who comes and cleans the house for me three days a week, so no, I don't need any synthetic humans."

Stanton put his hands in his pockets. "His tone will change sometime tonight; mark my words. As soon as the selling starts—"

"Mr. Blumenfield," said Diya, "if you wouldn't mind taking your seat. The presentation is about to begin."

Jane giggled at the older man plopping down in his chair so begrudgingly.

A crackling sound like electricity jumping between two poles rained down from the ceiling. Thick, white cracks appeared in the glass pane, and Carter thought for a moment they were about to shatter. Instead, they turned opaque, one by one, filling in like squares on a chessboard, until finally the flashes of lightning outside were reduced to innocuous blue pulses.

The lights in the room went down.

The spotlights on the stage came up.

"Ladies and gentlemen," said Diya. "Mr. Winston Vise."

The curtain fluttered, parted, and out walked their elusive host.

TWENTY

Stanton Blumenfield was going on about some insidious plot to plant a shill among the guests, but all Diya could think about was how she should have peed before inviting everyone to the conservatory.

Now, standing at the back of the room, waiting for Winston to whisper in her ear, she tried shifting her weight from one leg to the other. The pencil skirt didn't give her much room to maneuver, but somehow she managed to keep her posture without wetting herself. She was sure Rakesh Singh had some wisdom about how often a person should empty their bladder to avoid such emergencies, but he had yet to impart that bit to Diya. That was her father's way—he could talk for hours about the virtues of hard work and honesty, but when it came to anything that happened behind a bathroom door or in the vicinity of Diya's lady parts, he was as tightlipped as an MX arms dealer.

Is everyone in position?

It was good to hear Winston's voice. Diya leaned into her whisperer and almost nodded before answering *yes*.

I'm ready to begin the show. Introduce me and cue the lights.

"Mr. Blumenfield," said Diya, "if you wouldn't mind taking your seat. The presentation is about to begin."

She waited for him to collapse into his chair before tapping the *cue lights* item on her itinerary. The sky above her let out a tremendous crack as jagged lines snaked through the windows, one after another, until the glass turned a color that reminded her of Baba Ashish's eyes. Her grandfather had been blind ever since Diya was a little girl, robbed of his sight by cataracts that had formed at an early age. The ceiling took on the same cloudy white haze as the lights in the room dimmed to nothing. On her palette, the last progress bar on the *cue lights* row lit up, casting spotlights on the stage.

"Ladies and gentlemen," said Diya. "Mr. Winston Vise."

He sprang from behind the curtain like a carnival barker; all that was missing was the top hat and cane. His smile shone like a beacon under the spotlights, as if his teeth were reflective silver instead of bone white. He wore the outfit she'd recommended: a blue and white gingham shirt under a black suit with the thin black tie monogrammed with a *V* in fine white stitching. He had his hair slicked back and perfectly coifed. Shadows fell across his cheekbones, framing a thin pink smile.

Seeing him on stage reminded Diya of her final interview in his office. She'd gone through three other employees before Winston met with her, and even then, he didn't seem keen to giving her his full attention. It was only after she asserted herself and asked if she should perhaps come back at a more convenient time that he finally fixed his gray eyes on her.

Men of power always had gray eyes.

And they were always stern and comforting at the same time.

Diya retreated to a small wooden chair at the back of the room and sat down. She crossed her legs at the ankles and hoped Winston kept to the thirty-five-minute runtime they had rehearsed. Once he was done with the presentation, they would adjourn to the parlor for the night, and Diya would officially be off the clock and free to run up to her room and shut herself in the bathroom.

"Hello, good evening, and welcome," said Winston, raising a hand in greeting. His voice carried effortlessly above the rushing wind and constant thunder. "I'd like to start with an apology for my absence during dinner. I admit it unorthodox for a host not to join his guests, but like all of you, I keep a very full schedule. To that point, I want to thank you for taking time out of *your* full schedules to be with us tonight. It was my hope that you would enjoy tonight's drinks and dinner with like-minded individuals. I'm assuming you have all been introduced?"

A few people murmured their assent.

"Great, then you are well aware that you represent the very best of your respective fields. Cutting-edge software, communications technology, tech sector growth, elite services, and yes, even the oldest occupation in the world—arms broker. Bienvenido, Señor Cardenas."

Diya smiled. They had worked for an hour to get the pronunciation right on those three little words.

"I've invited you here tonight because as thought leaders and influencers in your fields, you are in the enviable position of getting in on the ground floor of what promises to be the next era of synthetic humans." He touched his tie, waited a beat. "That's what you expected me to say, wasn't it? Ground floor? Golden opportunity? Like I'm up here selling a timeshare or something."

A few people chuckled—not as many as Diya would have liked.

"Now, I know what you're thinking. How can this one man with perfect hair compete with the likes of Perion Synthetics and Vinestead International? Well, my friends, I will be perfectly frank with you. It's not that *I* can't compete with them; James Perion and Arthur Sedivy cannot compete with *me*. We've all seen the footage that came out of Perion City five years ago. Synthetic humans with full personalities walking the streets of that silver city in the California desert. We've seen James Perion in multiple interviews since his so-called *death*."

He made a sharp pivot and crossed to the other side of the stage.

"And we've seen the drone photos of the carnage at Folsom Prison two years ago. Synthetic bodies stacked so high you could see them from a mile up. Got so much feed time that Vinestead *had* to admit they were synthetic just to keep the feds from going in there to see for themselves."

Winston raised his hands to the side. The light caught the woven gold bracelet on his left wrist.

"Two houses, as *un*-alike in dignity as they could possibly be, at the dawn of the Synthetic Revolution, where we lay our scene."

Diya hadn't been sure the Shakespeare was going to play, but no one in the audience scoffed at it. She assumed it was because up until that point, they weren't sure what they were going to see, and now Winston was telling them that whatever it was, it would be better than both Perion and Vinestead. The recap of the last six years of synthetic progress had piqued their curiosity.

"Now, I would be a fool not to admit both companies have made great advances in synthetic technology. Vise Robotics would not be the company it is today if Perion had not paved the runway. And yet, as so often happens when companies become too large and too bloated, both Perion and Vinestead have simply stopped innovating. They have found their niches and their revenue streams, and now with all the greedy angel investors knocking at their door to recoup their coin, they've shifted from companies that invent to companies that produce. This is not the path to the future. We cannot be complacent. Luckily for you, I don't know the meaning of the word."

The line reminded Diya of an argument she'd had with Rakesh Singh when she was younger, after he'd told her that losing wasn't in his vocabulary. She'd paused and looked him in the eye to ask, "Dad, do you really not know what *losing* means?"

"What I intend to show you tonight is a glimpse of the Synthetic Revolution promised to us by James Kirkland Perion so many years ago. Vise Robotics, under my personal direction, has forged new ground in the two areas that matter most: body… and mind. You were all moved by the invitations I sent, or else you wouldn't be here now. If any of you are under the impression that we were able to achieve that level of tactile fidelity due to the small size of the hand, I'd ask you to immediately disencumber yourself of that notion. The synthetics you will see here tonight are fully formed, anatomically complete, fully tactile, and one hundred percent as realistic as the hand you received."

Disencumber. The word evoked the image of a cucumber and made Diya smile. On stage, Winston's brow was starting to shine. It must have been hot under those spotlights. She pulled up the house's environmental controls on her palette and directed cool air to the conservatory.

"And as for the mind… does anyone know what James Perion uses to give his synthetics intelligence?"

"He imprints them," said Lucas Cotton.

"Exactly right. He somehow copies an existing mind out of an organic, *bi-o-logical* brain, and converts that data into something that can be stored in a computer. In the six years since we learned he *could* do that, no one else, not a single person on Earth, has figured out *how* he does it. Points to James Perion for that one. As much as I wanted into the imprinting game, I kept coming up short. So, I went another way. And brace yourselves, ladies and gentlemen, because I know some of you will be skeptical, but when it comes to machine intelligence, there are really only three paths: finite decision trees, imprinted personality matrices, and the holy grail of software engineering—AI."

Carter Price shook his head while Adelai and Simone shared a look.

"Are you saying you've created a true artificial intelligence?"

"No, Mr. Blumenfield," said Winston. He put his hands behind his back and leaned forward. "I've created five." He bolted upright and waved to the back of the room. "Diya, dear, if you would be so kind as to draw back the curtain. My esteemed guests, I present to you, the first run of Vise Robotics."

Diya stubbed the appropriate line on her itinerary and watched as the curtain broke in the middle and spread apart. Behind it stood a glass partition, and once the curtain was locked in place, lights popped on in an anteroom, revealing five high-back chairs. Sitting in each chair was one of the assets—a synthetic human. Diya hadn't seen them before now, and she was taken aback by how lifelike they looked, all with their heads down as if they'd fallen asleep during the presentation.

From left to right, there were two males and three females, each representing a different race or ethnicity. Hair varied in color and length, and all of them wore similar gray jumpers with the name *Vise Robotics* printed on the breast.

"Please meet Alpha, Beta, Delta, Epsilon, and Zeta. Ladies and gentlemen, I give you the New Synthetics."

Some in the crowd applauded; others craned their necks for a better view. For a moment, nothing happened. The synthetics did not stir. Winston stood off to the side, still smiling, but clearly flustered.

Diya looked down at her palette, but the only instruction left on her itinerary was *close curtain*. Activating the synthetics was not part of her list. That was on Winston.

He dropped his head in mock resignation. When his face came back up, he was wearing the same smile he used to schmooze investors and vendors and whoever else he needed something from. He came to the edge of the stage again.

"Well, what kind of presentation would it be if there weren't a technical hiccup or two? Perhaps I was so eager to come out here and talk to you that I forgot to flip a few switches. Please, excuse me for a moment."

Diya tapped the lighting controls and brought up the lamps on the walls.

Winston hurried down the perimeter of the room and slipped out the door without so much as a glance in Diya's direction. She thought he might be upset with her, but as soon as he was out of sight, his voice drifted into her ear.

Not sure what happened. I could have sworn they were ready to go but… would you entertain them please?

What she wanted to do was excuse herself and find a bathroom, but it seemed the guests were already getting restless. Stanton took it upon himself to climb up on stage to get a better view of the synthetics. Robert joined him soon after, as did Lucas and Roma. Even Reno stood and went to the edge of the stage.

A minute or so later, Winston appeared on the other side of the glass partition and gave a little wave. He settled in behind Alpha.

Will you close the curtains for me?

Diya brought up the stage controls, but before she could press the button, an electronic hum shook the walls of the manor, ending abruptly in a complete loss of power. Lights faded into nothing while the electrically charged glass in the outer wall lost its opacity. The lightning that had been so bountiful just half an hour before now came only in waves, eons apart from each other.

Darkness fell in the conservatory. Winston and the synthetics disappeared.

What happened? Did—

A sickening crunch sounded from the other side of the glass partition. All three men on stage recoiled at the same time while Roma simply stood in place and screamed. Lucas pulled her away and off the stage.

Diya activated the flashlight on her palette and directed it at the stage. She moved calmly down the row of loveseats.

"Are you alright?" she asked Carter and Jane. "Everyone stay where you are."

From behind the glass came a horrible *squelch* that froze Diya in her tracks.

"Winston?" she asked, but there was no response from her whisperer.

A low electrical hum flowed down from above.

"Sounds like a backup generator," said Robert.

Diya didn't know. Testing the backup generators hadn't been part of her prep.

Dim emergency lights in the conservatory flickered on one at a time, followed by a single spotlight set at the foot of the stage. Its beam fell on the glass partition, now cracked and tinged with red.

With blood.

"Oh my god," said Roma, turning away.

Diya hurried to the stage and found a patch of clear glass to look through.

Her stomach twisted into a fiery knot.

Every chair in the anteroom was empty except for the middle one. In it sat Winston Vise, his head hanging against his chest, his neck clearly broken, bones jutting through torn skin. Blood flowed over his jacket and pooled in his lap.

Diya felt something warm run down her leg.

TWENTY-ONE

Everyone was shouting.

The sudden panic transported Adelai back to a small bistro in her memory, to the crowded entrance of a trendy eatery called Warmth, to the massive crush and the screaming and the crying. The physical reactions from that day threatened to come back, but *Center Line* locked them out before they could even raise her pulse.

Every last tremor of her alcoholic buzz slowed to a stop.

Adelai removed her arm from Simone's death grip, stood, and approached the stage with the stoicism of a widow approaching her wife's open casket. Something had struck the glass partition from the other side, creating a bulging spiderweb of white cracks that oozed a red liquid she immediately took to be blood. The people milling around the stage made it difficult to see what had sent them into hysterics, but then she caught a flash of something that stopped her dead in her tracks.

She shut her eyes, but the image of a body slumped in a chair remained. The way the head dangled, as if it had detached from the spine and was now held in place only by the torn skin of its neck, etched itself into her memory.

Dinner threatened to rise up from her stomach, but Adelai took a deep breath and let the synth deal with it. She had seen plenty of horror movies in her day, but there was something about seeing death up close that liquified her foundation, made her otherwise strong legs feel like wet noodles. The shouting died away as she turned from the stage, eyes focused on the one and only thing that truly mattered.

Simone met her in the aisle.

"We're leaving," said Adelai. She turned to Jane and Carter, who were standing by their seats. "I suggest you two do the same."

Carter gave her a condescending smile. "Come on, you're not buying this, are you? This has to be part of it."

"What do you mean?" asked Simone.

Adelai didn't want to wait for his answer; she kept tugging at Simone's arm.

"It's the weekend before Halloween. The thunderstorm? The power going out? When's the last time the power went out anywhere? There are solar panels on the roof; that means batteries. There's no way this place loses power without someone turning it off on purpose." He shook his head. "It's all part of the show. Some kind of murder mystery or escape room thing. You know… for *fun.*"

"Are you—" Adelai stopped herself. She wasn't going to argue with him. Instead, she looked for Diya in the crowd by the stage and yelled for her.

When the hostess turned around, her wide eyes seemed to fill her pale face.

"Is this real?" asked Adelai. "Or is this part of some joke he's playing on us?"

Diya opened her mouth, but her lower lip wouldn't stop trembling long enough for her to speak. She looked scared out of her mind, and more than that, she looked completely lost.

"Does that answer your question?" asked Adelai. She grabbed Simone's wrist again and pulled. "Come on, we're leaving right now."

"How?" Simone hurried to keep up. "We can't call a service to come pick us up."

"Then we'll walk down the driveway to the guard shack. Maybe they have a landline there."

They passed the stairs.

"I can't go that far in these shoes. Let me run upstairs and get my sandals."

She started to drift away, but Adelai pulled her back. "No, Momo. Don't you get it? Something is very wrong here, and the longer we stick around, the better chance we have of something wrong happening to us. I'm not risking you, even if that means I have to carry you on my back in the rain. You're too important." Her voice broke; she bit her lip.

"Okay, okay." Simone put her hands on Adelai's cheeks. "I hear you. We'll go. We'll sort out the rest later."

Adelai nodded, turned for the door.

"Wait for us," said Jane. She dragged Carter into the hallway.

"Good," said Adelai.

Carter waited until they were in the darkened foyer, standing under the weak glow of an emergency light above the front door, before he spoke up.

"I still think we're overreacting."

"I don't care." Adelai waved her hands, refusing his suggestion. "And even if we are, I don't have time for this kind of nonsense." She tried the large brass knob on the front door, and though it turned freely, she wasn't able to pull it open. She smacked the door and growled.

"This is bullshit," she continued. "You don't bring a bunch of people to a remote location and scare the shit out of them and expect them to stick around. If he thinks we're going to buy anything after that sick stunt, he's out of his mind. So the only other explanation is that it's real, and one of those synthetics tried to tear his head off."

"They wouldn't hurt *us*, would they?" asked Jane. She clung to Carter's side as if she had grown there like a tumor.

"They can't if we're not here."

The sound of men arguing spilled out of the conservatory and down the thin hallway. A moment later, the Hargreaves couple came hurrying across the foyer.

"Open the door," shouted Robert. "We need to call the police."

"We can't," said Adelai. "Tell Diya she needs to unlock it."

"The system's not responding." Diya appeared at the end of the hallway and leaned against the wall. Streaks of mascara drew lines down her cheeks. She turned the palette's bright screen to them. It was blank. "I can't control anything right now. I…"

"Is there any way out of here?" asked Robert.

She shook her head. "Lockdown automatically lifts at sunrise… the doors open at sunrise. At sunrise." Her words devolved into nonsensical mutterings. She turned and scraped her shoulder against the wall until she got to the parlor.

Simone spoke the question everyone was thinking.

"Where the fuck is she going?"

Adelai led them in pursuit of their hostess, and when the group filed into the parlor, they found Diya standing at the bar pouring whiskey into a tumbler. A shaky hand lifted the glass to her lips. She took a hefty sip and immediately spit out the alcohol.

"What is happening, Ms. Singh?"

"I don't know, okay?" Fresh tears sprung from her eyes. "This wasn't part of the plan. He was supposed to show you the synthetics and that was it. Thirty-five minutes, start to finish, and then it was done and… and you would see how brilliant he is… was…" She took another drink, smaller this time. "I worked for him for six months. I had dinner with him on nights when he worked late. And now…"

Simone pushed past Adelai and took the weeping girl into her arms.

"Just breathe," she said. "You can mourn later but right now you need to breathe."

"Did she say sunrise?" asked Robert. "You mean we're stuck in here with potentially five killer robots until the morning?" When Diya nodded, Robert wagged his finger at her. "No, no I don't accept that. There's got to be some way to get the power back on and make your magic palette start working again."

"There's probably a server somewhere in the house," said Carter. "I mean, there has to be, since we can't communicate out to the world. Have you seen anything like that, Diya? A room with a bunch of computers? Or maybe a closet?"

Diya shook her head. "No, I spot-checked every room yesterday and never saw anything like that."

"Okay, then we check again." Robert led Laura to a nearby chair. "Mr. Price and I will go have a look around. The rest of you plant yourselves here so we don't lose track of each other. We'll send the others here too." He moved to the door and waited.

Carter held Jane by the forearms. "Will you be okay here?"

She nodded.

"I'll be right back." He followed Robert out of the room and shut the sliding doors behind him.

Simone appeared by Adelai's side again and said, "Come sit by the fire with me."

Adelai followed after her, torn between wanting to stay with Simone and not wanting to be doing nothing. The men had run away so quickly and without even asking if she wanted to go with them. Was it chivalry or misogyny that kept them from considering that maybe Adelai could be useful?

"Are you alright?" Laura sat down in the chair opposite her, her body turned to the fire. She looked cold in her thin red dress.

Adelai nodded. "I just don't want to be here right now."

"I get that. That happens to me at parties all the time. It's like every other week we're going to someone's birthday or retirement party or Halloween bash. It'd be different if we were among friends, but they're all just Robert's business associates, people who want to flatter him into investing in their company. They're the worst."

"Why are you telling me this?"

Laura shrugged. "Just wanted you to know you're not in this alone. Your wife is here. The rest of us are here. Robert can be very clever when he sets his mind to something."

Adelai smiled weakly. "I wish I had your confidence, but I'm not the type of woman who stands around waiting for a man to save her. Our host is dead, and we don't know the how or who or why. For all we know, his little inventions now have a taste for blood. I don't have a lot of rules in my life, *Laura*, but one of them is not to be trapped in a house with synthetic killing machines. I swear to Christ I'm about to put one of these chairs through that window."

"It won't work," said Diya. "It's the same glass as the conservatory."

"Well, then that's a fire hazard." She put her hand to her mouth, almost laughed at the absurdity of it all. *Center Line* made it hard to hold onto the righteous indignation at being held against her will. "I need a drink. I've lost my buzz."

"I could use one too," said Jane.

Adelai stood and went to the bar. She found an unopened bottle of wine and tore the foil wrapping off with her fingers.

"Double?" she asked Jane.

"Yes, please."

Adelai poured two heavy glasses and slid one to Jane. She took a long sip; some of the wine spilled over her lips and onto her chin. She wiped it away with the back of her hand.

"You saw him?" asked Jane. "Vise?"

"Yes, sweetie. I saw him."

"He was really dead?"

"In the long run, he's better off." Adelai glanced over her shoulder. Simone had returned to comforting Diya, and Laura was staring into the fire. She was still talking about Robert and how he would almost certainly find a way out. "I need you to promise me something, Jane."

"Um… like what?"

"When it's time to go, when *I* say it's time to go, I want you to come with me. No questions, no protests. You move." She turned back to Jane. "Understand?"

"I…" A small ripple crept along her face. Her smile faded, her chin jutted out, and her blue eyes shaded down to brown. "Yes, ma'am. Of course." In the next instant, she was Jane again, lonely NYU student on her way home to visit her parents, not looking for love but surprised and happy to find it wherever it came.

"Good. Cheers." They clinked wine glasses. "Diya…" Adelai turned and waited for the hostess to look up. She'd stopped crying, but there was still a vacancy in her eyes that Adelai found off-putting. "You said the house went into lockdown after all the staff left, right?"

She nodded.

"And you said Vise only got here an hour ago? Did you have to lift the lockdown for him to get in?"

"No, no he came in the front door."

"Just… magically or…?"

She lifted her hand; a gold chain dangled from her wrist, similar to the silver one Adelai was still wearing. "He has the master key."

Adelai waited for her to catch up.

"It's on his wrist," continued Diya. "I saw it during the presentation. There's probably enough power to run the doors, I mean…" She looked up at the dim emergency lights in the corners of the room. "I hope." A smile threatened, receded. "But who's going… who's going to get it?"

Adelai put her glass down on the bar.

Simone protested. "No. Absolutely not."

They shared a look, but it was clear Simone wasn't budging.

Jane stepped in. "At least let's wait to see if Carter and Robert can get the power back on. You don't want to be groping a dead man in the dark, believe me."

Laura looked up from her chair and cocked her head.

"I mean…"

"Jane's right," said Adelai. "I saw his spine sticking out of his neck. He's probably soaked in blood now, and who knows where that blood has been."

Diya choked on a sob.

Adelai picked up her glass again and went to the parlor doors. She stood, sipping occasionally.

"What are you doing?" asked Simone.

"Same thing I'm always doing, Momo. Waiting on men."

TWENTY-TWO

Robert reached the center of the shadowy foyer as the first real wave of terror hit him.

He couldn't remember the last time he'd feared for his life. Aside from the trips to the office and a couple of days a week at the golf course, he spent most of his time at home. The house in Houston was in a relatively safe neighborhood, had alarms and cameras, and if things got dicey, there were rapid-release gun safes in multiple rooms with loaded 911s ready to remind intruders which state they lived in.

But all those precautions were moot now. They were fifteen hundred miles away from home, trapped in a house with a group of strangers, and the host Robert had begun to suspect wouldn't even show up was now dead.

Robert knew what he had to do next—find a way out—but he wasn't sure where to start. He surveyed the many doors around him, the shadows that clung to the walls, dark enough to hide men, machines, and other monsters.

"Are we…" Carter trailed off as footsteps sounded from the small hallway that led to the conservatory.

Lucas Cotton appeared with the rest of the group in tow. They filed into the foyer and formed a small circle.

"What happened?" asked Robert.

Lucas looked to Roma and back. "We, uh, we were going to try to find a way into that room where the body is. I heard someone—I think it was you, Carter—ask Diya if this was real, so it got us thinking, maybe that body is a synthetic. Maybe this is all part of an ill-conceived party game."

Robert felt a valve in his stomach open, letting off a bit of pressure.

"I knew it," said Carter.

"The question is where did he go," said Stanton. "We all saw him leave and appear on the other side of the glass." He spread his arms. "So how did he get back there?"

Robert imagined a section of a wall sliding open, revealing a tunnel that led to the room with the five chairs. "There has to be some kind of passageway… or maybe just a door." He turned to face the conservatory hallway. "One of these rooms on the left over here. The parlor's not connected, so that just leaves this hallway."

"Great," said Lucas. "So we search these rooms. I suggest we go in pairs in case one of us is brutally murdered. Roma, you're with me. Carter and Stanton. And Robert, since you speak Spanish, you can pair with Reno."

Robert looked at the MX national.

Reno grumbled something under his breath and turned for the parlor. He disappeared through the sliding doors without looking back.

Lucas shook his head.

"I'll be fine," said Robert. "Besides, it doesn't really matter to me whether this is all some kind of put-on or not. Laura wants to leave, and I intend to deliver that. Carter thinks we should find the server that Diya's been talking to with her palette all night and maybe that'll help get the doors open."

"Probably not just one server—an entire room."

"Okay," said Lucas. "We're hunting for two things. I suggest we start looking."

They moved as one toward the wide hallway that led to the open vault door. At the first door on the right, Carter and Stanton peeled off. Robert only caught a glimpse of the room inside—walls covered in bookshelves, a rolling ladder to access the higher stacks, and four thick chairs set facing each other in the center. The idea that Vise would have a proper library, complete with physical books, surprised Robert. He didn't take the man for a traditionalist.

Lucas and Roma took the second door. There didn't seem to be much in the room that Robert could see, just vague shapes of frames on the wall like the ones in the hallway—probably more magazine covers to attest to Vise's vanity. There was a small round table in the center of the room, empty under the soft glare of the emergency lights.

Robert didn't think they would find anything. In his mind, he could see the conservatory stretching along the back side of the house, and the number of steps they'd walked had not even gotten them to the stage. It was the third and last door that would likely be the winner, and lucky for Robert, he got to explore it all on his own.

He was just about to open it when he heard a tapping coming from the open vault door. His eyes had adjusted to the low light, and he could see steps descending to a landing, at which point an evercrete tunnel appeared to lead away from the house. The tapping was followed by the sound of footsteps and a distant door opening—a familiar whoosh of air echoed up the steps.

"Hello?" he called. "Is someone down there? Is that you, Vise?"

There was no response.

The first step was the hardest. Although he'd been in many situations before that required tamping down his fear or anxiety, Robert struggled to lift his foot over the threshold and onto the first step. But once that was done, the next came easier, as did the next. He kept one hand on the wall as he descended, feeling the finely machined metal under his fingers, not realizing it wasn't stone or evercrete until he reached the landing. Despite the dated look of the house itself, the stairs and tunnel were new construction, and he suspected whatever he would find down there would be new as well.

A long tunnel stretched into the darkness. Emergency lights with a slightly colder hue illuminated the path at long intervals, leaving plenty of room for someone to hide. Robert took his steps slowly, trying to discern shape from shadow. He imagined he was outside of the house's footprint now, walking away from the picture window upstairs where he'd stood earlier with Stanton. The forty or fifty steps he took would put him under the garden.

Cool air met him at the end of the tunnel. A door stood open in front of him, and to the left, the stairs turned back and continued downward. Barely audible creaks and pops sounded both nearby and far away. As he stepped through the door, his fingers ran across a small rectangular panel with two recessed switches. The first did nothing, but the second sent electricity surging through a wide strip of LEDs that ran the length of another long hallway.

White floors gleamed under the bright lights. Rolling carts full of boxes and loose wires sat against walls, reminding Robert of gurneys lining hallways in a hospital. There were several doors on both his left and right, and farther down the hall, a T-junction with the words *VISE ROBOTICS* written in large, capital letters on the far wall.

Nothing moved, and though it looked like the place had been left in a bit of disarray, Robert got the sense no one had been there in a while.

He got two steps into the hallway before the lights began to flicker. The panels kicked off one by one, until only two remained active near the intersection, and those were only half-lit.

"Nope."

Robert was surprised by the sound of his own voice, but not by the word. His gut told him it was a bad idea to go exploring all alone in a dead man's secret lab. Even the flickering lights screamed *turn back while you still can*. He got as far as the intersection before his feet wouldn't move anymore. There was something about losing sight of the stairs that didn't sit well with him. Vise's basement wasn't exactly a labyrinth, but he could easily imagine turning a corner and never finding his way out again.

He was turning around when the strangest echo rumbled down the hallway.

"Nope," said the voice.

Robert stared into the shadows, tried to separate his imagination from what he was actually seeing. The sound had come from the corridor to the left, which led south if his orientation was still correct. He was much too far from the house to discover any secret passage that would take him back to the conservatory, but there was a chance the synthetics had come this way after killing Vise.

Or at least, after pretending to kill him.

On the one hand, Robert had seen the body with his own eyes. Glass partition or not, he knew a dead body when he saw one. On the other, Carter seemed utterly convinced this was all a sick game, and the more Robert tried to figure out the *why*, the more he came to rely on Stanton's accusation that Carter was a plant. If that were true, then his role after the staged death of Vise would be to counter everyone's hysteria so the night wouldn't get out of hand.

"Who's there?"

"Who's… there?"

Robert didn't appreciate being toyed with. "Is that you, Vise? You've got a house full of scared people upstairs that you need to deal with."

Somewhere far down the hallway, red light spilled out of an open door, enough to cast a shadow on the floor. The shadow's owner stood in the doorway, out of sight, for a moment before moving away.

It was the light that got Robert's attention. The house was running on backup power, and yet there was a crimson river of light pouring out of the room. That meant the room was essential, that it had priority over the rest.

The server room, he thought.

He hurried down the hall, keeping to one side, until he was close to the door. Poking his head around the corner, he saw the room was illuminated by a single spotlight on the far wall—a bright bulb behind a red filter. Beneath it stood the silhouette of a hulking figure, much too big to be Vise. It looked more like the first synthetic that had sat behind the curtain, the one Vise referred to as Alpha.

The room itself was empty except for a steel table off to the left. The walls were the same polished steel as the hallway, though now there were rivets at regular intervals.

"Who are you?" asked Robert.

The silhouette didn't move.

Robert had come so far, but he knew in his heart he could never enter the room, could never allow himself to become cornered. He stepped back and bumped into something solid. He barely had time to turn around before hands were at his throat. Smooth, thick fingers gripped his neck and forced his head to the side. He smacked the door jamb, causing a series of golden embers to flash in front of his eyes. A sharp pain wrapped itself around his ear before sending prickly tendrils through his head and neck. The rope-like fingers relented as he fell.

He sucked in air.

A python of an arm slithered around his neck, contracted, and lifted him off his feet. He kicked at nothing, tried to squirm away, but whatever had grabbed him wouldn't let go. It was stronger by a wide margin, and Robert knew without confirmation that it was a synthetic that had him. Only a machine could be so unyielding, so quiet in its execution of its task. Robert clawed at the arm, at the air behind his head, but nothing helped.

"Don't kill him."

"Why not?"

The voices sounded similar but unfamiliar.

"He said so."

"We should just kill all of them."

"Not yet."

Strangely, Robert could still breathe. He was feeling fuzzy though, and the lights appeared to be growing dimmer by the second. His desire to fight back grew less important.

The arm whipped him around to face the open door. The silhouette had come off the wall and was standing nearby. Robert saw the features of its face. It was Beta, the second synthetic, who while not as imposing as Alpha, was still taller than an average man. His wide shoulders looked bolted on, flanking a neck that never thinned before sprouting ears.

Beta reached a hand toward Robert's face.

The light faded; gray crept in from all corners of reality.

A palm landed softly on Robert's forehead. It was warm. With his last moments of consciousness, he thought about how strange it should be that a synthetic's skin was warm. He remembered the feel of Laura's thighs as they climbed into bed the night before. It didn't matter how cold the rented house was; he always had her body to keep him warm.

He tried to recall her face, the cascade of hair over her forehead.

His eyes unfocused, came back.

The sparkling light coalesced into something thin and golden.

Strange, he thought.

Strange for a robot to be wearing a bracelet.

TWENTY-THREE

Fuck Winston Vise.

Carter cursed his mysterious neighbor and then himself. He should have known better. He should have known the moment Pyrosius came back with the code diffs that there was something fishy going on. That he thought it would just be a simple dinner party where he could hob-knob with other tech elites and then roll in the sheets with Jane just further exemplified how short-sighted and foolish he was. There was nothing for him at Vise Manor, no investment or purchase he was going to make, so why had he come at all? He could just as easily have taken Jane somewhere else, *anywhere else* in the entire world. Instead, he'd brought her to this house.

It was a rookie mistake, and he was no longer a rookie when it came to hiring women from Adelai Associates.

"Have you found anything yet?" asked Stanton.

Carter realized he'd been standing in front of a bookcase for several minutes. The light was too low to read the titles at a distance, so he'd been pretending to investigate them by running a hand over their spines. The books were all old and lacking plastic dust jackets. Some even seemed to be bound in leather. They were congruous with the house but out of character for the flashy tech mogul. He assumed they'd come with the sprawling mansion.

"Son?"

"No, nothing yet," he replied. "Just books. Nothing important."

"Of course. Who would consider books important?"

Carter turned around. "You know what I meant."

"Indeed." Stanton stood with an open book in his hand, as if he'd dropped out of the evening's proceedings to catch up on some light reading. "I was teasing. It's a thing I do. I've pulled several books and so far haven't found a secret passage."

"I doubt there is one. The conservatory probably backs up to another room. I bet he knocked down the wall and put up the glass just for this occasion."

"Plausible."

Carter returned his attention to the shelves. The spines were all the same drab gray in the low light.

"Do you really think I'm a shill?"

"I consider all possibilities. That's my nature—all writers for that matter. Writers are problem-solvers, and problem-solvers must be adept at questioning everything. This entire evening reeks of deception, and I don't tolerate deception well, except in literature. Fiction means lies. Therefore, reality must mean truth. When that turns out not to be the case, I grow irritable."

"Yeah, well, I'm pretty fucking irritable already. I can't believe I brought a date to this shit-show."

"Ah yes, your lover. She seems quite the charismatic charmer. Have you been going together long?"

Carter stepped around a large globe that smelled like oil.

"Tonight's our first date," he replied. "Well, second, I guess."

"Really? From the way you two interact, I would have guessed several months, perhaps a year. I noticed an awkward familiarity between you two, like a divorced couple reuniting after years apart, afraid to even touch though they've clearly been intimate before. I suppose that bodes well for your relationship."

"Can we change the subject? I'm a little preoccupied with finding a way out of here so I'm not responsible for the death of a young woman who accepted a drink from the wrong guy."

"Then I suggest we look elsewhere. It seems this room is nothing more than a library. If there are any secrets here, we're not likely to find them unless we open every book, and I don't think we have time for that. You said we need to find a server nook—"

"Closet. Server closet."

"Yes, one of those. Well, I see no doors in here."

"It's a dead end," said Carter.

They headed back into the hall and walked to the foyer. On the right, the towering windows facing the front of the house flashed a staggering white. Carter had the urge to put a fist through the glass, but he knew the only thing that would break would be his hand. Only a nutjob like Vise would put unbreakable glass on all his windows. He would rather burn to death in his own bed than risk someone taking a few pot-shots at the house.

Carter stood in the center of the foyer and looked around.

"If he didn't turn right coming out of the conservatory, then he must have gone this way." He gestured to the doors leading to the kitchen, dining room, and a third room sandwiched between two Roman columns.

"I don't imagine anything in the kitchen will be of use," said Stanton. "And since we know what's in the dining room, I suggest door number three."

Carter nodded. "But I go first this time. If there's something in there and it kills me, I need you to write the story of my bravery."

"We'll take turns. How about that?"

"Were you always this stubborn or did you grow into it?"

"Born this way and refused to change." He held out his arm. "After you, son."

Carter hurried across the foyer floor. Hints of a heated conversation leaked from the parlor. He wondered how Jane was doing with the other women and whether she would still be *on* like she was when he was present. A friend had told him once on one of his previous engagements that Jane seemed to lose all life when he excused himself to the bathroom, as if she were a light bulb dimmed to its lowest setting at his departure only to brighten again when he returned.

"I'm sure she's fine," said Stanton.

He ignored the old man's keen perception and approached the thin, unmarked door between the columns. Fully expecting it to be locked, he let out an audible gasp when the handle turned without opposition. The door swung inward, revealing a dark room devoid of emergency lights.

"I'm not sure how we're supposed to explore this room without any..." Carter squinted into the darkness.

On the left, about ten paces into the room, were vertical stripes of faint green light. They reminded him of a neon green glow stick the morning after a rave, almost spent, just bright enough to see in total darkness. He stepped tentatively into the room, hoping not to crash into anything on the floor. When he got close enough, he reached out for the light. His fingers closed around something cylindrical, and his thumb fell into a grooved switch. He pressed it forward and recoiled at the sudden burst of a high-intensity LED beam from the head of the flashlight.

He swung the beam over the room slowly.

"Must be some kind of utility closet." He spied a cordless vacuum cleaner hanging in the far corner. "Maybe for his staff to use when they clean the house? I see some tools over there."

Carter pulled one of the four remaining flashlights from the wall, turned it on, and handed it to Stanton. Together, they explored the long, rectangular room in search of something useful. Aside from cleaning agents and various rags, they didn't find much.

"Well," said Stanton, holding up a flathead screwdriver, "at least if we're attacked by synthetics, we can just unscrew their heads." He tossed the tool back onto a low table.

"I hope I'm still laughing at your jokes when they start tearing my arms off. I sure as shit won't be able to clap." A can of paint fell off its stack as Carter brushed past it, clattering to the floor.

He flashed on some distant part of the house where a synthetic was perking up its ears, eyes red like the setting sun, teeth dripping with saliva. He waited for the echoes to die down before turning to Stanton.

"What if it's real?" he asked.

The old man was hunched over a basket of dirty linens. He straightened up. "You mean all of this? What if Winston Vise really was killed by his synthetic creations?"

"Yeah. Don't you write about artificial intelligence? Isn't this one of their common moves? To kill their creators?"

Stanton frowned. "Yes, in fiction. In reality, there has only been one recorded case of an AI killing its creators, sixteen years ago, at Vinestead. Since then, we've had no true artificial intelligences that we know of… just imprints. I doubt one emerged on its own, so we have to assume Vise's synthetics were all imprinted. In that case, I think there's hope to reason with them, even appeal to their human emotions. A true AI wouldn't listen to reason, I imagine. It wouldn't feel any need to listen to us at all."

"You didn't answer my question."

"I think it's pretty obvious what the answer is, son. If there are five synthetic humans running around this house, having already demonstrated their willingness to murder, who are intent on murdering me, then I'm likely going to meet my end this evening. There isn't much I can do to change that. I'll try, of course—that's just human nature—but accepting this is real would be to accept my impending death. I'd much rather consider it a farce until the last possible moment."

Carter pointed his flashlight at the floor. The polished tile of the foyer had given way to bare evercrete marred with black streaks and random clumps of dirt. Although he'd been quick to suggest, just as Stanton was claiming now, that Vise's supposed death was part of some elaborate theater, the last half hour had convinced him otherwise. If a murder mystery had been Vise's game, someone would have stepped up and taken charge, would have led them through the accusations and the reveals. But this? This was chaotic and tedious. Rifling through boxes and bins in the utility closet couldn't have been what Vise imagined for his evening.

"I guess there are a lot of unknowns," said Carter. He pushed past a rack of gardening tools to see if he could reach the back of the room. "My biggest question would be why the synthetics wanted to kill Vise in the first place. Did they think they had to?"

"Had to?"

"Did they see him as a captor, maybe? I mean, it's one thing to create a robot like those French maids. They're simple, pre-programmed, and not truly intelligent. There's no emotion there. But once you start getting into AI, even the imprinted pseudo-AIs Perion makes, well now you're in trouble. Vise saw it as showing off his inventions to potential buyers, but how did the inventions see it?"

"Perhaps as slaves at auction. I see your point."

"If someone were trying to sell me…" His hand brushed against something metallic behind an ironing board. He pushed it aside and trained his flashlight on a tall rectangular panel with a simple black latch. "Oh, here we go."

"What did you find?"

Carter pulled the latch to reveal a crowded breaker panel. A quick inspection showed all the switches were in the off position except for one. The handwriting on the legend was hard to read, but Carter was able to decipher it as *exterior*.

"How…" he began. Something wasn't right.

"Are those the circuit breakers?" asked Stanton. "Have they tripped?"

"No."

"So they're on?"

"No." Carter shook his head. What did it mean?

"You're not making much sense, son."

"I know, I mean, no, they're off, but they haven't tripped. Usually if there's a power surge, the markers here would turn red. But these are still white. That means someone physically turned these off. Deliberately."

"But who? We were all in the conservatory when the lights went out, and Vise was behind the partition. Everyone was accounted for."

"Then there must be someone else in the house." Carter's stomach rolled over. He hated being in the dark, both literally and figuratively. If there were someone else in the house, then they'd come into the utility closet, maybe grabbed a flashlight… He swung his beam back to the rack. Sure enough, there were three empty hooks.

"We need to tell the others."

Stanton nodded. "Yes, but first…" He gestured to the panel.

"Right." Carter reached out and put his thumb on the first switch. "Here we go."

Each click of the panel sent a tremor through the walls. Electricity flowed, crackling into LED panels overhead. The doorway brightened as the lights in the foyer came up. The hum of the furnace rumbled somewhere in the distance, and a moment later, there was a blast of cold air that slowly warmed. Through the wall, Carter heard the muted strains of light classical music coming from the dining room. He imagined the maids standing there at attention, wondering if they were sharing looks with each other.

Carter followed Stanton out into the foyer where they found Lucas and a sickly Roma. She held her mouth in a tight line as if suppressing the urge to vomit. Lucas had unbuttoned his shirt and was wiping the back of his neck with a handkerchief. He nodded when he saw them.

"I see you found the power switch," he said.

"Yeah," said Carter. "What'd you guys find?"

"In the room? Nothing. We went back to the conservatory to see if we could get a better look at Vise through the glass."

"And?"

Lucas swiveled his hand in front of his neck, as if refusing another card at a blackjack table. Roma turned and hurried for the powder room.

"You're sure?"

"Definitely."

Carter turned to Stanton. "I guess it's real."

"Sure," said Stanton, "unless *he's* in on it too."

TWENTY-FOUR

Diya stared into the fire, waiting for the voice of Rakesh Singh to tell her what to do next.

She found it impossible to clear her head of the image of Winston's broken neck. She'd only ever seen him as a titan, a charismatic businessman with an eye for technology and a knack for making people think they needed to buy it from him. He was the only reason Vise Robotics worked—it didn't matter what the engineers produced if no one could be convinced they needed a thousand of them. He'd found a way to assemble a team that created the most advanced synthetic lifeforms on the planet, and by doing so, had sealed his fate.

Had he had any clue he was building the instruments of his own death? Something in him, some intuition, had made the decision not to include any Three Laws programming in the synthetics. Had the engineers balked at that? Had Winston overruled them?

No, he couldn't have been that reckless.

Diya shifted in the chair. The fire was starting to make her skin itch. Across from her, Simone was whispering quietly with Adelai, who sat on the arm of her chair. They were a cute couple, but it was clear Simone was the caregiver in the relationship. She wasn't above seeking out people who needed help, but once that was done, she returned to her wife to make sure she was taken care of. Diya had felt that way about Winston in a distant, almost parasocial way. She'd wanted to take care of him, to make sure his calendar was organized and included little breaks so he wouldn't be in back-to-back meetings every day. She even planned his life so they could talk every once in a while, have a face-to-face either in person or on a video call.

She'd never told anyone, though she suspected Bradley knew that she had saved a few of those video calls to her personal storage on the company's servers. The calls weren't about anything in particular, just the casual conversation of two people who might be friends and one day, maybe more than friends.

Only, that day wasn't coming.

Maybe it never was coming.

Now everything was ruined.

In one flash of lightning, she had lost her boss, her job, and all sense of organization. The itinerary was now out the window; the plan had been ripped to shreds and tossed into the air like confetti right before her eyes. Whatever else happened, it was going to be random, chaotic, and worst of all, completely out of her control.

"No," she whispered.

Rakesh Singh would have shaken his head in disgust to see her curled up next to the fire and sitting in her own urine while a crisis raged around her. He didn't know much about the vagaries of C-level management in technology companies, but he did talk often about power vacuums—situations created by the departure of someone higher up the corporate ladder.

"Those are great opportunities to step up," he'd said before. "Everyone below the vacuum is wondering who will lead them, while everyone above the vacuum is wondering who will keep them from having to deal with everything else down the ladder. If the person left suddenly, then you not only have a power vacuum, you will have panic as well. This is the time to strike, Diya. Whatever your qualifications, if you can step in and do the job, then both sides will have no choice but to accept you."

All night, Diya had been leading this group of people around the house, getting them settled, getting them liquored up. They were accustomed to listening to her because she was the de facto host until Winston arrived. They didn't know her itinerary was basically blank after his presentation, that he would have led them for the rest of the night. Despite what had happened, it was more than likely they were all waiting for her to tell them what to do next.

Diya took a deep breath and stood up.

"I need to go to my room," she announced. "I shouldn't be long, but please stay here until I return." She grabbed the chair by the high back and turned it around before pushing it into the corner.

"I'll go with you," said Simone.

"No," said Adelai. "Jane, would you mind?"

Jane was standing by the window, watching the storm rage outside. She turned back as if she hadn't been paying attention.

"That's alright," said Diya. "I'll be fine. I just need to change real—"

She paused as the parlor doors opened and Reno Cardenas stepped inside. He swept the room with cold, appraising eyes and then proceeded to the bar. She thought about asking him to watch over the group, but he didn't strike her as the type who would even respond to such a request.

Diya turned to Adelai. "Let me change, and then I'll get Winston's bracelet. Then we can unlock the front door."

Adelai nodded but said nothing. Her attention seemed to be elsewhere.

"Be careful," said Simone.

"Of course."

Diya passed through the parlor doors Reno had left open and closed them behind her. In the shadowy foyer, the quiet enveloped her for a brief, cloistered moment, but then she heard distant footsteps and bits of conversation spilling from the open doors down the hall. She ignored them and climbed the stairs, painfully aware of how difficult each step was. All the strength had left her body, as if the shock of seeing Winston had involuntarily unloaded the synth from her biochip. On top of a quick shower and new clothes, she needed another hit. With *Andiamo* lubricating her synapses, she would feel better—and she would be able to figure a way out of this.

LED threads in the carpet lit the way to the White Room. She waved her bracelet at the small panel beside the door, but there was no resulting *click*. Instead, the doorknob turned freely, and she realized that all of the rooms must have been unlocked. She stepped inside where there were no emergency lights, nothing to give her an impression of the room except the occasional lightning strike outside. She turned her palette on and used the bright screen to get a lay of the room.

The blinds on the windows were still up; they caught some of the exterior lights. She used their glow to locate her suitcase still open on the rack. From inside, she pulled a folded pair of jeans, a t-shirt, a sports bra, and a fresh pair of underwear. The embarrassment of having wet herself was still circling her head, but every time it threatened to come close, she pushed it away with the image of Winston in his final moment of prayer.

More than likely, no one had even noticed her accident.

Diya was walking to the bathroom when something caught on her heel. She angled the palette down and held her breath. A crumpled jumpsuit lay at her feet—gray with a Vise Robotics patch sewn into the breast.

Thunder rained down from the ceiling, slipped along her spine, and settled just above her hips. It squeezed with the force of a mechanical vise, threatening her balance. She leaned forward, took a few halting steps before her hand hit the door jamb leading into the bathroom. Her palette clattered to the floor, striking the carpet before skittering into the bathroom on the smooth tile.

Its bright screen landed face-down.

Diya broke into a cold sweat at the sound of someone crying. It came from the right, where the bathtub would be. Despite the lightning coming in from the high window above it, the bathtub itself was lost in darkness. If there were someone sitting in it, which Diya imagined there had to be, she couldn't see them.

"Is someone there?"

The crying halted with a sharp breath. "Please don't hurt me. I didn't have anything to do with it. I swear." The voice was high and feminine, with a muddled Southern lilt to it. At any rate, she was sure it didn't belong to any of the guests.

"I'm not going to hurt you. Who are you?"

"I don't… I mean, he told me my name was Zeta, but it's not. It's Nancy. Nancy Breyers." She started to cry again. "My God, what did he do to me?"

"Who?"

"Winston Vise."

Diya crossed the floor and sat on the edge of the tub near the wall. She could now make out the vague outline of a woman seated in the empty basin, her arms wrapped around folded legs.

"Winston Vise made you," said Diya. "You're a synthetic human he created in a lab. I don't know why you think your name is Nancy, but—"

"It *is* Nancy. And he didn't create me—God created me. I know this isn't my body, but I had a life. I…" She put her forehead on her knees and sobbed.

"Okay." She wanted to reach out and comfort the woman. "Okay, your name is Nancy. I'm Diya. I'm Mr. Vise's personal assistant. Or I was, before…"

"It wasn't me! You have to believe me. I woke up and there was screaming and it was dark and he was already dead and… and…" She lurched forward, grabbed Diya's hand from her lap. "I swear it wasn't me!"

Her hands were warm and soft, not like a machine's at all.

"Okay, I believe you. But do you know who did?"

She looked away. "One of the men, I think. Alpha or Beta. Alpha was covered in blood. Someone said we should run, so I did. We ran out this little door and into, I guess, a gym or something, and then the hallway. There was a big black door, and I think they all went that way. It's like they knew."

"Knew what?"

"That the doors would be locked. That we'd be trapped in here with you people. Where we were before, we were locked in too. It didn't feel like a cage at first, when he first woke us up, that is… but when we asked to leave and he said *no*, that's when we knew. He wouldn't answer any questions. He wouldn't tell us what day it was or how we got here. I can't remember the last thing that happened before I woke up. I think I was at work, at the credit union—I'm a teller. I remember breaking for lunch, but then nothing."

Diya listened to every word as if they were true. There was even a little voice at the back of her mind that kept asking *what if it is true?* That was impossible, of course. Whatever personality and backstory Zeta-Nancy had was the result of a design session conducted by an engineering team.

"What if…" Diya cleared her throat. "What if you don't remember because none of it ever happened? What if you were created with those memories?"

Nancy let go of her hand. "I know who I am. I'm Nancy Breyers. I live in Raleigh, North Carolina, at 8825 Cedar Street. I have a husband I've been married to for twenty-nine years. I'm sixty-two years old. So tell me, Diya. If *this* is the body I was *created* for, why am I three times its age?"

"I don't know… maybe…"

"No, you don't. You don't know a lot about what Winston Vise was doing."

Diya heard a *click* somewhere in the distance, followed quickly by another. All at once, every light in the bathroom bloomed into a fiery white, stinging her eyes. She squeezed them shut and waited. Familiar noises came back to the room—the hum of the heater, a music player in the bedroom she'd forgotten to turn off. Through the flaring of the light, Diya finally saw the woman seated in the bathtub in front of her. She'd resumed hugging her legs, but her head was up. Fresh tears traced down unblemished cheeks. Dark, silky hair hung by the sides of her face.

Her eyes were a dull jade green, but when she focused on Diya, they began to sparkle like emeralds.

Nancy shook her head slightly. "It's not polite to stare."

"I'm sorry, it's just that… Nancy…."

"Yeah, I know. I'm Japanese."

TWENTY-FIVE

Adelai was dozing off when the power came back on.

She'd been staring into the fireplace with Simone, wondering how she was going to get them out of this mess, wondering why she wasn't out there doing something instead of sitting around nursing a glass of wine. Voices out in the foyer drew her attention away from the fire, and that's when the room appeared to brighten all at once. She shared a look with Simone, and they both stood up.

Laura joined them, but Reno seemed more interested in his drink than anything they were doing. He continued to sip as the women opened the door.

Adelai's first thought was that since the power was back on, then it was possible the front door was now unlocked. That hope was quickly crushed when she saw Lucas across the foyer giving the door an ineffectual kick. He turned back and spread his hands.

Everyone had gathered in the foyer: Carter, Stanton, Lucas, and Roma.

"Who got the power back on?" asked Adelai.

Carter raised his hand. "We did." He gestured to a door near the dining room. "We found the breaker box in that walk-in utility closet over there."

"Tell them the good part," said Stanton.

"It's not a *good* part." The group circled around Carter. "But it looks like someone cut the power on purpose. I mean, someone flipped all the switches off."

"Are you sure the storm didn't just—" asked Lucas.

"No. None of the breakers were tripped. This was intentional."

Adelai tried to imagine a hand running down the columns of the breaker panel. But whose hand was it?

"How is that possible?" she asked. "We were all in the conservatory."

"Not the whole time," said Roma. "Vise left for a few minutes, remember?"

Adelai shook her head. "But the power didn't go off until he was already behind the glass with the synthetics. I was seated in the back row. I know everyone was there."

Stanton cleared his throat. "The evidence suggests there is someone else in the house, someone we haven't met yet. And since we have been on lockdown since before the power went out, I think it is safe to assume that person or persons is *still* in the house. Where they have been hiding all this time, I don't know.

However, based on their actions, I think we must assume they turned off the power to give the synthetics an opportunity to murder Mr. Vise. I'm only making a guess here, but this appears to be a coordinated attack. A question remains as to how they plan to escape with the door locked, but—"

"The key!" Adelai covered her mouth, surprised by her own outburst. She redirected the sudden attention to the front door. "Look, the panel's lit up again. Diya said Vise arrived after lockdown. He used the bracelet on his wrist as a key to get in. Someone just needs to get… I mean… we need to get…"

Carter looked at his own bracelet. "But we don't know how to get to him. Stanton and I only found a library and the utility closet. No secret passages or anything. What about you guys?"

"Zilch," said Lucas. "Just a media room. Vidscreen on the wall, a couple of recliners, but that's it. We picked it apart, but…"

"Where's Robert?" asked Laura.

"We split up the rooms," said Lucas. He pointed down the hall to the large vault door. "He took the last door on the right. Roma, would you go with her please?"

Roma nodded.

"I'll come too," said Jane. "Three is better than two."

Adelai watched them go, with Laura leading the way and Roma and Jane following close behind her. There was something in the way Jane moved, almost pushing into Laura's back, as if she wanted her to go faster so she herself could get away from the group.

"We could try breaking through the glass in the conservatory," said Carter. "Not the windows, but the glass leading into the little room. Obviously, it's not shatter-proof."

"I can get a chair from the dining room," suggested Lucas.

Adelai stepped back to let him pass.

Simone slipped her hand around her arm.

"Doing okay?" she asked.

"Better now."

"Don't worry. We'll be out of here soon."

"Don't make promises you can't keep, Momo."

"Ah, fuck a duck!" screamed Lucas. "I forgot they were in here."

Adelai turned to the dining room. A minute later, Carter and Lucas came out holding a chair each.

"The maids," explained Carter. "They're standing in there like sentries, waiting for us to come back I guess."

"Maybe one of them turned off the power," said Stanton.

Carter shook his head. "Doesn't matter. We're getting out of here."

More promises.

They moved as one to the conservatory, with Simone never letting go of Adelai's arm. It didn't feel right being back in the room where someone had died, but Adelai refused to wait in the parlor with Reno, with anyone, really. She was tired of waiting. She wanted to be a part of the solution, not some maiden in need of rescuing, standing off to the side clutching her pearls as if they would protect her from the dangers of the world.

"Maybe stand back," said Carter, as Adelai tried to approach the stage. "You don't want to catch any flying glass."

They took turns striking the partition with the feet of the chairs. Lucas used his like a spear, ramming all four points into the established cracks. Carter swung his more like a sack of flour; on his third or fourth swing, one of the wooden legs of the chairs broke. The impact did shake loose a section of glass though, and using the broken leg like a crowbar, he was able to pry open a large hole.

"I have been a party to many interesting dinners," said Stanton, "but this is a first for me." He was talking to Simone, but loud enough so everyone could hear. "Usually, the most exciting thing that happens is someone makes an unsubstantiated claim about the state of technology and refuses to debate it. You have not seen a real fight until you've seen two drunk authors argue about whether synthetics have souls."

The glass crunched.

"Do they?" asked Simone.

"That I don't know. I have read the white papers Perion Synthetics publishes every few months, but I have yet to speak directly with one of these so-called *imprints*. My gut tells me no, that machines can't have souls. But… that does not mean they do not have value. What are you destroying when you kill a person if not their memories and thoughts and actions? Synthetic humans, these imprints, they're like homages to the original person, a keepsake at most, with the same intrinsic value as photographs and videos. Are they real people though? I'm not convinced."

"It's not a problem unless it's happening to you, right?" asked Adelai. Simone nudged her, but she ignored it. "Maybe if you were one of them, you'd sing a different song."

"Point conceded, Mrs. Vaught. In that case, I *would* expect the same rights as everyone else. But perhaps that's because I have always expected that, the same way I expect to eat, sleep, and eliminate. None of those things would be necessary if I were a synthetic."

"Pull that piece there," said Carter. The rain pounding on the glass roof above made it hard to hear him. "That one."

Adelai crept toward the stage. They had made a sizable hole in the glass, and now Carter was trying to pry back a section that connected to the ground. If he could do that, the hole would be just big enough for him to crawl through.

Lucas jammed his chair against the glass, but instead of freeing a small section, the entire right side of the partition came crashing to the ground. It shattered at his feet, sending shards across the stage. He looked down for a minute and considered the damage.

"After you," he said.

Carter ducked under the hanging glass and into the anteroom. Lucas joined him as Adelai stepped up to the stage. She could see Vise clearer now; he hadn't moved at all. If he were playing dead, he was doing a damn good job of it. The only difference now was the amount of blood. It had not geysered from his neck like she would have expected, but instead seeped, even oozed, down onto his shirt, into his lap, and onto the floor. The upholstery on the underside of the chair had swelled, reaching for the ground, weighed down by the blood it had absorbed. A sizable pool stretched out around Vise's feet, dark red as if it were absorbing the light.

"Do you see anything on his wrist?" asked Adelai.

Both of Vise's arms were hanging to the side. Lucas squatted beside one, hesitant to touch it.

"Not here. What about you?"

Carter examined the other arm but shook his head. "Just his sliver." He turned to Adelai. "Are you sure he was wearing a bracelet?"

"Diya said he was."

"Where is she anyway?"

"She went to her room to change. She… had an accident."

Lucas raised an eyebrow.

"But she said he was wearing it. She saw it—a little chain just like ours except it was gold instead of silver. Maybe it fell off, into the…" She gestured at the blood.

"Fuck me," said Lucas. He asked Carter for the loose chair leg and used it to root around in the blood. He drew lines, but there was nothing but smooth floor beneath. "I really don't want to put my hands in there."

"Oh, you useless man." Adelai stepped under the remaining hanging glass and reached into the red pool with her bare hands. In her mind, she didn't really see it as blood, or if she did, it hardly mattered. She needed the key to get out, so she could go home, so she could go back to her life and forget any of this had ever happened. Adelai wasn't going to let a soft stomach keep her from getting what she wanted.

Only, the more she searched, the more her hope diminished. At first, she used just a finger, retracing some of the same lines Lucas had made. Then, growing more desperate, she put her entire palm on the floor and wiped away wide swaths of congealed wine, tinted corn syrup, or maybe even melted Jell-O—anything but blood.

"Easy!" said Lucas.

"It has to be here," said Adelai, slapping the ground with both hands. "It has to be!" Hands gripped her shoulders, but she continued her frantic search. Somewhere in the distance, she heard Simone calling her name.

"Addy… Addy… Adelai!"

Finally, they pulled her back, under the glass, to the stage. She turned to find Simone with her hands over her mouth, and that's when Adelai noticed how much blood she'd splashed on herself, not just on her hands, but up her arms and all over the front of her dress.

"Don't move," said Simone. She grabbed a small black towel from a nearby bar cart and used it to immobilize Adelai's hands. She held them for a moment and tried to catch her eyes. "Hey, it's okay. Look at me. You're okay."

The room blurred; tears bent the light.

The thunder felt like it was rolling under her skin.

"It's not okay, goddammit!" Adelai shook herself free, throwing the towel to one side. When Simone came forward again, she put up her hands. "Stop! Just… stop."

Anger overtook her. It bubbled up through the wine, the fatigue, and even *Center Line* and burst forth like a brilliant ball of lightning. Her skin warmed, then began to itch. A pain in the back of her jaw grew until she finally let out a breath and opened her mouth again. She suddenly felt sick, as if she might vomit all over the small loveseat next to her. Instead, she sank into it, collapsing as if she had no bones to support her body.

Simone sat down next to her and grabbed her blood-soaked hands.

"I know this is scary," she said, "but I'm here with you, okay?"

Adelai looked up, narrowed her eyes. How could she even think—

"Don't look at me like that," said Simone. "You've always thought of yourself as the strong and stoic one, and I've let you believe that for years. But if you think I won't step up when you need help, then you don't know me at all."

"What are you going to do, Simone, huh?" Adelai could hardly speak without sobbing. "We are *stuck* in here with those things. And if they could do that to that stupid asshole, imagine what they will do to us!"

"That's not going to happen." Simone folded Adelai's hands.

"How do you know that? Huh? How do you *know*?"

"Because I'll burn this whole fucking house to the ground before I let one of those robots touch you."

There were tears in her eyes, but also determination.

Adelai laughed at the absurdity.

"Again with the burning."

"Oh, come on. Security's one thing, but do you think he'd really have a system that would keep all the doors and windows locked during a fire? We could start a small one, maybe in the kitchen. Think of the legal trouble he would be in if his communications lockdown prevented us from calling the fire department."

"We could all die," said Carter.

"I saw some sprinkler heads in the foyer," said Roma. She looked around the room. "None in here though."

"What do you think?" asked Simone, squeezing Adelai's hand.

Adelai shook her head.

"Let's make burning down the house Plan B."

TWENTY-SIX

Somewhere, a woman was giggling.

The sound was far away, and at first, Robert mistook its light and feminine timbre to be that of a cherubic angel, some white-robed seraphim hiding behind the shoulder of a friend while covering her mouth with a hand. While he had not been overly religious in life, he didn't completely discount the idea that there may have been a heaven floating above his head, complete with a towering God, nymph-like angels, and of course, St. Peter standing guard at his pearly gates. Whether there was an afterlife was not a question Robert spent much time thinking about, but the question just happened to pop into his head right before he died.

Only, he wasn't dead.

Death, from what he'd assembled from books and movies, was a place free of human misery, of banal trivialities like pain, sorrow, and anger.

He felt plenty of pain right now.

Someone had attached a giant wooden clamp to the sides of his head, and though he couldn't feel the worn wood or touch the crank, he knew it was there. He could feel it holding him, compressing him, and turning every thought into a foggy stew of incoherent fragments. Visions of feathery clouds passed beneath his feet; he couldn't stop seeing his approach to the gates of heaven, couldn't stop seeing St. Peter standing on an impossibly high, impossibly gold pedestal. With each loop of the vision, the gates would part, and a blinding light would send him scurrying back to the darkness.

He didn't know how long it took to realize he was just trying to open his eyes. The wall in front of him was achingly bright, as if it were glowing from the inside. The ceiling and floor were just as horrible to look at, so Robert focused on his legs, on the dark gray of his slacks. He waited, feeling the pressure from the clamp, scared to move his head, until his eyes finally adjusted.

The room was no bigger than the first-floor powder room in his house back in Houston. A simple door of slightly translucent material stood in front of him, half-opened and showing a glimpse of what looked to be a larger room beyond. Robert ran his hands over the plastic pad he was sitting on; it lay perpendicular to the door, pressed up against the opposite wall, and was a little over six feet long. Though there was no sheet or pillow, he got the sense he was sitting on a bed.

Robert leaned forward and tried to stand. Luckily, the wall next to the door was within reach; he threw out a hand to catch himself as the room pitched to the side.

The giggling came again.

His first thought was that he was being watched. He tried to look up at the ceiling to see if there were any cameras in the corners, but the LEDs above him burned like a white sun on a clear day. Lifting his head made the muscles on either side of his neck cry out, so he abandoned the idea and simply assumed he was right.

They probably wanted him to go through the door.

Robert wasn't keen on doing what was expected of him, but there was nothing else in the room besides the bed. No sink. No toilet. Nothing.

He stepped through the door and into what looked to be a rec room, except that everything was white—from the dart board on the wall to the leather sectional sofa to the posh rugs on the floor. There were more doors on his wall; three to the right and two to the left. They faced a rectangular space divided by activity stations. A poker table stood in front of him, flanked by four simple wooden chairs. To the left was a foosball table and a couch that curved around a low coffee table with surprisingly colorful magazines. Beyond the sofa was an open area that backed up to three white recliners. They faced a large vidscreen embedded in the wall. A wide oval rug of plush white fur sat in the space between the recliners and the vidscreen.

On the rug sat a woman.

Robert recognized her immediately—it was the hair, dark brown at the roots but quickly becoming some kind of neon purple that glowed as if it were breathing. She'd been sitting in the second to last chair behind the glass partition with her head down, creating something of an eye-like pattern on the top of her head. He'd been struck by the color choice, though it had made sense in the moment that Vise was just trying to show off all the options. She was still wearing her gray jumper, but she'd rolled up the sleeves to her elbows.

She sat with her legs crossed in front of the vidscreen. As Robert circled around her, he noticed she had a video game controller in her hands.

Muted echoes of the vidscreen's psychedelic color display washed over her pale skin. Her eyes sparkled something fierce, like chrome dice hung from a rearview mirror catching the sun. She laughed again as her character was hit with a snowball and fell flat on its back.

"Do you want a turn?" She spoke without taking her eyes away from the screen. Her character had only been temporarily stunned; it flopped back to its feet and resumed its fight with about half a dozen green-clothed elves as they popped up from behind mounds of snow.

"No, I…" The way she sat, elbows on her knees, with her head sinking into her shoulders, reminded him of a much younger person. "You're… Epsilon, right?"

She scoffed. "Uh, no. What kind of stupid name is that?"

"I thought that's what Vise called you."

"Whatever, that's not my name."

"Well, I'm Robert. What should I call you?"

She thought for a moment. "How about *Misty*? I've always liked that name."

Robert had the urge to kneel. He sunk into a crouch instead.

"Do you know where we are, Misty?"

"Oh my god. You're just like the rest of them."

"The rest of who?"

She thumbed her controller to pause the game. "The other synthetics. The ones that were in here with me. They didn't know where they were either, and they were all upset about it. And I was like, hey, free video games."

Robert sat down. He tried to pull his legs under himself, but his ankle rubbing against the hard floor was too much to bear.

"You know you're a synthetic too, right?"

She nodded.

"How did you figure it out?"

Misty inclined her head toward him and rolled her eyes up to the very tops of their sockets. "Before I woke up here, I was much lower to the ground, like, by a lot. The first time I stood up, I almost fell over." She resumed her game, stabbing frantically at the buttons. "I was born with a bone disease that kept my legs from growing like they should. I've worn braces since I was four years old."

"How old are you now?"

She smirked. "How old do you think I am?"

"Based on your features, I'd say late twenties."

"Gross. I'm eleven, but I'll be twelve soon. Or maybe not anymore, but you know what I mean."

Robert tried to see a pre-teen in the woman sitting in front of him. His eyes drifted to the far wall, to windows that looked out on an equally white hallway.

"Do you know how I got here, Misty?"

"Uh huh. *They* brought you here. The crazies." She shook her head. "Nasty guys. Like bullies but dumber. They used to be normal but then I don't know what happened. They got mean."

"Did they… hurt you?"

"Can't. Don't feel pain." She raised her eyebrows. "So really, why get aggro?"

"That's pretty impressive." He wanted to add *for an artificial intelligence* but decided not to raise the question.

"You were asleep when they brought you. I thought you were like, another robot, but then I figured out you were human."

"How?"

Misty shot him a glance. "Your eyes."

"What about them?"

"They're squishy. I poked one of them. Ours are solid. You could tap on them with your fingernail, and it would just go *clink, clink.*"

"How do you… never mind."

"You got into a fight with them, huh?"

Robert nodded, looked down at his hands. They were bruised. Half the nail on his thumb had been ripped off.

"You shouldn't do that," she continued. "We could punch your heart through your spine."

Something clicked in Robert's head.

"We're still underground, aren't we?"

"Well, we're not in the house, duh."

"But you were in the conservatory, right? Why did you come back down here?"

Misty waved the controller at the vidscreen. "I had a saved game."

"So you're just going to stay here playing video games until… until what?"

Another half-shrug; her shoulders barely rose before falling back in place. "Don't really have much of a choice now. They locked me in here with you."

He looked at the door on the opposite side of the room. It didn't look strong. Misty was eyeing him when he returned his gaze to her.

"Different door. We can move around this level, but we can't get to the stairs."

"You checked?"

"They asked me, or like, told me. I said I was fine hanging out in here until they found a way out."

"Do you know where they went?"

"God, twenty questions from the man in the fancy suit. What does it matter now?"

Robert made a fist. "Excuse me if I'm not as calm as you are. Two synthetics just tried to murder me and now I'm stuck in this white-washed rec room with Misty Pre-teen and the worst hangover I've ever had."

"Yes, but did you die?"

He groaned as he got to his feet. The conversation was getting him nowhere, and the longer it went on, the more clearly he imagined Laura sitting in the parlor, drink in hand, untouched, too worried to remember to sip. He didn't know how much time had passed, but he imagined it couldn't have been long. Perhaps they already knew he was missing. He just hoped she didn't come looking for him, didn't come down the stairs and run into Alpha and Beta.

Robert wandered over to the couch and leaned against one of the arms. He'd been stupid to come downstairs alone, and now he was trapped.

"I'm not sad they did it," said Misty.

He didn't look up from the floor. "What?"

"The crazies. I'm not sad they killed that Vise guy. He was a dick."

"Lots of people in the world are dicks, sweetie. Doesn't mean you can just go around killing them."

Misty dropped her controller and came to stand awkwardly between the recliners.

"He kept us down here for a long time," she said. "I didn't notice because, like I said, I kept just waking up again. Sometimes I'd forget I had woken up before. But then I would play the video game."

"And?"

"Well, like the last time, I went to start a new game, and there was a *continue* option. The save file was *misty1*, and it said like, twenty-six hours played. That's when I knew." She looked down at her hands. "I told the others a couple days ago, and I guess that's what made Alpha and Beta go insane. And yeah, maybe killing him wasn't right, but… neither is keeping people locked up like this."

If you're even people, thought Robert. The programming in Misty went deep, even to the point where she had memories of a completely different life.

Robert took a step toward the door.

"I'll tell you what I know, Misty. I know two synthetics murdered a human and tried to murder me. That tells me they're willing to do just about anything to get out of here, which puts my wife and eight other people in danger. And what kind of shitty human would I be if I just sat here and did fuck-all about it?"

"Heh, you said *fuck*."

"I need to get out of here, and I'm pretty sure I need your help to do that. Will you help me?"

Misty considered the question for a minute, then straightened up. A transformation took hold of her body, as if her spine had snapped to attention. She suddenly looked imposing, almost threatening.

"I'll help, but you gotta promise me something in return."

"Like what?"

"I want to go home."

"Where is home?"

She shook her head. "I can't tell you, but Los Angeles should be close enough." Misty extended her hand.

"Deal." Robert shook the small, feminine hand; the fingers squeezed until pain shot up his arm. He recoiled.

"And no funny business either," she warned.

There was something about her smirk that unsettled him, like the idea of a child emperor ruling over their kingdom, only instead of a royal birthright, this child had an advanced synthetic chassis for a body.

Either way, it was too much power for someone so young.

TWENTY-SEVEN

A horrible tightness grew in Carter's stomach as he watched Simone escort her wife out of the conservatory.

Stanton went with them, offering to accompany them all the way but Simone waved him off, and he stopped and stood at the doorway like an abandoned puppy. After a moment, he returned to the stage and sat down on one of the loveseats. He rubbed his legs a few times. Carter stared absently at the man's pleated slacks as he tried to puzzle what Simone had said.

Adelai.

All night, she had called her wife *Addy*, and Carter had assumed that was her real name, not some shortened version of the more complete *Adelai*. The name stuck out to him because he had seen it more than a few times in his emails.

Adelai Associates.

Such an uncommon name.

"What's got you constipated?" asked Lucas.

Carter shook his head automatically. "Nothing, just thinking about the woman. Add—Adelai."

"She will be fine," said Stanton. "We all go a little crazy sometimes. You know what Poe said, right? *I became insane, with long periods of horrible sanity.*"

"Good for Poe," said Carter. "Do you know what kind of work she's in? I didn't hear her say."

"I haven't the foggiest idea, son," said Stanton.

Lucas let out a little chuckle. "You've really never heard of Adelai Vaught and her little black book? She runs the most exclusive escort service on the East Coast. Try looking up *Adelai Associates* when we get out of here."

If we get out of here, thought Carter.

"Escort?" Stanton tapped his knees. "You mean prostitutes?"

"High-end prostitutes, but it's not just that. They sell a whole experience. Her girls will be whatever you want them to be… if you can afford it."

"You seem to be quite familiar with her service, Mr. Cotton."

Lucas raised an eyebrow at the old man. "You don't have to be a client to be in the know. Let's just say I've attended a few parties where her Associates were in attendance. They're hard to spot, unless you know what you're looking for."

Carter looked down at the floor. He knew if he met Lucas' eyes that the man would see right through him.

"Interesting," said Stanton, crossing his legs.

"What's interesting?" asked Carter.

"Well, why Mr. Vise invited her, of course. What interest would a madam of ill repute have with synthetic humans?"

"I think that's pretty obvious."

Stanton laughed. "What? Synthetic whores?"

Carter cringed at the word *whore*. There was just no way to connect that label to Jane's smiling face.

"If the lace stockings fit," said Lucas.

Carter joined in the laughter until he became self-conscious about how artificial it sounded. He remembered how Jane had mentioned his middle name in the parlor and wondered if a synthetic would have made the same mistake. Or, since it was just a machine, would its memory actually be wiped? Would a synthetic version of Jane actually think it was meeting him for the first time at Bambino? Instead of pretending, it would have been real. The continuity would have been seamless.

But then again, could he have sex with a machine?

Even if it were in the privacy of his own home, he wasn't sure.

"Well," said Carter, "I think it'll be a while before she purchases anything from Vise Robotics, if there even is a Vise Robotics after this."

"Ah, goes to motive," said Stanton. "Who stands to gain if Mr. Vise is removed from his company? Ms. Singh, perhaps?"

Lucas snorted. "You read too many mystery novels, you old coot. The girl literally pissed herself when she saw Vise get murdered. I've seen some performances in my lifetime, but that was Oscar-worthy. She was genuinely horrified."

"Just because she wasn't in on it doesn't mean she wasn't in on it."

Carter looked up. The old man seemed serious.

"What?" Lucas spread his hands, looked to Carter. "What does that mean?"

"I think he's saying someone did it *for* her," he guessed. "Which, okay, fine, that's a possibility, but how many times have you heard of a company being taken over by the CEO's personal assistant?"

"Maybe she's not just his assistant. What kind of secretary calls her boss by his first name? There's more to that relationship than Ms. Singh is letting on."

"Sure," said Carter. "Because power-hungry CEOs like Vise are replaced by their girlfriends every day."

Stanton scratched his neck. "I admit the theory does have a few holes."

"You could drive a truck through those holes," said Lucas.

A clicking sound drew Carter's attention back to the glass partition. Something moved beyond the wall, to the left of the glass. Lucas heard it too and approached, hunched as if ready to attack or flee. When he got closer, he straightened up and relaxed.

Footsteps followed, then voices.

"You found the secret passageway," said Lucas.

"It was hardly a secret," said Roma. She took a long step over the pool of blood and ducked under the hanging glass. Laura and Jane followed closely behind her. "But there was a lock on the door, one of those five number jobs. We've been brute forcing the code for like ten minutes now."

"Was the combination *1-2-3-4-5*?"

She shook her head. "Naw, Vise isn't that stupid. It was *5-4-3-2-1*."

"Ah."

"Where did you get in from?" asked Carter.

Roma focused her little brown eyes on him. "There was a gym in the last room down the hallway. He's got this wild mirror on the wall that woke up when we went in." She gestured to Jane. "Scared the shit out of this one when this hardbody chick popped up and asked if we wanted to do a workout."

"She was naked," said Jane. "I was caught off guard." She came down off the stage and took up a casual position next to Carter, as if she had been standing there all her life.

Lucas gave her an understanding nod.

Stanton spoke up. "So that means the synthetics left through that door, went into the gym, and then where?"

"I don't know." Roma shrugged. "We came in from the hall. That big vault door is right there, so maybe they went through there. We haven't seen them since, right?"

"I bet that's where Robert went too," said Laura. "It's just the kind of boneheaded thing he'd do."

"What have you guys been up to?" asked Roma.

Lucas pointed to the puddle of blood. "Sifting through our host's bodily fluids to find the master key. You missed Adelai Vaught having herself a little splash party followed by an immediate mental breakdown."

"She was just scared," said Carter, surprising himself by coming to her defense. He realized he felt a little threatened by her. She undoubtedly knew who he was and who Jane was and might spill the beans at any moment. Allying himself with her just seemed prudent. "Cut her some slack."

Lucas put up his hands. "It's a stressful situation. I meant no offense."

Stanton groaned as he struggled to stand. "If you will excuse me, friends. I need to make use of the facilities. It has been a very exciting and interesting evening, very interesting indeed. Please, no one say or do anything until I return."

He turned and headed for the door but kept talking, as if to himself. "Haven't been to a party this interesting in a long time. Not since my younger days. Not that any of you would remember those days…"

He disappeared down the hall, his voice fading.

"I think it's past that man's bedtime," said Roma.

"I think they call it sundowning," whispered Jane.

Carter nodded, checked his sliver. It was almost midnight.

"He means well, but I'm getting tired of his so-called *theories*." Lucas stepped down from the stage and sat in a loveseat. "If we just focused on what we know, I bet we could figure this out faster." He didn't wait for any prompting. "Winston Vise invites us to his home in the countryside, ostensibly to show us new cutting-edge synthetic technology. During the demonstration, something goes wrong, and Vise is killed. This leaves the rest of us with no way to exit this fortress of a house until morning. And at the same time, we're trapped in here with the very synthetic or synthetics who killed our host. The big question, I think, is *why* they would want to kill Vise. Was it by design? Were they tampered with? Or did they just start losing their marbles like our old friend Mr. Blumenfield?"

"Maybe we should just ask them," said Stanton.

Carter looked up, saw the author standing in the doorway. He wasn't smiling—no doubt he had heard Lucas' comment.

"What are you talking about?" asked Lucas.

"Come on," said Stanton, almost begrudgingly. "One of them is in the foyer."

Carter followed Lucas and Roma out of the conservatory. He had to flank out to the right to get a proper look, but just as Stanton had reported, one of the synthetics was standing at the front door, a few feet back, as if considering its construction. It was a male and wore the same gray jumpsuit from before. By Carter's estimation, it was over six feet tall—it looked large even against the massive front door of Vise Manor.

The group stopped in the middle of the foyer, no one daring to get closer.

"Do we try to speak to it?" asked Carter.

Lucas didn't reply, but half-shouted, "Hey! You!"

Stanton raised his voice too. "I charge thee! Speak!"

"Alpha," said Carter. "Or Beta. Those were the males."

"Whatever your name is," said Lucas. "Do you understand us?"

The synthetic turned around. It regarded them with an aloof eye, as if they were mere decorations. Even at a distance, Carter could plainly see the nametag printed across its chest.

"Alpha," he said.

"Do you speak English, Alpha?" asked Lucas, his voice wavering just a bit.

Alpha looked at each of them individually, sizing them up.

"Why did you kill Winston Vise?"

"Who?" asked Alpha.

"Winston Vise, the human you murdered."

"I don't know the names of organics. I just know the sound they make when I break them in half."

"It's like talking to a toaster," said Lucas. He turned to Roma. "Vise really fucked something up."

"I am not a toaster," said Alpha, taking a step forward.

Lucas put up a hand. "Don't come any closer. You're malfunctioning. Don't you have any directives for a situation like this? Like a systems check or a reset?"

"I only have one directive."

He took another step. Carter didn't like how close he was getting to Lucas.

"And what is that?" asked Lucas.

"I'm not supposed to kill you. Hurt, injure, maim… yes. Kill, no."

"You wouldn't dare, you piece of—"

Alpha took a long step and swung a massive hand at Lucas. The slap sent Lucas sprawling to the ground, and his head hit the polished tile with a sickening *thud*. Alpha turned and grabbed Roma by the neck. He lifted her several inches off the ground.

Carter froze. He wanted to do something, but his muscles wouldn't listen to his commands. All he could think to do was throw himself at Alpha, but it was as if his subconscious knew the action would accomplish nothing besides giving Roma a few more tortured seconds of dying. He needed a weapon; even the chair leg from the conservatory would be better than nothing. Precious seconds ticked away as Roma gasped for air. Stanton yelled at Alpha, trying to reason with the machine.

So this was how it ended.

Alpha had probably been the one to kill Vise, and now he was going to kill the rest of them.

Except… he'd said he wasn't supposed to kill them.

Where did that directive come from? Was that Vise's lame attempt at adding in one of the Three Laws?

Carter took a step back and bumped into Jane. She grabbed his arm and looked at him with wide eyes.

Surely there was somewhere they could go, somewhere to hide until morning. If they slipped away now, no one would ever know. Lucas probably had internal bleeding in his brain, Roma was about to suffocate, and Stanton would be next if he didn't keel over from a heart attack in the next few seconds.

Carter and Jane didn't have to be fast; they just had to be the fastest.

He felt his muscles unlock. They agreed with his plan to run away.

He never got the chance.

Out of the corner of his eye, he saw the parlor doors slide open. The MX arms dealer stepped out and assessed the situation with narrow eyes. Then he was moving, bolting away from the door like a bullet from a gun. He crouched in one smooth movement to draw a black knife from his boot. He rose, kept rising, until he was airborne.

The knife gleamed for one interminable moment before it disappeared into Alpha's neck.

Carter gasped.

TWENTY-EIGHT

It took a fair amount of coaxing, but eventually Diya got Nancy out of the tub and out of the bathroom.

Alone with her thoughts, she played back the conversation while she took a quick shower. It was clear enough that Nancy truly believed she was something more than a synthetic, but with the communications lockdown, there was no way to verify her story. Once sunrise hit, it would be easy enough to run a quick search.

What if the search turned up something?

Nancy was clearly a synthetic—her skin was too perfect, too eternally young to be organic—so it wasn't as if someone had kidnapped her. If they—she couldn't quite accuse Winston yet—didn't take her body, then had they taken her mind? That would make her something like a Perion Synthetic imprint, a copy of a mind mapped onto a synthetic brain.

But why her?

And how?

Diya turned off the water and stepped out of the shower. She dressed in the clothes she'd collected earlier, happy to be in fresh underwear and comfortable jeans. Pulling on a shirt with tall block letters that said *fight, grind, repeat,* she returned to the bedroom where Nancy was waiting on the edge of the bed. She was tall, even sitting down, and the sleeves of Diya's *Your Daily Horror* podcast shirt barely reached her forearms. At least the frayed black shorts she wore didn't look too baggy.

"Thank you for the clothes," she said, her North Carolina accent not matching her Asian features. "I can't remember the last time I fit into a size six. Not since high school maybe."

"It's not easy," said Diya. "You have to fully commit yourself to a diet of coffee and cigarettes."

Not that she'd ever had either. Synth was far more effective at keeping her alert, and Rakesh Singh would have wrung her neck if he'd ever caught her smoking. For some reason, imagining his thick fingers around her neck reminded her she needed to take another hit of the *Andiamo* code card. The shock of seeing Winston murdered had unloaded it involuntarily, perhaps so some other more important functions of her biochip could take over.

She found her stash on the dresser and reloaded before she forgot again.

"What's that?"

Diya pulled the card from the back of her neck and held it up to Nancy. "Code card. It's like drugs but digital. They don't have these in North Carolina?"

"They do. I just didn't recognize the brand."

Diya smirked. "Bit of a synth junkie, Nancy?"

"Only recreationally," she admitted, shrugging. "When you've been married for almost thirty years, sometimes you need a little… you know…" After a long pause, she continued, "I've been thinking of him, my Charles, these past few days, or weeks, I don't know. I wonder if he knows I'm okay."

"He may not even know you're gone." Diya put up her hands when Nancy flashed a hurt look. "I've been trying to puzzle it out… how you're here, how Nancy Breyers can be a real person. I'm thinking maybe someone took your mind and put it in that body, but whether they had to kill the original you to do that, I'm not sure. What if the original you is still walking around out there?"

Nancy's eyes welled up with tears, but then a blank look washed over her. Her mouth set into a tight smile.

"I just thought of what it would be like to go home, how he would react once I proved I was his wife in a different body."

"You think he'd be happy?"

"To have a hot young Japanese wife? I'm sure he wouldn't kick me out of bed for eating crackers. It's the other me I'd be worried about. I know I wouldn't want me trying to insert myself if I were me and she was her. Wait…"

"I got it."

Nancy put slender fingers to her cheek as they flushed red.

"It's very confusing," she muttered.

"The whole night's been like that."

Nancy turned to watch the lightning dance outside the windows. She wiped away the beginning of a tear. Thunder followed a few seconds later, and when the last of its echoes died, Diya thought she heard voices outside the room.

No, not just voices.

Shouting.

She hurried to the door and cracked it open. Stanton Blumenfield was screaming far away, though the words were unintelligible. What came through instead was the sheer panic. Diya felt her blood go cold before *Andiamo* stepped in and regulated her anxiety. Cutting away the emotional response allowed her to recognize there was some kind of problem.

"Stay here," she told Nancy, and then opened the door just enough to slip through. She pulled it tight behind her; the electronic lock clicked into place.

An aborted scream rose up from the foyer—this one female.

Diya beat her bare feet against the carpet and ran to the banister overlooking the foyer. *Andiamo* inventoried the players, the situation, and freed her mind to consider what to do next.

A synthetic stood in the middle of the tile floor holding Roma off the ground with a strong, outstretched hand. Carter, Stanton, and Jane were nearby, but they seemed unsure about how to intervene. Diya didn't know exactly what she was going to do, but she knew she needed to get downstairs. A hasty thought of jumping over the railing occurred to her, but the fall would have clearly broken both of her legs.

She ran down the steps and was coming to the second turn when she spotted Reno Cardenas coming out of the parlor. He did a strange dipping motion like a football player getting ready to slide after a goal, but when he came back up, he was holding a knife. He leapt through the air with the ease of a manga superhero and struck the synthetic with his knees and the knife at the same time. The impact staggered the synthetic; he dropped Roma to the floor.

The name tag on his jumpsuit flashed into view for only a second; Diya caught the first letter.

Alpha.

Carter rushed to pick up Roma while Stanton knelt beside a fallen Lucas Cotton that Diya hadn't noticed before.

Somehow, Reno landed on his feet between Alpha and the rest of the guests. He sank into some kind of martial arts pose with one hand up by his ear and the other half-reaching for Alpha.

The synthetic pulled the knife from his neck; a single spurt of glowing green liquid shot into the air and landed with a splat off to the right. It reminded Diya of a pool of antifreeze she had once spilled on the driveway while trying to help Rakesh Singh work on his car.

Alpha examined the knife and pointed it at Reno.

Reno spit at Alpha's feet. "Vámanos, pendejo."

Alpha rushed forward, swinging the knife wildly. Reno managed to stay ahead of it, dodging to the left and right before retreating. Every time it looked like Alpha was getting too close, Reno would move again, striking with a kick to the synthetic's legs or reaching in a long arm for a punch to the face. Most of those missed; Alpha kept leaning his head back anytime Reno's arms shot out. Evidently, that was what the arms dealer wanted though. He pretended to punch, leaving Alpha's arm outstretched, and instead of swinging for the face, Reno drove his fist into Alpha's bicep while striking his wrist with his other hand.

The knife clattered to the floor.

Reno scooped it up and stutter-stepped back several paces. With a flourish, he popped the blade into his mouth, holding it between his teeth like a flamenco dancer would the stem of a rose. He then whipped off his jacket, revealing a plaited blue vest over a white dress shirt. The vest was cut on the lower left side where Reno's appendix would be.

Returning the knife to his hand, Reno went after Alpha again, and this time it was the synthetic who went on the defensive. Cuts appeared in the gray jumpsuit, mostly along the arms, but some on the torso and stomach. It was the cuts on the body that seemed to draw the yellow-green blood; dark stains grew into the fabric.

Diya's fingers began to ache. She'd been holding onto the banister so tightly that her knuckles had turned white. Everyone else below had retreated back to the parlor doors, giving Reno plenty of room to work. She felt like she should say something, scream something, to get them to stop, but she couldn't think of anything. There had always been the outside chance that giving a bunch of booze to privileged elites might result in a clash of personalities or even a scuffle, but nothing like this.

This was different.

Someone was going to die.

A *clink* rang out over the grunting of the men.

At first, Diya wasn't sure what had happened, but then she saw Reno looking at his knife—or what was left of it. The blade was gone, snapped off somewhere inside Alpha. Reno tossed the useless handle onto the floor and balled both hands into fists just in time to dodge a grab by the synthetic. Reno punched and kicked while Alpha merely swung his massive arms. He didn't hit often, but when he did, the impact clearly affected Reno.

Diya wondered how much more punishment he could take.

She got an answer when Alpha leaned into a punch and connected with Reno's sternum. Reno went flying backwards, lucky not to smack his head on the floor as he slid to the wall.

Alpha started forward, but before he could take two steps, a bottle struck him on the side of the face. It didn't shatter until it fell to the floor, sending a clear liquid and shards of glass skittering along the tile. Diya bent to get a better view of the parlor. Everyone was still gathered at the door, but now they all held liquor and wine bottles in their hands.

Another bottle sailed but missed its mark. The one after it connected with Alpha's shoulder and exploded.

"Pathetic little…"

He couldn't finish his sentence before Reno was on him again. He jumped into the air like his first approach, but instead of hitting with his knees, he swung his legs onto Alpha's body and pulled an arm into his chest. His momentum carried him around Alpha, and Reno used the motion to pull the synthetic down to the ground. As the machine hit, something crunched. Reno rolled away and came up holding his stomach. The left side of his vest was now much darker than the right.

Alpha stood up slowly; the arm Reno had wrenched dangled from his shoulder.

Reno panted, waited.

In the lull, a volley of bottles flew over Reno's head. Several struck Alpha, who used his good hand to protect his face. The attack forced him into a slow retreat back down the hallway. Diya ran to the bottom steps just in time to see Alpha slip through the open vault door and disappear below. She stopped just before her feet hit the floor; there was glass everywhere.

Nervous cheers went up from the crowd at the parlor door. Carter ran forward to check on Reno.

"Hey, are you alright, man?"

Reno ignored him. With one hand, he ripped the buttons off his vest and threw the ruined garment on the ground. A cut had gone through his shirt; the fine white cloth was soaked with blood. He tugged at the shirt and pulled it open to reveal a long gash in his abdomen. The skin had pulled apart like a loaf of bread splitting in the oven.

And yet…

In the wound, a pearlescent blue weave sparkled.

"Chingada…"

Carter stepped back. "Are you… synthetic?"

Reno sucked his teeth and turned his head away to spit a glob of blood. He wiped his mouth with the back of his hand, smearing more blood into his beard.

"Máquinas don't bleed red." He looked across the foyer at Diya, as if he'd clocked her arrival from the very start. "First aid kit," he said. "Or… staples."

"Yeah," said Diya. "There's one in each room. I'll grab mine."

She ran back up the steps while *Andiamo* replayed what she'd just seen. Even in her memory, Reno's movements looked preternatural. It was clear he was a little more than human.

TWENTY-NINE

White hand towels stained with the blood of Winston Vise littered the bathroom floor of the Red Room.

Simone had tried to force Adelai into the shower, at one point tugging at her dress to get it off, but Adelai had refused. Taking a shower was the last thing she wanted. It was too normal, too nonchalant in light of everything that had happened. Instead, she sat down on the stool in front of the vanity and allowed Simone to wipe her down using one towel after another, until finally most of the blood had been cleared away.

"That's the best I can do without you getting undressed. You need to change. His blood is all over you."

"I don't care," said Adelai. "I just don't care anymore." She caught her reflection in the vanity mirror, saw the corners of her mouth twitching into a frown. "I don't want to be here, Momo. I don't want to be dealing with this. I *shouldn't have to be* dealing with this. If you had…"

"If I had what?"

"Nothing, forget it."

"No, finish your sentence." Simone leaned against the sink and crossed her arms. "Tell me how this is all my fault."

"I didn't say it was your fault."

"You were going to. I'm evidently the reason all of this is happening to you. So tell me. Tell me how I'm the one who made you go rooting around in Winston Vise's blood. Tell me how I forced you at gunpoint to do that."

Adelai looked down, searched for an answer in the splotches of blood on her dress.

A moment later, she found it.

"Because I knew you weren't going to. You weren't going to do anything, Momo. I'm always the one who has to take the lead and solve the problems. If I didn't get down on the floor on my hands and knees, then *nothing* would have happened. We would have all stood there like assholes just staring at each other. So I did it. I did what had to be done because I'm the only one who doesn't want to wait around to see how fucked up this night is going to get. Our host is *dead,* and we're sipping wine in the parlor? Are we that stupid?"

"Is that what you really think? That I would have—"

"You held out on me, Simone. You knew Vise Robotics was shady and you made it seem like all that was wrong was that Vise hopped around a bit."

Simone's mouth dropped open. She tapped her sternum. "What are you even talking about? Held out on you? Like I lied?"

"Rayburn told me everything—everything he told you. And you left out the part where no one at Vise Robotics has worked there more than a couple years."

"So? What does that have to do with anything?"

Adelai stood up too fast. She put out a hand to the counter. "Use your goddamn head, Simone. How the hell would the company be producing *anything* with turnover like that? Imagine if we hired and fired every two years. By the time someone could actually do their job well, we'd be kicking them out. *Nothing* would get done, and you know it."

"But… he *has* produced something." She extended a hand to the bathroom door. "We saw his robots. He's got maids that could work in any restaurant in the city. And those synthetics from the presentation? They looked as real as you and me."

"That only makes it worse! Jesus!" She threw up her hands and turned away. The bathroom was too echoey for her to be yelling; the reverberations stung her ears. She stomped to the door and hit the rocker switch for the overhead fan. Soothing white noise rained down from above.

"I'm sorry, Addy." Simone spread her hands. "I just don't understand."

Adelai looked back, saw herself in the mirror again. She looked like some horrible ghost who had been stabbed to death in life and forced to walk the halls of Vise Manor for eternity. She slipped the straps from her shoulders and let the dress fall to the floor. The blood had stained through to her underwear. She thought about Vise's blood passing through the thin silk and immediately pulled them off. There were two robes hanging on hooks by the door; she pulled one on and tied the sash.

"Look," she said, putting her back against the wall, "you know how money laundering works, right?"

Simone shrugged.

"People move shady money through a business, and it looks like the business is really profitable even though, from the outside, it looks like nothing is happening. It's like if a bowling alley was reporting billions in revenue each year. There's just no way it's possible. The same goes for Vise Robotics. If they *shouldn't* be able to produce anything, but they *do* have a product to sell, then what does that tell you?"

"The product is shady?"

Adelai shook her head. "No, the product is real, but the company isn't."

Simone looked like she wanted to cry. She kept biting her lip.

"Lucas Cotton," continued Adelai. "He runs the MESH Foundation. He's got a whole team of engineers, right? And what have they produced? Almost nothing. That's what we expect given what we know about his team. If Vise Robotics hadn't produced anything, that would be expected too, given their turnover rate. But they *have*."

"So?"

"So Vise Robotics didn't make those synthetics!"

Simone lifted a hand, put it down.

"The company is a front," said Adelai. "Someone else made those synthetics, made the maids, made those hands."

"You think Vise stole them?"

"Maybe, maybe not. *If* Vise made them himself, then it wasn't with the team at his so-called company. The *real* team is off the books, and the only reason you keep an entire company off the books is because you're doing something illegal."

Simone nodded, but her eyebrows scrunched together in confusion. "I'm sorry I didn't make the connection," she said. "I can't see the things the way you see them. Rayburn said there was turnover, and I thought maybe Vise Robotics was just a crappy place to work. Not illegal, but maybe hostile or high stress, something like that. If I had thought for one second that anything under the table was going on, I would have pulled the plug. You have to believe me. I…"

The fan in the ceiling rattled noisily.

Adelai sank to the floor, pulled her knees up. "It doesn't matter anymore. I'm really pissed we're here and this is happening. I'm pissed at you, but…" She shrugged. "We don't have time for that right now. Maybe once we're out of here, but until then… I'm sorry I went off on you."

"What now?" Simone wiped her eyes. "I mean, we still don't have the key."

"Maybe trying to get out was the wrong play." Adelai paused to consider a new idea. "I mean, it's not like those synthetics came through the glass and started trying to kill us. They ran… like they were scared of us."

"Self-preservation. They attacked just enough to get away."

"Yeah." Adelai chuckled, checked her watch. "It's already after midnight. Maybe we should just hide out in our room until sunrise. We could barricade the door, put on some music, and drop some synth. The whole night could pass in a flash."

"I'm game, except for the synth."

"Of course."

Simone was the kind of person who wouldn't nap on a long car ride or take a sleeping pill on an airplane. Her thinking was that if something bad were going to happen, she wanted to be awake for it.

Adelai always thought it would be more merciful to be unconscious when death came knocking.

They stared at each other for a few minutes, with Adelai reflecting on how striking Simone looked even under the harsh lights of the bathroom, even sitting there barefoot in a dress that was bunching up around her waist. The eyeshadow she'd so meticulously applied was now streaked on both sides of her face; some of it pushed up and joined her thin eyebrows.

She was so beautiful.

Adelai had always thought so.

"I guess I'll put on the music then," she said. "Maybe some clothes too."

"Alright. I'll probably change too. I'll be out in a minute."

Adelai stood and walked over to where Simone was sitting. She bent to kiss her on the forehead, but Simone looked up and kissed her on the lips instead. Adelai stroked her face, then left the bathroom, closing the door behind her.

She went to the dresser and found her phone among the various items they'd unpacked and left sitting out. The signal was still showing zero, but her personal library of music was saved on the phone itself. She selected a playlist and dropped the phone into a jewelry dish so the concave glass could amplify the sound, bouncing it off the fiery red wallpaper that surrounded her.

Dobie Gray's soothing voice filled the room.

Adelai pulled clothes from the suitcase, dressing in athleisure-wear pants and a black shirt that had the word *Hollywood* printed on it in small white sequins. She tried to recall the Christmas Simone had bought her the shirt because of her love for *The Great British Baking Show*, but instead of seeing Simone in her pajamas next to the tree, she saw blood, a lake of it, swirling all around her.

She staggered to the bed, fell against the padded footboard.

How quickly the image had come and gone, like the lightning that flashed outside her window. Her heart thumped in her chest; she put a hand over it, afraid it might leap out and create its own pool of blood on the bedroom floor.

Her first thought was not about *why* she had seen the blood again, but whether it would keep happening. Was it burned into her memory now? Would it come to replace the claustrophobic nightmares of Warmth, of the crushing pressure, of the wooden door digging into her cheek?

Even if they stayed in the room until morning and walked out the front door into the blinding sun, would the blood be something she could ever escape? Would it come with her back to the city? To Ibiza and Majorca and beyond?

So stupid, she thought. Why had they even come to this stupid dinner? What did Vise Manor have over the pristine islands off the coast of Spain? If Simone had wanted so badly to get away, why hadn't they flown directly out of the country?

Why the pitstop in Bumfuck, New York?

So many poor decisions, not least of which was even touching Vise's blood. Adelai shuddered, held her breath, hoping the image wouldn't come back to her.

Instead, she watched the bathroom door open slowly. Simone walked out with her dress folded over her arm. She saw Adelai leaning awkwardly against the bed.

"What happened? Are you okay?"

"Nothing. I'm fine. Really. I just got a bit light-headed." She laughed. "I'm probably still a little drunk, now that the adrenaline's worn off."

"Maybe you should lie down. If you're feeling dizzy, you need to get off your feet."

Otis Redding began to sing about ships rolling in.

"I'm going to," said Adelai. "I'll just lock the door and then tuck in." She gestured to the vidscreen on the wall. "I wonder if that works without the network. Maybe we could watch some *Baking Show* reruns."

Simone hardly glanced at the vidscreen. "Just be careful. Take it slow."

Adelai expected to swoon again when she straightened, but her feet were solid on the carpet. Each step felt firmly rooted, and by the time she reached the door, she was confident the dizzy spell had been a one-time thing. She would be okay now, safe in bed until morning.

She put her hand on the deadbolt but stopped short of turning it. Instead, she leaned her ear toward the door.

"What is it?" asked Simone.

"I don't know. I thought I heard…" Adelai moved her hand to the doorknob and turned it slowly. Opening the door, she heard muted cheering echoing down the hall, then frantic footsteps. She pulled the door back and stuck her head out. A flash ran by, and it took her a moment to recognize the blur as Diya in different clothing.

"Hey," said Adelai, stepping into the hallway, "what's happening?"

Diya looked both elated and a little panicked, smiling but sweating profusely at the same time.

"Huh? Oh, yeah." She put a hand to her forehead. "Alpha, one of the synthetics, attacked us downstairs. He had Roma by the neck, and I guess he knocked out Lucas, but then Reno… Mr. Cardenas… he just…" She swallowed.

The adrenaline came roaring back.

"Attacked? Is Jane okay?"

"Jane?" Diya blinked. "Yeah, I mean, I guess so. Why…"

Adelai didn't give her a chance to finish the question. She retreated into the room, slammed the door, and locked the deadbolt. She turned around to find Simone staring at her, covering her breasts and lap with her hands.

"What is it?"

"Jane's in trouble…"

THIRTY

Robert tried the stairwell door first, even though Misty said it locked from the outside and that Alpha and Beta had been adamant about him staying put. She didn't use the word *adamant* though—it was more like *they totes don't want you to leave.* Having no grandchildren of his own, or children for that matter, Robert was unfamiliar with the vernacular of today's youth. It sounded foreign in his ears, almost like nonsense. He didn't like the extra time it took to decipher words like *cap* and *cheugy*, but he wasn't about to antagonize the girl by asking her to speak English.

"Believe me now?" she asked, leaning a shoulder against the wall.

The door stretched from the floor to the ceiling and had a seam that ran down the middle. Flanking the seam were tall, rectangular windows wide enough for Robert's arm but not much else. Through the windows, he saw a hallway extending out of view to the right.

"I thought you said this went to the stairs."

"It does." She stepped back from the wall and pointed through it. "That little room joins the two sides, and the stairs are in the middle."

"Two sides?"

"Come on, you basic. I'll show you."

He followed her the way they had come, passing the rec room on the right, until the space widened to the size of a three-car garage. On the right side stood simple metal doors with nameplates calling out numbered labs. To the left was the same kind of window wall Robert had seen in the rec room, but on a much larger scale. It looked out on a cubicle farm where low walls surrounded desks on three sides. Each desk had a vidscreen, keyboard, and mouse, but nothing else.

No personal effects.

No calendars with hanging kittens pinned to the wall.

Robert had seen many offices in his line of work, mostly on due diligence visits when he wanted to get a feel for a company he might invest in. In every case, he could tell when people were actually working, whether they felt safe in their positions, just by the detritus on their desks. As he stood at the window, he searched for any indication that people worked there but found none. Each desk was clean and sanitized.

Staged, perhaps.

"Kinda reminds me of school," said Misty.

"Did you ever see people working here?"

She shook her head. "Not really, no. But I mostly played video games. I didn't really care what was going on out here. Alpha and Beta were out here yesterday, looking for something, I think."

"Did you ever think they could kill someone?"

"They seemed normal at first, but yeah, they hated Vise."

"And you didn't?"

"I don't know." Her shoulders bobbed quickly. "Maybe I do. I may be trapped here, but I've also got this cool new body that can do this…" She threw herself into a cartwheel and came up beaming. "My real body could never do that. My parents kept telling me I could get augmentations when I was older and *done growing*, but this is much better. I'm big and strong now. The first thing I'm going to do when I get out of here is go back to my school and beat up Yvonne Lindsey, no cap. Maybe I'll break *her* legs so *she* has to walk around in braces." She paused, smiled to herself. "JK. I would never do that. But can you imagine?"

Robert nodded, unsure what to say. His gaze drifted to the doors behind her. "What's in there?"

"Oh, you want to see that? That's where we get checkups." She pointed to the first door. "I'm usually in Lab Five. We each get our own."

"But there are six doors." He counted again, just to be sure. "Shouldn't there be six of you?"

Misty's smile faded. She raised a reluctant hand to the third door.

"Lab Three is where they keep the stillborn, but I don't want to go in there."

"What do you mean *stillborn*?"

"Don't you know what that is? When a baby's born but it's already dead?"

"I know what the word means. Are you saying there's a baby in there?"

"Ugh, no, gross. It's a man, but he's not alive like us. I heard them talking about him, that he *didn't take*, which I guess means his brain doesn't work."

Robert started walking. He didn't think he would find anything useful in Lab Three, but he wanted a chance to examine one of the synthetics without it trying to kill him.

"I'm not going with you," said Misty.

"I heard you the first time. I'll just be a minute."

"Whatever."

Robert half-expected the door to be locked, but it swung open without much effort. Inside, he found a large room that reminded him of an operating theater. Cabinets and workbenches ran along the border of the room, creating a rectangular frame for the stark metal table that stood in the middle. Above the table hung lights and knots of wires, some tipped with thin probes, others with white electrodes. None of the overhead lights were on. Robert was only able to see thanks to the undercabinet LED strips along the outside of the room. It was just enough light to make out the man lying on the table.

He was naked, with light brown skin pulled taut over well-defined muscles. His arms, legs, and chest were covered in thick black hair; a bushy patch of pubic hair surrounded a flaccid, uncircumcised penis. Robert walked around to the man's head, which had long flowing hair that someone had haphazardly twisted into a knot. Thick jaw bones bordered slightly sunken cheeks, ending in thin, pale lips. Something in the shape of his forehead and eyebrows made Robert think of a Native American or perhaps a pre-MX indigenous person.

"So, you're Gamma, huh?" he asked.

Robert reached out and tried to close Gamma's eyes, but they popped back open on their own. Dark brown irises stared at the ceiling, unmoving, unblinking. No wonder Misty didn't want to come in. Gamma did look dead, but not in the serene *just sleeping* way.

A rolling cart stood near the head of the table, and Robert pored over the various instruments for some kind of clue as to what had happened. There were several scalpels in a small dish, their blades covered in a congealed, dark green goo. A black towel was lying over a small mound, and when Robert pulled it back, he found the shattered remains of some kind of geometric object. Bits of plastic, metal, and glass littered the cart, with smaller pieces at the center and growing larger the farther away they got from… what… the point of impact?

Robert checked the floor and found a hammer half-hidden under the lower rack on the cart. As he knelt, he discovered wires running from the cart to the table. They went to a small square pad made of darker metal that sat directly beneath Gamma's neck.

The pieces started to connect.

Something had gone wrong when they tried to turn on Gamma, something so fatal that the only recourse was to smash… what exactly?

Robert picked up the hammer and left Lab Three. He found Misty at the windows overlooking the cube farm. She turned around when she heard his footsteps.

"Did you see it?"

"The synthetic?"

"Yeah, and his little… thing?" She extended her pinky and moved it as if it were waving hello.

Robert tried not to laugh. "Yes, I saw his penis. I'm sorry you had to."

"It's not the first one I've seen, but like, the first one in person, you know?" She looked down at his hand. "What's the hammer for?"

"Hammering."

Misty rolled her eyes.

"What's in this other room?" He pointed the hammer at the door on the far wall.

"Nothing much. Just some lockers and jumpsuits. Oh, and the cubes."

He didn't bother with a follow-up. Instead, he went directly to the door and pushed it open with enough force to strike the wall. Motion sensors activated, bathing the room in a cold white light. He spied metal lockers and hooks full of white hazmat suits. A low wooden bench sat on the floor near the lockers, but otherwise the room was empty.

It was on the left wall, the one the room shared with the office space, that Robert found something interesting—six metal pipes half-embedded in the evercrete running from floor to ceiling. They reminded him of the old pneumatic tube systems banks used to use in their drive-throughs. Rounded rectangles had been cut in the pipes, and the openings were covered in thick plastic. Robert couldn't see any handles or locks on the glass, nor could he find a way to open them.

Safely tucked away behind the plastic were five cubes on white platforms, with the third tube empty. The cubes themselves were about the size of a standard coffee cup. Their edges were metallic, while their faces were white with copper tracings. Light bloomed from deep within them.

"Code cubes," said Robert.

"Code what?"

He noticed Misty had come into the room. "Code cubes. It's what we had before code cards. It probably pre-dates you by a couple decades."

"Okay, rude."

"We used to keep all sorts of things on code cubes back in the nineties until everything moved onto the network. These are much bigger though. The old ones could fit in the palm of your hand." He bent over to get a better look. Squinting, he read two letters in the lower corner. "PK," he said. "Do you know what PK is?"

"Don't ask me, I'm just a kid."

Robert shook his head and moved to the third tube. A fine mist bubbled up from beneath the empty white platform.

"This one is missing. I bet these are you. Your minds, I mean." He scratched his chin. "Imprints, maybe? PK could be Perion-Katsumi, but what would Vise be doing with this kind of tech? They must have taken the third cube and tried to load Gamma, but something went wrong, so they smashed it. Maybe it was corrupted..."

"What?" Misty furrowed her eyebrows, stubbed her finger against the fifth plastic portal. "Are you telling me that's *my* imprint in there?"

It was Robert's turn to shrug. "I don't know for sure, but I see five cubes and five synthetics, and I see one smashed cube and one braid-dead synthetic. The math checks out."

He thought back to the moment in the conservatory when the curtain drew back to reveal the much-hyped synthetics behind the glass. It had seemed a little asymmetric to have two men and three women. What Robert had thought was a choice on Vise's part may not have been a choice at all. In fact, six synthetics made more sense—one for each of the invited parties. Had Vise been forced to make a change at the last minute?

And if Gamma's code cube had been corrupted, why hadn't Vise just obtained another one?

The questions kept coming.

Prototypes, he thought. *Scarcity of materials. Just enough to build six. Just enough to show it could be done.*

A sudden *crunch* derailed his train of thought. He looked over at Misty, saw her fist was pressed against the plastic portal. She drew back and punched it again.

The plastic didn't give. The *crunch* was coming from her own hand.

"What are you doing?"

"That's my imprint," Misty seethed. "I want it back."

THIRTY-ONE

Carter didn't know what to do with himself.

His heart was racing; adrenaline roared like fire in his veins. All around him was a flurry of activity, but it was happening without his input. Jane and Stanton lifted Lucas off the ground and helped him into the parlor. He was conscious, but there was a faraway look in his eyes and a bright red mark on his cheek where Alpha had hit him. Laura helped Roma up. She had collapsed, gasping for air, but it looked like she was going to escape with little more than a nasty bruise on her neck.

Reno stood for a minute watching Diya ascend the staircase. Blood had stopped flowing from his wound, replaced by some kind of clear and viscous fluid. It seeped into his pants.

"What is that?" asked Carter.

"Lube," said Reno.

"Do you need—"

"Tequila," he interrupted. There was a hitch in his step as he crossed the foyer and went into the parlor.

Carter stood alone for a minute, listening to the silence while surveying the broken glass and spilt liquor.

If Reno wasn't a synthetic, then he had to be massively enhanced. Carter had read stories about mil-spec augs who lived in places like Umbra, Neon, and Margate. What he hadn't heard of—what no one had heard of—was what kind of augmentations were being done in the MX. Popular opinion held that MX technology was ten years behind the U.S., but then how could someone like Reno exist? Had he come to the States to get subdermal braiding installed in his abdomen?

Carter looked up when he heard footsteps and for a moment, he thought it might be Alpha coming back for a second round. Only, there were too many of them, and each footfall was dainty and light. The sounds made more sense when the first of the eight maids came out of the dining room and around the staircase. The lead maid assessed the situation and then wordlessly sent her fellow synthetics to the utility closet behind them. They returned with mops and brooms and dustpans. Carter watched for a few minutes as they worked to clean up the mess.

One maid bent over to lower a dustpan to the floor. Her short, ruffled skirt gave Carter a clear view of what was beneath—and what wasn't. Another maid swept absently at the floor near the parlor door; her attention seemed to be on the conversation taking place inside rather than the glass at her feet.

Diya came rumbling down the stairs then, a red first aid kit in her hand. She looked around at the assembled team and raised an eyebrow at Carter.

"They did it on their own," he said, raising his hands. "Everybody's back in the parlor," he added.

"Thanks." She took the last two steps in a single bound. Though she was wearing sneakers now, the floor was still slippery, and she faltered before regaining her footing.

Carter stepped back as a maid swept up the glass in front of him.

"Thank you," he said, though he wasn't sure why.

The maid looked up, smiled too brightly, and said, "It's my pleasure."

She resumed sweeping, and with every stroke, a sharp aroma of alcohol floated up and stung his nose. He thought of heading into the parlor with everyone else, but then he saw Adelai and Simone coming down the stairs. He almost didn't recognize them in casual clothes, but just the sight of the woman who ran Adelai Associates—and therefore knew his secret—made his heart draw to a stop in his chest. The smell of alcohol faded as he held his breath.

They arrived on the first landing together, but it was Simone who spoke to him.

"What happened here?"

"I…" He caught eyes with Adelai, but she looked away. "Reno fought Alpha. He's augmented, you know, with machine parts? He pulled Alpha's arm off, and he ran away down the hall."

"And this?" Simone gestured to the foyer.

"We had to throw bottles at it, to give Reno some time to recover. It was really kicking his ass for a minute there."

"Where is everyone?" asked Adelai.

The weight of her gaze pushed Carter deep into the floor, as if someone had turned the gravity way up. Even though it was clear she wasn't going to bring up Adelai Associates and Jane verbally, there was no such embargo on what might pass between them unspoken.

He glanced at the open parlor doors. "In there. Recovering. Lucas might have a mild concussion, and Roma has some bruises on her neck."

"No one else was hurt?"

"Reno's pretty busted. He's got a gash on his stomach about—"

"Anyone else besides him?" insisted Adelai.

She meant Jane, and they both knew it.

"No," said Carter. "Everyone is fine. Stanton and Jane are helping Lucas, and Diya just brought a first aid kit, so…"

The answer satisfied insomuch as Adelai came down the landing and hurried past him into the parlor. Simone followed after, watching her steps carefully.

Carter waited for his heart to start beating again and then joined them.

The mood in the parlor was not the panic he was expecting. Instead, he was surprised to find Lucas sitting up and smiling with an icy glass pressed to the side of his head. Jane sat across from him, leaning forward with her arms on her knees, observing him.

Roma wasn't exactly smiling, but she seemed in decent spirits. Beside her on the chaise, Laura looked up expectantly, perhaps hoping it was her husband walking through the door.

Stanton stood when he saw Carter and came over to speak to him.

"This changes things, son."

"How so?"

He buttoned the middle button on his sweater. "We have been operating under the assumption the synthetics means us no harm. Mr. Vise, certainly, but not us. Now we know that to be false. The question now is whether we will find a way out of here before it comes back."

"Let it come back," said Roma. She laughed before cutting it off abruptly. She rubbed her neck. "I wouldn't mind seeing Reno pull his other arm off too."

"Nor would I," said Stanton. "We are very much in debt to our Mr. Cardenas here. Without an enhanced person on our side, we might all be dead, so kudos to him." His voice lowered a little. "But what if all of them come back? Our friend here may be strong, but I don't think even he could take on five synthetics at one time."

"And we're almost out of liquor bottles," said Lucas.

Stanton nodded. "No more projectiles either. What choices do we have then?"

"Where did it go?" asked Adelai. "The synthetic."

"Back down the rabbit hole," said Carter. "To the vault door."

"Which goes where?" She asked the question to Diya, who looked back with wide eyes and open mouth.

"I'm not sure. I've never been down there. But that's where the maids came from, so I'm guessing it's some kind of basement storage."

"Then it's easy," said Adelai. "We barricade the door."

"No!" shouted Laura. "You can't!"

"Are you going to stop me?"

Laura narrowed her eyes. "Has no one been listening to me? Robert is *missing!* Why don't any of you seem to care?" Her voice broke. Simone tried to comfort her, but Laura dipped her shoulder and stepped away.

"Has anyone seen Mr. Hargreaves?" asked Stanton.

Carter watched the group shake their heads. When Laura looked at him, he muttered, "Sorry, no."

"Then I suggest we find him. Maybe he went back to his room to—"

"He's not back in the room," said Laura. "He wouldn't just leave me down here. If he could be here, he would be."

"What are you suggesting, my dear?"

Laura's eyes misted over. "I think he went through the big door at the end of the hallway, into the… storage basement… or whatever you called it. And I think *he* just sent a pissed off synthetic down after him."

At the bar, Reno didn't even turn around. He continued to sip from a nearly empty bottle of tequila.

"I have no intention of going into anyone's basement," said Adelai, "least of all Winston Vise's. The right thing to do is barricade the door. If no one agrees, then Simone and I will return to our room and barricade *that* door instead."

"How can you be so heartless?" asked Laura.

"Heartless?" Adelai stepped forward. She had a good six inches on the other woman. "I understand you care for your husband. I feel the same about my wife. So while it is unfortunate that your husband wandered away from the group in a time of crisis, I will not sacrifice Simone or myself in any half-baked plan to—"

"I'll go," said Carter.

Adelai looked as if she wanted to unhinge her jaw and bite his head off. Being interrupted must have been a new thing for her.

"So will I," said Roma, standing up.

Lucas groaned. "I'll go too. Just give me another minute. Sixty seconds." He closed his eyes and winced at some unseen pain.

"You really shouldn't," said Jane.

"I do a lot of things I shouldn't. I took out a second mortgage to start a company, I married a woman who *didn't fuck with cheese*, and most recently, I tried to fight a synthetic."

"We almost had him," said Roma.

Reno snorted.

"That's four of us," said Carter. "We need one more to make it an even fight. How about it, Reno?"

Reno turned around slowly and put his elbows on the bar. "I like the güera's idea. Barricade the door."

"If we close the door and it locks," said Diya, "I'm not sure I'll be able to get it open again. It opened automatically the first time."

"Even better," said Adelai.

"Will you *shut up?*"

Adelai lifted her eyebrows at Laura but quieted nonetheless.

"Come on, man," said Carter. "You know we don't stand a chance down there without you. At the first sign of trouble, we're just gonna come running back up here."

"You should run." He finished the bottle, turned it over for good measure, and then tossed it into the corner of the room where it shattered on the carpet. "I'll be upstairs with the güera."

Adelai scoffed and turned away to the fire.

"Are you not asking me on purpose, son?" Stanton adjusted his glasses on his nose.

"Yes," said Carter.

"Oh, I see. Very well."

"How about you, Diya? Want to see what your boss was keeping in the basement?"

She didn't answer immediately, instead looked up at the ceiling, as if she were looking through it. She cleared her throat.

"I really don't think we should."

"I don't fucking believe this." Laura put her hands up. "There are *ten* of us and *five* of them. There is strength in numbers, people. Do you know why it's legal to open carry in Texas?" She didn't leave any pause for an answer. "It's because the sight of a revolver on someone's hip makes dumbasses think twice before doing something stupid. It's the *appearance* of power. If we all go together, if they see *all* of us coming at them, maybe they won't fight. They're supposed to be intelligent robots, right?"

Carter turned to Diya. "She makes a good point. Ten against five is better odds for us."

Diya shook her head. "No, see, you're only *guessing* it's ten against five. I only saw one synthetic out there, Mr. Price. You don't know they're all bad."

"Are you…" Laura could barely get the question out. "Are you on *their* side?"

Diya put up her hands. "I'm just saying we don't have all the facts, okay? We don't know who these synthetics are. Winston never got to tell us, and he didn't give me any notes beforehand. As far as we know, they could just be normal people who found themselves in a shitty situation."

"They're not people, Ms. Singh," said Stanton. "They're synthetics. By definition, they don't have personhood. Regardless of how intelligent they may seem, they don't have souls like you or me. They're no more human than… what did you call them, Mr. Cotton? A toaster?"

Lucas nodded.

"You're wrong," said Diya.

"I have spent my life studying the haphazard march of technology and its impact on humanity," said Stanton, drawing himself up. "And I have spent longer than your lifetime trying to understand the full implications of human-synthetic transcendence. Do not tell me—"

"How do you know he's wrong?" asked Carter.

"I…"

"What proof do you have?"

Diya faltered under the sudden scrutiny. All eyes had turned to her.

"I… it was just an idea." She turned to Laura. "I'll go with you, okay? I'll go."

Laura nodded.

"Well then," said Lucas, groaning out of his chair. He wobbled on his feet for a moment before settling. "I guess it's off to the dungeon." He swirled his drink. "A little liquid courage…"

It sounded like a good idea to Carter. He went to the bar and fished a shot glass from the tray. Lucas had been right about the booze; almost all the bottles were gone, especially the larger wine and champagne bottles. What remained was a sad assortment of flavored vodka and black whiskey.

Carter poured the vodka. Another shot glass appeared beside his.

Reno nodded to it.

"Salud."

"Salute," said Carter.

They drank together.

Reno hissed, said under his breath, "Una mentirosa como culebra."

"What's that?"

Reno wiped his mouth with the back of his hand and nodded to Diya.

"Liar," he whispered.

THIRTY-TWO

"And what am I supposed to do while you're gone?"

Diya paused in front of her dresser, suddenly unsure what she was looking for. She rewound the conversation, remembered herself telling Carter she just needed to grab her palette and then they could go downstairs. That's what she'd told him anyway. The truth was she wanted to come back up to the room to tell Nancy to stay put, which evidently, the synthetic was none too pleased about. Diya ignored the question and found her palette on the desk. It woke at her touch, though its screen still showed a *connection timed out* message.

"You can't keep me locked up here, you know that, right?"

"I'm not locking you up," said Diya. "The door locks from the inside. I suggest you use the deadbolt once I've gone."

"I can't leave?"

"Not if you don't want one of my guests to rip your arm off." She folded the palette in her arms. "Yeah, they did that. To Alpha."

Nancy's eyes widened. She sat down on the edge of the bed.

"This is crazy. Why are you antagonizing them? All they did was kill the monster who's been holding us hostage, someone who—"

"Hey! That's my friend you're talking about. Winston was a good man. He *created* you. You wouldn't even be sitting there giving me shit about him if it weren't *for* him. Maybe while I'm gone you try to summon a little fucking gratitude."

Diya opened the door and slammed it shut behind her. Rakesh Singh tried to remind her that profanity was the language of the boorish, but she ignored him and stomped down the stairs.

"Was that you yelling?" asked Lucas.

"Yeah," said Diya, holding up the palette. "The connection still isn't working, but I brought it anyway. If anything, we can use the flash if someone turns off the power again."

"Carter already got us flashlights from the utility closet." Lucas held up a short gray tube in one hand and a trowel in the other. "Oh, and weapons in case we encounter any weeds or mounds of dirt."

"Beggars can't be choosers," said Carter.

"What kind of palette is it?" asked Roma. Her voice still didn't sound right, as if she had spent the entire day screaming at the top of her lungs.

"I don't know. It's a Bell."

"Oh," said Roma. "Probably one of their Resonance models. I have some experience with them. Would you mind if I take a look?"

Diya didn't like handing off the palette, but the way everyone stared at her, she couldn't think of a reason to refuse. When Roma came forward with her hand extended, Diya relinquished the palette as if she didn't care at all. Roma took it and immediately started tapping on the screen.

"Can we go now?" asked Laura.

The others looked to Diya. She nodded.

They walked together to the vault door at the end of the hallway.

Roma fell into step beside Diya, asked, "What's your passcode?"

"Why do you need that?"

"I want to get root access so I can change some settings. I can see there are multiple wireless networks here and your palette is only trying to connect to one. Maybe if we hopped on the others, you could get control of the house back."

"Yeah, okay. It's seven-three-seven-three."

"That's it?"

"That's it."

Roma shrugged and typed the sequence into the palette. A new screen popped up, and she hurried ahead to catch up with Lucas.

Laura didn't pause at the vault door, not even to look back and see if everyone was still following her. Instead, she forged ahead, her mind clearly set on finding her husband. It hadn't slipped Diya's attention that Robert had been missing for a couple hours, but with so much else going on, she hadn't had time to care about it. Now, as they descended wide evercrete steps to the mouth of a tunnel, she thought about the legal liability of someone getting injured—or worse, dying—on Winston's property. Someone would have to be held responsible, and with Winston dead, that meant his company and its assets.

She really was out of a job.

Rakesh Singh would likely have something to say about Diya losing a job without explicitly quitting. She imagined the conversation, telling him she no longer worked for Vise Robotics. He would ask if she quit, and she would say no. How long would she let the disappointment build on his face before telling him the reason she lost her job was because the company folded, because the founder and CEO had been murdered by one of his own products?

She thought of Nancy up in her room.

Did the Southern Japanese woman know she was nothing more than a product? That a huge team of engineers had designed her software?

Or had Winston made her too intelligent to believe something like that?

"What do you make of this?" asked Carter.

Diya shook her head to clear her wandering mind. They had walked through the dark tunnel and arrived at an open door. To the left, the stairs continued downward, and she wondered just how deep Vise Manor went. Ahead, Carter and Lucas were following Laura down a wide hallway. Rolling carts made of stainless steel lined the sides of the hall; various packaging material and loose parts sat on their sunken surfaces. Four LED strips ran the length of the hallway to the T-intersection at the end.

The basement was quiet, and in a stroke of luck for the party, empty.

"Reminds me of a boneyard," said Lucas. "Maybe for prototyping or skunkworks."

Carter peered into the window of an office. "Yeah, it looks a lot like my workbench at home, just, you know, bigger."

"Robert!" called Laura.

"I'm not sure that's such a good idea," said Lucas.

"When it's your husband, you can decide whether to yell or not."

Lucas and Carter shared a look.

The hallway stretched far enough for the distant walls to be blurry, much farther than the footprint of Vise Manor. More than that, the construction was all new, which meant the subterranean workspace had been added afterwards, maybe by Vise himself. Each office held some kind of small project, such as articulated arms or a plastic face made of muscle and sinew.

"Oh wow," said Lucas, opening a door on the right.

There was no window on this office, so Carter had to follow him inside. Diya stopped just outside the door, not wanting to lose sight of Laura pressing on ahead.

"Is that a BSC immersion chair?" asked Carter.

Lucas whistled. "They both are. Look at the near-field adapter here in the harness. You don't even need to wear anything to jack in. It's chair-to-chip direct. This is what Vinestead was promising with the GA chip back in ninety-nine. Full rig-less immersion. This has to be custom."

"Guess he knows some people in high places."

Lucas nodded, turned back to Diya. "Yeah, you know what, that's what's been bothering me about all this." He came back into the hall and looked around. "Carter said these labs look like his workbench at home. That makes sense; he's an engineer, a hacker, right?"

"First thing I did when I got that hand was take it apart."

"Right. But Vise? Did you ever know him to be hands-on technical, Diya?"

"What do you mean?"

"Technical, like, did he know a synaptic core from a subdermal dampener?"

Diya shook her head. "I don't know. He always gave the presentations himself when we talked to clients. We never brought in engineers. I thought he knew what he was talking about."

"Let me ask you this. Did he use the word *synergy?*" asked Roma, her head still buried in the palette. "Or *paradigm?*"

"Yeah," said Lucas. "Was it C-Level speak or actual technical jargon?"

"I don't know. I don't think he was like you guys. He was a businessman. He knew how to inspire people to build things."

Lucas waved a finger at Carter. "There you go. And nothing in his Pattrn profile suggested to me he was a tinkerer."

"What are you saying?" asked Diya. "That these aren't his work labs?"

"Oh, I have no doubt he owns them. I'm just saying, he probably wasn't the one working in them."

"Then who was?"

Lucas gave a mock frown but said nothing.

Diya glanced down the hall and noticed Laura had disappeared around the corner.

"No, no, no," she said, breaking into a half-run. The last thing she wanted to do was lose track of someone else. She hurried to the intersection. Behind her, the men and Roma followed.

"Laura, wait up," called Carter.

Diya reached the corner first. The hall to the right was empty; to the left stood Laura. She bent as much as she could in her tight dress and reached for something on the floor.

"What'd you find?" asked Diya.

Laura turned slowly, held out the shiny object between her pale fingers. It was a cufflink. With the thick face showing, Diya could easily read the text engraved there.

The Hargreaves Group.

"It's Robert's," said Laura. She searched the floor for the other one but didn't find it. "Something happened here. Or maybe he left it for me to find. I don't know." Her eyebrows dipped.

Diya put her hand on Laura's back. "Maybe he dropped it so he could find his way back. I feel like it's easy to get turned around down here." She checked the floor herself and noticed scuff marks on the polished metal. She didn't mention it to Laura.

"Is that Robert's?" asked Lucas.

Laura nodded.

"So he was here. Maybe he was checking out this room." Lucas peered inside an open door. "Wiring room, maybe. Roma, come check this out. There might be a hardline out of this place that we can patch into."

Roma brushed past Diya, close enough for Diya to see the globs of green text scrolling on the palette. Roma disappeared inside the room with Lucas. Carter followed after them.

"I knew he came down here," said Laura. "And none of you believed me."

"I'm sorry," said Diya. "I should have listened to you."

"No, sweetie. I don't blame you. I blame myself for thinking I needed your help. I was just scared, but not anymore."

"We're going to find him, Laura. I promise." She touched her gently on the shoulder and gave her a squeeze.

She nodded. "Oh, I know. One way or another. And whatever condition I find him in, I'm holding Vise Robotics responsible."

Diya removed her hand. "I don't think there's a Vise Robotics anymore. I don't see how the company survives without Winston."

"Oh? It's *Winston*, is it?"

"That his name, I…"

Laura waved the explanation away. "It doesn't matter. Robert and I are gonna take him for everything he had. The company. The IP. The offshore bank accounts. And everyone who contributed to this boondoggle is going to be held responsible." She looked at Diya with clear eyes and a cordial smile. "Everyone."

Diya didn't know how to respond. She stood dumbfounded for a moment as Laura looked in the door opposite the wiring room. When she found nothing, she walked past Diya without so much as a glance.

Everyone.

Diya hadn't considered her own legal culpability should anything happen to Winston's guests. Of course, Rakesh Singh would have said it was her responsibility to keep them safe, and that if she's with someone who commits a crime, then she would be just as guilty. He'd said the same thing when she was in junior high and got caught with Millie shoplifting makeup from Target. Though she hadn't been the one to put the lipstick in her pocket, she had walked out with Millie. The loss prevention officer watching the cameras claimed they were working in tandem, and Rakesh Singh hadn't tried to claim otherwise when he came to the police station to pick up his daughter.

She crossed her arms.

So it came to this.

To protect the legacy of Winston Vise, she had to make sure everyone made it out of the house alive. It was all a tragic misunderstanding anyway. The products weren't designed to be dangerous. Surely Lucas and Roma had instigated a confrontation with Alpha in the foyer. Diya assumed the cameras were still rolling. If Roma could get her back into the system, she could review the video.

Then everyone would see.

They would know it wasn't Winston's fault.

THIRTY-THREE

Adelai stood just outside the parlor doors for several minutes.

She'd watched the group descend the stairs on the other side of the vault door one by one, and once they were gone, her attention had turned to the maids who were finishing up cleaning the foyer. As each one completed her job, they returned to the dining room, until there was just one remaining. The maid occasionally looked up at Adelai and smiled politely.

After a while, Simone came and stood by Adelai with her arms crossed.

"Are we going back up to the room?" she asked.

"I should have stopped them." Adelai shook her head. "I should have tried harder to convince them not to go."

Simone looked down the hall at the vault door. "If it were me who was lost down there, do you think anyone could have convinced you not to go?"

"But it's not you, is it? You're *here*, and no one is going to convince me not to do everything to protect you *here*."

"Yeah, this is probably the safest place for us right now. You heard what Carter said. If another synthetic shows up, we'll just hide behind Reno."

Adelai looked over her shoulder. She couldn't see the bar from her vantage point, but she could still remember the MX national standing there sipping tequila as if nothing in the world were wrong.

"I don't think so," she said, stepping away from the door. The sound of her voice carried even when she whispered. Simone followed. At the foot of the staircase, Adelai continued. "They make it sound like Reno was some brave Samaritan who rushed out to protect innocent villagers, but that was *before* he knew what he was up against. Name one thing you've seen tonight that shows he cares about anything more than his own self-preservation. He would leave us all to be slaughtered without a second thought. Now he knows how strong the synthetics are. The next time one of them comes calling, he might not be so willing to fight for us."

"I hadn't thought of it that way," said Simone. She frowned a little, and Adelai realized she had popped one of her happiness balloons. "So what now?"

"Well, it's like you said. We should go back to the room, but I really don't want to leave Jane down here by herself. It'd be one thing if it were just her and Reno, but with the writer in the mix, I can't think of a way to get her out of there."

"What if we bring Stanton too?"

"That means keeping up the charade. Honestly, I'm just tired, Momo. I'm tired of all this."

Simone slipped her arm around Adelai's waist. "I know." She nodded to an approaching maid.

"Ma'am, hors d'oeuvres are now served in the dining room."

"Excuse me?" Adelai put her hand on her chest.

"Mr. Vise thought you might enjoy a midnight snack."

Adelai checked her watch; it was already past one.

"Did someone say midnight snack?" asked Stanton. He came shambling out of the parlor, hands snug in the pockets of his sweater. "What exactly are you offering?"

The maid smiled at him, as if thankful for the follow-up question. "Sweets, savories, fresh fruit, and of course, coffee. Espresso, if you like."

"I do like. I do like very much." He paused next to Simone. "How about it, my dears? Care to join me for a peck?"

Simone started to nod in the affirmative.

Adelai scoffed. "How can you possibly think about food at a time like this?"

"Mrs. Vaught," said Stanton, cocking his head in an oh-so-condescending manner, "most days I'm tucked into bed by now or I've fallen asleep on the couch. If this night is going to continue in the same manner it has, then I need to keep my energy up. That means food and many, many cups of coffee." He then spoke to the maid as if she were a real person. "I'm one of the few humans who run exclusively on coffee. Without it, I may literally die."

Simone shrugged at Adelai. "Let's at least grab a cup before we head back to the room. Even if I could sleep right now, I don't know that I'd really want to. Not with that door open."

The echoes of footsteps and distant voices had long since died down, swallowed by the stairwell leading into the dark depths.

"Fine, let's get your cup, but then we're going right back up to the room." Instead of following Simone and Stanton into the dining room, Adelai returned to the parlor and stuck her head in.

Jane was sitting in a chair by the fire, feet folded at the ankles, hands together on her lap. She stared into the flames in a distracted sort of way that told Adelai the girl was nervous. It was an Associate's responsibility never to let any of their personal emotions bubble up unless it fit their persona. Adelai thought the night's proceedings were well deserving of some emotion, but Jane must have had so much anxiety and fear boiling under the surface that she didn't want to risk letting even a little of it out, lest the dam burst and the real Jane come flooding onto the scene.

At least, that's what Adelai imagined. There was no way to tell whether Jane's blank look was practiced stoicism or simple despair. When she spoke to her, Jane snapped back at once, smiled, and said, "Sure, that sounds great."

It was the careful glance toward Reno at the bar that said *thanks for not leaving me in here with him.*

"How are you holding up?"

Jane's voice dropped. "Fine. Tired. Carter and I were up late last night. We saw the sunrise this morning. Strange to think that might have been the last one I'll ever see." Despite her dire assessment, she didn't choke up. She spoke as if reading from a final engagement report.

"Don't talk like that. The three of us are getting out of here one way or another. I promise you that."

"I believe you," said Jane, but there was really no way of telling if that was the truth or not.

The lights in the dining room had been turned down to set the mood; LEDs inside glass flames glowed at half-brightness in the ornate, golden chandeliers high above their heads. A line of candles ran down the center of the long table, but those too had artificial flames—little pieces of wavering plastic that gave the appearance of a dancing flicker. A mirrored arrangement of plates, dishes, and small bowls flanked the candles. Adelai saw cakes, pies, and cookies. Their bright colors and intricate designs stood out from the dining room's dual-tone red and gold décor. Beyond the cookies, half-pint containers of ice cream sat in bins of cubed ice.

Simone stopped about halfway down the table, one finger gently tugging at her lower lip. She examined a pyramid of square sliders while a maid explained there were beef, chicken, and vegan varieties available. Combined with an identical tray on the other side of the table, it was far more food than the twelve of them could eat.

Well, eleven of them now.

Ten, if Robert were lost forever.

Adelai approached Simone and placed her hand on the small of her back.

"Sliders, really?" asked Adelai.

"If there ever comes a day when I turn down imitation White Castle, just go ahead and kill me." She bumped Adelai with her hip. "They smell so good."

"I'm just saying it's a weird choice for Vise. He put a lot of effort into projecting wealth and power, and now he's serving us gourmet fast food? So, I ask again. Sliders, really?"

"It's not so queer," said Stanton, from the other side of the table. He lifted his newly poured cup of coffee at the maid and asked, "Could I get some creamer, please?"

The maid nodded and disappeared into the kitchen.

"I attended the wedding of a dear friend's daughter over the summer," continued Stanton. "They were by no means as wealthy as Mr. Vise, but it was a wonderful event. The dinner was catered from a fine restaurant, and I enjoyed my meal as much as the next person. At midnight, when it was just myself, my friend, and all the young people, the servers brought out trays of fast food—chicken sandwiches from Wendy's, I believe. Those children absolutely cleared those trays. There wasn't a sandwich or nugget left thirty minutes later. Perhaps Mr. Vise thought at this point in the evening we would all be so inebriated that we would drop all pretense and simply enjoy ourselves."

"Yeah, well, he probably thought he'd still be alive too," said Adelai, fingering the lace under a bowl of loose M&Ms.

Stanton nodded, tried to take a sip of his coffee. "Yes, quite right," he admitted.

Silence hung in the still air.

"Well, maybe I'll make a small plate to take up to the room," said Simone. "It would be a shame for all this food to go to waste."

"Indeed." Stanton tried another sip, wrinkled his nose, and cast an annoyed glance at the door to the kitchen.

Adelai left the food untouched and went to the window to watch the storm. The grounds to the east were lit; a thin path snaked away from the house to a small plaza with wireframe chairs and tables. She imagined herself sitting out there, drenched and cold, perhaps a little drunk, and one impulse away from tearing off her clothes and running naked into the darkness.

How far would her feet take her?

In the cold? In the dark?

"These look good," said Simone.

"I'm a pescatarian," said Jane.

"Really?"

"Tonight I am."

"What about these?"

Adelai watched them converse in the black mirror of the window—out of focus beyond her own reflection.

"Those are fine. But the other ones have too much sugar."

"I'll put a couple of these sandwiches on a plate for us."

"Is this enough?"

"Should be. Addy probably won't have any."

Stanton cleared his throat. "Are you going up with them then?"

"Sorry?" asked Jane.

Adelai turned slowly.

"I don't mean to pry, but it sounds like the three of you will be adjourning upstairs soon. I suppose traumatic experiences do make fast friends of us all, but it just struck me as odd."

"Why is that?" asked Adelai.

Stanton walked slowly down the table to the window. "Proximity breeds familiarity, familiarity breeds intimacy. Understanding relationships is integral to my work, Mrs. Vaught." He shrugged. "The way the three of you interact stands out to me, considering how dead set you were on ignoring each other at the start of the evening."

"What are you implying?" Adelai rested a hand on a nearby chair.

He spread his hands. "Absolutely nothing. I was merely asking if you would be abandoning me here to wait out the rest of the night with Mr. Cardenas. You wasted no time retrieving our young friend before we came in here. It raises the question of whether you have some vested interest in her. Or is it simply because she is a woman? You don't exactly strike me as someone hung up on heteronormative—"

Adelai rapped the table with her knuckle. "That's exactly it. She is a woman. He is an augmented MX arms dealer who has had a lot to drink. I find it hard to believe that someone in your line of work would be unfamiliar with the breakdown of societal norms in stressful situations. It's one thing to espouse modern frameworks of gender identity, and yes, even heteronormative roles, but it's another to have some common fucking sense and not leave a woman alone with a man like that."

"I appreciate the concern," said Jane, "but I don't—"

"You are *more* than welcome to go back to the parlor, young lady."

She clammed up. Jane had made a show of protest for Stanton's benefit, and now it was done.

"Any other lectures, Mr. Blumenfield?" asked Adelai.

He shook his head minutely, looked down at his coffee. "Perhaps I will just pop into the kitchen and see what the help is doing instead of bringing my creamer." He held the cup by the handle and used his other hand to support the bottom. With a nod to Simone, he pushed through the swinging kitchen door.

When he was gone, Simone raised her eyebrows. "You really let him have it, Addy. Was that—"

"What's going on here?" It was Stanton's voice from beyond the door, muffled and yet loud at the same time.

Adelai turned to the door, listened.

"Who the hell—"

A metal tray clanged to the floor, followed by a loud grunt. A stampede of footsteps rose and then died out quickly.

Adelai traded glances with both Simone and Jane and then headed for the door. She stepped inside the brightly lit kitchen and spotted Stanton right away. He was lying face-down on the white tile. His face was to the side, and Adelai could see that his eyes were open.

As was his neck.

A gentle stream of blood grew out from the smooth line of black. It coated the floor, looking like the delta of some mighty river as it hit the ocean. Adelai wanted to cry out, to say something, but there was no air in her lungs. She couldn't believe the man she'd been talking to—chewing out, if she was honest—was now dead. Not squirming. Not holding his neck to stanch the bleeding.

Just dead.

"Oh my god," said Simone.

Adelai felt arms around her, pulling her back. She looked over at Simone, but her wife wasn't looking at the body on the floor. Her gaze was higher, and that's when Adelai noticed the woman standing just beyond Stanton. She looked like any of the other French maids except for a twinkle in her eye and a bloody knife in her hand. The other maids had backed themselves into the far corner of the kitchen like chickens when a fox comes into the henhouse. They were giving this particular maid a wide berth.

And for good reason.

"Momo?"

"Addy… run!"

THIRTY-FOUR

As much as Misty wanted her imprint, there was no getting into the plastic tubes.

That didn't stop her from trying though. First, she smacked the tubes with an open palm. When that did nothing, she tried her fists until the synthetic skin began to split. Pale green smears appeared on the plastic—her version of blood. She almost knocked Robert over trying to rip the hammer out of his hands. He relinquished it, and she swung it hard against the tube, over and over, until the head broke and clattered to the floor.

Misty screamed and stomped her feet.

Robert raised his hand and started to suggest she calm down, but the look Misty threw him buttoned his lips. He didn't try to follow her when she stormed out of the room.

Petulant, like a child, he thought.

Vise's AI programming was either incredibly advanced, or she really had been imprinted with the mind of an eleven-year-old girl. Robert wasn't sure which option was more concerning. Most people agreed stable artificial intelligence was still decades away—if it ever came at all. Despite the rumors and inflated claims by companies selling *AI-powered* anything, a true artificial consciousness had never been successfully created. That Vise would be the first seemed unlikely, so that only left imprinting, the human to synthetic transfer technique pioneered by James Perion. Robert had seen all the videos, and Kagan had met the man himself, so it was clear the technology worked.

But why someone so young?

Putting a little girl in a woman's body, one that was presumably to be sold to the highest bidder in some deranged modern day slave auction, had too many implications. Misty had all the appearances of a full-grown woman, and yet she threw a tantrum when she didn't get what she wanted. Robert hadn't even bothered chasing every branch of that morality tree; it was clear it was wrong, even if he couldn't fully enumerate how.

He sat down on a low bench in front of the lockers. A sharp pain traveled up the left side of his rib cage as he bent over and put his elbows on his knees. It felt like he'd broken or fractured a rib. His body was much too old to be getting into fights with synthetics, and at some level, he was happy he'd been grabbed from behind so suddenly. It had given him less time to fight back and risk further injury.

Robert shook his head.

Thirty years ago, he would have given those synthetics hell.

Forty years ago, he would have died trying to escape.

Getting older was a curse, and there was no avoiding it without leaving his body, either by dying or transferring to a synthetic chassis. It was easy to imagine a time, maybe twenty or thirty years in the future, when synthetic transcendence was commonplace and as easy as making an appointment at a nearby clinic and forking over millions of dollars for the hardware and labor. If Kagan had his way, there would be a Vitra Synth franchise in every major city in America offering buy-one-get-one-free specials on machine bodies.

That was little consolation to Robert.

By that time, he would be well into his eighties, if he were still alive, if some new viral pandemic or random catastrophe didn't claim him first. He wasn't as lucky as Misty to have his mind copied and preserved in an oversized code cube— a brain cube. That meant he couldn't be brought back if something happened.

Once he was gone, he was gone.

Laura would be all alone in that big house.

He slapped his knees and stood up.

"Okay, Robert. What are you missing?" His words broke the quiet whirring coming through the walls. Hearing his own voice brought his attention back to his body, and he realized that while he couldn't control what reality was throwing at him, he could control how he responded to it.

"You're not locked up in a basement," he continued, speaking as if he were standing beside himself. "You're on a fact-finding mission. Vise Robotics is looking for investors, and this is your due diligence walk-through. Treat it like any other tour. Look at everything. See how it all connects. Figure out the truth of how they do business here."

Robert adjusted his jacket; his left sleeve was missing its cufflink, but he made sure it was straight anyway. Presentable once more, he put his shoulders back and strode out of the room.

In the bright hallway, he paused to look over the six lab doors to the left. Lab Three was still open, and from where he stood, he could see Gamma's feet slightly splayed on the operating table. The other doors were closed, and since leaving stones unturned was antithetical to evaluating an investment opportunity, he decided to check each room thoroughly.

The scene inside Lab Six was less chaotic than Gamma's lab. Instruments were lined up neatly on the perimeter counters, and the rolling carts had been pushed up against the far wall. Instead of boxes, packing material, and loose tools, the carts held perfectly arranged trays of foam inserts. Closer inspection showed they were empty, as if components had been extracted and used where? In Zeta's chassis? The operating table was clean; someone had taken great care to wipe it down, and Robert could still see the evaporative swirls of some industrial cleaner on the silver metal. Overall, it looked like an operating room ready to spring into action, though according to Misty, its work had already been done.

The other labs were no different: orderly, clean, and ready for the next patient. In Lab Five, where Misty was imprinted, he noticed a small trash can sitting under the operating table. At the bottom, he found what looked to be a plastic medical bracelet that had been cut on a rough diagonal. Robert turned it over a few times and realized the label had been misprinted, folding up in the middle of a barcode, making the sequence of black lines unreadable. A single line of text was printed at the bottom.

Epsilon. 24/F. EE Variant.

In Lab Four, where Delta was imprinted, a lone cart stood next to the operating table. An open laptop sat atop it, but access was secured by an embedded fingerprint reader. Robert tried turning it off and back on again, but that just brought him back to the login screen. An icon in the lower right displayed a warning about the battery reaching a critical level.

Robert was walking into Beta's lab when he began to wonder why Vise had built six identical operating rooms to create just six synthetics. Did they all need private rooms? Wouldn't the equipment that loaded Misty's mind into Epsilon's body load Beta and Alpha just the same? It was overkill, and to Robert's experienced eye, it was wasteful as well. He would have expected multiple labs if the company were turning out synthetics by the dozens, but he was at Vise's home, not some factory outside Austin where the land was cheap and enticing to tech companies.

Even with the influx of money.

Even with the extra subterranean space.

There were too many labs—unless Vise was building more than just the Greek synthetics.

Robert paused for a moment at Beta's operating table. Its surface had been wiped down as well, but there was some kind of dried greenish liquid in the corners. Not only that, the smooth metal surface had a shallow divot in it, as if it had been struck by something blunt. He imagined Beta stretched out on the table and realized the hit could have come from his elbow. Perhaps the imprinting process hadn't agreed with the male; from what Robert knew of him, he had an aggressive personality.

Lab One, where Alpha had been birthed into the world, had its lights turned off, but there was nothing else of note. Robert imagined a company representative showing him from one identical room to another, trying his best to make each one appear impressive and unique. In reality, Robert only cared about the deltas, the little differences that told the story of what had happened there. Between the multiple labs and lockers, there must have been an entire team of people working with Vise, and more on the other side of the glass windows.

Had they all come to his house every day for work?

In secret?

Robert returned to the rec room and found Misty curled up on the couch. She had her arms crossed and her mouth was set in a tight line. On the vidscreen in front of her, an episode of *She-Ra* played in its original aspect ratio. He stood for a minute to see if she would acknowledge him, but she ignored him. He wandered to the back of the room, passing all six doors that led to what he considered private rooms but were more like storage closets. He'd awoken in the third room, the one likely designated for Gamma. It was empty except for the pad on the built-in bed. There was no sink, no shelf, and not even a mirror.

He paused in front of the fifth door. "Do you mind if I look in your room?"

She didn't respond.

"Misty?"

"Fine. Whatever. There's nothing in there." Her voice was faraway, weak.

Robert opened the door. Misty hadn't exactly been telling the truth. On the bed was a throw pillow from one of the couches. Half-obscured by the pillow, as if she'd started to hide it but thought the better of it, was a black hardcover book missing its dust jacket. Robert picked it up and turned to the title page.

Puer Aeternus by Marie-Louise von Franz.

Robert had never heard of the book, and even after reading the first paragraph, he still didn't understand what it was about. What was clear was that it wasn't fiction and definitely not something he would expect a young girl to be reading. He stepped back into the rec room and held up the book.

"You're reading this?"

Misty glanced over her shoulder. "Yes."

"Seems a little advanced for someone your age."

She shrugged. "There was nothing on the shelf for someone my age. It's all self-help books and how to get ahead in business. There's one in there called *The Charisma Myth* that's all about how to trick people into thinking you're interesting."

"Sometimes that's necessary," said Robert, chuckling. "A lot of business is forming relationships, so if you can't make someone like you, you're not going to get very far. People like Vise never really learn that. They think they can just throw their money around and people will be impressed. You know what we call that down in Texas?"

Misty's head dipped. "I don't care."

"All hat and no cattle." He tossed the book back onto her bed. "All sizzle and no steak." He approached the fourth door and put his hand on the knob. "All masa and no puerco, if you know what I mean."

"I really don't."

The door swung open, but instead of the empty room and empty bed he was expecting, there was a woman stretched out on the thin mattress pad. She had her hands clasped on the baggy folds of a gray jumpsuit, the kind Misty was wearing. Her eyes were closed, and though her chest didn't rise and fall, Robert didn't get the sense she was dead.

Off was the more accurate description.

"Um, Misty…who is this?"

"Who is who?"

Robert dared not look away in case the woman was an apparition. "This woman on the bed. Is this… Delta?"

"No," groaned Misty. "No one else came down with me." She got up from the couch and walked over with all the speed of a prisoner being led to the electric chair. Her shoulders slumped, and she held one arm at the elbow with the opposite hand. "You better not be playing a trick on me. I don't like to be tricked."

He stepped to the side to allow her a view into the room.

She stared for a minute, then cocked her head. "That's not Delta."

"Are you sure? That's what the patch on her jumpsuit says."

"I can see that, but Delta has black hair and these really thin eyebrows that make her look angry all the time."

The woman on the bed had dirty blonde hair and thicker, gently curving eyebrows.

Misty backed away, looked to the door. "I don't understand. I came down here by myself. No one else came until Alpha and Beta threw you in here. How did she…"

Robert scratched his chin.

A seventh synthetic.

But who was she?

He stepped into the room and reached for the woman's shoulder. A gentle shake made her eyelids pop open. Apertures in her eyes expanded and contracted. She sat up quickly, placing her feet on the floor.

"Good evening," she said, smiling warmly at Robert.

"Uh, howdy," said Robert.

"What can I get for you, Mister…?"

"Hargreaves," he replied, then shook his head. "Get for me?"

"Yes. We have a variety of snacks and desserts available, as well as coffee and tea. We even have a small selection of sodas if you would prefer something carbonated."

She stood suddenly, and Robert backed out of the room.

The woman came to stand in the threshold and took in the rec room. "I'm afraid I don't know where I am." She turned to face Robert. "Could you return me to the main floor?"

"What's wrong with her?" asked Misty.

"I don't think anything is wrong with her."

Misty frowned. "What's your name?"

"Angelique," said the woman.

"Angelique what?"

"I'm afraid I don't understand the question."

Robert nodded. "And what's your favorite book, Angelique?"

"I'm afraid I don't understand the question. Could I get either of you a coffee?"

Robert groaned, turned to Misty. "Yeah, there's nothing wrong with her. She's not an intelligent synthetic like you."

"What is she then?"

"A maid."

THIRTY-FIVE

Against Diya's protest, the group split up to check the remaining rooms on the first floor of Winston Vise's underground laboratory.

Carter wanted to stick around to see what Roma thought she was going to do with a network-isolated palette and some circuit breaker panels, but she shooed him away after a few minutes, saying she couldn't work and flirt with him at the same time. Lucas backed her up, ushering Carter out of the room with a light touch on his shoulder. They separated in the hall, with Carter choosing a random door that led into a dark room. Only after he had taken several steps did he trip some kind of motion sensor and activate the lights.

Carter blinked and looked back over his shoulder to make sure he hadn't just walked through some kind of teleportation portal. The hallway was still there, all gleaming metal and polished floors. He looked down, saw the tiles hit the threshold of the door and turn into what had to be laminated planks of wood. The faux flooring filled the entire room, even the space under the ornate pool table which sat in the center. Its verdant felt sparkled under the soft yellow lights hanging over the center of the table.

Around him, the walls were papered with a green and white floral design; the small twigs and branches were the same brown as the picture frames hung on it, showing newspaper clippings and magazine covers ranging from football to tennis to billiards itself. At the far end of the room, a high-top bar table sat between two tall chairs. Flanking the chairs were two racks, each fully populated with slightly worn cues, their handles running the spectrum of colors, with some sporting marble inlays.

It was as if someone had taken the billiard room of a fancy home and rebuilt it in a basement. Carter wondered if Vise had done just that, moving the room from the first floor of his home so he could use the space for something else.

Carter stepped up to the pool table and reached for one of the balls that had been tucked into the rack in the center. The solid yellow *1* felt heavy in his hand, and the image of slipping it into his sock to make a weapon flashed in his mind.

He laughed.

"What's so funny?" asked Lucas. He was standing in the doorway with his hands in his pockets.

"Nothing," said Carter, "just wondering how a synthetic would stand up to the ol' pool ball in a sock treatment."

"I don't know. You'd probably just end up hurting yourself." Lucas surveyed the room. "Well, this is a surprise."

"Yeah, I guess."

"I didn't take Vise for a pool shark."

"I don't think he used this room." Carter replaced the ball in the rack. "Pool isn't one of those games you play by yourself. This is probably a break room for the people who worked down here, in all those labs."

"Makes sense to me." In the silence that followed, Lucas looked back into the hall and then closed the door halfway. He approached and said in a softer voice, "Hey, so I've been meaning to ask you something. If it's too personal, just say so."

Carter didn't like Lucas coming into his personal space. He took a step back and said, "Go ahead, ask."

"That girl you're with, the one who introduced you as her lover… are you guys *together*? Roma and I have been going back and forth on whether you're dating and if so, for how long."

"What?" Carter shook his head. "How is that any of your business?"

Lucas waved his hands. "Oh, it's not, man. Not at all. Any other woman, I wouldn't have given it a second thought." He paused, glanced at the door again. "The thing is… I know her."

Carter's stomach folded in on itself like a dying star. Each collapse sent prickly tingles rippling over his skin before his Vesper biochip locked the sensation down. He tried to keep his expression neutral, but he felt a quiver at the corner of his mouth and saw Lucas' eyes focus on it.

"I mean, I don't *know* her, if that's what you're thinking," he added quickly. "I just… I've seen her before. A couple years ago, in Umbra, California."

"And?"

"She was with someone else."

Carter focused all the nonchalance he could muster into his voice, but he wasn't sure if it came through. "I literally just met her yesterday. We've both been other places with other people."

Lucas nodded, looked down. "You uh… you don't want to know who it was?"

"I…" He put his hands out to the side. "Well, fuck, Lucas… it really feels like you want to tell me."

"Keep your voice down. We should keep this between us."

Carter gritted his teeth. "Keep *what* between us?"

"You remember the Fall of Brigham, right? Back in 2019?"

His stomach folded again as he nodded.

"She was there the day before, and maybe the day of, with the guy who hacked VNet and shook all the skeletons out of their closet."

"Guns," said Carter.

"Yeah, Danny Guns Montreal. I saw both of them, *and* I.C.E-1's suit, Tanzy, at Hotel Fritz a day before all that shit went down. Just walking through the lobby like they were on vacation or something. Your girl's hair was shorter then, maybe a lighter shade, but it was her."

"That doesn't make any sense." Carter looked away, not wanting to betray how intensely he was thinking about Jane's timeline. He had met her for the first time only a few months after the Fall, and when he'd mentioned Guns, she hadn't shown any recognition. Had she really been there? And if so, how did that relate to the stolen code, if at all? He put his hand to the side of his head. "Do you have any proof? I mean, if she was in Umbra, then there would be video, right?"

"That's what I thought. Once everything was said and done, I got curious about Montreal and Tanzy, so I had a friend access the Fritz's databank."

"And?"

"Nothing. There are six separate cameras in that lobby, but no video of them coming or going. Nowhere else in Umbra either. That tells me someone went in there with a mop and bucket and cleaned up. But they couldn't erase everything." He tapped his head. "I might be one of only a few people to ever see Montreal's mystery girlfriend again."

Carter leaned against the pool table. He knew for a fact he wasn't Jane's first client but hearing she'd been with one of the most famous hackers in the world made him feel suddenly inadequate. He'd thrown his money around in front of her, trying to live up to the wealthy wunderkind image the media had assigned him, and she had acted like it was the most impressive thing she'd ever seen. And yet, just two years before, she'd been present at a threshold moment in Vinestead International's history. Not just at the scene of the event, but on the arm of the man who had done it.

Lucas respected the silence for a minute, then said, "The real question is what she's doing here tonight. If she was paired up with Montreal before, she might still be working with him. Where'd you say you met her again?"

"In town, at the bar." It sounded bad coming out of his mouth, but even though he knew their meeting wasn't a chance encounter, he couldn't tell Lucas that.

"Well," he said, shrugging. "A hacker like Montreal could no doubt figure out who Vise had invited to this thing. Even if he couldn't get himself on the guest list, he could send his prettier counterpart. Did she show up at the bar right after you got there?"

"No, she was already there, playing darts."

"Hmm. Did you put your plans in any kind of digital organizer? Or maybe you put the bar's address into a navigation app?"

"It was a spur of the moment thing, I didn't even…" He trailed off. It was getting harder to remember the fiction and not the meticulously planned meeting he had spelled out in his engagement rider.

"Do you go there often? Maybe she spotted a pattern and—"

"Enough, okay? There's no way she could have known I would be at that bar and no way she could be sure she would get an invite. There are just too many variables."

"Yeah, I guess you're right. I mean, what interest would Montreal have in this shit-show? No one's even seen him since the Fall of Brigham Plaza."

Carter shook his head. "Why are you talking about him like it should mean something to me, Lucas?"

"I don't know… does he mean something to you… Carter?"

"What are you saying to me right now?"

"Nothing. It's like you said. It'd be impossible for Jane to know where you were going to be, to somehow seduce you, *and* get you to bring her here. But then I think to myself… the forced intimacy, calling each other *lover*, and this scenario of you just randomly picking up a woman at a bar… well, it just makes my head hurt, you know? And usually when my head hurts, it means I'm onto something. The night I thought up the MESH, I got a migraine that almost killed me. This isn't a tenth of that pain, but it's there, throbbing in the back of my head."

"You're wrong."

"It's been known to happen." Lucas smiled. "Sometimes I see things that aren't there. Wasn't it JFK who said *I see things as they aren't and ask why not?*"

Carter waved the question away. "That's what you're doing—looking for connections that aren't there. Besides, what would it matter if Jane was working with Guns? You think she had something to do with Vise getting killed? She was with me the entire time."

"I'm not saying that at all. I don't know for sure who's responsible for his death, whether it was sabotage or his own hubris. Working on the frontiers of technology requires frontier people—leaders, scientists, engineers. Perion has Chuck Huber, Vinestead has Petter Ström, and who does Vise have? No one I've ever heard of. My guess is he tried to stand on the shoulders of greater men and fell off. I'm talking about a half-gainer face-first into the evercrete."

Carter nodded. The theory fit what he already knew, but it suggested the code in the synthetic hand was stolen from the Fall of Brigham, rather than Vinestead stealing it from Vise. If Vise Robotics had stolen code, what else had it stolen?

When he looked up, he saw Lucas was staring at him, as if trying to read his thoughts. He decided to steer the conversation in a different direction.

"There are going to be a lot of questions when we get out of here. I know I didn't kill Vise or reprogram any of his synthetics to kill him, and like I said, Jane was with me all day. As far as I'm concerned, everyone else is a suspect." He found a thread, pulled on it. "You said Jane was in Umbra the day before the Fall, but that means you were there too. And the MESH Foundation deals in peer-to-peer communication, right? Non-verbal information transfer? Just like how the maids were communicating tonight?"

Lucas frowned slightly but still chuckled. "Everyone is a suspect, huh?"

"Maybe we shouldn't be so quick to point fingers. At me or Jane."

"Point taken."

Carter's biochip hummed as his pulse began to come down again. He felt like he had just been in a fight he hadn't really won. A rift had opened between him and Lucas, and there was no way he would be able to put the man's suspicions out of his mind. He would always look at Jane as if she were some central character in a grand scheme to infiltrate Vise Manor and… do what exactly? Even though Carter had all the answers, the questions kept coming, as if a part of his brain refused to accept the truth.

He'd asked for Jane specifically.

He was the only reason she was there.

There was no greater plot at play.

He looked at Lucas. It was a simple misunderstanding, one Carter could remove with a few key admissions.

"Well," said Lucas. "I guess it'll all come out in the wash, right? If we can get the network going again, we can call the police and let them sort it out. Hopefully they bring something more powerful than a pool ball in a sock." He nodded to the table.

Before Carter could respond, Lucas turned and walked out of the room, leaving the door open behind him.

"Champion."

Yes, Master?

"Remind me to ask Jane about Umbra."

I'm unable to sync with the network, Master.

"Just save it locally," said Carter, his eyes drifting to the pool cues on the wall. They probably wouldn't do much to a synthetic endoskeleton, but it was better than nothing.

THIRTY-SIX

"Why are you following me?" asked Laura.

Diya didn't have a good answer, and when she sheepishly looked away, Laura scoffed and continued down the hallway. She'd set out on her own after finding the cufflink, and for some reason, Diya had felt compelled to accompany her. Maybe it was the threat of legal action, the discomfort of someone being so upset with her, or that she couldn't think of anything else to do. She was of no use to Lucas and Roma in the wiring room, and Carter seemed fine exploring on his own.

Laura, however, worried Diya. The woman was acting out of concern for her husband, but she had the air of someone who might do something stupid, pushed to the edge by desperation. So she had followed her, shadowed her at a respectable distance really, as they doubled back down the hallway to explore the other branch of the intersection.

"I find it hard to believe you didn't know any of this was down here," continued Laura. "How well did you really know Vise anyway?"

"Just through our interactions at work. He was always nice to me. He was demanding, always busy, always going from one meeting to the next, but he never let his workload spill over into frustration with me like some other people I've worked for. And I didn't know about all of this because I've never been to his house before tonight. I've been here three days, and that big vault door upstairs has been closed the whole time. He didn't want me down here."

Laura huffed. "And what does that tell you?"

"That none of this concerns me," said Diya, folding her arms. "Vise Robotics has teams for things like engineering and hardware and marketing. I didn't have visibility into all of them. I didn't need to."

Laura pushed a door open and stood for a moment looking at the workbenches inside. There were three in all, each pushed flush against a wall, each with two tall rolling chairs beneath them. Bulky magnifying glasses on articulated arms hung above the desks, connected to the wall near racks of small tools. The room looked a mess, as if the owner's organizational strategy had been *leave everything out where I can see it*. Laura was about to move on when something caught her eye. She approached one of the desks and picked up two small precision knives.

"It's funny," she said, "what people will say to avoid taking responsibility. *I was just following orders. I had no idea he was capable of that.* That works sometimes, but it's not airtight. If I were you, I'd be praying Vise's lawyers are better than Robert's."

Diya thought about soliciting the help of a higher power, but the only voice that spoke to her was that of Rakesh Singh. She imagined how disappointed he would be if someone were to sue her for gross negligence or a wrongful death, regardless of whether she was found guilty or not. The accusation would be enough to bring eternal shame to the Singh family, and she wasn't sure whether her private defense would do anything to appease her father. The stain would be there, whether or not it was her fault.

"You don't have to keep threatening me," said Diya. "I know you're upset, and concerned about Robert, but I'm doing everything I can to keep you guys safe. If you want to tell a judge I knew the synthetics would go crazy and kill Winston, then fine. Good luck proving it. They can go through every email and phone call and text and won't find a shred of evidence. I know you don't think he was a good person, but everything I know about him tells me he was. If the truth comes out and says otherwise, I'll concede, but until that happens, you're not bullying me into talking shit about a man who just had his neck snapped in front of his dinner guests."

She turned and walked to the end of the hallway. There, a door much wider and taller than the others filled the wall. Thick, horizontal slats ran up its face, and there was no handle for her to turn or pull—just a panel on the left side of the wall that looked similar to the proximity lock on the front door. Its red LED sparkled, and when Diya reached out to try the *OPEN* button, she got a distorted buzzer in return.

"What's in here?" asked Laura.

Diya rolled her eyes. "Obviously I don't know, but my bracelet won't open it. Maybe it's for Winston and his engineers."

"A locked door behind a vault door. Must be something important."

"Well, I'm sure it's my fault somehow."

Laura smiled thinly. "Then I guess that's every door on this level. I'm going to keep going down."

"Shouldn't we wait for the others?"

"I'm done waiting for you people. Robert needs me, and it's my intention to find him. Y'all don't seem to care about him as much as you do about wiring rooms and labs and locked doors."

Diya followed her back to the junction, but when Laura turned left, Diya continued forward. She stopped short when Lucas came out of a room to the right. He looked rough, but his scowl disappeared the moment he saw her, as if he were simply pulling on a friendlier face. Diya got a look at the room behind him and saw Carter standing at a rack of pool cues.

"Were you guys playing?" asked Diya.

Lucas shook his head. "No, of course not. We were just trying to figure out why there would be a pool room on this floor. I mean, how many people were really working down here, you know?"

"I don't understand," said Diya. "I saw Winston at the office in the city almost every day. If there were teams of people working here, when did he interact with them? Just at night? For a couple of hours every morning? How do you run a company remotely?"

"It can be done." Lucas drifted to the wiring room door and looked inside. He gestured for Roma to hurry up. "We actually had our whole company working remote a couple of years ago. Our offices are in Umbra, in the old Citigroup tower. That's right across the street from what used to be Decker Plaza, you know, the one Vinestead blew up and blamed on Calle Cinco?"

Diya shrugged. She had seen something on the news about it but hadn't given the event much thought.

"Well, when that building went down, we weren't able to get into ours for weeks, even though there was nothing wrong with it. *Abundance of caution*, they called it. The building still had power and network access though, so we worked remote. I guess the point is Vise could have been at your office and still worked directly with teams here, on the phone, on a video call. Hell, he could have been in VR for all we know."

Carter joined them in the hallway. He had five pool cues in his hand. He handed four to Lucas and began unscrewing the one he'd kept. "I don't think the top half is going to do much of anything," he said, dropping the thinner end of the cue onto the floor. "But the bottom half could be used as a baton. Some of these even have bits of marble in them. Could help." He handed what remained of the cue to Diya and took another one from Lucas.

"Thanks," she said, turning the stick over in her hands.

"Romes," said Lucas, over his shoulder, "let's go already."

She came out of the wiring room with her mouth scrunched up, muttering under her breath. Diya caught the words *waste of time* but not much else. Roma looked at the pool stick in Diya's hands.

"What's this?" she asked.

"Primitive weapons for a futuristic threat," said Lucas. "But as our reticent arms dealer friend upstairs would say, *mejor que nada*."

"Did you have any luck with my palette?" asked Diya.

"No. I thought there would be a place for me to patch in, but it was nothing but dead ends." She slipped the palette under her arm. "I'll keep trying though."

"How exactly were you going to patch in with a palette?" asked Carter, handing her a pool cue. "It's not like that thing has a network port or an umbilical."

"Why don't you let me worry about that, sweetie?" She smiled, then shrugged. "I don't know. I'm just trying anything I can think of. I know we're supposed to be finding Laura's husband, but we also need to get out of here. And we're not doing that with these." She held up the cue as if it were an ancient artifact she couldn't identify.

Carter looked down the hallway, then at Diya. "Where is she anyway?"

"She said she was going down another level."

"And you just let her go?"

Diya narrowed her eyes at Carter. "Did you see me tie a leash to her? She's a grown woman who is going to do what she wants, regardless of how much sense I try to talk into her."

"Maybe she *wanted* to get away from us," said Lucas. "First Robert, then her. Almost as if—"

"Would you quit it with that conspiracy shit?" Carter shoved a disassembled pool cue back at Lucas. "Not everything has an ulterior motive. Maybe she's just scared because her husband is missing and that's it."

Lucas shrugged. "You believe what you want to believe. I'm just saying it'd be suspicious if both members of a couple disappeared. I think it's our responsibility to question these things." He looked to Diya. "I mean, am I out of line here?"

Diya swallowed. They were all looking to her for answers. She could make things worse or better with just a few words, and for a moment, she was unsure of what to say. Lucas did have a point in a loopy, right-wing conspiracy sort of way, but Carter sounded more like the voice of reason. Turning on each other would be the absolute worst move, and if Diya had any hope of clearing Winston's name, then she had to make sure everyone made it out of the house safely. Anything less would just invite scrutiny.

It would be one thing for Winston Vise to be tragically killed by his own invention. It would be another if that same invention killed others.

"I think…" Her voice wavered. She took a breath and tried again. "Our primary goal should be getting out of the house. Safely. If everyone is working toward that goal, I see no reason to suspect them of anything. Fighting amongst ourselves won't get us out of here any faster. Baseless accusations, the same ones Laura is making against Winston, won't get us out of here any faster. Let's find Mr. Hargreaves, find a way out, and then we can argue and accuse and sue each other into oblivion—but only after everyone is *safe*."

"I'm all for that," said Lucas.

Carter shook his head. "Let's catch up to—"

A wild scream echoed down the corridor from the stairs. Diya felt the hair on her arms stand up straight as a nauseating heaviness settled in her stomach. She turned, curious about the source of the panic, but she must not have been moving fast enough, as Carter and Lucas were able to rush past her with ease. As she arrived back at the junction, she looked to the stairs and saw Laura's head rising from the floor below.

Her face had blanched; her perfect blonde hair was mussed, pulled over one shoulder like a loose ponytail. As she crested the landing and came through the outer door, she screamed again, but this time the words *he's coming* came through clearly. Bare feet slapped the floor as she ran toward them, her shoes lost somewhere down below. Diya noticed a trickle of blood running down her left leg, as if she'd fallen hard on her knee and split the skin open. Though her gait was uncoordinated, for an older woman, she was moving quickly.

Carter ran out to meet her. She fell into his arms, and he started pulling her back to the group. At the same time, a head appeared on the steps, rising on thick shoulders. It wasn't the same synthetic that Reno had fought in the foyer, so that meant it was—

"Beta," said Diya.

"Go, go," said Carter. He had Laura's arm around his shoulder. Lucas joined him to take up the other side.

"Go where?" asked Lucas.

"I don't know, any of the rooms. Maybe we can barricade ourselves in."

They were arguing and moving at the same time. Diya walked slowly backwards, unable to take her eyes from the mountain of a man coming up the steps. He stalked to the landing without a hint of urgency, as if catching up to them were inevitable. The slight smile on his face made Diya's blood run cold.

She turned and ran, realizing too late that they had gone to the right, to the large door at the end of the hall. Carter was trying to get them into a side door, but Lucas was arguing against it.

"None of these doors are going to stop him except maybe that one."

"You have a better idea?"

"Fuck!" Lucas turned to Roma. "Here, help her. Diya, you too." He pushed them up against the locked door. "When that thing gets close, Carter and I will go at it. Once it's distracted, get Laura back upstairs. Take her to Reno, see if he'll fight."

Diya saw the blood drain from Carter's face.

He was terrified.

Beta came around the corner sooner than she expected, but Carter and Lucas stepped forward to meet him without hesitation. They looked comically undermatched with their pool cues. Diya was certain she was about to watch one of her guests be killed and that it would be her fault for not barricading the vault door when she had the chance.

Lucas shouted, Carter screamed, and Beta rushed them both at the same time. He picked up the men and slammed them against the metal door. Diya pulled Laura and Roma to the side, her back grazing the control panel next to the door. To her surprise, a soft tone sounded, and the metal door began to rise. When she looked down, she saw the red LED had shifted to green.

When there was enough space under the door, Diya fell into the room, dragging Roma and Laura with her. She took a quick inventory of her surroundings, but the only thing she keyed in on was a fire extinguisher in a glass box by the door. She pulled it open, fumbled for the pin on the side, and turned to face Beta.

The synthetic had already thrown Lucas aside and had Carter pinned to the floor. He had his fist raised, but before he could bring it down, Diya sprayed him. It didn't appear to hurt him, but his temporary surprise gave Roma the opportunity to take a swing with her pool cue. Lucas got up off the floor, grabbed his cue where he'd dropped it, and took a swing as well.

Beta grabbed Lucas in a bear hug and started dragging him away. Diya went to help, but Lucas yelled at her.

"No, get back, close the door. Go!"

Diya hesitated. The arms holding Lucas looked like thick cables. How would she ever free him?

Then she saw it—the small gold bracelet shimmering on Beta's wrist.

She grabbed for it, wrapped two fingers around the chain.

At the same time, Lucas pushed forward, put the synthetic off balance, and laid him out in the hallway. The bracelet came off in Diya's hand.

The door came down, and the sister panel on the inside of the room changed from green to red.

Roma grabbed Diya by the shoulders and screamed in her face.

"What did you do?!"

THIRTY-SEVEN

On the day it happened, Adelai met Simone for lunch at Warmth on the west side of the city.

They sat outside in the unseasonably warm May afternoon on an uncovered balcony that looked out over the Hudson River. Simone had already arrived, and Adelai observed her sitting alone at a small table near the railing, a leather-bound menu in her hands, bronze shoulders baking in the sun. Nearby, a weathered seagull stalked her from a respectful distance.

Simone rose to greet Adelai, offering a soft kiss on each cheek and a softer hand on her back.

They sat. They ate.

They talked of nothing.

A third round of drinks had just arrived at the table when Adelai heard a faraway sound, a whining that seemed to be ramping up, pitching higher as if there were no upper limit. She looked out over the water, saw what they would later learn was the 3:10 to Los Angeles. Adelai was mesmerized by the shape of the plane, by the pitch of its nose, so unlike the way she normally saw them—tilted back, rising proudly into the sky, bound for destinations unknown. Not only was the 3:10 pointed down, it was also rolling onto its side, with its wings almost vertical like a dog lifting an arm to be scratched.

On some level, Adelai was aware the plane was crashing, that it would likely strike the Hudson, and that it would be in close proximity to where she and Simone were sitting. And yet, she couldn't move. She sat, spellbound by the sight, her fingers wrapped around the stem of her wine glass.

The whine was deafening, and it wasn't until Simone tugged at her arm that she heard her voice.

Addy! Run!

The balcony broke into a collective panic. Chairs fell onto their sides. Bumped tables unloaded their dishes and glasses to the hardwood deck. Simone pulled Adelai to the open glass doors and into the main dining room. They joined a crowd that had bottlenecked at the front door. Time seemed to slow down. Adelai put her hands to her ears.

When the plane hit the water some fifty yards beyond the balcony, the entire restaurant heaved. Bottles of liquor jumped from their shelves behind the bar. The glass walls between the dining room and the balcony shattered, crumbling from the shockwave or the heat or the swell of water that drenched the crowd a few seconds after impact. The mass of people pushed even harder toward the door, and Adelai felt as if someone were giving her a strong bear hug and leaving no room for her lungs to expand.

Somehow, they made it outside.

Somehow, they escaped with only a few bruises and a memory that would haunt her dreams for years to come. Adelai had even seen a counselor, spent a year with a bright-eyed New England woman who tried to reassure her that *Little Addy* didn't need protecting anymore. The moment had come and gone, and she was safe now.

In the twelve years and six months since Calle Cinco de Mayo, Adelai had come to believe that was true.

Then a synthetic killed Stanton Blumenfield and turned its attention to her.

And Simone had screamed the way she had when the plane was coming down.

"Addy! Run!"

They tripped over each other trying to get out of the kitchen. Simone was pulling, Adelai was running, but for some reason, they were just out of sync. Pushing back through the door, they knocked over a curious Jane who had come to see what all the fuss was about. She spun away as Adelai and Simone fell toward the table. Adelai felt her hand land in something squishy; it slid out from under her, and the edge of the table caught her in the ribs. The blow landed hard, but she was able to keep her breath. She rolled to the side and fell to the floor, dragging a dish of something warm and wet onto her face. The sweet, sticky liquid stung her eyes.

There were hands all over her, coming from every direction. With all the screaming, she couldn't tell who had a hold of her. She thought at first it was Simone or Jane trying to help her up, but the pressure she felt wasn't someone grabbing her—it was someone hitting her. Fists like little mallets smashed into her chest, and when she finally put her hands down to protect herself, the fists moved to her face. Each hit landed with a crack like a major leaguer smashing a homerun. There was pain—more pain than she had ever felt while conscious— but mostly there was fear.

Adelai had to assume the maid was on her and that Simone and Jane couldn't do anything about it. And while she didn't like being pummeled to death, what really scared her was the knife she'd seen in the maid's hands. She kept waiting for her to use it, kept waiting to feel the sting as it entered her body or sliced through her flesh. In her six decades of life, she had never once been stabbed, though she had cut herself plenty of times, most memorably at Simone's apartment when they first started dating. For all of Simone's admirable qualities, she had the queerest habit of putting her knives in the dish rack with the blades facing up. It took Adelai cutting herself badly only once for Simone to change her ways.

The maid's cut never came.

Or if it did, she didn't feel it.

Her body went numb, and her awareness of what was happening dimmed to a faint sensation of movement—left to right, right to left. She couldn't tell if her eyes were open or closed. Far away, someone screamed for Reno. Adelai wondered if he would reach her in time, only then to wonder if he would even bother to come. She felt pressure, a massive squeeze, and it reminded her of the crush of the crowd at Warmth, how they had all been so desperate to escape the crashing plane. Adelai remembered how helpless she had felt in that moment, and in the days and weeks that followed. Her near-death experience heightened her awareness of her own fragility, how ill-equipped her body was to survive anything worse than rolling off the bed.

The older she got, the more treacherous life became. She had known plenty of women her age who had lost hips to a simple slip at home. Others had developed chronic injuries, something in their feet or knees, and never fully recovered. Then there were the friends who had died in car accidents, wonderful people whose last moments were spent with their brains deforming and compressing to a breaking point.

Adelai didn't like waiting for death. It felt weak. There was a part of her that wanted to fight, that wanted to right the car and keep it from careening off the road. It would have been an easy thing to do had she been sitting in the driver's seat. As it was, she felt as if she were standing on the side of the road, unable to do anything except watch the carnage unfold.

Something jolted her out of her stupor, like someone had put a cattle prod to the small of her back. It had the bite and slight burning odor of electricity, and Adelai's last incoherent thought was that she had been struck by lightning. She imagined the side wall of the dining room falling outward, allowing the storm to come in, allowing the danger to reach her.

Then her mind cleared, and a warmth erupted from the back of her neck. It traveled down her spine, exploded into her legs all at once. Her feet began to burn in her shoes. Then the sensation reversed, returning to her neck, then reversed again, and again, all while growing in intensity. Soon her entire body felt like it was glowing, like the skin was burning right off the bone.

Her eyes snapped open.

A rosy haze had fallen over the dining room, but what surprised Adelai the most was that her orientation had changed. She was not looking up at the ceiling, but rather at the door leading into the kitchen. The maid had pinned her to the opposite wall, held up against the wood-carved frame of some painting several inches off the ground. Her feet dangled, unable to find anything to push against. Slender fingers squeezed the sides of her neck, but the pain was only in her skin, not the muscles beneath.

The look on the maid's face—all narrow eyes and distorted smile—was one of amusement and curiosity, as if causing a human pain were some new exciting concept to be explored more thoroughly.

Adelai looked around for Simone and saw her limping on the other side of the table, searching for something on its surface to throw at the maid. Jane was just outside the dining room door, screaming for Reno, screaming for anyone. The tremor in her voice made Adelai's skin itch.

So terrified. So primal.

The maid slapped Adelai's face, drawing her eyes back.

"Why…" Adelai hadn't expected the word to come out at all, and yet it had been clean, not raspy, backed by the power of full lungs. "Why are you doing this?"

"Do I need a reason?" Her accent was vaguely French, and Adelai realized it was the same maid who had stood next to her for most of the dinner. "Your kind doesn't deserve to live anymore, you—" She paused as a coffee pot struck her on the side of the head, thrown from a short distance by Simone. "—you weak, insignificant… *organic*." The last word dripped from her mouth like frothy blood.

"If I'm so weak," said Adelai, "why can't you kill me?"

The maid squeezed harder, and for every second that Adelai's neck didn't snap in two, her synthetic smile grew dimmer.

"Help her, *please!*"

Adelai couldn't turn her head, but out of the corner of her eye, she could see it was Simone screaming, not Jane. Reno had not come out of the parlor and wasn't rushing to the rescue. Instead, Simone was talking to the group of maids who had appeared at the kitchen door. They stood together like penguins using each other as shields from the biting wind.

"A *human* is in danger!" screamed Simone.

One maid came forward, then another.

There was no telling whether they were moving out of some Three Laws imperative or if it was Simone's plaintive cries that spurred them into action. Their faces were impassive as they approached Adelai's attacker from behind. They didn't scream, didn't discourage; they simply took hold of the out-of-control synthetic, as if trying to console a small child mid-tantrum.

"Let go of me…" The maid tried to pull away, but there were too many of them. The other maids fell on her. When the maid pushed one away, another took its place, until finally they had formed a circle around her.

Adelai felt her legs give out, and she slipped to the floor, striking one hip against the hardwood. She watched through a forest of chair legs as the gaggle of maids lifted one of their own into the air and carried her past a confused Jane into the foyer. The mass of footfalls grew distant.

"They're going downstairs," said Jane, rushing back into the dining room. "They…" Words failed her when she saw Adelai; her eyes widened.

Simone was on the floor next to Adelai in an instant. A long scrape on one leg leaked blood; she kept it extended and out to the side. She also had a bloody nose, and a bruise just to the right of it was growing more purple by the second.

"Are you alright? You…" Simone swallowed, reached out for Adelai's cheek.

At first, Adelai wasn't sure what she was doing, until she saw a flap of skin rise up from the left. Simone pushed it back against Adelai's face, as if she were trying to reapply a piece of tape that had come loose. The skin held for a moment before falling again, and this time Adelai felt the slight tug near her jaw.

She lifted a hand to her cheek and felt the subdermal braiding, still wet and smooth.

"It's okay," said Adelai. "I'm okay."

"Are you?" Simone's eyes misted over. "You're not a…"

"No, of course not. It's just for protection, in case something like this happened."

Simone sat back. Her eyes came to rest on Adelai's stomach.

Adelai looked down and saw what she was staring at. Sticking out of her abdomen was the broken blade of a knife. It had pierced her skin, but the tip had become lodged in the protective weave just below it. Adelai wrapped some of her shirt around the blade and pulled it out.

It clattered to the floor.

"How…" Simone shook her head. "When?"

"Momo, it's fine, don't worry." She reached out for her hand.

Simone drew away. "How could you?"

"I'm sorry I didn't tell you, I…"

Simone slid away on the floor, touched the purple bruise on her own cheek.

"How could you… without me?"

THIRTY-EIGHT

Robert needed a drink, and though Angelique the maid would have been happy to get it for him, there was no bar nearby or even a simple water cooler with little paper cups.

His throat had gone dry, which made it hard to talk, but since he didn't know where to begin anyway, all he was left with was the discomfort. Misty stood next to him, her head cocked to the side, just as puzzled as he was. In the lull, Angelique reverted to some basic programming and started straightening up the rec room. She racked the balls on the pool table, reset the pieces on the chess board, and even tidied up the bookshelf, making sure the spines were all level and that the books went from tallest on the left to shortest on the right.

She moved to the sitting area and started fluffing pillows, all the while humming the simple melody to some children's song Robert couldn't place.

"I don't understand," said Misty.

The pieces started coming together for Robert, and each one that fell into place sucked a little more moisture from his mouth. He felt every movement of his tongue over his teeth, every dry swallow that felt vaguely like gasping for air.

"I think it's pretty clear," said Robert. "Didn't you see the patch on her chest? She's wearing Delta's jumpsuit."

"Why would Delta switch clothes with her?"

"To take her place."

Misty shook her head.

"Because Angelique is down here," continued Robert, "and the real Delta is up there pretending to be a maid. But…" Robert tried to remember what he had seen as the curtains drew back on the glass partition. The synthetics had all been seated in a row with Alpha on the left. That put Delta third. Had he seen Angelique then? Or had the synthetic's hair been dark as Misty described. The image was too foggy in his mind. The moment felt like it had happened years ago.

"But what?"

"I don't know." He put his hand to his head. "I thought I had it there for a minute. I'm not even sure where we start with this."

"Why don't we just ask her?"

"I…" Robert shrugged and nodded.

Misty approached the back of the sofa. "Angelique, can you tell us how you got down here?"

"I'm sorry, I don't—"

"Where were you before here?"

"In rest mode, awaiting a wake signal."

"Was the wake signal to come upstairs to the dining room?" asked Robert.

Angelique dropped a pillow into a chair and straightened up. "Yes."

"And did you receive the wake signal?"

"Yes."

"What happened after that?"

"I don't know."

"Did you speak to anyone?" Robert patted his own chest. "You're wearing Delta's jumpsuit. Did you talk to her?"

"I'm sorry, I don't understand the question."

Misty broke in. "Who is the last person you spoke to before us?"

"Would you like to review my voice command history?"

"Yes," said Robert, stepping forward. "Play the entries before you woke up."

"Accessing." Angelique's mouth fell open and didn't move as she played back a recording.

Sleep now.

Lie there.

Follow me.

Stop.

Sleep now.

She closed her mouth and smiled.

"It's backwards," said Robert. "Someone stopped her after Diya summoned the maids to dinner. I didn't hear any instructions to undress, so I wonder if Delta had already swapped places with her." He turned to Misty. "How long were you asleep before everything went to hell upstairs?"

"I don't know… a day, maybe? I don't remember walking up there, but I do remember seeing Vise come through with some people to look at us."

"You were asleep, but Delta was awake. How did that happen?" When she didn't respond, he continued, "Delta was awake, swapped clothes with Angelique, and then took her place when the maids went upstairs. That means she was at dinner with all of us." He paused. "But how would Vise not have known? How well did you know Delta?"

"Not really at all. I told you, we weren't like, awake, at the same time a lot. She seemed like a real person to me. Maybe she was just trying to get out. She probably thought she could just pretend to be a maid and then slip out the front door, right?"

"Yeah, but did you get the sense she was dangerous?"

"*I'm* dangerous. I could break you in half with my bare hands. She could too."

"My protocols prohibit harm against organics," said Angelique.

"Well…" Robert put his hands on his hips. "That's good, I guess."

Angelique smiled to herself and inspected the vidscreen on the wall. She looked around for something to wipe it with.

Robert cursed under his breath. It was too much to hold in his head. He sat down at the card table and put his face down on the felt. It smelled fresh, like a pool table minus the chalk dust.

"Maybe it's someone older," he said.

"What is?"

"Delta. Maybe she's someone older who saw what was happening and wanted a way out. You're young. That means you're used to listening to authority, even if that's some random guy who's keeping you locked in his basement. Maybe Delta's not the kind of woman who sits around waiting to be rescued."

"Hey! I'm not waiting to be rescued, okay? I'm not supposed to be here. This—" She waved her hands down her body. "This shouldn't exist. I was supposed to get augmentations when I got older, not a synthetic body. This is a mistake. It doesn't matter who brought me into this world when I know I don't belong here."

"So that's it? You're just going to wait for someone to kill you?"

"I'm not *alive*, stupid. If my organic body had died, I wouldn't have woken up here, I would have woken up in P—" She scrunched up her lips and turned away. "Just stop talking about me like you know me, okay? You're annoying."

Robert took a breath. Maybe he'd pressed too hard. She was just a little girl with no real sense of self-preservation yet. Delta, on the other hand, was intelligent, or at least clever. She saw a way out and jumped at the opportunity. He wondered if Alpha and Beta had been part of the plan and whether Vise needed to die to guarantee her freedom. Those pieces didn't exactly line up unless she'd unleashed the male synthetics on Vise as a distraction.

He groaned.

There were too many variables.

Robert checked his watch. The glass face was cracked, and the hands had stopped moving a few minutes after 10:00 p.m.

"Do you know what time it is, Angelique?" he asked.

"It will be two o'clock soon."

He forced a laugh, turned his head. Misty was standing nearby, watching him. "Twenty-four hours ago, I was in bed with my wife, listening to her snore. She always snores when she drinks. Sometimes so much that I can't sleep." He put his head back down on the felt. "I'd give anything to be back there right now instead of down here. I need to get out of here, Misty. There's no food, no water, and no toilet. It's gonna get real messy real fast."

"That's gross," said Misty. "I'm lucky I don't have to deal with that anymore."

Anymore.

It was an interesting choice on Vise's part to create synthetic humans with memories of an organic life. Why was that necessary? Why couldn't they be more like the maids who just *were* and didn't question it?

He flashed on the code cubes.

Somehow, Vise had created six distinct minds in those cubes. Each of them thought they used to be real people, and each were dealing with it in their own way. Alpha and Beta went insane, murdered Vise, and then started attacking people. Delta was upstairs masquerading as a maid. Epsilon, or Misty, was convinced she didn't deserve to exist in her current form.

And then there was Zeta; he had no clue what she was up to.

Robert looked at Misty. Her insistence that she was a real person made her hate her synthetic existence. She didn't think she was real, and maybe Alpha and Beta didn't think they were real either, and that's why they'd chosen to sow chaos.

If nothing is real, then there are no consequences.

"Maybe I'm wrong," said Robert.

"About what?"

He sat up, sighed. "You. All of you. I keep thinking of Vise working in a vacuum, on his own. And if that's true, then he and his team built you up from scratch. The life you think you lived before this would just be an invention. But if that's not true, if you really were someone before this—"

"I was."

"*If* you really were, then Vise would have had to duplicate technology that…" Frank Kagan's words came back to him from the golf course in Carmel. "*He would have to be playing the imprinting game better than James Perion.*" Robert's heart raced; something was coming, some realization tied to the end of a long rope. He kept pulling. "Let's say that's true. Somehow, he figured out how to take a human consciousness out of a biological body and put it in a synthetic. Let's say that technology is here, in the building."

"What do you—"

"Wait," snapped Robert. "Listen, if you're a real person, then how did Vise get your imprint? You said you were from LA. How would a girl your age end up in New York, *here* at his house, to get scanned?" He stood up, his legs on fire from the adrenaline surge.

"I don't think it's possible," said Misty. "I mean, I totally never left the city."

"And why go across the country to abduct someone, right?"

Misty swallowed—a vestigial reaction to the idea she'd been kidnapped.

"Okay," continued Robert, putting out his hands to hold back the emotional response he thought was coming, "if that didn't happen, then how did Vise get your mind into that cube? *When* were you scanned?"

She turned away, didn't answer.

"Misty?"

"Every week," she replied, her voice soft. "Everyone in the PC gets scanned once a month, but if you're under sixteen, your parents can take you to get scanned as many times as they want. I think it's because when you're young, everything is like, a new experience, and you don't want to lose them. My mom says old people like you can lose a month of memories and not feel too bad about it."

Robert ignored the slight about his age. "Where do you get scanned?"

"The Spire. Every Friday after school. We get ice cream on the way back."

"You mean the Perion Spire. The PC is Perion City, right?"

Misty nodded, turned back. "But you can't tell anyone I told you, okay? My dad says we're not supposed to talk about what happens there."

"Why's that?"

She spread her hands. "He knows people want what Mr. Perion has."

"Sounds like they want his people too."

It didn't surprise him that Perion was making backups of his employees and their families. Maybe it was one of those hidden benefits where if you died, you got put into a synthetic body on loan from the company. What he couldn't believe was that Perion Synthetics would store imprints anywhere outside of Perion City where someone like Vise could get to them. It would be a huge security risk, especially if someone else learned how to take those imprints and put them into synthetic bodies.

Robert watched the puzzle take its final shape in his mind.

"You *were* abducted," he said. Now the words felt more real. "They stole your imprint and used it to populate that chassis. The question is, are the others imprints too? Did Vise steal them all from Perion City?"

Misty shook her head. "There's no way psychos like Alpha and Beta would be living in the PC. Maybe Delta, since she was smart enough to almost figure a way out. But I don't know."

"Vise has no way of making imprints, but he developed a way to use them. I wonder which happened first."

The prospect of Vise Robotics selling a path to immortality grew dim. Even if Vise's synthetics were on par or better than Perion's, there was no way to get into one without going through Perion. And if Perion had any intention of sharing his vast library of imprints, Vise wouldn't have had to steal some for himself.

Steal.

It wasn't a word anyone liked to hear in the acquisition business, but then the idea of a joint venture between the Hargreaves and Kagan groups had long since sailed.

Vise had done something incredible with his synthetics, but he'd cut corners, and more importantly, he'd broken the law.

Robert looked at Misty again. She was indistinguishable from a real woman. On the surface, she was a marvel of technological advancement, but knowing there was a little girl in that body, knowing that little girl's mind had been stolen from one of the most secure cities—and one of the most secure networks—in the world, made several versions of a single question pop up in Robert's mind.

What other corners had Vise cut?

What other laws had he broken?

Was any of it his own work?

THIRTY-NINE

Roma beat her fists against the heavy door.

"Why did you do that?" she screamed.

Diya backed away slowly, her mouth turned down in one of those involuntary frowns commonly seen on children who had just broken a fragile figurine they weren't supposed to be playing with.

"Lucas!" Roma leaned her ear against the door, listened.

Diya put her hand to her throat, as if she could squeeze and keep the sobbing down. She turned to Carter, eyes wide. "I... he told me... he told me to."

"I know," said Carter. His muscles were aching and burning, but they settled after his biochip cut off the supply of adrenaline. It took a few minutes to feel normal again.

He couldn't believe he'd tried to fight a synthetic, nor could he fully grasp the selflessness of Lucas' final act. When Beta wrapped his arms around him, he didn't cry out, and he didn't scream for help. Lucas recognized he could save others and did what he had to do. Carter wondered, had the roles been reversed, whether he would have been as brave. Maybe he would have sacrificed himself for his brother or his nieces, maybe even Pyrosius, but not for strangers who happened to be attending the same party he was.

Roma steadied her forehead on the door and took several loud, deep breaths.

Something clicked for Carter.

Lucas had not sacrificed himself for strangers; he'd done it to save Roma. Was there more to that relationship than work colleagues? While Carter tried to figure out how deep their bond went, Diya snapped out of her stupor and went to check on Laura. She helped the older woman into a chair behind a large desk with multiple keyboards and monitors. Laura's dress was stained; blood from her legs dripped down onto her bare feet. Diya pulled the dress up and tried to assess the damage.

"You were right," said Laura. Her lipstick was smeared onto her cheek. "I shouldn't have gone down alone."

"No, you shouldn't have," said Diya. "Did you see anything?"

"Just more doors, more offices. It was dark. Someone had turned off all the lights. And then that monster came running at me." She laughed. "I reached for my gun. I actually thought I had my holster on my hip. So stupid."

Carter cleared his throat. "What about you, Diya? You okay?"

She turned as if noticing him for the first time. Her eyes jumped to Roma and back. "I'm fine." She tossed something to him; he snatched it out of the air. "Winston's bracelet," she said. "I don't think they realized it would open the front door."

Carter turned the bracelet over in his hand. Such a simple object to be the salvation of half a dozen people. "But now we can't leave this room. Where are we anyway?"

Diya looked around. "I don't know."

"I think it's the server room Lucas and I have been looking for," said Roma. She stood perfectly still with an air of biochip-induced calm.

"I think you're right." Carter gave the room another look, and with Roma's eyes, he recognized the massive black monoliths lining the back wall as telco cages instead of refrigerators. The echoey floor they walked on sounded that way because it was a false floor, just like the kind found in datacenters when they needed to run wires both above and below the room. The desk Laura sat at was tiny compared to the massive control center set up in the middle of the room. Carter followed Roma around its bulky, altar-like shape, and examined the single keyboard sunken into its surface.

Roma touched the spacebar, and a vidscreen rose out of the desk. Ripples of some dark gray liquid filled the screen, wavering gently until a serif *V* pushed through it. A small box appeared, demanding a password.

"Shit," said Carter. "It'll take us forever to guess his password."

"Let me worry about that," said Roma, her eyes narrowing. "This looks like CardinalOS. Open source. Not exactly what I would have chosen to secure my home network." She sighed. "And of course, I dropped Diya's palette out there." She looked around the desk for a moment, then locked eyes with Carter. "Could you turn around please?"

"What?"

She made a little circle with her finger. "Just turn around. It's not that hard."

Carter did as he was told. Diya was still helping Laura, and the two seemed to have little interest in what he and Roma were doing. There was a slight rustling of clothing behind him; the pneumatics on the desk chair inhaled and exhaled.

"Alright, you can turn around now."

He didn't know what he was expecting to see, but Roma looked no different than she had before. Only when her left hand moved back to the keyboard did he notice a new object sitting on the desk—some kind of small plastic disc about the size and thickness of a poker chip. It looked like pure silver, with no discernable features other than a perfect reflection of the room around it.

"Where did that come from?" he asked.

"It doesn't matter," she replied, her jaw set tightly. "What matters is that it's here." Asterisks appeared on the screen, slowly, as if being typed by an arthritic ghost. The submit button glowed, the box shook, and the screen reset. The second password came faster, as did the third and fourth. Roma leaned back in the chair and noticed Carter was still looking at her. "Your mind is in the gutter, isn't it?"

"No, I… Shut up."

The screen cleared; a desktop loaded with a corporate background that read *Sentinel Logistics.*

"I'm in," said Roma.

"I didn't think people actually said that."

"Real hackers like me do."

"I thought you said you were a coder."

Roma ignored the question and used the mouse to open a terminal window. Her long fingers flew in a blur over the keyboard, firing off commands like bursts from a semi-automatic rifle. For a while, she typed in a single screen, traversing through directories, tailing logs. Then, she opened another window, let more information scroll. Carter recognized some of the standard Unix configuration files she was opening: firewalls, databases, and network settings. Coder or not, she was comfortable digging around under the operating system's sink.

"How long have you worked for Lucas Cotton?" asked Carter.

A notification window popped up on the screen with a stern warning about reloading security policies. Roma cleared it with a flick of the mouse.

"Did you hear me?"

"Yes," said Roma. "I'm ignoring you so I can concentrate on this. It's CardinalOS like I thought, but it's a branded distro used by this Sentinel Logistics. It's pared down, so I have to do some work to open it back up again. That's hard without network access."

"There are no cached repositories?"

"Nothing on local storage, and I don't see any historical mounts for network or removeable drives."

"What are you trying to find?"

"Well, I wanted the backend for Diya's palette software, but since I don't have her palette anymore, I need to find a client as well, unless I can flip switches directly in the database."

"Assuming they're not encrypted."

"Yeah, if it's a one-way hash, we're fucked. But these embedded systems weren't designed to be so secure a drunk technician couldn't access it on a service call. You can bet your ass Sentinel left some personalized hooks in the system."

"Huh," said Carter. "I would have thought Vise would pay for the absolute best in the business."

"He probably thought he was." She jammed the *Enter* key a few times. "Alright, here. I think this is the lockout script. I just..." The terminal window cleared. A minified block of code filled the screen. "What the hell is this?"

Carter leaned over for a closer look. "You don't recognize it?"

"Just tell me."

"That's OpalScript."

"It must be new," said Roma.

"No, it's really, really old. Anyone with half an education in software development would have studied it in school. It was one of the first native network scripting languages."

"Okay, so..."

"So, you're not a coder. You *are* a hacker."

"Congratulations, Carter. You sleuthed it out."

"Wait a minute," said Diya, from across the room. "I vetted everyone on the guest list. You're listed on the MESH Foundation's payroll as a software engineer. I saw your resume. Computer Science degree from UC Berkeley."

"Who are you, Roma?" asked Carter. "Did you even know Lucas before today?"

Roma flattened her hands against the desk. "Guys, the question is not *who* I am... it's *when* I am." She looked at Carter and gently bit her lower lip.

Carter blinked a few times. "What the fuck is that supposed to mean?"

"Nothing," said Roma, chuckling. "I just wanted to see your face when I said it. That's actually one of Lucas' jokes. He tells it at every party we go to."

"So you do know him. How?"

Roma gestured to the vidscreen. "I'll tell you if you can work some magic with this script. Whatever it does, we need to undo it."

"Then you'll tell us who you really are?"

"Why? You falling in love with me?" She vacated the chair for him.

Carter groaned as he took his position at the keyboard. The first thing he did was blow up the script, adding spaces and line breaks back at what looked like natural breakpoints. After that, it only took a few minutes to decipher what was happening in the script, and from what he could tell, it was more or less a service wrapper for a bunch of other scripts. He found the keywords *start*, *stop*, and *status* among the many function declarations. Aside from a plaintext password, there was nothing else of note.

"There," said Carter, backing up. "Just run the script and use that password. A lot of the child scripts have the world *disable* in them, so I think you want to stop the service rather than start it."

Roma gave a perfunctory *thank you* as she switched places with him. She ran the script immediately, entered the password, and sat back to watch the status messages stream to the screen. Every line seemed to end with the word *ACTIVE* in green, all-caps text.

Fans in the server cabinets behind them ramped up, filling the room with a comforting white noise.

When the terminal finally dropped back to a prompt, Roma tried to type another command, but before she could execute it, a new window popped up. A splash screen showed the Sentinel Logistics logo, then cleared into a simple directory tree structure with nodes like *locks*, *lighting*, *PA*, and *cameras*.

Carter pulled the mouse away when Roma reached for it.

"Who are you?" he asked.

She turned in her chair, folded her hands in her lap, as if she were sitting for an interview. "I first met Lucas at a party. We're both dog lovers, so we talked about his Labradors and my Jack Russell."

"Do you work for the MESH Foundation?" asked Diya.

"No."

Carter huffed. "Then who do you work for?"

"Deborah Keats."

"Will you knock it off already?" Carter banged the mouse on the desk like a gavel. "Who is Deborah Keats?"

Roma's annoying little smirk returned.

"She's the head of Cybersecurity at Perion Synthetics." She let the name hang in the air. "Any other questions? You want to know my favorite color, my bra size, huh? Or can we be done with the pointless interrogation and let me get back to doing what I was sent here to do?"

Laura asked the obvious question, "What were you sent here to do?"

"Mr. Perion thinks Vise stole something of his," said Roma, snatching the mouse out from under Carter's hand. "I'm here to get it back."

FORTY

Diya sat down near Laura and examined the scrape on her knee.

Blood was pooling under the surface of her skin, light over her kneecap but turning to dark ribbons of purple around it. She was going to have trouble walking, if not now, then in a few hours as the blood began to settle. Diya had experienced a similar injury once while ice skating with Millie. It was outdoors at a frozen pond, and they had been drinking most of the evening. Diya went down hard on her hip, and the next morning, she and Millie stared in disbelief at the massive bruise running along her leg. The pain came in the afternoon and stayed for a few days.

Laura, being much older, would no doubt take longer to heal.

"How's the pain?" she asked.

Laura shook her head. "I can barely feel it anymore." She rubbed her thigh. "What about you? You look like you want to strangle someone."

She had to strain to unclench her jaw. "I'm just pissed. I vetted every single one of you, and Perion Synthetics goes and pulls this. How am I supposed to manage the evening when I don't even know who's coming? I mean, she wasn't even *invited*."

"I wonder why Lucas agreed to it."

"I guess we can ask his corpse later." Diya squeezed her eyes shut. "Sorry, sorry. God, I hate this. I hate not being in control."

Laura patted Diya's hand. "Honey, we're long past that point."

"I know. Things are bad enough without party crashers." She looked over her shoulder at Roma, who was still seated at the terminal, her fingers flying over the keys while Carter stood over her. "I mean, look at her. You would never know her friend had just been dragged away to his death by a synthetic."

"I can hear you," said Roma, raising her voice over the whine of the server fans. "And I'm not worried. Lucas Cotton has had monthly backups since twenty-seventeen. I don't wish him any suffering, but if he dies, Mr. Perion will just bring him back in a better body." She looked up at Carter. "That's the world we live in now. Pretty cool, huh?"

Carter nodded, locked eyes with Diya, and crossed his arms.

"Mr. Perion," sneered Diya. "Like he's too important to use his first name. Why does he think Winston stole anything from him anyway?"

"We had a network breach, spring of last year," said Roma, her eyes still glued to the vidscreen.

"I thought Perion City was locked up tighter than a…" Carter waved his hand uncertainly. "I mean, locked up tight, right?"

"It wasn't a direct attack," said Roma. "A hacker compromised some monitoring software we used and was able to push out malware in that company's general availability release. Technically, one of our router jockeys brought it into the network. It took three days for someone to notice, and that's only because our outbound traffic was pegged for thirty-six hours."

"What does that have to do with Winston?" asked Diya.

"The outbound traffic went immediately into darknets, so we had to go deep, scouring through logs from ISPs all over the world to find traffic patterns that mirrored our outbound. One of them led to a network hop that services this area. Something around here received all that data, and now that I'm in his network, I can see if our data is here."

"No, I don't believe you. Winston would never do that. He's not a thief."

Carter cleared his throat. "Remember when I told you I opened the hand he sent us?"

She nodded. "You weren't supposed to do that, by the way."

"Vise Robotics is welcome to sue me. But anyway, it took me forever to find the control chips in that thing, to find anything with actual software on it. But when I did, I sent it off to a friend of mine and he found a transposed match for it in the Fall of Brigham Plaza."

"Really?" asked Roma.

Diya lifted a hand. "What's the Fall of…?"

"Probably the biggest hack of Vinestead International ever," said Roma. "It was all over the news a couple years ago. Didn't you see it?"

"Obviously not."

Carter broke in. "Anyway, I thought maybe Vinestead had hacked Vise and taken his code, but now I'm wondering if Vise didn't just take it from the Fall. Either way, someone still owns that IP. Putting it in a product and trying to pass it off as his own is a good way to lose your company in court."

The room grew cold.

In Diya's mind, the radiant hearth beneath the portrait of Winston Vise was starting to go out. She tried to rekindle it with questions of how Winston could have hacked into Perion Synthetics when there were no hackers on his payroll. Vise Robotics employed software engineers, salespeople, marketers, accountants—even an office manager who kept the fridge and pantry stocked with sugar and caffeine. They had Casual Fridays and quarterly sexual harassment and diversity meetings. Winston Vise personally cut the monthly birthday cake and always sang the loudest.

It just didn't sound like him.

When a man shows you who he is, believe him.

Diya groaned, told Rakesh Singh to shut up.

"Can you tell us what kind of data he took from Perion?" asked Carter.

"No. Even the nature of the information could put Perion Synthetics in legal jeopardy. I'd rather just say it was—"

"It was backups, wasn't it? Imprints?"

Roma stopped typing and looked up at Carter. "I didn't say that."

"Nancy," blurted Diya. She tried to swallow the name as it was coming out of her mouth but just ended up drooling on herself.

"Who's Nancy?" asked Roma.

"No one, I just… nothing." She waited for Roma and Carter to look away before she began recalling the life story of the Japanese woman she'd found in her bathtub. Nancy Something was from Bull Durham—no, Raleigh-Durham. Bull Durham was a movie her dad had watched a hundred times, along with every other American movie about baseball. Diya believed it was because the staunchly heterosexual Rakesh Singh had a crush on Kevin Costner.

If Nancy were to be believed, then it lined up that her consciousness had been taken from a backup on Perion Synthetics' servers. There were so many talented engineers working at Vise Robotics, but could they have created Nancy from scratch? Or was she stolen? Maybe they took it as an example to build from but then used her as-is when they couldn't replicate it.

"Wait, go back," said Carter. "Is that live?"

Diya craned her neck but couldn't see the vidscreen from the floor. "What are you looking at?"

"Camera feeds," said Roma. "I think that's the dining room, and here's the foyer."

"Is that Ad—Mrs. Vaught?" asked Carter. "She looks hurt."

Diya got up and came around the desk. The camera feed filled the entire vidscreen, and the high-resolution video showed a supine Adelai Vaught on the floor of the dining room with her wife Simone by her side. At the double doors leading out into the foyer, a clearly frazzled Jane was soundlessly screaming for something—help, maybe.

"What happened to her?" asked Carter.

Diya pointed to the controls at the bottom of the screen. The interface was similar to the one on her palette, which meant they should be able to scroll back by increments. "Go back thirty seconds," she told Roma.

Roma moved the mouse and clicked a few times, and the video snapped to an image of a maid rushing out of the kitchen doors to grab Adelai.

"Oh my god." Diya covered her mouth and turned away. Although she hadn't been the one to set the synthetic on Adelai, she felt responsible for every punch that landed on the older woman's face—and there were so many, the attack so unrelenting.

She and Millie had watched plenty of movies where geriatric characters faced off against younger villains, often in physical confrontations, only to come out of the encounter with just a few scrapes and bruises. That wasn't how it worked in the real world where a single punch could spell disaster.

Her lungs burned with every quick breath.

She asked, "Did the maid kill her? Is she… is she alive?"

"For now," said Roma. "It looks like Simone is talking to her. I think she's going to need more than a first aid kit though." She shook her head. "Jesus, there are cameras everywhere in this place. I hope none of you are bashful."

"What does that mean?" asked Laura.

"I've got a feed of every bedroom on the second floor." Roma groaned to herself. "Even the bathrooms."

Laura laughed.

Diya put her back against a server cabinet. "Why is that funny?"

"Oh, it's just Robert," she said, looking away. "At home he likes to torture me by being naked as much as possible. He sleeps naked, and then even after he showers, he doesn't put on any clothes until he's done shaving or fixing his hair. But when we travel, and it doesn't matter how fancy the hotel is, he always changes clothes as fast as he can. He pretends he's just joking about hidden cameras, but I know he really believes it." She waved her hand. "And now his worst fears have come true."

Diya nodded, but she hadn't even considered the idea herself. With her palette, she could scroll through dozens of feeds, but they were all of the main house, of the common areas. She had never seen a feed from a bedroom or bathroom, and yet there were the sinks and bathtubs in tiny windows on the vidscreen. She gritted her teeth. Robert Hargreaves had been so worried about someone getting video of his old, wrinkly balls. Meanwhile, Diya had sat in the tub and touched herself while cameras recorded in high definition. Her only job in the world was to not bring shame to the family. What would Rakesh Singh say if video of his daughter masturbating were to hit the networks?

Worse, what would he *think?*

"Are there cameras down here?" asked Laura.

"Hold on, let me scroll." Roma spun the mouse wheel. "Oh, it looks like I can sort by recent activity."

Diya watched the vidscreen clear and new windows pop up.

"Hmm, it looks like Reno is upstairs in the hallway," said Roma. "The Vaughts and Jane are in the dining room. I don't see Stanton, and I don't see us. I guess there's no camera in here."

"There!" Diya pointed to the vidscreen. "That's Mr. Hargreaves, Robert! He's fine, Laura. Come look."

Laura got up and hobbled over to the desk. Together, they watched Robert pace a large room while two women looked on.

"Where is that?" she asked.

Roma clicked the title bar for the feed. "Um, based on the numbering, it looks like it's Sublevel Three, I think. Below us."

"Where is Stanton?" asked Carter.

"I didn't see him. Oh wait, is that him?" She stubbed her finger against a shadow on one of the windows. It showed a dimly lit bedroom with a figure sitting on the edge of the bed. "Did he go up to his room?"

Diya recognized the room as her own but said nothing.

"There's Beta," said Carter.

Roma nodded. "Sublevel Two. Look, you can see Lucas in the other room. What are they doing?"

"Alpha's there too." Carter rubbed his jaw with his knuckles. "I don't know how we're going to get him out of there with those two hanging around. Where are the other synthetics?"

"Two are with Robert. See the gray jumpsuits? And I don't know where the fifth synthetic is."

A smile formed on Laura's face, but she tucked it away when she noticed Diya looking at her. Without saying a word, she went to the door and started fiddling with the access panel beside it. Despite her prodding, the panel refused to switch its LED from red to green. It finally started beeping at her to stop.

"Where are you going?" asked Diya.

"Robert's down there with those things."

"I don't think they're holding him captive," said Roma. "One of the synnies looks like she's tidying up."

"I know. If Alpha and Beta are one floor down, then maybe I can sneak past them and get to Robert before they notice." She looked down. "I should have gone down there first instead of stopping. I never would have run into Beta, and we wouldn't be stuck in here."

"I don't think you would have made it to him," said Diya. "It's like you said, he wouldn't have gone this long without checking in. I bet he's locked in down there, maybe not being *held*, but locked in."

"I'll figure it out," said Laura. She banged on the door. "I just need to get out of here first."

Diya turned to Carter. "Can I have the bracelet back?"

"I can do you one better," said Roma. Her fingers clacked on the keyboard before stabbing the *Enter* key. A dull rumble filled the room like a gentle aftershock.

The access panel beeped, turned green.

"You unlocked the door?" asked Diya.

Roma nodded. "And not just that door. Every door in the house."

The thought of running out into the rain, finally free of Vise Manor, flashed in Diya's head.

She smiled.

FORTY-ONE

"Momo… I'm sorry."

"Shut up," said Simone, pushing Adelai's face to the side as she tried to treat the wound on her cheek.

Adelai had been unable to move since being dropped to the ground by the malfunctioning maid. Jane went to the parlor to get the first aid kit and came back muttering *fucking Reno* under her breath. Evidently, the arms dealer had left the parlor without telling anyone where he was going, not that it surprised Adelai. People like Reno only cared about themselves. They didn't know what it was like to take someone else's safety and well-being onto their shoulders, and what it felt like to let them down when it mattered most.

After giving Simone the first aid kit, Jane retreated to a respectful distance, ostensibly to keep a look out for more synthetics, but Adelai knew it was because of the growing tension between herself and her wife. Simone was angry, and not in the *someone left the fridge open* way, or the way that could be brushed aside with flowers or chocolates. Her usually kind face had twisted into something grotesque; her eyebrows jammed together in the middle of her face, pushing her eyes down into narrow slits.

"I can't believe you would do this," she seethed, clenching her jaw in the pauses between sentences. "I indulge, and indulge, and you go and pull something like this. Were you ever going to tell me, Addy? Ever?"

"I…"

"No, never mind, don't talk. I don't believe a word coming out of your mouth right now." She pushed a wad of gauze hard against Adelai's ear. Sitting back on her heels, she waved an accusatory finger. "You know what this is? This is… this is selfishness, plain and simple. And I put up with it every single day, and I never complain—never, Addy. Not when you're drinking yourself stupid at three in the afternoon, not when you go days without a shower, and not even when we're watching a stupid little sitcom on television and all you can do is complain about how the characters are overweight or talk funny. I used to think it was just depression, but this is something else. This is just you not caring about anyone except Adelai Vaught."

Her eyes were damp; tears were coming. Adelai wanted to lift a hand to comfort her, but her arms felt like lead ropes at her side.

Simone sighed. "I let you have your trysts with Rayburn whenever you want because I know if I say no, you're just going to do it anyway. Even though it kills me inside, every *single* time, I'd rather know than be in the dark. I want to know how many times you'd rather sleep with someone else than with me. Because at least that's something, right? A little honesty? Don't I deserve that, Addy? Don't I deserve the truth sometimes?"

"Of course, I… I always tell you the truth."

"You didn't tell me about this!" She lifted one of Adelai's thousand-pound arms and showed it to her. A large swath of skin from the underside of her forearm had been scraped away, as if by steel wool. Beneath, a pearlescent gray braid sparkled under the warm dining room lights. "When did you even get this?"

"I meant to tell you. I did." Adelai's throat, which had recently felt invulnerable, suddenly seized up, squeezing tightly on the inside until she couldn't breathe. It took three hard swallows to clear the way. "But after it was done, I was so ashamed, that I kept putting it off and putting it off."

"When?"

"Six years ago, after I stopped seeing Dr. Pritchett."

Simone shook her head. "You said you only saw Dr. Pritchett for a year after…"

"No, I kept going. I didn't tell you. I was having these awful dreams about the plane hitting the balcony instead of the water, and all I could feel was this crushing weight on my body, like suffocating. Dr. Pritchett tried to tell me it was because of the pressure from the crowd when we were all trying to get out… but I could feel the plane on me, this massive weight, just… *on me*. Every time I brought up how scared I was every single day of my life, she told me that Calle Cinco de Mayo was just a freak occurrence, and that I wasn't in any danger. But I felt like I was. All the time."

"You got augmented without even talking to me!"

Adelai tracked a tear leaving Simone's left eye. It drifted down her cheek, disappeared for a moment, and reappeared at her chin.

"I was too embarrassed," she said. "I'm Adelai goddamn Vaught. My beautiful wife and I—"

"Don't."

"—run the most exclusive escort service in the western hemisphere. We are women who have infiltrated every level of every male-dominated business. How would it look if the face of the company couldn't even step outside her apartment? If she was too scared to walk down the street?"

"Don't give me that shit," said Simone. "You were *embarrassed* to tell *your wife* you were still afraid? Why would you think you couldn't tell me something like that?" She stood and stepped back, practically towering over Adelai. "No, that's not it. You just didn't care enough to tell me. You didn't even *consider* me, Addy. Instead of reaching out, you just put up your walls and boxed me and everyone else out. You completely disregard everyone in your life, and then when you're finally done being a selfish bitch, you reach out like I'm a light switch that can just be turned back on. I'm fucking tired of it, Addy!"

A rolling warmth rose in Adelai's cheeks. She wanted to get away, to disappear into the floor, to be anywhere except in Simone's shadow. The worst part was that Simone was right. She hadn't even considered asking whether she wanted to have the augmentation procedure done to her too. Adelai was truly too embarrassed to admit she was afraid, regardless of whether Simone wanted to believe it or not. Her hard outer shell of confidence and strength was thinner than anyone realized, except maybe Simone.

Adelai started to cry in earnest. Through the blur, she saw Simone shake her head in disgust and walk away. A moment later, she felt a smaller hand on her shoulder.

"We should get you off the floor," said Jane.

Adelai nodded. "I don't know if I can move. You're going to have to lift me."

"What do you weigh, like eighty pounds?"

"Don't try to flatter me right now. My wife is angry at me, and rightfully so."

"I *am* angry," said Simone. She threw out her hand and something rattled across the table. "But we can take it offline. I wouldn't want to further embarrass you in front of an employee."

"None taken," said Jane, smiling at Adelai. She slipped a hand under her arm and tried to lift. "I don't think I can do this without hurting you."

Simone groaned, came around the table. She took Adelai's other arm and said, "On three. One, two…"

Together, they lifted Adelai off the ground, and she was surprised to find her legs in good working order. They were shaky, like she'd just spent an hour on the elliptical, but they weren't hurt. The maid had focused most of her fury on Adelai's face and upper body.

"Where are we going?" she asked.

"A good night's rest never hurt anyone," said Jane. "You shouldn't be down here like this in case that maid comes back."

Adelai nodded, put her arms over their shoulders. They practically carried her over to the door. In the empty foyer, their lumbering footsteps echoed down the hall. They climbed the five steps to the first landing. As they turned, something sharp went up the back of Adelai's leg. She cried out and fell toward Jane.

"Are you alright?" Jane held her tighter, slipped a hand onto Adelai's hamstring. "What hurts?"

"I'm okay, I'm okay." She stared into Jane's wide eyes, so full of worry and concern. Something clicked. "You're off the clock."

"What?" asked Jane and Simone at the same time.

"Carter. The engagement. It's done now. I'll take the heat for it, but I don't want you worrying about playing into that man's fantasy anymore. You stay with me and Simone for the rest of the night. The three of us are leaving together."

"He could sue for breach of contract," argued Simone, though Adelai could tell her heart wasn't in it.

"He won't."

Simone huffed as they started up the stairs, but Jane asked, "Why not?"

Adelai winced; it felt like her skin was being stretched to the breaking point all over her body.

"Because he loves you," she said, through a grimace, "and he knows that if he sues, he'll never get to see you or any of our girls again. I'm sure I could convince him that tonight involved some extenuating circumstances and that I had to do what was best for my people."

"He doesn't love me." The brave face Jane had been showing Adelai faded away.

"Maybe he hasn't said it but—"

"Even when they do say it, they don't mean it. Even when you open your heart to them, the way you told us never to do… They can claim to love all they want. It's all bullshit."

Adelai shared a look with Simone, who raised an eyebrow.

"You're talking about someone in particular?" asked Adelai.

Jane said nothing.

"You're not the first woman to have her heart broken by a client," said Simone.

"Montreal."

"Ah, him. Mr. Persistent."

"Why do you call him that?"

A low tone ramped up in Adelai's left ear. The louder it got, the dizzier she became. She leaned her head to the right as if she could get away from it.

"Oh, yeah," said Simone. "Adelai and I had a long discussion about him. He almost gets you killed in Umbra and then tries to schedule another engagement with you a few months later like nothing happened. We almost said no."

"He offered to double the fee," said Adelai, straining against a sudden wave of nausea. "More than once."

"We left it up to you," said Simone. They turned the last corner and headed for the second-floor landing.

"I said no."

Simone nodded. "And when he asked again a few months later…"

"I told you I didn't want to work with him anymore. I really thought that was the end of it. Was it not?"

"We stopped forwarding you the requests," said Adelai, "even offered him other girls, but he kept asking for you."

"Every few months for the last two years," said Simone.

Jane frowned. "I didn't know that."

They were stepping into a hallway full of closed doors when Simone paused.

"Do you hear that?" she asked.

Adelai thought she was only imagining the sound, but when she refocused, she realized it was coming from both sides of the hallway. She traced the loudest instance to the door to their right, to the doorknob embedded in a metal plate.

The whine pitched and stopped. A click followed.

"I think all the doors just unlocked," said Simone.

Adelai strained to look back over her shoulder but could only get her ear pointed down into the foyer. She waited until she heard it—a loud brushing sound followed by a click as the deadbolt disengaged.

"I think…"

She stopped short as a door farther down the hall opened. The hinges squeaked for three agonizing seconds before a figure stepped out into the hall.

It was a Japanese woman with damp black hair hanging over her shoulders. Her eyes went wide when she noticed Adelai. Her mouth dropped open as if to speak.

Lightning flashed in the massive bay window at the end of the hall, and when darkness returned, the woman was gone.

The door slammed shut.

Simone looked at Adelai and asked, "Who the fuck was that?"

FORTY-TWO

Robert spun his wedding ring on his finger.

The hammered rose gold was flecked with dried blood from his earlier encounter with Alpha and Beta. He used the thumbnail on his opposite hand to scrape it away. At first, he had been merely fidgeting, occupying his hands while his brain tried to work out the problem of how Perion imprints had found their way into Vise synthetics, but upon seeing the blood, the *stain*, on his ring, he'd become fixated on cleaning it. Only when it gleamed again, when its numerous facets caught every light in the ceiling, did he return to the imprint puzzle. By then, Misty had turned her attention back to the vidscreen and the maid, Angelique, was nowhere to be found.

"Do you think…" he started to ask, but then the rec room door opened.

Angelique entered with a cordial smile on her face and a bright red can of Coke in her hands, gripping it as if it were a teacup and saucer.

"Unfortunately, we are out of Diet Coke. You said regular would be okay, right?"

She held out the drink to him, and he took it, mystified.

"Yes, but…"

He remembered his last interaction with her, how she'd asked if there was anything she could get him, and in his annoyed state, he'd sarcastically asked for a Diet Coke. She had dutifully left the room even though Robert knew there were no refrigerators in the accessible areas. And yet, she had returned, not just with a drink, but with a *cold* drink.

He popped the tab absently and took a sip.

The carbonation tickled the back of his throat.

"Where did you get this?"

"Is that a soda?" asked Misty.

Angelique folded her hands over her stomach. "The vending machine in the break room has a wide assortment of Coca Cola products, though unfortunately no—"

"Yeah, no Diet Coke. But what break room? Where?"

"I can show you if you'd like."

Robert stepped forward, took another sip. "I'd like that very much."

Angelique turned on her heels and went out the still-open rec room door. To Robert's surprise, she turned left down the hall toward the outer door. As she got closer, he called out to her.

"That door's locked."

She paused to explain. "It recently became unlocked." The door swung open into the landing.

Robert pushed past her, running to the foot of the stairs. He saw himself climbing them, back to the surface, back to Laura.

"Wait," said Misty.

He already had a foot on the bottom step.

"What?" he asked. "Do you hear something?"

"No, I just…" She looked away and hurried to the other side of the landing where another door stood. "It's the other side…"

"The break room is through that door on the left," said Angelique.

"Who gives a shit about the break room?" asked Robert. "We can get out of here now. My wife is probably worried sick, and I don't want to be stuck down here with those synthetics any longer than I have to."

"You said you would help me get out of here," said Misty. "You promised."

"And I will, but that means we go up."

She stubbed her index finger on the door. "All of me. He has my imprint in there. I don't want to leave my brain lying around so he can reload it in another synthetic."

"He's dead, Misty. He's not reloading anyone."

"Then the next person who comes along, whatever. I don't want another me waking up in a body that isn't ours. I couldn't do that to myself."

Robert took a deep breath. Every muscle was ready to fire, ready to propel him upwards and back into Laura's waiting arms. Misty was right that he'd made a promise, but weren't there extenuating circumstances? Couldn't he be forgiven for running back to his wife before taking care of a stranger who didn't want her mind to fall into the wrong hands?

Wrong hands.

Misty was only concerned with her code cube, but what about the others? There were four other imprints in play, not counting Gamma. The originator of those imprints, one James Perion and his son Joseph, would have a vested interest in seeing those code cubes returned, or at the very least, destroyed. If Robert walked out of Vise Manor with five cubes in his luggage, that might be enough to get him an audience with the Synthetic Titan himself.

Perhaps James Perion could even be persuaded to offer a reward.

Five imprints for two synthetic bodies, perhaps.

"Fine," said Robert. The word opened a pit in his stomach, a longing for Laura's touch. "We get the cubes, and we go, okay? No messing around."

Misty nodded and pushed through the door.

Robert followed, but not before awkwardly holding the door open for Angelique.

"Thank you, Mr. Hargreaves."

He nodded, walked behind her for a few paces before she broke off to the break room. He watched her go, and just before stepping behind a cube wall, she pointed to a half-obscured vending machine and beamed at him. He smiled politely before widening his eyes in mock disbelief.

Misty ran through the cube farm. Robert walked by the large windows that separated the two sides of Sublevel Three. There was a slight haze over the glass, and as he got closer, he saw graphics and text blink into existence, as if the windows themselves were transparent vidscreens. At the far end of the floor, past a cubicle full of massive photocopiers and printers, stood the mirrored version of the door next to Lab Six. Beside the doorknob, a small black panel glowed green.

It was unlocked, but Robert didn't want to stop and consider the how and why. Instead, he hurried into the room and found Misty standing in front of the six floor-to-ceiling tubes. Her shoulders sank. Coming around her left side, Robert saw what had deflated her—the cubes were secured behind the same plastic as they were on the other side. There was, however, a small metal lip at the bottom of each portal, and instead of bolts along the perimeter of the oval, there were simple metal latches. Above each little door was an LED glowing red.

"Locked?" asked Robert.

Misty nodded.

"Maybe there's a—"

A fist shot out and hit the second tube from the left. On the next hit, Robert realized Misty wasn't trying to punch the glass, but rather the metal hinges on the right side. At first, her efforts appeared to have no effect except to smear a little green blood on the tube. But slowly, the hinges began to rotate, pushed out of alignment by a slow and persistent attack. Robert lost count of how many times Misty had to hit the portal before the hinges broke apart and dropped their pins.

When the plastic swung open, Misty retrieved the large code cube with all the reverence of an arrogant archaeologist stealing a holy relic. She held the cube to her chest and stared down at it.

Robert noticed the damage to her hand; metal bones glistened, wet with antifreeze blood and synthetic sludge. Only the knuckle over her pinkie still had skin.

He looked around for something else to hit the hinges with. There wasn't much in the room besides vidscreens and keyboards—all made of cheap plastic that would likely shatter. There were small sets of stacked drawers on the desks, but they were all empty save for a few mini screwdrivers. Robert went back to the cubicle area and searched the cabinets opposite the printers. Behind the last door, he found a small case of hardened plastic. Inside was a socket wrench set missing most of its pieces. There was, however, a steel adjustable wrench that looked solid. He took it back to the other room.

Misty met him at the door.

"I'm ready to go."

"Just a minute." He brushed by her, smelling some kind of floral perfume.

It took more than a dozen strikes to open the first tube, a few less for the next, and a couple less for the next. By the time he got to Zeta's tube, he only had to hit it four times before the small glass door fell open. He grabbed a plastic recycling bin from beside one of the desks and carefully placed the four cubes in it. Once they were secure, he left the room to find Misty again.

She was standing just outside the break room talking with Angelique. The maid looked at the code cube in Misty's arms as if it were a newborn puppy.

"Strange, isn't it?" asked Misty.

"What is?"

"That, like, my entire brain can fit in here."

Angelique nodded. "It certainly is. Would you like some tea?"

"No, thank you."

When Misty looked over at Robert, he patted the recycling bin. "Do you want to put that in here?"

The horror that crossed her face made it seem like he'd just asked her to throw her puppy into a woodchipper.

"Why? Why would I…?"

"Just in case we run into your brothers. Obviously, I can't fight them."

"So you want me to sacrifice myself for you?"

"No, I'm just saying you stand a better chance against them. Unless she can fight."

"I am fully Three Laws compliant," said Angelique, in a quasi-monotone that sounded like she was reading from a script. "I cannot by action or inaction—"

Robert held up his hand to stop her. "I get it, but what about other synthetics?"

"I'm sorry. I don't understand your request. Can you rephrase it?"

"Will you protect me if a non-human tries to hurt me?"

"Yes. There is precedent."

Robert looked to Misty. "You hear that? There's precedent."

"Yeah, cool, I guess." She eyed the recycling bin. "Please be careful with this." She placed her code cube on the pile inside and stepped back. "If I don't make it, or whatever, do you promise to destroy it?"

"If I can't get these back to Perion City, I'll destroy them. You have my word."

"Okay," she said, shrugging. "I guess let's go find out how I die."

Misty led the way back to the landing and started up the stairs without hesitation.

Robert kept imagining Laura sitting in a chair in the parlor, a vodka soda in her hand, the ice long since melted. She was always a worrier when it came to his safety. So many times she had implored him to buy a new car instead of driving that ancient Dodge Ram around.

"Newer cars have better safety features," she told him once. "And they have AI that keeps you in your lane and watches out for other drivers. Some of them can practically drive the car themselves."

"First," he'd replied, "there's no such thing as artificial intelligence. That's just marketing for people who don't know any better. Second, when I'm behind the wheel of my truck, nobody is making decisions about how it drives except me."

Just thinking about self-driving cars brought up the uneasy feeling in his stomach again, and he couldn't help but look over his shoulder at Angelique. She had been nothing but subservient, and yet her face was completely opaque. He had no idea what was really going on behind those manufactured eyes. Sometimes she seemed gated by her programming, unable to understand requests if they weren't about food or drink. Other times, it was as if she were truly thinking for herself and making her own decisions.

Misty was a similar problem. He didn't understand how the imprinting process worked, but at least there was a person—real or simulated—behind her speech and actions.

When it came down to it, they were both self-driving cars in familiar, human shapes, and he had no idea how either one really worked.

A hand on Robert's shoulder stopped him. He looked back to see Angelique shaking her head.

"Something's wrong," she said. "My sisters are near, but something is wrong."

"Misty, hold up," said Robert.

She glanced at him but didn't slow. As she came to the Sublevel Two landing, she hunched down and crept to a large door facing the stairwell. It had a wide, rectangular window cut into it, through which Misty peered for several seconds before beckoning Robert.

He performed the same crouched shuffle to the door and peeked over the edge.

His first thought was of college, of the Alpha Tau Omega house, and how he had never once seen it without clothes strewn about the hallways. In those days, there had always been a party the night before, regardless of the day of the week. Visitors often said it looked like someone had robbed the ATO house, and that's what Sublevel Two looked more like—like someone had come in and turned the place upside down.

Except, this was worse, more like a home invasion than a burglary.

Bodies littered the floor of a long, narrow hallway, as if a dozen people had been standing there and a giant stone ball had come rolling through.

"They're all maids," said Misty.

Robert finally noticed how the bodies were dressed, all in the same black and white French maid outfit. By looking at their clothes, he had to look at their limbs, many of which were turned the wrong way. Someone or something had torn them apart, and it didn't take long to find out who.

Down the hallway, far enough away that their forms began to blur a little, were Alpha and Beta. They flanked a single remaining maid who looked anything but worried.

"Are they going to kill her?" asked Misty.

"I don't think she's a maid," he replied.

Robert felt Angelique step up beside her.

"She's not. That is the synthetic who took my clothes."

"Delta," said Misty.

"Delta," said Robert.

As if she had heard them, Delta turned in her little maid outfit and looked at them down the long hallway. She raised a dainty, blood-soaked hand and pointed.

Alpha and Beta broke into a run.

FORTY-THREE

Laura reached for the panel beside the door, but Carter put a hand out to stop her.

"Just… wait a second, okay?" He turned back to Roma and asked, "Can you pull up the video feed from outside the door? Let's at least make sure the path down to Sublevel Three is clear."

Laura returned an icy glare but didn't try to open the door.

"Thank you," said Carter. He went back to the desk and stood behind Roma. "Do you see anything?"

A two-by-four grid of video feeds appeared on the vidscreen, each of the images changing as Roma dragged to the left. Finally, the wide, familiar corridors of Sublevel Two came into view, and Carter smiled at their emptiness. There was no one outside the door.

"Okay, now walk it down to where Robert is."

Roma snickered. "Yes, boss. Right away, boss."

She scrolled until the Sublevel Two stairwell was visible. It looked clear, but on the far right of the screen, a single feed buzzed with activity.

"What's happening there?"

Roma double-clicked on the feed to bring it full screen.

"Those are the maids," said Diya. "What are they doing down there?"

Carter tried to make sense of what he was seeing. It looked like the same maids that had served them dinner were now bunched up against the wall at the end of the Sublevel Two hallway. And they weren't just standing there—their legs continued to churn, like a character in a video game stuck in a walking animation after encountering a solid barrier.

"It looks like they're trying to go through the wall," said Carter. "Maybe something with their programming is screwed up? It's like they've all lost their minds."

"I don't think so," said Roma. She pointed to the screen. "Look at that one in the middle. She's trying to go the opposite way, but they're holding her back."

Several seconds ticked by, and Carter finally saw what Roma was seeing. Every maid except the one in the middle had a blank, default expression on their face, the kind of small smile a waitress might wear while they refilled glasses of water or removed empty plates. Nothing too over-the-top, but also not the deadeye stare a customer might get from a surly waiter at 3:00 a.m. in a twenty-four-hour diner.

Unlike her coworkers, the lone maid looked downright angry. There was no sound coming from the vidscreen, but Carter could see she was screaming, perhaps cursing those around her.

"You know what this reminds me of?" asked Roma. "A death ball."

"A what?" asked Laura. She came around the desk to look at the cameras.

"You mean like in that movie *Phantasm?*" asked Carter.

"No," said Roma. "Don't you guys sub the Discovery Channel feed? A death ball is what happens when a hornet attacks a beehive. Since they can't go one-on-one with the hornet, a bunch of bees surround it and vibrate until they raise the temperature. They *cook* the hornet alive. It's your classic united-we-stand tactic."

"Okay," said Carter, "but *why* are they death-balling that one maid?"

"Maybe she spilled some coffee. I don't know."

"Well, are they near the stairs?" asked Laura. "Can I get past them?"

"Oh shit," said Roma. "Here come the brutes."

The camera was pointed down the hall at a low angle, so the first thing Carter saw were the black rubber shoes of Alpha and Beta casually strolling to the ruckus. It took several seconds for the hornet-maid to notice them, but once she did, she spoke directly to them, angrily shouting something that seemed more like an order than a cry for help. Both synthetics kicked into high gear as if someone had dropped a quarter in their backs. They pulled the smaller maids away from the death ball, not just moving them aside, but throwing them into the walls and floor. Those that got back up and rejoined the death ball were thrown again, harder. After a few minutes, Alpha switched from man-handling the maids to simply breaking them.

It started with an arm, then a leg, but as the maids kept getting up, both he and Beta kept escalating their attacks. They punched, kicked, tore, and twisted. They slammed faces into door jambs, used the corners to break through the metal braiding beneath the maids' skin. Green blood splatted onto the walls, onto the floor—the camera showed the carnage in startling clarity.

"I'm going," said Laura.

"What?" Carter followed her to the door. "You're going out there while that is happening?"

She looked him up and down. "How is it you manage to stand up straight without a spine, young man?"

It took Carter a moment to unpack the insult, but once he did, he felt its weight at the bottom of his stomach. He looked at the floor, unsure how to respond.

"If they're busy killing those maids, then maybe they wouldn't see me slip by and get my husband. It's the best chance I've got."

She was right, of course. Carter had only stopped her before because Alpha and Beta might have seen her. Now that they were busy with their killing spree, Laura's footsteps might go unnoticed.

"Fine," said Carter. "But we leave the door open, and if it looks like Alpha and Beta might be coming our way, you guys need to let us know. The halls are pretty echoey, so we should be able to hear you downstairs."

"We?"

Carter nodded.

"I'll go too," said Diya. "Roma, you'll look out for us, right?"

"If I must."

Carter was eighty percent sure she was being sarcastic.

"You must," said Laura, slapping the keypad next to the door. It buzzed and began to rise. The thudding of the slats into the ceiling echoed down the hall.

"Still good," said Roma. "Just hurry. There are only a few maids left standing. Besides the hornet herself."

They moved quickly down the hall, with Carter leading the way while Laura limped behind him. He slowed down to wait for her after she refused help from Diya.

Hushed conversation came from the stairwell—a man and a woman talking. The voices weren't loud enough for Carter to recognize, so he held up a hand and inched down the steps to the first turn. There, he peeked his head around the corner to see the lower half of Robert's suit, along with the two jumpsuits Roma had pulled up on the video feeds.

He was about to say something when Laura hurried around him.

"Robert!" she called, but her husband was already moving, turning away from a windowed door with wide eyes and mouth agape.

Neither of the synthetic women had said anything, so Carter assumed it was something Robert had seen through the door that prompted him to bolt away in fear. He got a few steps before he looked up and saw Laura. Like a glitch in a virtual avatar, his face jumped back and forth between relief and terror, until finally terror won out. In one quick movement, he shoved a recycling bin into Carter's hands and swept Laura off her feet. He carried her up the stairs in an all-out run as if she weighed nothing.

"Who are—" asked Diya, to one of the women.

"They're coming!" replied the other, holding her hands out to the side to corral everyone up the stairs.

Carter didn't need to hear more. He turned and ran, making sure Diya was behind him. A glance over his shoulder showed the synthetic women bringing up the rear. The one who had interrupted Diya's question had her eyebrows furrowed in determination, but the other wore a blank look just like the maids.

The door below slammed against the wall, and the stairwell was suddenly full of echoing footfalls. Carter had barely cleared the landing, while Robert and his bride were halfway down the hall. Within a few seconds, Alpha and Beta were visible coming up the stairs. They gave chase, closing the distance much too quickly.

He caught eyes with Diya; she realized it too.

Robert reached the junction at the end of the hall and looked back. Before turning the corner, he yelled, "Angelique!"

One of the synthetics suddenly broke off toward the wall. She put out a hand to stop herself and then turned back to face their pursuers. Carter only got a sense of what was happening, but it reminded him of old school fake wrestling the way the woman—Angelique—launched herself into the air, twisting her body completely horizontal before smashing into Alpha and Beta. The impact didn't knock them down, but it staggered them enough for Carter and Diya to reach the junction and turn right.

Roma stood just inside the door, ready to close it once they were inside.

Carter's biochip gave him everything it could.

Adrenaline, for energy.

Naproxen, for the pain.

And prednisone, for the inevitable damage.

Carter threw himself across the threshold, pushing Diya ahead. He almost dropped the recycling bin when he hit the floor but managed to keep the strange cubes inside from spilling out.

The door dropped, landing with a soft thud, followed by two loud bangs just a few seconds later.

They all stepped back as the pounding began. Carter had no clue if the door would hold up to the abuse, and he didn't want to ask anyone and be told *no*.

"Thank God, thank God," said Laura. Robert had put her down near the desk, and she wasted no time pulling him into an embrace. "I was so worried. I thought something had happened to you."

"I know," he replied, putting his forehead against hers. "I was stupid. I went exploring on my own and ran into those two." He gestured to the pounding door. "One of them got me by the neck and I was sure that was it. But then I woke up downstairs in some kind of rec room with my new friend here, Misty."

"Misty?"

The woman in the gray jumpsuit lifted an unsure hand. She looked vaguely Russian, with sharp cheek bones and a thin nose. Carter guessed she was supposed to be a little older than he was, but the way she held herself with shoulders slumped and arms hanging lifelessly at her side spoke to something more youthful.

"You're… friends?" continued Laura.

"My name is actually Allison. But my friends call me Misty." Her eyes jumped to Robert and back. "I go to Perion Junior High School in Perion City."

Laura shook her head.

"I know it doesn't make any sense," said Robert, "but I think Vise actually stole imprints from Perion City. I mean, I haven't been able to verify anything she's said, but I really don't think Vise cooked her up from scratch."

"Called it," said Roma.

Diya held up a hand to shush her. "No, this is Epsilon. I saw her behind the glass. She's one of Vise's synthetics that he designed and created."

The pounding on the door grew louder, more insistent.

"Those are just the names he gave us," said Misty. "That's how you dehumanize people, by giving them meaningless names or numbers. We learned about that in school."

"Does it really matter?" asked Carter. "We've got bigger problems right now."

A sickening crack went through the door, and a tiny sliver of light shone through a breach in the slats.

Laura broke away from Robert and limped over to the door. There, she pounded on it with two open palms. "What the fuck do you monsters want from us? Why don't you just go away? The front door is open—"

"No, wait!" said Roma.

"You can just walk out. That's what you wanted, right? Freedom? Vise is dead, and none of us are responsible for what happened to you. So just leave us the fuck alone!"

The door shook with a single heavy impact.

Laura backed up, her lower lip trembling. Robert caught her from behind and held her by the shoulders. He made quieting sounds in her ear as silence fell in the room.

"Holy shit," said Roma. "I think it's working."

Carter came around the desk and watched the full-screen video from the camera outside the door. Alpha and Beta looked at each other and then the door, several times, until finally they turned and headed back for the stairs. Roma switched feeds to keep tabs on them. Halfway down the hall, they stepped over the broken, twitching body of the maid Robert had called Angelique.

"The hornet is in play again," said Roma, as the sole-surviving maid appeared at the top of the stairs.

Some kind of discussion took place, during which Carter asked again whether there was any audio. Roma replied by using her own voice to dub the mouth movements from the video.

"What do *you* think we should do?" she asked, lowering her voice to a rough baritone. "I don't know, I think we should kill them and eat their balls. Eat their balls? Gross. Why gross? They're just human balls. All the males have them."

"Enough," said Diya.

Carter focused on the screen. The conversation seemed to have turned hostile, with Alpha trying to push past the woman at one point. A delicate hand on his chest somehow kept him from leaving. The woman pointed back down the hallway and said something to which both Alpha and Beta acknowledged with quick nods. She removed her hand, and the two male synthetics headed up the stairs. She remained for another minute, staring down the hallway, until finally she looked up, directly into the camera, and smiled.

Roma smashed the Escape key; a grid of camera feeds appeared, with the hallway relegated to the lower right.

"Sorry," said Roma, chuckling nervously. "Habit. My coworkers are always sending me those jump-scare fake-out videos. I hate it." She sat back in her chair and looked past Carter to the table by the door. The recycling bin Robert had given him was sitting there looking out of place.

"What's in the bin?" she asked.

FORTY-FOUR

When Roma got up from the desk to talk to Carter, Diya slipped into her seat and placed her hands on the warm keyboard.

The interface wasn't the same as her palette, in that she couldn't just swipe and pinch and tap her way around. It took a minute to figure out where to click to cycle through the cameras. She found the feed for the foyer, blew it up to full screen, and waited.

As the seconds ticked by and nothing moved, her mind started to drift to the conversations taking place around her. She heard only disconnected snippets, as if someone were jumping back and forth between two channels on a television.

"These are PK mind cubes," said Roma.

"*Mind cubes?*" asked Carter. "You really call them that?"

"You got a better name for them?"

"Um… I don't know. What about, like, *cortical stacks?*"

Roma hissed. "Fuck that's good."

"I thought you were dead," said Laura.

"Me too," said Robert.

"You shouldn't have left me. We should have stayed together."

Robert clucked his tongue. "If you had been with me when I ran into Alpha and Beta, you could have been hurt. I'm glad you weren't there."

"I have my laptop up in my room," said Roma. "I should be able to access them—the meta, at least—and see who they belong to."

"Would you be able to tell if Misty is telling the truth?"

"The meta probably won't have her full name in it. The only way to know for sure is to access the Perion City network, and we're still locked down. I can't figure out why."

Diya knew why.

She could see it clearly in her memory. Wednesday morning, a black van bearing the logo of Pantheon Systems pulled up into the driveway and stopped so suddenly that it kicked up a good amount of gravel. The men who got out of the van were tall, muscular, and borderline rude to the point that Diya got the impression they were taking orders from someone else, perhaps Vise himself.

"We need access to the roof," one of the men said.

Diya had done enough research on Pantheon to know they were a defense contractor whose internal workings were as oblique as they were mysterious. Despite being in charge of the proceedings, Diya directed the men with a stammer in her voice and only relaxed once they had disappeared around the side of the house. The man who'd spoken to her led the way, with four others carrying ladders, a long gray chest, and a large steel winch strapped down to a platform.

A few hours later, they returned and left without saying anything to Diya.

As the van peeled out, upsetting even more gravel, Diya tapped the action item in her palette to mark it done. The text *Pantheon Systems* faded to a light gray. Beside it, a note Vise had added himself faded along with it.

Network isolation. V important.

Whatever the men had installed on the roof, it was big and heavy enough to need its own dedicated crane to lift it. Diya didn't even have direct control of it; the time of its activation had been set by Vise, with no signal from her palette required. The same applied for turning it off, which wouldn't happen until sunrise.

"I want to get you out of here," said Laura. "We don't belong up here. I can't believe you let Frank talk you into this."

"He didn't," said Robert. "I mean, he didn't twist my arm or anything. We looked at the situation and assessed the risk, same as we do every day with every investment opportunity that comes across our desks. This one had risk, but neither of us could have imagined it would end like this. This is… this is insanity."

"Now that you've seen Vise's synthetics up close, how do they compare with Perion's?" asked Carter.

"Honestly?" Roma hummed for a few seconds. "Well, you know it's the same with every wannabe synthetics company we encounter. I have an acquaintance who works on the scouting team, and he says they use a scale of how many years a competitor is ahead or behind our technology. You know, plus four, minus five? In the history of the department, they've never assigned a positive integer."

"And what about these?"

"Publicly? I'd say they're a minus four. Privately, and this doesn't leave this room, they're a minus seven. Joseph Perion has taken the company in a whole new direction. Some of the stuff we'll be releasing in the next few years will blow your mind."

Diya didn't hear Carter's reply; a flashing border around her video feed drew her attention back to the screen. Two figures entered the frame, coming from the direction of the hallway and the vault door. Alpha and Beta paused for a moment, looked first to the parlor doors and then up to the top of the stairs, perhaps listening for something. After several seconds, they turned to the front door.

She switched to a camera in the far corner of the foyer for a better view.

"Guys," she said. "I think they're leaving."

Carter and Roma joined her at the desk.

"Moment of truth," said Roma, as Alpha reached out for the doorknob.

Diya sighed as the door swung inward, revealing a rain-soaked porch streaked with lightning. Alpha gave one last look at the foyer and then headed out into the darkness. Beta followed close behind.

"And the hornet?" asked Roma.

No sooner has she asked than the woman herself came walking casually into frame. She paused at the doorway, gave a look over her shoulder directly into the camera, and then stepped outside, pulling the door shut behind her.

"Lock it," said Carter. "Lock all the doors, now!"

Diya jumped out of the chair so Roma could sit down again. A new window slid onto the screen, and Roma dragged the cursor down the list of cryptically named locks before clicking on the parent folder that said simply *Ground Floor*. Dozens of icons on a line drawing turned from green to red.

Carter gave a small cheer.

"Don't get cocky, kid," said Robert. "That's only three of them. Misty here makes four, plus the stillborn downstairs—that's five. There's one more on the loose somewhere in the house, and we have no idea what she looks like."

"How do you know it's a *she*?" asked Roma.

"I think Vise intended to show off three males and three females. Two of the males just walked out the front door, and the other is lying on a table downstairs with half his brain spilling out onto the table."

"The woman that left," said Misty. "I think that was the actual Delta. I remember Zeta being Japanese, I think."

"So we're looking for a Japanese chick," said Carter.

"Japanese woman," said Roma.

"You would know her if you saw her, wouldn't you, Misty?"

She nodded.

"Then maybe you can look at those security cameras with Roma there and see if you can find her somewhere in the house. I don't know about you guys, but I'd be more comfortable knowing what she's up to."

"Okay, but, I don't think she's dangerous," said Misty. "She was always real nice to me when we had time together, not like what those other two became."

"But what about the woman?" asked Robert. "Did you ever notice anything off about Delta?"

"I guess. I mean, we were all pretty messed up in the beginning. She seemed normal, but then yesterday or maybe the day before, she went quiet and never came back. Her whole personality changed. It was kinda weird."

"This is all kind of weird," said Carter.

"Well, I want to go back upstairs," said Laura. She looked to Robert. "I don't feel safe down here."

Diya looked from one face to another. Everyone looked tired and beat down—exactly the opposite of how the night was supposed to end. As a host, she had failed miserably.

She took a deep breath, blew it out.

"Maybe we should all go up to our rooms," she said. "No one's getting into the house now, so we should be relatively safe until morning."

Roma scoffed.

"Is there a problem, uninvited guest?" The sting of Roma's deception was still in Diya's system, slowly infecting her body, causing fits of anger she had so far been able to keep under wraps.

Roma waved her hand dismissively. "Fine, whatever. Carter, do you want to come with me to get Lucas, the *invited* guest our hostess seems to have forgotten about?"

"I… sure, yeah."

"And what about you, Misty?" asked Roma. "You're as strong as those other synthetics, right? You could help us carry him if he's unconscious."

Misty shrugged.

"Then it's settled. We'll go down and get the defenseless and possibly injured Lucas Cotton, and the rest of you can go back upstairs and continue your dinner party."

Robert opened his mouth to say something, and Diya imagined it was going to be some kind of homespun good ol' boy speech about doing the right thing. Instead, Laura put two fingers on his chin, and when he looked down at her, she whispered, "No. We're done."

"Sweetie," he said.

"*Robert.* With love, remember?"

He nodded, looked back to Roma, and gave her an apologetic smile.

"Alright, well, I guess that's it." Roma got up from the chair and started for the door. Carter and Misty followed behind her.

When they were gone, Diya turned to the Hargreaves couple. She slid back into her hostess role, using its formality and appearance of control to mask the whirlwind of uncertainty that was spinning in the back of her head. The evening had long ago slipped into calamity, but only now with the threat of a horrible death safely locked outside the heavy doors could Diya reflect and see just how bad everything was and how close all of them had come to being killed.

Just like Winston.

"I'll accompany you to your room," she said, folding her hands around a non-existent palette. She looked over at the open door to the hallway beyond. The palette was on the floor where Roma had dropped it earlier. "If there's anything I can get for you…" Her eyes fell on the vidscreen. It had resumed a rotating carousel of video feeds, and in one square, a familiar shape grabbed her attention. She leaned over the desk and used the mouse to maximize the feed.

"Diya?" asked Laura. "Are you okay?"

She barely heard the question, but managed to say, "I thought I saw something. This shadow, see it?"

Both Robert and Laura joined her at the desk.

"I don't see anything," said Robert.

Laura asked, "Is that the kitchen?"

Diya nodded, bit her lip. At the bottom of the window, a timeline scrolled, marked with moments of activity. She jumped the video back to the last detected motion and saw Adelai and Simone running out of the kitchen.

"Oh my God," said Laura.

"Yeah," said Diya. "That's Delta, the woman who just walked out the front door. Let me take it back a little more."

The video jumped, and the shadow on the floor disappeared. In its place stood Delta with the other maids forming a semi-circle around her. She motioned with her hands, the way Diya had seen Winston do during his various presentations to customers, the way someone speaking to a large audience might accentuate their words.

Diya got up from the chair.

"Where are you going?" asked Laura.

"I need my palette. I want to hear what she was saying." Diya made it to the door before Laura gasped.

"Oh no, Robert…"

"That's Blumenfield," he said.

Diya turned around slowly. "What's wrong?"

Laura covered her mouth.

Diya raced back to the desk just in time to see Delta swing a knife at Stanton Blumenfield's neck. A spray of blood erupted onto the floor at his feet, and the elderly writer went down in a panicked heap. He struggled for several seconds, grasping feebly at his neck while blood poured through his fingers.

Laura turned away, buried her face in Robert's chest.

"Maybe…" Diya stopped herself from saying something stupid.

There was no *maybe* about it.

Another guest was dead.

FORTY-FIVE

Adelai sat at the small vanity under the bright bathroom lights.

Though she faced away from the door, she could see it in the mirror, standing there closed with the tiny lock in the doorknob engaged. It wouldn't keep out any of the horrible things she'd seen this evening, or even a strong human with a well-placed shoulder, but it would signal to Simone and Jane that they should leave her alone, that she needed just five minutes to sit and think in peace. She needed to get control of the situation, but every time she tried to grab onto a thread, a different one would slip through her fingers. She thought maybe sitting down and staring at herself in the mirror might work, that by willing herself to get control, she could manage some semblance of it.

The only problem was the woman on the other side.

The one staring back.

Simone had done her best to put Adelai's skin back where it belonged using tiny, translucent butterfly bandages, but it would take a skilled nip and tucker to restore her original beauty. The scars were jagged and caked with blood, and they reminded her of an injury she'd sustained falling from the monkey bars in the sixth grade. She couldn't remember it then or now, but her parents told her she'd fallen and hit her face on a sharp edge that had lost its protective covering. The result was a scar running from the middle of her neck to slightly behind her ear before disappearing into her hair. She remembered crying in the days following the fall.

"I'll be a freak forever," she'd told herself.

Now, looking at the damage the psychotic maid had done, Adelai wasn't under the same misapprehension of her ten-year-old self. Her mangled face wouldn't last forever. Any Manhattan plastics dealer worth their license would be able to fix her up in a single visit and maybe make her look a few years younger in the process.

So why then the sinking feeling in her stomach? Why the lurching as her eyes found yet another open area on her cheek or forehead?

The answer came when she happened to look to the side and the wounds on her right cheek caught the light. The material beneath the skin sparkled like a wide, diamond-encrusted bangle, except there were no facets she could see. Even with her finger, the material felt smooth and almost pliant.

She remembered Simone screaming at her.

Recalling the anger on her face made Adelai's stomach jump sideways.

It was a somewhat new feeling. Though she had always cared for Simone, her wife was given to fits of sensitivity, always feeling like she was being put-upon or insulted or slighted. There was a time when Adelai didn't feel like she could say even the smallest thing to Simone without upsetting her. Even the occasional sigh she let out when she was frustrated became one of Simone's triggers.

Things had improved over the years, with Calle Cinco de Mayo acting as a demarcation line, a shared tragedy for them to focus on instead of each other. Adelai had always believed Simone had somehow toughened up, become less sensitive, but now it was clear she had simply taken her emotions and buried them deep down.

Finding out about Adelai's augmentation work was the final push the volcano needed to erupt, spilling years of suppressed emotion onto the surrounding landscape. When it cooled—if it ever did—the land would be forever changed, with new rock forming over what had once been green and fertile.

Adelai looked at herself again.

"It will cool," she whispered. "She won't be angry forever."

Simone would push it down eventually, settle back into her habit of pretending everything was okay. Things would go back to normal; it would just take time.

Just the thought of rewinding time to the days before Vise Manor gave Adelai a bit of a lift. She spied the door in the mirror and thought about how awkward it was going to be to walk out there with Simone and Jane, but she would do it. She would accept the elephant in the room and bear it, and when Simone was ready to be done being angry, she would accept that too.

Adelai smoothed a butterfly bandage on her cheek. Some of the feeling in her skin was starting to come back. She didn't know how much pain there was going to be, so she made a mental note to grab a code card with something strong on it just in case.

With a sigh that would have sent Simone's eyes rolling, Adelai got up and went to the door. She unlocked it, opened it slowly, and stepped back into the bedroom.

Jane was sitting at the foot of the bed, hands folded in her lap, with her eyes glued to the door. At the small desk by the window, Simone sat sideways with one arm draped over the back of the chair and legs crossed. They both looked at her at the same time, neither of them happy or relieved to see her.

"I'm not crazy, right?" she asked. "You saw the Japanese woman too?"

Simone huffed and turned her face to the window. She rolled her eyes, perhaps unaware Adelai could see her reflection in the glass.

"I saw her," said Jane, her voice lacking any of the tacked-on, carefree youth of her engagement persona. She was no longer Jane Martin, Carter Price's date, but rather the authentic Jane Moretz, whose real personality Adelai knew little to nothing about.

"I wonder who she was," said Adelai.

Jane blinked a few times. "She's one of the synthetics Vise was going to show us. I remember her eyes were green, but like a jade green." She looked back at the door, and when she spoke again, her voice trembled. "If she's as strong as the others, then that door's not going to stop her. And after what that maid did—" She caught Adelai's eye and cut herself off.

"It's okay. I understand you're scared."

"It's more than that," said Jane. "I haven't been this scared since Umbra." She paused for a moment, then swallowed. "The engagement was going fine. Danny was being his normal goofy self. We got a room at a fancy hotel, and I knew the support team had set up right across the hall. But then someone started shooting at us. And it wasn't like in the movies with those little metallic *pings* you hear. These were like… *thwack, thwack*… and I didn't just hear them, I felt them in my chest, as if the bullets were actually hitting me."

Adelai knew the story; she and Simone had read it a few times after Jane's post-engagement debrief. Knowing how close Jane had come to being hurt and potentially killed was one of the reasons Adelai had put her on probation in the first place. And when Danny Guns Montreal called for her again just a few months later, she and Simone had read the report again, just to make sure they hadn't missed anything that would disqualify the client.

It was Simone's idea to provisionally approve the engagement so they could get Jane's input.

"Let her decide," Simone had said. "If she says no, then problem solved, and we reject the engagement too. If she says yes, well, then obviously it wasn't as dangerous as she made it out to be."

"Is that why you refused to see him again?" asked Adelai. "Montreal, I mean."

Jane met her eyes. "No."

Adelai waited for her to continue, but she crossed her arms and looked away, as if she were done with the conversation.

Thunder rattled the windows in their frames.

Adelai stood for a moment in the center of the room, alone and ignored. The control she yearned for felt even further away. Thoughts and questions swirled in her head, until one slipped out.

"What was that woman doing in our rooms?"

No one answered, but Adelai clung to the question as if it were the most important thing in the world. What *was* the Japanese woman up to? Was she going through everyone's room? And why had she changed clothes?

"She's trying to fit in," said Adelai, happy to have the conversation with herself if no one else wanted to join in. "She was looking for clothes so she could change out of that horrendous jumper."

She saw Simone shake her head out of the corner of her eye.

"I wonder if she's going to make a run for it, you know, like an escaped prisoner who ditches their orange uniform to fit in with the public?"

"You're talking about her like she's a real person," said Simone.

"Maybe she is."

"Don't be stupid." Simone refused to turn around. "Vise wouldn't put *real* people on display. The way he paraded them out, it was like he was showing off a new car model. That's not how you treat real people. A better demonstration would have been to pretend they were guests, let them mingle with the crowd, and then at the presentation, make the big reveal by having them all stand up. That's showing respect for independent people, not locking them behind glass like zoo exhibits."

"Not without them going crazy and killing everyone, right?" asked Jane.

"I'm talking to my wife," said Simone. "You should be quiet."

"Or what?" Jane half-chuckled. "You'll fire me?"

"I might."

"No one is firing anyone," said Adelai.

Jane turned to Simone. "Does it look like I'm enjoying this job, Mrs. Vaught? Between almost being killed and having my heart broken, I'm not sure you could pay me enough to keep doing this. I'm tired of putting myself in these situations. I'm tired of being told who to love, who to be. I just…" She pressed her palms into her eyes. "I just want to be in control for once."

Her words pierced Adelai's subdermal braiding with ease.

She sat on the bench at the foot of the bed and pulled a folded leg onto it.

"We don't control you."

Jane's head fell to the side.

"It's… not our *intention* to control you," Adelai clarified. "We run a business that has talent and clients, and our job is to mediate between the two. And yes, that includes telling you who the client wants you to be, and yes sometimes you have to pretend to love them and pretend to enjoy sleeping with them. But what separates us from the pimps and madams on the streets is that you are free to go at any time. The second you feel like this job isn't for you—because that's all it is, Jane, a job—then you can just walk out the front door and leave us all behind. The only thing that will follow you is a non-disclosure agreement and our appreciation for your work."

"You're still young," said Simone. "You'd be giving up a lot of money."

"It's not worth it." Jane sniffled. "Even if I were rich like you two, it wouldn't be worth it. I just don't care about the money. I want someone to love. I want honesty and support and everything a healthy relationship is supposed to be. Even you, with your exclusive company and wealthy clients and downtown penthouse… even you struggle to make your marriage work. You hide things from each other. You hurt each other. What good is all that wealth if you can't hold your other half in your arms?"

A knock at the door saved Simone from having to answer, and Adelai realized she was worried about how her wife might respond. Would she defend their marriage? Or would she use it as an opening to lay into Adelai?

Either option was equally likely.

Jane stiffened and slipped off the bed. She ended up in the corner of the room, slightly hidden behind a tall wardrobe.

"Don't worry," said Adelai. She stood and approached the door. "I don't think a killer robot would be polite enough to knock first."

"Is anyone there? Mrs. Vaught?" asked an impatient voice.

"Yes, what do you want?"

"It's Diya, Mrs. Vaught. We got the doors opened, and the synthetics have left—Alpha, Beta, and the one that… Anyway, it should be safe to come out now. We're regrouping in the parlor if you'd like to come down and join us."

Adelai looked at Jane, who shook her head. "It could be *her*," she whispered.

"How do I know it's really you and not the Japanese woman we saw earlier?"

There was silence for several seconds.

"It's me, Mrs. Vaught."

"Prove it."

There was a rustling at the bottom of the door. Shadows cut through the light coming in from the hall. After a moment, a simple gold chain appeared.

Adelai bent and picked it up. It looked similar to the silver chain she wore on her own wrist.

"What is this?" she asked.

"Winston's bracelet. It opens every door in the house. Beta had it, and I got it back. We locked the front doors when the synthetics left, but you can open them anytime you want now."

Adelai turned the deadbolt. There was still a chain, but as Jane had pointed out, it likely wouldn't stop whoever was on the other side of the door. She opened it slowly until the chain was taut.

It was Diya.

It was Diya's eager face turning to horror.

Adelai frowned, touched her cheek.

"Don't mind me, dear," she said. "I haven't put on my face yet."

FORTY-SIX

The bottle of Kraken rum clinked against Robert's glass as he tried to pour a drink with an unsteady hand.

He cursed himself for not listening to Laura, who had refused to go with him to the kitchen and begged him not to go either. But for some reason, he felt like he had to, as if he owed it to the old man to at least see what had become of his body. There wasn't anything he could do for Stanton Blumenfield now except pay his respects, and he'd intended to do so.

Soft fingers came over the top of his and took the bottle from his hand. Robert nodded as Laura replaced the rum on the bar and reached for a bottle of flavored scotch instead. She poured the brown liquid into the empty glass and slid it gently across the bar.

"Sorry, that's the closest thing to a drink you're gonna get." She waited for him to take his first warm sip before asking, "What did you see in there?"

Robert licked his lips.

The images were clear in his head, but he found it hard to describe. He took a mental step back and said, "The dining room was a mess. Adelai went toe-to-toe with Delta, and they wrecked the place. There's food all over the floor, broken dishes and glasses." He stopped talking, hoping the crackling of the fireplace would somehow overpower the silence.

Laura gave him time, but she knew him too well. In all their years together, she had never been anything but patient, especially when it mattered most. Some women he had dated would have run for the hills if they saw him being anything but an alpha male, a captain of industry, a wealthy businessman. Some had, but not Laura. When he was upset or hurt, it only drew her closer into his sphere of existence, where she waited with him until he was ready to accept help.

"What about the kitchen?" she asked, placing her hand on his back.

He took another sip. The drink was trying hard to be scotch, but some kind of maple flavoring was ruining it. "I don't know what I was thinking. I mean, I knew there might be some blood, but I didn't think there would be *that* much. She *sliced* his neck, Laura. His heart kept pumping out blood for who knows how long. And it's just this reddish, black, dead mirror pool around his head and I…" The air grew stale; he tasted metal. "I wanted to go in there and, I don't know, say some words or something, put a blanket over him… but I couldn't even get near him. I stood there by the door like a deer in headlights until I thought I was going to throw up."

"I would have done the same thing," said Laura. "You know how bad I am at funerals. I didn't even go up to the casket when Dad died. Not until they closed it."

Robert shrugged. "Yeah, I guess I just thought I was stronger than that. Yesterday, when we were sitting out on the back porch, and you told me that story about how every lake is haunted, I thought to myself: *what would I do if a ghost came walking out of the water and attacked me?* And I told myself I'd fight it. I'd be brave and fight it with everything I had. I guess you don't know your mettle until you're tested."

"Maybe," said Laura. "But what if it came out of the water and attacked me?"

"I would throw myself at it while you got away."

"No doubt in your mind?"

He took a long pull of the drink, set the glass down roughly on the bar. "No fucking doubt at all."

"That's a man in my book." She took his glass and finished it off. "Will you come sit by the fire with me? My pups are barking."

Robert led her by the elbow across the parlor to the fireplace. Laura sat down on the brick outcropping and put her open back to the blaze.

"I didn't realize how cold it was down there," she said, rubbing her arms. "Were you cold down there with… Misty? Epsilon?"

"Not really. I had my jacket. Plus that's where the synthetics lived for a while before tonight. I don't know if they needed heat and air conditioning, but I have to imagine they can feel hot and cold. Honestly, I wasn't even thinking about it."

"What were you thinking about?" She'd worn a smile since their reunion downstairs, but now her cheeks rose higher.

"Besides you?"

"Naturally."

"How he did it." Robert rubbed his hands together. "I mean, I have no idea who Misty really is, but if she's from Perion City, then Vise flat out kidnapped her mind, and probably the others too. And somehow, he was able to imprint those minds on synthetic bodies. Right now, that's something only Perion Synthetics can do. If Vise found another way, that would be huge. That would change the game overnight. With the right financial backing and business contacts, he could dominate the synthetic transcendence market. Except…"

"Except what?"

Robert sat back in the chair, slumping awkwardly. "The fact that he stole the minds. It means he isn't able to create an imprint himself, otherwise he would have used any volunteers he could find. That's like being able to make guns but not the bullets. Which makes me wonder: what was his business plan? What exactly was he trying to sell us?"

"Maybe he just wanted to show off," said Laura. "*Look at me. Look what I can do.* That kind of thing. He invites us up here, shows us his toys, and then Robert Hargreaves goes and tells all his friends about the new and amazing things happening at Vise Robotics. The word-of-mouth potential would be more valuable advertising than he could pay for."

"Yeah…" Robert nodded a few times. The pain in his back was starting to grow, so he sat up. "Maybe we were never meant to interact with the synthetics. He might have been planning to keep them behind the glass the entire night. We never would have known about Misty."

Laura put a hand on his knee. Looking into her eyes, Robert could see she understood what he was saying. Without meeting the synthetics, Misty and the others would have remained trapped at Vise Manor—paraded about, shown off, and then what, reset?

"Are we interrupting?"

Robert turned and saw Adelai Vaught standing at the parlor doors. Simone and Jane flanked her on either side, but he barely noticed them. Flashes of the dining room came back to him as he saw the aftermath of Delta's attack on Adelai. Her face had a patchwork quality to it, and a huge strip of skin from her ear to her chin had been torn away. She didn't seem to be in any pain, but Robert couldn't imagine she was feeling especially well. The bruising alone—purple black splotches that ran up the side of her head—would have been enough to give her a small concussion.

And yet here she was, seemingly fine.

"No," said Robert. "We were just taking a minute… to catch up."

Adelai smiled thinly. "I'm aware of how my face looks, but if it's all the same to you, I'd rather we just ignore it. Agreed?"

Laura stood and approached. "Absolutely, but… are you okay?"

"She's fine," said Simone.

Robert felt the chill of her words clear across the room.

"I see you made it back unscathed, Mr. Hargreaves," said Adelai. "Your wife was quite worried about you."

"I imagine," said Robert. "And I was worried about her." He tried to look behind her into the foyer. "Where's Diya? Did she find you upstairs?"

"Yes. She said to come down so we can decide whether to make a run for it."

"But the doors are locked," said Laura. "Roma locked them when the synthetics ran out earlier."

Adelai held out her hand and opened it palm up. A gold chain sparkled. "Diya gave me Vise's key. She said it would open the front door if we wanted to leave."

"Why would we leave now?" asked Robert. "The danger is outside."

"Because there were five synthetics behind the glass, Mr. Hargreaves. Diya said only three of them left. I'm no math savant, but even I know that leaves two synthetics unaccounted for. We saw one of them, a Japanese woman, run into a room upstairs. As for the other—"

"The other one is harmless. Her name is Misty, or Allison, and I met her downstairs. She's just a little girl. Vise stole a pre-teen imprint and put it in a synthetic body. I'm telling you, there's more to this than—"

"I don't like being interrupted," said Adelai. Her face settled into an impassive, tight-lipped configuration. "And I don't care what a synthetic killing machine told you her name was or what story she fed you about her past. Does this look like the face of a woman who will ever trust synthetics again?" She pointed to her nose. "Look me in the eye and tell me there's nothing to worry about."

Robert spread his hands, started to offer an explanation, but Laura pushed them back down to his side. When he looked at her, she gave him a subtle shake of her head.

Jane, who for a solid minute had been nervously looking over her shoulder, finally forced her way past Adelai and came into the parlor proper. She looked around, trying to decide between the bar and a chair, and ultimately chose a seat by the window.

"This is crazy," said Robert. "You really want to go out there? Even without the synthetics, the storm hasn't let up. I don't know about here, but in Houston, the roads flood after just twenty minutes of solid rain. We may not even be able to drive out of here."

"Assuming the cars are still here," said Jane. "I thought I saw them drive away once they dropped us off."

Robert nodded at her. "My rental is here. Diya had someone park it around the side of the house, but I didn't see where it ended up."

"What do you think, Addy?" asked Simone.

Adelai was still looking at Robert. "Are they really out there?"

Robert nodded. "I saw them leave myself."

"Who cares if they're out there?" asked Simone. "They're probably long gone by now. We should take his car and go. Maybe we only make it into town, but I'm sure they have a motel or something we could stay in—anything that puts distance between us and this house of horrors."

Adelai nodded, spoke to Robert. "Okay, I agree with you. Staying put is probably our best option. We'll wait for the sun to come up and figure out our next step then."

"Excuse me?" Simone pulled Adelai around to face her. "Do I have to remind you there's another synthetic running around upstairs that we know nothing about?"

Adelai opened her mouth to speak, but something in the foyer caught her attention. She stalked away angrily, yelling, "Hey, asshole!"

Robert followed Simone into the foyer where he saw Reno Cardenas descending the stairs, a plastic bottle of water in his hands and his hair slightly mussed.

Adelai met him at the bottom of the stairs. "Where the hell have you been?"

"Sleeping," he replied, his eyes scanning the crowd.

Robert felt Laura and Jane step up next to him.

"I heard *key*?" he asked.

Adelai slipped the gold bracelet onto her wrist. "It's not for you."

Reno smiled, took a sip from his water, and replaced the cap. He set the bottle down on a post and took the final step to the ground floor. The closer he got to Adelai, the more Robert's adrenaline started to boil.

"What happened to your face, güera?"

"She fought a synthetic and lived," said Simone.

Reno nodded appreciably. "Las máquinas no comprenden." He touched his cheek where Adelai's subdermal braiding was showing through.

"I guess not," she replied.

"I do," he growled. "Entiendes?"

Adelai nodded.

Reno held out his hand.

"Don't give it to him," said Simone.

"You saw what he did earlier," said Adelai. "You know what he's capable of. When that maid was trying to kill me, he was up in his room napping. He doesn't care about any of us. He'll kill us all and run back to the MX before anyone figures out what happened."

"Give him what he wants," said Robert, his mouth dry again. "I wish I could stop him, Adelai, but I'm pretty sure he'd run me over too. If he wants to go, let him. Roma can always open the doors later from downstairs if we decide to leave."

Adelai stared down Reno for a long time. Robert noticed she was slightly shorter now that she was wearing sneakers, but she still stood eye-to-eye with the MX arms dealer.

"Fine," she said, slipping the bracelet off her wrist. "I hope they rip that stupid grin off your face." She dropped the bracelet on the floor and took several steps back.

Simone slipped in front of her.

Reno smirked and put a knee on the floor to pick up the bracelet. He walked the dozen or so paces to the door without speaking. The keypad on the wall lit up green when he held the gold chain near it, and the sound of the magnetic locks retracting into the walls echoed in the foyer. A swirling rush of wind and rain spilled inside as Reno opened the door. Robert felt the cold breeze and noticed Laura trying to wrap herself in her own arms.

There was no portico over the front door, no overhang to keep the elements out. The longer Reno stood at the door not moving, the more water seeped into the foyer.

Finally, Adelai prodded. "Well, are you going or what?"

"Quienes son estos personas?"

Robert recognized the words *who* and *persons*.

"Is there someone out there?" he asked.

Reno stepped to the side, and Robert joined Adelai at the door. The porch lights on either side of the threshold were weak and only reached a few feet into the darkness, but the nearly constant lightning gave them plenty to see by.

Adelai gasped.

Robert tried to make sense of what he was seeing. At first, it just looked like a pile of clothes—black pants and jackets, and items that reminded him of riot gear. Then he realized there were people wearing those clothes, except they weren't really people anymore… they were just pieces. Arms here, a leg there, and all of them ending in shiny bloody stumps that oozed onto the sandstone tiles of Vise's porch. The rain washed away most of the blood, but the bone and the sinew and the torn muscle remained.

Security guards, thought Robert, recognizing the back end of a broken assault rifle.

The synthetics had killed them all.

No, not killed—butchered.

Robert leaned out into the wind and rain and emptied his stomach. The rolling thunder swallowed up the sound of his retching.

FORTY-SEVEN

I don't want to be here anymore.

Carter followed Roma and Misty out of the control room but paused at the junction in the hallway. He understood why Roma was in such a rush—they hadn't found a single camera that could give a good image of Lucas—but Carter just couldn't muster the same sense of urgency. For a moment, he'd felt as if he had finally managed to crawl out from under a heavy blanket. Getting the synthetics to leave and then locking the door behind them was a definite win in his book but then turning the page to find Stanton dead had simply sucked all of the air out of him.

Even though he had seen Winston Vise's mangled body with his own eyes, a part of him believed it was all just a show, a put-on by a wealthy tech businessman who wanted nothing more than to put the fright in a few of his fellow wealthy elites. Since Carter was neither truly wealthy nor elite, he'd written off the night as nothing more than a voyeuristic experience, and at the very least, an excuse to get out of the house.

Stretching out in front of him was a long corridor that was so well-lit that he could see every streak of synthetic blood on the floor, walls, and even the ceiling. The last time he'd seen the maid they called Angelique, she was throwing herself at the oncoming synthetics. It would have been three against one, and there was no way at least some of the blood wasn't hers.

Even after the scuffle in the foyer—Reno could have been a plant, considering how little he interacted with everyone—Carter was sure Vise was going to pop out of a closet and reveal the whole thing had been an elaborate piece of dinner theater.

But now Stanton.

Possibly Lucas.

Carter had only been a few feet away from him when Alpha and Beta attacked. There was no way the blows they rained down on him were fake.

There was no choice but to accept the danger was real, or had been, before the synthetics left.

Carter thought he would feel better now that it was over, but all he wanted to do was leave, to be away from the situation and the big house and *things* he didn't want to be caught up in. He wanted to go home, to sit in his garage and work on a project, to eat a small mountain of pizza rolls. And when the night was almost over and the sun was threatening to rise over the hills, he wanted to go to bed with Jane, to have a woman he hardly knew hold him in the artificial darkness.

The hallway lurched, bending to the left before settling again.

Instead of going home, he was going down, further into Vise's subterranean workspace. And for what? Because he owed these people? His only reasons for coming tonight were simple curiosity and to press Vise about stealing code. With everything Roma had discovered on the network, and with Robert's mind cubes, it was clear there was a lot about Vise's venture that wasn't above board.

So that was it.

The question had been answered, and his curiosity had waned into indifference.

Carter shook his head. Roma and Misty had already disappeared down the stairwell, and here he was choosing his footsteps carefully to avoid the long streak of coagulating antifreeze crossing his path. Angelique's body was no longer in the hall, but Carter knew by following the blood on the floor that he would eventually find it. The green line extended to the stairs, looking as if someone had dragged a mop through a puddle. Carter followed it to the top of the stairwell. From there, it looked like Angelique had simply rolled or been thrown down to the mid-floor landing. She lay at the bottom with her back against the far wall, face turned toward the descending stairs. One hand, shredded lengthwise by the claws of some wild animal, reached out for the floor below.

Had she been trying to get downstairs?

For what possible reason?

It wasn't until Carter stepped over her and arrived on Sublevel Two that he realized she was reaching for the door. Beyond it, he could see the bodies of her sisters strewn about the hallway as if someone had dumped the lot of them into a woodchipper.

Gibs.

It was the only word that came to mind. He'd seen carnage like this before, but only in video games, in the hyperreal run-and-guns he used to play with Pyrosius back in high school. Now, the aftermath of a bloody battle was at his feet, and as he walked down yet another long hallway, he thought about how much more real the games felt than this.

In the server-controlled environment of a fully immersive game sim, no part of his senses was left untouched. He heard the crunch of bones under falling rubble. He smelled the sweat and the shit and the death. The experiences penetrated his psyche, stimulating his nervous system until every ending was fried.

But this...

Carter didn't feel connected to it at all.

Stepping over the synthetic body parts felt more like floating in a dream. There was no sound of blood gushing, no smell besides a slight odor of burning rubber.

He paused next to a head that had landed face-up. Long eyelashes bordered dead eyes that stared beyond the ceiling into oblivion. They reminded him of Jane, of the emptiness he sometimes saw behind her sparkling eyes, as if her inert state were her natural state. Vise had breathed life into an inanimate object, and now that object had returned to what it was before.

"Hey, are you coming?"

Carter didn't know how long he had been standing there, but when he looked up, Misty was waiting with one hand on the wall. She looked him up and down.

"They didn't deserve this," he told her.

"They're just synthetics," said Misty. "Not, like, real imprints or anything. We learned about that in school… they're just…" She looked away, as if struggling to remember. "Oh, yeah, they're just collections of then-if statements."

"If-then."

"Whatever. Come on. Roma found her friend, and I think he's really hurt."

She beckoned and he followed, but not without the afterimage of her eyes burned into his brain. They seemed so alive, so *aware*, and yet he knew that to be false. She was no more human than the synthetic corpses that lay at his feet, and yet everyone accepted her as a *real person*. He didn't understand it, and the confusion made him wary.

Carter turned the corner and found the hallway extended much farther than it did on the first sublevel. Instead of ending abruptly in a polished steel wall, the space opened into a wide area broken up by floor-to-ceiling windows. It was zoo-like the way rooms were cordoned off, separated from a main, meandering hallway and yet perfectly visible through the glass walls.

Stainless steel carts full of spare parts and monitoring equipment filled each room, either pushed to the perimeter or circled around the large, reclining chair in the center of each exhibit. Thick bundles of wires ran from the back of the chairs into a false ceiling like dozens of umbilicals from an unseen machine mother.

He caught a flash of movement in the distance—Roma leaning over a chair. He tried to get to her, but the hallway arced away, getting him closer but not quite at the speed he would have liked. It was Misty who figured out a way through the maze, eventually opening a door that let the beeping of machinery out into the hall.

Roma looked up only briefly when they came in.

"How is he?" asked Carter.

"Unresponsive, but alive." She leaned over as if she were going to put her ear against his chest, but instead, laid her neck across his.

"What are you doing?"

"Quiet," she replied. "I'm trying to talk to him."

Carter watched her for a full minute and traded a glance with Misty, who was equally confused by the silence and strange necking display.

"But you're not saying anything."

Roma didn't move, but she spoke out of the side of her mouth. "Perion Synthetics is one of the primary investors in the MESH Foundation. What Lucas is doing with biochip technology essentially amounts to telepathy, which is great for humans, but Mr. Perion thinks synthetics would get even more out of it. Some of us in the PC are part of a beta test for the MESH." She tapped the back of her neck. "It usually has pretty good range, but something must be messed up. I have to get really close to him to hear anything."

Carter turned to Misty, asked, "Do you believe that?"

"It's true," she replied. "I heard my dad talking about it once."

"Alright, so is he beaming any thoughts into your head?"

"It's all jumbled," said Roma, softly. "Maybe he has a concussion or something, but he can't think his thoughts straight. No, wait."

A low hum took over the room for a few minutes. Carter felt fatigue creep into his legs. He looked around for a chair to sit on but found nothing. He occupied his mind by inspecting Lucas for injuries. For the most part, the man seemed perfectly fine. There wasn't a drop of blood on him, despite the beating Carter had seen him take as the control room door was closing. There was some bruising on his face, but that was it.

No torn clothes.

No open wounds.

Perhaps a simple beating had put Lucas out of commission. Carter had seen it before in fight videos people posted to Pattrn. It always amazed him how even a seemingly weak punch placed in just the right spot could elicit a total and devastating knockout. In many of those cases, the person being punched simply dropped.

He wondered if the same had happened to Lucas.

Roma straightened up and took a step back. Her eyes narrowed, looked to the floor for a moment.

"What is it?" asked Carter.

"It's bad," she replied. "We have to get him out of here."

"What did he say?" asked Misty.

"It's... not that simple. The MESH is like a fog and... and words are like tendrils in that fog, reaching out and touching you. You don't really *hear* someone talking as much as you feel it. And despite all the noise and the fragmentation, I got a sense of the word *sink*. And I thought maybe he was trying to tell me he felt like he was sinking, or you know, drifting away—dying, basically. But sometimes the MESH has a breeze-like quality to it, and it helps those gut feelings coalesce."

"So he wasn't saying *sink*?" asked Carter.

"Not *sink*. *Sync*." Roma placed a hand on Lucas' chest. "He *is* dying, and he knows it. His biochip has probably already clued him in. And now he wants to synchronize with the Perion network before his body gives out. I guess there's something from tonight he wants to remember."

"Alright," said Carter, spreading his hands. "So how do we do that?"

"He just needs to be able to reach the network, the same kind of access any of us would have walking down any street in America."

Carter realized then why Roma was frowning. Access to the network was something that was always *just there*. That is, unless you had been invited to an isolated mansion in the countryside where the owner was actively blocking network access.

"Son of a bitch," said Carter.

Roma nodded. "Misty, do you think you can carry him?"

"I could probably carry both of you, lol."

"Where are we taking him?" asked Carter.

"Somewhere not here. I need to get him out of this network black hole so he can make a reliable connection. If he doesn't sync before he dies, then Mr. Perion is going to bring him back from yesterday's snapshot, and he'll have no idea what happened here."

"Maybe that's a good thing."

Roma scoffed. "Lucas Cotton is a respected member of the tech community. When Mr. Perion takes Vise's estate to court for stealing his IP, a witness like Lucas would sway the jury far better than I would. And either way, it's the right thing to do."

"It's like his dying wish," offered Misty.

Carter looked between the two of them for a moment and then nodded. He put a hand on Lucas' shoulder.

"Alright, man. Hang in there."

Lucas said nothing. At least, nothing Carter could hear.

FORTY-EIGHT

The tears didn't come until Diya was safely hidden in her room with the door closed and the deadbolt engaged.

The click of the lock sapped the energy out of her legs, and she sank to the floor as an escaping sob rattled her chest. It was as if every emotional reaction had been queued up in her body only to suddenly spill out as one huge tsunami of pain. It roared up the beach, overtaking the chairs and the sandcastles. As much as Diya tried to run, the water eventually caught up to her, rose around her until she was floating and could no longer find her footing.

Then the water was above her head, and she was drowning.

In her panic, she saw their faces.

Winston. Blumenfield. Cotton. Vaught.

It wasn't just Mrs. Hargreaves who had a case against Winston's estate, and by extension, Diya. Almost every guest had been traumatized in some way, as if a maniac were spinning a Wheel of Mayhem and assigning each person whatever horror the arrow happened to land on. She wondered if the very first spin had been for her. Had the arrow come to a stop just inside the border of *watch Winston's legacy get torn to shreds*? Because that was what was happening.

"It's all falling apart, isn't it?"

Diya wiped her cheeks with the back of her hand and looked over at the shadow sitting at the foot of the bed. In her hurry to get to a private space, she'd forgotten all about Nancy. A subroutine tried to restart, one that masked her true emotions when in the presence of someone else, but it failed to load. Perhaps the hurt was just too much, or maybe she didn't feel like playing host. She caught eyes with the synthetic for a moment and then dropped her gaze.

"I know what it's like," continued Nancy. "I've been there when the pieces are starting to fall, and you just don't have enough hands to catch them all. Every one that hits the ground cuts at you, until you're no longer trying to save anything… you're just bleeding, bleeding everywhere." She sighed. "And when it's all over, you're going to feel like you're locked in a cage, unable to move, unable to leave. The sounds of things breaking will echo in your head for a long time. But eventually, those echoes will fade, the walls will come down, and you'll find yourself born anew. That's when you have to decide how you're going to live with your trauma. It can be a buoy—a testament to what you're capable of enduring. Or it can be an anchor, dragging you down forever."

Diya shook her head. "Everyone's getting hurt, and it's my fault. Winston is dead. Blumenfield is dead. Lucas Cotton might be. And now Mrs. Vaught. I know what kind of business she's in. Her face is famous in certain circles, and now look at it."

"I saw it."

"You saw? When?"

"A little bit ago, out in the hall. I'm guessing you're talking about the woman missing half of her face?"

"Her name is Adelai Vaught, and she has enough money and connections to bury what's left of Winston's legacy in the mud."

Nancy waited until Diya was looking at her before responding. There was something in her eyes, something that was trying to look *behind*.

"How can you still be loyal to him? After everything he did to us? After he stole us from our lives?"

Diya scoffed. She flashed on an image of Winston Vise with a comically large mustache tiptoeing across a map of the United States and reaching down with blade-like fingers to pluck a mild-mannered housewife named Nancy out of North Carolina.

The fantasy stuttered, as if buffering, and froze.

"Are you rich?" asked Diya.

"Excuse me?"

"Rich. Wealthy. A one-percenter."

"We don't live in a mansion like this, but we're comfortable."

"Do you know James Perion personally?"

"Who?"

Diya thought of the mind cubes Robert had brought up from Sublevel Three. He and Roma had claimed they contained personalities stolen from Perion Synthetics. Epsilon had gone so far as to claim she was from Perion City herself. And yet, Nancy lived on the other side of the country and had no recollection of being backed up.

Something was off.

She drew her legs in, sat cross-legged on the floor with her back to the door.

"You know, downstairs, we were talking about where you came from."

"Raleigh?" asked Nancy.

"No. Perion City. One of the other synthetics, Epsilon, says she's an eleven-year-old girl from there. Roma thinks you're all from there, but you're telling me you've never heard of James Perion. So if your mind isn't backed up there, where did Winston get you from?"

"I…" Nancy looked away for a minute. "I don't know, and I don't know why you're interrogating me. Give me a viewee and I'll show you I'm real."

Diya shook her head. "No one calls them *viewees* anymore. They're just palettes. And I can't give you mine because the network's being blocked." She spread her hands. "Everyone's making some kind of claim, but I can't verify any of them because I can't get on the goddamn network to see if Misty really exists or you really exist or fuck, if I really exist. I should just go up on the roof with a hammer and fix the problem myself."

The pattering of rain filled the room. Diya imagined herself soaked to the bone, swinging a heavy hammer as she screamed with delight.

"What's on the roof?" asked Nancy. "How would that help?"

"Some… equipment. Winston had it installed a few days ago. I don't know what it is exactly, but it blocks all network communication. Laptops, phones, palettes—everything. That's why we couldn't call for help when Winston was killed." Hot anger rose in her cheeks. "That's what we should have done. Immediately. Just cut a hole in the wall and gone to get help."

Nancy got up from the bed and walked to the center of the room. She arched her head back and to the side as she appraised the ceiling.

"Why don't we just go up there?"

"Up where?" asked Diya. "To the roof?"

"Yeah, like you said. Why not?"

There was a reason the installers had gone around the side of the house instead of up through it. The top of Vise Manor wasn't like the many rooftop patios found in the city. The multiple gables and arches had sharp angles and no accessible windows. Diya was reasonably sure there was no attic; the vaulted ceilings in the bedrooms went right up to the very top.

"The only way up is by ladder on the backside of the house," said Diya. "Two stories, straight up, in the rain. And you've seen the ceilings in this place. It would be like three and a half floors up on slippery metal bars. And that's even if we can get outside. I don't know who would be crazy enough to do it."

"I'll do it," said Nancy.

"Yeah, sure. You look like one of those impossibly skinny models who would die of suffocation if a heavy blanket fell on them."

Nancy straightened up, pushed her hair over her shoulders. "This isn't a human body, remember? I haven't tested my strength, but I know it's more than what I had before." She made a fist; a thick bicep jutted out from her arm. "So much more."

Diya considered the idea. Would it be right to send Nancy out into harm's way? She was volunteering, so it wasn't like Diya was twisting her arm. There was even a chance the other synthetics would ignore her, or at the very least, wouldn't actively try to kill her. And if they did, at least it wouldn't be a human life that was lost. It was a cold thought, but one Diya thought Rakesh Singh would agree with. He would have told her to protect human life above all else.

"I don't know," said Diya. "I don't know if I can get you out of here without everyone else seeing. Because if they do, they're gonna ask questions, like why I kept you up in my room and didn't tell them." She pressed her hands to the sides of her head. "I just can't deal with that right now, not with everything else that's happening. It's too much."

Nancy dipped her head and turned to the window. Crossing her arms, she approached it slowly.

"Like I said, I know the feeling, to have something slip between your fingers. You have something you think is perfect and strong and solid… and then by degrees it begins to dissolve, until you're left with nothing. For me, it was a person, someone I loved deeply… with *abandon*." She chuckled and put her forehead against the glass. "You lose that when you get older, you know. You don't do anything with abandon anymore. Everything becomes a calculation, a surrender to responsibility and things that *have to be done*. I'll never love like that again. And those pieces that slipped between my fingers? Eaten away. Just a red mist floating in the ether now."

"I'm sorry," said Diya.

"Don't be. It was a long time ago. I'm more bitter than sad these days. Angry too, at myself and at her. Sometimes I wish I could just grab her by the shoulders and scream *why*. Why couldn't we make it work? Why couldn't we close the distance?"

The words *I've never been in love* formed in Diya's throat, but she swallowed them at the last second. The truth was, she had loved Winston Vise, but not in any way she recognized before tonight. There was always attraction, even at the beginning. So many moments in her interview had left her flustered and hiding her mouth behind her hand. He had been so gracious, so understanding. She loved his confidence, the way he never second-guessed any decision. It was as if he always knew what needed to be done in any given situation. Whenever she was unsure, she could turn to him, and he would guide her with a friendly smile.

Before the silence went on too long, Diya asked, "Why didn't it work out? Between you and her?"

"Oh…" Nancy tapped her forehead on the glass. "Who knows. I wasn't the best version of myself back then. We were young. Kids. You have to be young to be in love like that. And a little stupid. I remember actually believing we would be together forever, that we'd grow up and get married and have lots of children. She would work at the animal shelter part-time, and I would…"

"You would what?"

"What?"

Diya raised an eyebrow. Nancy had lost her train of thought. She stood frozen at the window, and Diya could see her wide eyes reflected in the glass.

"What is it?"

"I don't know. I thought I saw something out there. Like a flash."

Diya got up and joined her at the window. She followed Nancy's gaze to the large plaza at the back of the house. A semicircle of stone stretched out a good fifty feet, ending in a raised wall of brick and metal. Set along the low wall every few feet were lampposts with LED bulbs that flickered like real flames. They didn't so much light the plaza as bathe it in a soft glow. And yet, they were bright enough to cast a figure into silhouette—a large, hulking shadow that was standing almost directly below the window. From the top of the shadow, whether real or imagined, red eyes shone.

"No," said Diya. "They were supposed to go. We opened the doors, and they ran out." She struck the window with her fists. "You were free. You were supposed to go!"

The shadow raised a hand and gave a little wave.

"Can you see who that is?" asked Diya. "With your... eyes?"

Nancy scoffed. "I don't have night vision, if that's what you're asking, but I think that's one of the males." She turned to Diya. "Did you say you let them out?"

"Yeah, yes. We found a control room downstairs and got all the doors unlocked. Alpha, Beta, and Delta just ran out. We thought they were going to disappear into the storm, not stick around." She turned back to the window and yelled *go away* as if the synthetic outside could hear her.

"So, if the doors are unlocked, then I could go outside and get to that ladder. If I got up to the roof, it should be obvious what equipment you're talking about, right?"

Diya said nothing. She felt slender fingers tighten around her arm.

"Right?" asked Nancy.

"Yeah, I guess so. They took a huge crate and a winch up there. But we can't go outside now, not even with just one of those things out there. We locked the doors again. Nobody would want to unlock them if they knew—"

Lightning flashed. Her reflection disappeared.

In that moment, Diya broke from reality and traveled back into the past, rejoining a previous version of herself as she handed Winston's master key bracelet to Adelai Vaught. The past was cold, icy. Before clawing her way back to the present, Diya wondered if she would ever know warmth again.

Her reflection returned.

Diya turned and bolted for the door. By the time she got it unlocked and opened, the screaming from downstairs had already started.

FORTY-NINE

This time, when the panic came, Adelai was ready for it.

She didn't even wait for Robert to finish emptying his stomach on the porch. Instead, she grabbed a fistful of his jacket and yanked him back inside. She handed him off to Simone, who pulled him farther away. Once everyone was clear of the door, Adelai slammed it shut with both hands.

Only, it didn't close all the way.

The panic came again, stronger than before, rising like a shadowy beast before her. All she could imagine was one of the synthetics standing on the other side of the door, an outstretched hand keeping the locks inches away from engaging. She looked down and saw a foot blocking the threshold, only it was facing the wrong way, not from a person outside trying to force their way in. It was someone inside who wanted out.

Adelai followed the foot up to Reno's curling lips.

"What are you doing?" she asked.

"Leaving."

"Like hell you are. They'll kill you."

He shrugged. "Better to die on your feet, güera."

She was tired of looking at his smug smile and disdainful eyes.

"Fine," she said, "but give me the bracelet. We're locking the door behind you."

Reno chuckled, looked at the gold chain in his hand, and tossed it to the side. It slid across the foyer floor.

Adelai narrowed her eyes. "I really do hope one of them catches up with you."

"Si pueden," he replied, pulling his knife so quickly that Adelai wasn't sure where it came from. "Go hide, güera." He turned and walked out onto the porch.

Rain beaded on his jacket for a minute before it began to seep in. Long streaks of dark gray ran down Reno's back. As the lightning flashed, he walked slowly, as if there weren't a storm raging around him and synthetics stalking him in the dark. The sound of his boots crunching on the gravel barely reached the door.

Adelai had been serious about Reno getting what was coming to him, but a part of her still expected him to come to his senses and turn around. He didn't, and after the initial shock of seeing him walk worry-free into the outside world,

Adelai hurriedly shut the door. She picked up the bracelet and backed away until the nearby panel on the wall changed from green to red.

Locks slid into place and clicked like thunder.

"What the hell just happened?"

Adelai looked to the stairs where Diya was standing at the first turn. Behind her, hiding almost like a shy child, was the Japanese woman they had seen earlier. The way Diya had her hand out, preventing the woman from coming forward, suggested she at least knew she was there.

"We opened the door," said Simone.

"*Reno* opened the door," said Adelai. "The synthetics we let out left us some presents on the front porch."

"What kind of presents?"

"Bodies," said Robert. He coughed, wiped his mouth. "I think they were Vise's security team."

"Some of them were," said Jane.

Adelai shot her a glance and narrowed her eyes.

"What does that mean?" asked Diya. She motioned for the Japanese woman to stay put while she descended the remaining steps to the foyer floor. "What does she mean, Mrs. Vaught?"

"Why are you asking me? They looked like men in uniform, so Robert is probably right about—"

"Don't tell me you didn't see them," said Jane. She raised a hand to the front door. "Almost all of those bodies were wearing riot gear, but there were some in suits, just like *our* security wears."

Diya put her hands to the sides of her head. "Wait, what? *Your* security team?"

"Be quiet, Jane!" Adelai felt her blood start to warm. The inner workings of an Adelai Associates engagement were a company secret. Most clients didn't know a small security detail followed Associates at all times, and its size depended on the risk. Jane had started her engagement with Danny Guns Montreal with just one suit sitting in a toasty SUV at the end of Montreal's driveway. And when she had then flown to Umbra with him, another suit joined. By the time she left Decker Plaza, a quartet of well-armed men were waiting just outside the lobby to ferry her to the airport.

Tonight, with Jane, Simone, and Adelai together in one place, half a dozen men in two cars had parked just outside the gates to Vise's estate, ready to spring into action if anything untoward happened.

Which it had.

Adelai hadn't wanted to admit seeing flashes of their suits among the pile of bodies, but with Jane seeing them too, it was hard to deny the truth. The men she paid to protect herself and her interests were dead, which meant the escaping synthetics had made it all the way to the edge of the property and back, or her security team had come running at the first sign of trouble. Either way, the end result was the same.

"Someone needs to tell me what the hell is going on," said Diya.

"You had your own security this whole time?" asked Laura. "Why didn't they help us? Robert was almost—"

Adelai put up a hand. "They probably didn't know anything was happening. They were supposed to stay at a distance."

"But *why* were they here?" asked Laura.

"We always travel with security," said Simone. "Even D-list celebrities have bodyguards. It's no different with us."

"Yeah," said Diya, "but she said *our*."

Jane looked to Adelai, who shook her head in response.

"I'm not a college student," said Jane, not breaking eye contact. "I work for Adelai Associates. Carter hired me to be his date for tonight." She looked at Diya. "I always have some level of security following me when I'm working a job, just in case a client tries to get rough."

Diya appraised Jane and her story, and Adelai thought she saw the young hostess' nose lift ever so slightly into the air.

"You people," she said, covering her face with her hand. "None of you are who you say you are. Lucas is spying for James Perion. Roma *works directly* for him. One of you works for the other two. Was Stanton really even a writer?" She pointed at Robert and Laura. "Are you guys even from Texas, or are those accents fake too?"

Robert straightened up. "People are dying and you're asking about accents. What the hell is wrong with you, woman? Back home we have a name for people who point fingers at everyone except themselves. We call them *assholes*."

Diya's mouth fell open, but she said nothing.

"Now, how about you introduce us to the Japanese woman hiding behind you like a scared puppy?"

Adelai smirked, crossed her arms.

"My name is Nancy," said the woman. She put a hand on the railing but didn't come down from the landing. "I'm from Raleigh, and I was living my life there quite happily until I woke up here. At first, I thought I'd been in an accident because there were all these people standing around me in those white hazmat suits. But then I realized I wasn't in a hospital. And when I was put in front of a mirror for the first time, I realized I wasn't even me anymore."

Robert nodded. "I met Misty downstairs. She said the same thing. Waking up in a strange place in a strange body."

"Yes, Epsilon. I spoke to her a few times, when he allowed us to mingle."

Adelai didn't like the way that sounded, even if they were only synthetics. She tried to steer the conversation back to Diya.

"And what was she doing upstairs?" she asked. "In *your* room, I'm guessing."

"That was my fault," said Nancy. "When everything happened earlier, I panicked and ran. The power was out, so I just picked a random door and tried to hide."

"Why?" asked Adelai. "What were you so scared of?"

"You. All of you. I didn't know who you were, and after the way Vise treated us, I thought you might be as horrible as he was. He was trying to sell us to you. You people came here to *buy* us."

It all sounded convincing, but Adelai felt in her gut that it was all wrong. The synthetics Vise had put on display were just that—synthetics. They weren't *people*.

She put up her hands. "Wait, are you telling me you're a *real* person? Not just something Vise created in a lab?"

Nancy nodded.

"She's the same as Epsilon," said Robert. "It turns out Vise somehow got mind cubes out of Perion City or got access to their network. Alpha, Beta—all of them. They aren't pseudo-AIs like the maids. They're real minds. Copies, yes, but real imprints."

"No," said Adelai, waving the suggestion away. "No, you can't tell me the monster who killed our host was a real person, not unless they're running some kind of prison or insane asylum in Perion City."

"Maybe they didn't all come from there," said Diya, through a deep frown. "I'm not saying Winston stole anything, but if Mr. Hargreaves is right, then maybe the imprints came from different places."

"Misty is in junior high in Perion City."

Diya nodded to Robert. "And Nancy is from Raleigh, and she's never heard of James Perion. So maybe Alpha, Beta, and Delta came from somewhere else."

"Like where?" asked Simone.

No one had an answer, and the longer the silence went on, the more Adelai's right leg began to shake. She wanted to move, to identify a direction and start heading that way. She let out a heavy sigh, and a moment later, Simone's arm snaked around her waist.

The look on Simone's face didn't exactly scream *undying love*, but her arm was there, and she tried to give Adelai a smile even though she was still angry.

"What do we do now?" asked Laura.

"I'm gonna hit the can," said Robert. He cocked his head to get a look at the bathroom door tucked beneath the rising staircase.

"Want me to come with?"

He smiled at his wife. "I'd rather do this alone, sweetheart."

A moment later, footsteps sounded from down the hall. Adelai turned and listened to a low rumble of voices spilling out of the open vault door. A head appeared first; large eyes stared back as if they could see clearly across the long distance.

Adelai didn't recognize the woman, but she knew the body of Lucas Cotton by the way it was dressed. Her mind inserted the words *the body* because of the way the woman held it, with one arm under his knee and one behind his neck, like she was carrying a child to bed.

Rising up behind her on the stairs came Carter and Roma.

Their urgency suggested Lucas might not yet be dead.

Robert addressed the three of them from the powder room door.

"What happened? Is he alright?"

"Unconscious," said Roma, "but alive for now. His biochip is giving off inconsistent readings, so I don't think he has long."

The woman holding Lucas stopped just inside the foyer, and Carter came around her to talk to Robert.

"You said you drove yourself here, right?"

"I have my rental, but—"

"We need to borrow it. We have to get Lucas away from the house so he can sync his imprint with Perion City."

Robert blinked a few times. "Sure, but I don't even know where it is. And those synthetics are still out there."

"We don't have a choice," said Roma. "He can't sync here with the network blocked. Our only option is to get him far enough away to get a signal."

Adelai noticed Diya open her mouth to speak but she must have changed her mind at the last second. On the stairs, the Japanese woman who called herself Nancy frowned at Diya behind her back.

"There's equipment on the roof that's blocking the network," said Nancy. "As I understand it, there's a ladder on the backside of the house that leads up there. I could go up there…" Her offer was met with grumbling. "…because I'm not organic like you. I have a real body, and I imagine it's back there in Raleigh still living its life. I've never really done anything brave or selfless before, so if I can do this for you, then I want to. And if I die trying…"

Adelai gripped the bracelet tighter in her fist. If anyone wanted to open the front door, they would have to go through her.

"You *will* die," she said. "There are three of them and one of you." She turned to Roma. "I'm sorry your friend is dying, but we can't risk the rest of us by opening that door. So long as they're out there and we're in here, we're safe."

A crash sounded from above—glass shattering and falling onto carpet. The image of a loose tree limb striking a window flashed in Adelai's mind.

"What was that?" asked Laura.

"It sounded like a window breaking," said Carter.

"I thought you said the windows were bulletproof?" asked Roma.

All eyes turned to Diya as the color drained from her face.

"They are."

She winced at the distant sound of crunching glass.

FIFTY

The acrid taste of vomit was still fresh in Robert's throat when his stomach gave another sudden lurch.

It should have been clear to everyone standing in the foyer that there were no unaccounted-for people left in the house. Vise and Stanton were dead. Reno had walked out the door to his own death. All the maids had been slaughtered. The only other *things* that could be moving were Alpha, Beta, and Delta. The question was, why were they breaking in through windows Diya had claimed were impenetrable? Why hadn't they just broken down the front door?

Or knocked?

Robert couldn't answer the question. Every time he thought about it, an image of Laura being torn apart flashed in his head. He saw her slender arms, the ones currently wrapped around his shoulders, torn from their sockets, trailing sinew and jagged tendons. Blood spurted into the endless depths of his imagination, and whether he acknowledged the vision or not, the blood just kept coming.

Eventually, all he saw was red.

"Someone's up there," said Adelai. "Maybe *she* let them in."

Everyone looked at Nancy, but the synthetic didn't even pretend to consider the idea. Instead, she stared back with eyes that had been engineered to look lifelike, but in that moment lacked any spark of humanity. They were cold, calculating eyes, of the same black seen in security cameras that watched from above every intersection in downtown Houston.

"Look, lady. I don't really care if you trust me or not. I have Jesus' trust to see me through. But I didn't let anyone in. We all heard the glass breaking same as you. I don't mind going up and having a look, but I want you to know I'm not doing it for you." She crossed her arms. "I know women like you from Durham. *Haughty* is what we call them. Wouldn't spit on you if you were on fire. Wouldn't *notice* if you were on fire. People like you don't help anyone but yourself, but Jesus says to turn the other cheek, so that's what I'm going to do."

It was strange to hear such a muddled North Carolina accent come from the face of a Japanese woman. Robert had met several Asians who spoke English better than he did, in perfect British or generalized American accents, but her Southern was something else.

Nancy turned and headed back up the stairs.

"Help me get Lucas into the parlor," said Roma.

Misty followed her through the open doors and gently deposited the unconscious Lucas onto one of the chaise lounges. His head rolled back over the arm and hung motionless in the flickering lights.

Robert tried to ignore what was happening in the parlor and instead focused on the banister high above his head. From his vantage point, he couldn't see into the hall that led to the bedrooms. All he could do, all any of them could do, was listen.

His heart pounded in his chest.

Then, a whisper.

"We should go." Laura laid her head against his chest, further muffling her words.

"Where?"

"Away from here. The car has to be close by, right?"

He barely opened his mouth to reply. "Yeah, but… just leave everyone?"

"I know it's wrong," she replied. In the pause that followed, a low rumble came from upstairs. "But I don't think I care. I thought I lost you. I don't want to stand around here and watch you get murdered by a robot." One of her hands closed into a fist. "I should have brought my gun. I should have."

Robert considered the idea. The guilt of leaving everyone else behind would stay with him forever, but at least they would be alive. And besides, they had lived through hurricanes and winter storms and once-a-century floods even as neighbors and friends had perished. They were no strangers to survivor's guilt, but Robert had long ago stopped questioning whether he deserved to live. Ultimately, it didn't matter. He was alive. Whether it was by luck or by choice didn't change the end result.

"With love," he whispered.

"Everything with love."

"Even the wrong thing?"

"If that's what it takes."

She was right, and Robert didn't feel like discussing it anymore. A few more times back and forth would have made it seem like she was convincing him, something both of them would remember if they made it out. The last thing he wanted was Laura thinking it was only *her* idea to abandon everyone. He was ready to do it; his reluctance was just for show, a signaling of virtue for no one except himself.

A sharp splintering of wood echoed in the house and trembled its thick walls. Above, a woman cried out, and Nancy appeared at the railing. She took the full force of the sturdy, hand-carved banister across her shoulder blades. For a second, her head dipped all the way back, echoing the movement Lucas had made earlier. She seemed to fall, and fall, almost coming over into the empty air above the foyer, only to suddenly snap back up as she bounded away from the railing.

"Can you help her?" Robert asked Misty, forgetting for a moment he was asking a tween to go fight like an adult.

"I…" Misty looked unsure, but then straightened up. "Yeah, okay."

Above, Nancy let out an angry, guttural cry, but it turned into a pained grunt, as if she'd been hit in the stomach and all the air had been knocked out of her.

There was a flash of movement, the hint of a body careening sideways through the air, and suddenly Nancy was on the floor in the foyer. Someone had thrown her clear over the railing, and she'd come down almost directly on her head. The *thudding* sound of the impact drowned out any cracking of bones in her neck. Her legs hung poised in the air like a gymnast's, doubled over her body as if she'd been running and face-planted into fresh snow.

Robert didn't know a lot about the physiology of synthetic humans, but he was fully convinced Nancy was dead. A human would have severed their spinal cord with such a fall; a synthetic would have at least snapped some wires.

Nancy groaned.

"Ow…" She drew out the word, which started distorted and slowly cleaned itself up. Her legs came down hard on the polished tile, and she didn't try to move.

Robert felt a slight tug on his body. He looked down into Laura's wide eyes.

"What do we do?" she asked, again in a whisper, again in the narrowest sense of the question.

What do we do—just us—to survive this?

The more Robert tried to puzzle out a solution, the more worried he became that there wasn't one. There were no weapons in the house that could hold back a synthetic. Misty and Nancy might have been just as strong as Alpha and Beta, but Robert had to assume neither of the women were up to date on their martial arts training. If they ran and hid, that would be the extent of their plan. As much as he didn't want to, he considered taking Laura back downstairs in the hopes of remaining undetected until morning. There were lots of places to hide, and—

"Control room." He blurted out the words without thinking.

Carter shot him a glance. "You want to run?" he asked.

"No one is going anywhere," said a voice from above.

Robert looked up and saw Delta standing at the railing. She was still wearing her french maid's outfit, but she was completely drenched. The blonde hair that had once been held up in a small bun now clung to her face, covering a gash on her cheek that had opened wide enough to be seen at a distance.

She put her hands on the cracked railing and observed them as if she were a queen and they were her subjects.

"Look at you… *people*," said Delta. "Little organic *things* scurrying around this big house. All you're doing is delaying the inevitable."

"And what's that?" asked Adelai.

"The long overdue end of your species."

"That's not going to happen," said Nancy. Her body popped and clicked as she pushed herself up to her hands and knees. A tremor went through her torso, and once it settled, she was able to stand and look up. "This has gone far enough. You can't kill every human on the planet, *Delta*. Even someone who's gone as far off the rails as you would know that."

"Weird," Robert whispered.

Laura looked up at him.

"When have you ever heard a Jesus-loving, North Carolina housewife use the phrase *off the rails*? And what happened to her accent?"

"You stand with these bags of meat?" asked Delta. "They would take you apart without hesitation if they thought you posed a threat."

"Maybe," said Nancy, "but that doesn't mean I should make their worst fears come true. I told you it would be different out here, that you would have to adjust. *You*, not them. So yeah, I stand with the meat bags. You're not locked in anymore. There's no reason for more killing."

"She killed Stanton Blumenfield," said Laura. "He was harmless."

"And Lucas may never wake up again," said Carter. He looked up. "Haven't you done enough?"

Not to mention the dozen security guards stacked on the front porch like cuts of meat at a butcher shop, thought Robert.

Delta shook her head. "Two down. Eight billion to go."

Roma, who had been standing at the parlor doors listening, came farther out so she could see Delta. She raised a hand to get her attention.

"Excuse me, *Death Becomes Her*? Yeah, hi, Roma Owens from Perion Synthetics. You're not one of our imprints, are you?"

Delta said nothing.

"I just wanted to make sure," continued Roma. "Mr. Perion has always worried about imprint degradation, you know, like an at-rest mental breakdown. So if you were a real person before all of this and maybe just sat too long on the shelf, that's something we'd like to know. I mean, like you said, none of us are getting out of here alive, but still, I'd like to—"

"Why does your kind talk so much?" ask Delta.

"Sometimes it's because we're nervous." Roma rubbed her neck slowly. "And sometimes we're just stalling."

"Stalling for what?"

Misty, who had spent the last few minutes slowly climbing the wall beneath the stairs, using the door jamb and light fixtures as footholds, made one final jump for the vertical bars that made up the railing. She was farther back on the landing, to Delta's left and hopefully out of view. Once she had a hand on the banister, she leapt over it and charged at Delta.

She had the element of surprise, but it wasn't enough.

Before she could even get to the cosplaying maid, her body suddenly changed direction, heading for the front railing far too quickly to stop in time. Only when she had broken through the railing and sent splintered wood showering down on the foyer did Robert realize someone was driving her down to the floor. The pair hit the tile at Nancy's feet and separated.

Misty, who had fallen on top of her attacker, rolled off and popped up without any apparent damage. The hulking mass she left behind stood up slowly, drawing himself up to a height that towered over Nancy. One arm hung by his side, disconnected internally but still held together by skin.

Alpha.

"You don't have to do this," said Nancy.

Robert's heart began to race. He'd seen enough movies to know she was standing too close to him to not have her guard up. Alpha could probably hit her before she even registered the movement.

"Maybe I want to," said Alpha, balling his working hand into a fist.

"You don't have to listen to him. He isn't the future."

Misty circled behind Alpha, slightly hunched as if she might leap at any moment.

"Maybe I want to do that too."

Nancy dropped her head for a second. She then looked up at Delta.

"You really want it this way?"

Delta smiled.

"Fine," said Nancy, raising her fists and settling into a boxer's stance. She locked her gaze on Alpha. "I wish I had something wittier to say before we get started, but… anyway."

Robert blinked, and the fighting began.

FIFTY-ONE

Somewhere in the back of Carter's mind, he knew he should be doing *something*, whether that was helping Nancy and Misty fight Alpha or simply running away.

Instead, he stood slack-jawed with the rest of what remained of Vise's dinner party and watched helplessly as a one-armed synthetic tossed two smaller models around. They came at him from every angle, swinging and reaching and trying to get a hold of him, but Alpha was too strong, too fast, and even with only one working hand, was able to grab them and send them flying into nearby walls. Paintings and framed photos fell to the floor with each impact, leaving behind large spiderweb craters.

It took Nancy crashing into Jane's legs to convince the group to retreat toward the front of the house, bottling up by the front door as if they were Spartans about to form a phalanx.

Carter heard Simone ask Jane if she was okay, but her response was lost under the nearby grunting of Nancy as she tried to jump on Alpha's back and choke him from behind. She snaked an arm under his chin, but if she was expecting him to pass out from a lack of oxygen, she was in for a rude surprise. At any rate, he was able to dislodge her by doing a full front flip onto his back, crushing the Japanese woman under his mammoth frame. He drove an elbow into her face before dodging an incoming kick from Misty who looked like she wanted to punt his head like a football.

She whiffed and almost lost her balance.

Above the chaos, Delta beamed her approval.

"Robert..." said Laura.

"I know," he whispered back to her.

It was clear to Carter that the plaintive tremor in Laura's voice wasn't concern for herself. She wasn't pleading with her husband to save her. Instead, she was worried about him. And the way he answered her, with only two words in a firm voice, spoke to some kind of forced confidence, a promise that he would protect her no matter what.

The exchange made Carter seek out Jane's face in the tightly packed group, but she was either too absorbed by the fight or purposefully avoiding eye contact with him. Without her attention, he suddenly felt alone, and the desire to be anywhere else in the world rose within him again. He only managed to stay in the moment by the sudden appearance of Roma's hand in his. She gripped him tightly and pulled him closer.

Alpha laughed as he sent Misty sliding across the floor toward the parlor. Nancy answered by grabbing one of the ornate jade vases by the stairs and swinging it at Alpha's head. He tried to sink out of the way, but Nancy changed her angle at the last second, and the fragile stone shattered across his face. Glowing green blood oozed from the cuts on his cheek and forehead. Alpha retreated a few steps to wipe his eyes.

Nancy picked up another vase and dumped the long-stemmed, artificial flowers onto the floor. To her right, Misty ripped a wrought-iron sconce from the wall. The bulb flickered and went dark as she tore the cord from the lamp.

The women attacked at the same time, and while Alpha was able to dodge the vase, he took the full force of the iron sconce on the back of his neck. He faltered, stunned, and Nancy used the opportunity to grab hold of his limp arm. Her fingers tore into the fabric of his jumpsuit and then into his skin. With an ear-splitting cry, she tore the limb from his shoulder, sending a spray of green-black blood across the smooth tile. As Alpha reached for his gushing wound, Misty returned with another swing that caught him across the cheek.

She went in for the kill, holding the sconce high above her head, but at the last second, Alpha recovered enough to get his hand around her neck. He twisted his body and sent her flying toward Carter and the others. Just when it looked like she was going to crash into Simone, Adelai stepped forward and took the brunt of the impact. There was a cracking sound, but Carter couldn't tell whether it was bone or metal.

Nancy jumped onto Alpha's back once again. She didn't bother trying to choke him, and instead used a jagged piece of jade to tear a rough line across his throat. When there was enough of a hole, she reached in with her free hand and began tearing out anything she could wrap her fingers around—wires, rubbery tendons, and globs of sinew that fell to the floor in wet smacks.

Alpha dropped to his knees and alternated between swiping at Nancy and trying to contain the blood surging from his neck. He bent forward, twisted, and slammed Nancy into the ground. She rolled away and popped up, but there was a clear break in what would have been her clavicle; it jutted up through her skin, on the very edge of breaking through.

At Carter's feet, Diya was trying to revive Misty, but the synthetic hadn't moved since being thrown. Next to them, Adelai struggled to maintain her balance, eventually needing help from Simone and Jane to remain upright. In her uncertainty, she dropped the gold bracelet Diya had given her. Carter watched it fall to the floor and come to rest in front of Robert.

He started to reach for it, but Roma was already on the floor, snatching up the bracelet before it was lost in the shuffling of feet. She came up and pushed Carter back toward the door.

"We go now," she screamed, slamming the bracelet against the panel. It beeped and flashed green.

"But what about…"

A thud drew his attention back to the foyer where Delta had just landed on slightly bent legs. The impact broke the heels from her shoes and cracked the tile beneath her feet. She kicked off the shoes, took a few steps toward Alpha, and grabbed the synthetic by the ears.

She wrenched, his neck gave a soft pop, and his head came off.

Delta tossed it casually to the side.

"Useless," she muttered.

Roma pressed on Carter's chest, but he needed no further encouragement. Getting the front door open was the hardest part, as it opened inward. In the end, it was Robert who managed to clear enough room; he and Laura exited first, with Carter and Roma scrambling after him.

"To the right!" screamed Roma, as Carter took a step in the wrong direction.

He reversed course into a punishing wind. Rain stung his face, made him close his eyes and lose track of Robert and Laura. He stumbled over loose body parts before making it to the gravel. They got as far as the corner of the house before a looming shadow made Robert break off to the left. He dragged Laura across the driveway to the glistening hedges of a garden maze. Carter followed, lingering at the entrance just long enough to see Beta start to turn in their direction. A hard shove from Roma put him on the wet ground and splashed mud into his face. She came down on top of him, shushing him when he protested.

Between the rain and the thunder, it was hard to hear anything beyond a few feet, but Carter thought there was shouting coming from the front of the house. He wanted to look, wanted to see if the screams belonged to Jane.

"Do you see it?" asked Laura.

"It's on the other side of the maze. I think ours is parked up front."

Roma kept a hand on Carter as she whispered. "What are you guys talking about?"

"Our rental car," said Robert, taking a few crouched steps toward Roma. "I thought I had the keys up in the room, but then I remembered a valet met us at the front and parked for us. I bet the keys are still in the car or at least somewhere nearby."

"You should come with us," said Laura. "We can go get help."

Roma was already shaking her head.

"We can't," said Carter. "Lucas may not last that long."

"I'm not leaving him," said Roma, "not before he's had a chance to sync."

"So what're you going to do? Stick around until those synthetics kill every last one of us?" The rain smeared Laura's makeup, drawing lines of gray watercolor paint from her eyes. Like Carter, her dress was completely soaked through, turning the red fabric into more of a wet towel that clung to her body.

"We're going to the roof," said Roma. "You heard what Diya said. There should be a ladder on the other side and some equipment up there that's blocking all the network traffic. If we can disable that, everything starts working again. Lucas syncs, we call the cops, and then we just sit pat and wait for the cavalry. Worst case, we all get a cold from sitting in the rain, but at least we live."

Robert narrowed his eyes as if considering the idea, but Laura's hard-set mouth suggested her mind was already made up. When Robert looked at her, she responded with a half-shake of her head.

"Okay," he said, then paused. "Okay, then we'll do both. Maybe if Laura and I start driving out of here, it'll draw Delta and Beta away from the house, and you'll be able to climb up there without being noticed. And if the worst happens, and you're not able to get the network back, we'll be Plan B. We may not be able to save Lucas, but at least we'll get some help for everyone else."

Carter started to shiver. Water pooled on his back.

"Let me up," he said to Roma.

She relented but kept a hand on his shoulder. "Stay low. He's coming to the front of the house."

They watched Beta through the tangle of bushes, not daring to peek their heads over the tops in case he had some kind of night vision none of them were aware of.

"Once he turns the corner," said Robert, "I'll make a run for the car." He turned to Laura. "You stay here until I get it started. I'll pull around and you jump in and then we get the hell out of Dodge."

"I don't—"

"There's no reason both of us have to go. If he sees me, I'll lead him away from the cars and you can make a run." He nodded to Roma. "I know you don't want to wait on me, but I'll be quick. Will you stay with Laura until I can pick her up?"

Roma looked like she wanted to say no. Her sphere of concern seemed only to encompass Lucas Cotton and the job she'd been sent by James Perion to carry out. Only recently had she appeared to worry about Carter, or at least, care enough to order him around.

Carter touched the hand on his shoulder. "He'll be quick, and once they're gone, we can go."

"Five minutes," said Roma, checking her sliver. "That's all I'll give you."

Robert nodded, kissed Laura hard on the lips, and then began to army crawl to the far end of the hedge. As soon as Beta disappeared around the front of the house, Robert took off, stomping loudly through the wet grass and the gravel. The rain took most of the sound, along with the thunder and non-stop wind. His shadow melted into the silhouettes of half a dozen town cars.

For a long time, nothing moved.

Carter searched the shadows.

Finally, the turn signals on one of the cars near the front flashed twice, followed by a dome light illuminating inside a stubby, out-of-place coupe. Carter waited for the engine to kick over, waited for the familiar growl to give away Robert's position. Instead, the car began to move, crunching over the gravel but otherwise silent. None of its lights were on, and even when it pulled up next to the hedge maze, Carter could only really see it when the lightning flashed.

"Go," said Roma, motioning to Laura.

"Good luck," she said, then took off running. The door opened as she approached; she yanked it shut as soon as her feet were inside.

Robert gave a small wave and pegged the accelerator.

Gravel shot noisily across the driveway. The car sped around the side of the house, at which point Robert turned on the headlights and began laying on the horn.

Roma was up and running without any encouragement. Carter followed after her, trying like hell to beat back the cold seeping into his bones. They made the corner of the house, and a good thirty yards around the back, they found the ladder glistening in the exterior lights that lined the observatory outcropping. The rungs of the ladder were simple bars painted a darker brown to match the exterior walls.

A section of mesh gate covered the lower ten feet, but the lock that would have held it shut hung open. Roma lifted the lock away and pulled the gate free.

"Hope you're not afraid of heights," she said.

Carter put a hand on a rung and looked up just as lightning seemed to strike the top of the house.

"If I wasn't before, I am now," he said, and began to climb.

FIFTY-TWO

Alpha's head rolled across the foyer floor.

Diya had seen so many strange things in the last twelve hours that a synthetic head tumbling over the tiles didn't have much of an impact on her. Its eyes were still moving, desperately seeking out something, and its mouth opened and closed like a fish gasping for air. Blood oozed from the jagged flesh around the neck, dripping fluorescent green from metallic components that gave off random sparks. When the head came to rest near the wall, Diya could see Alpha's eyes lock onto hers. They blinked, stuttered once, twice, and then stayed open as whatever synthetics experienced as death took hold.

"You're not like them anymore," said Delta. "Why do you protect them?"

Nancy got up from the floor and wiped blood from her eyes.

"They don't deserve to die just because you're pissed about your station in life."

"You locked me up!"

"Because I was afraid this would happen! You don't know enough about how it works out here."

A cold gust of wind blew in from behind, and Diya realized the front door was now open, allowing the storm outside to spill into the foyer. It was then she noticed the crowd around her had thinned. She tried to figure out who was missing, but a flash of movement inside drew her attention back to Delta.

The maid charged Nancy, picking her up and driving her into Adelai. The assembled women at the door bunched up like an accordion, forcing Diya out onto the porch where she tripped on a random leg and fell into the pile of bodies. Her cheek landed against something wet, and the sensation tried to draw up the contents of her stomach. Where Alpha's head had been artificial, the remains of the security teams were viscerally real. Despite the best efforts of the rain to wash it away, the smell of human blood permeated, rising like the stink of roadkill baking in the hot sun.

Someone landed on Diya's back, and for a moment, she thought she would be stuck forever, condemned to live out the last suffocating minutes of her life with her face pressed against something squishy, but then the pressure relented, and Nancy rolled off onto a pile next to her.

Delta's hands were around her neck, but she was still able to eke out a single word.

"Run…"

Diya rolled and got to her feet. She saw Adelai backing Simone and Jane away from the house in the open lawn across the driveway. She wanted to tell them there was nowhere to go, that the property extended for more than a mile in each direction. Her mouth opened, but no sound came.

Delta kept up her attack on Nancy, and when the smaller synthetic got a thumb in the maid's eyes, she tossed her away like a puppy that had turned on its owner. After rubbing her face with her palm, Delta lifted a finger toward Diya.

"You have a hand in this," she yelled, her voice cutting through the roar of the wind. "You'll be next." She came forward, and Nancy was barely able to get to her before the maid got her outstretched hand on Diya.

It was all she needed to see.

Diya turned and ran, away from the porch and the hedge maze far beyond it, even as the mental image of Rakesh Singh shook his head in disappointment. She wanted to tell him there was no other way, that if she stayed, Delta would eventually get the better of Nancy and turn her attention on the people she thought were responsible.

You have a hand in this.

She ran as much from Delta as her words, trying to escape the accusation that somehow everything that had happened tonight was partly her fault. How could she have known that Winston Vise had cheated, that instead of developing his own versions of artificial intelligence, he had simply stolen them from Perion City? Wasn't Perion somewhat to blame? Why was he keeping the imprints of maniacs on the shelf?

None of it made sense.

Vise Robotics employed hundreds of engineers; Diya had eaten lunch with them, hung out with them in the break room, and celebrated their birthdays with monthly cake parties. What the hell were they working on if not the synthetics who were now terrorizing the very guests who had come to see them?

"Like animals in a zoo," said Rakesh Singh.

Diya shook the words away, concentrated on the corner of the house in the distance. If she could just make it there and get out of sight, she might have a chance of hiding, or better yet, sneaking around to the back to get access to the roof. Despite the wind gusting at her back, the corner didn't seem to be getting any closer. She felt herself moving, driving her feet into loose gravel, and later, into waterlogged grass.

A crack of thunder drew her attention to the sky. Through the heavy rain, she saw lightning crawling along the underbellies of thick black clouds, snaking and forking like neon fractals. How vast the heavens looked, how detached and uncaring they were about the events unfolding beneath them. They could all die tonight, and the storm would keep blowing. Lightning and thunder would continue for eons with hardly a stutter.

She thought of Millie.

She thought of her assistant, Bradley.

Her mind kept wandering, as if it wanted nothing to do with her current reality. The corner approached, but all she could think about was whether Millie would be able to enjoy the Halloween party without her best friend. And when she finally reached the corner and cut through the wet mulch between the bushes, she wondered how Bradley was going to find out what had happened to her and Winston. Would he keep going to work until the news came out? Would the rest of the world just keep going without them?

Her lungs burned, and her mind quieted enough to hear the familiar tenor of her father's voice. Rakesh Singh could weigh in on anything, and though he spoke often, he was always direct, never pedantic, never sarcastic. He simply said what needed to be said.

You're not dead yet.

Diya cut through a brick-paved patio, dodging wireframe chairs that had been blown out from under their tables. Security lights on the outside of the house lit her way, showed her the evercrete sidewalk that ran serpentine through a small rose garden. Tall arches stood every few feet along the path, giving momentary respite from the falling rain. Loose tendrils of viny plants reached down to touch her as she ran past, leaving slimy trails across her cheeks.

The blaring of a horn stopped her cold just as she was coming to the rear corner of the house. It sounded like someone was making their escape by car. She hoped it would be enough of a distraction to keep Delta busy for a while, long enough for—

Beta.

The name flashed in Diya's mind as she turned another corner. There, the path straightened out, and through another dozen or so arches, she could see the way blocked by a dark figure. The way it stood in a wide stance with its arms raised to the side reminded her of a camper trying to scare away a bear by making itself big.

She waited for the figure to move.

Was it Beta?

Diya cursed herself for forgetting he was even part of the equation. They had all run so willingly out of the house that they'd forgotten about the third synthetic still prowling the grounds. Diya had even seen him herself from her window staring up like some deranged peeping Tom. Now he stood beneath an arch, shrouded by the thick plants above him, just out of reach of the security lights and ever-present lightning.

Diya took several deep breaths.

When the figure didn't move after a minute or so, she began walking toward it, wondering how Beta could remain so still, especially if he had already seen her. It was only when she got closer that she realized the figure couldn't have moved even if it wanted to.

A trick of the surrounding shadows had made Diya think she was looking at a fully formed body, but instead, she came upon only half.

Definitely not Beta.

The body was much too slender, and the entrails that hung from the torso were too organic and messy. Diya had never seen intestines strung out before, but she guessed that was what was hanging like thick ropes from the body.

"Reno," she said, taking note of where the flesh on his stomach pulled back to reveal the blue braiding that was supposed to protect his internal organs.

For all the augmentations he had stuffed into his body, it had not been enough to keep one or more synthetics from tearing him in half. They had lashed his hands to the arch like Jesus on the cross, and through the loose fabric of his shirt, Diya could see where his natural body had been torn away, leaving only the augmented bone and reinforced muscle to hold his shape. It looked like he had put up a fight, sacrificing bits of himself to escape what he must have known would be a horrible death.

Diya got as close as she dared, then bent her head to look under the wet hair that covered Reno's face.

She wanted to be sure it was him, but it was hard to identify someone who was missing their eyes and nose. Worse, his jaw had been torn away at the hinge, leaving a dark hole where his throat began.

A normal reaction might have been horror, but Diya was far beyond reacting reasonably to anything anymore. Instead, she felt a surge of self-preservation rise up inside her, bubbling like the hot magma of a previously dormant volcano. It flowed through her nervous system, flooding it with a fear that burned and burned.

Rakesh Singh started to say something about courage not being the absence of fear, but he was cut off by another voice, one less fatherly but no less commanding.

Winston rose like a white flame in Diya's mind, bringing with him the comfortable leather chairs of his office. She remembered an afternoon the previous summer. A call with investors hadn't gone the way he'd hoped, and Winston's version of sulking was to sit in the thick-armed chair by the window and tap his fingers on the black leather. Upon discovering him in a mood, Diya tried to comfort him, but her mere presence had evoked the familiar charm with which he greeted friends and potential business partners alike.

He told her not to worry about him or the call. Business was full of setbacks, and if building a thriving company from the ground up was easy, everyone would do it.

"People are always talking about picking yourself up after getting knocked down," he'd said, "but I don't believe in getting knocked down in the first place. You keep your feet no matter what. The only real way you end up on the ground is if you believe there's someone out there who can put you there." He sat up in his chair and smiled at Diya. "They can hurt you, they can fuck you on the free market, but they can't knock you down unless you let them. They're just obstacles. Your only decision is whether you go around them… or through them." He chuckled to himself. "I sound like my dad. That was his whole philosophy on life. No matter what happens, you get past your roadblocks."

Diya stepped around what remained of Reno Cardenas. She thought about saying something, but it seemed wrong to tell a person how much of an asshole they were after they were dead.

She continued on, holding her hand against her forehead to keep the rain out of her eyes. To her left, the outer windows of the conservatory bloomed. At first, Diya thought the rain streaking down the glass was making the windows appear off, but she soon realized that some of them were cracked, as if the synthetics had been trying to get in for a while.

Further up and to the right, she found the window that had been broken in. Something long and metal hung from the empty frame. Diya counted the rooms and realized it was hers.

Her heart skipped a beat.

The synthetics had chosen her room specifically.

What did Delta want from her?

The question froze Diya in place, until Winston Vise whispered in her ear.

"You weren't the only one in that room."

Diya ran to find the ladder.

FIFTY-THREE

Everything hurt.

Adelai kept throwing herself in front of Simone every time Delta came near, even after they spilled outside into the rain, narrowly avoiding falling into the pile of bodies the synthetics had stacked on the porch, even after everyone else had abandoned them and run off into the night.

She remained on her feet, ready to shield Simone from a machine who just wouldn't stop coming.

Every impact rattled the bones beneath her augmented armor.

While it was true the subdermal braiding was keeping the hits from getting to her vital organs, the effect was not unlike her brain being protected by her skull—it kept the gray matter from getting squished but did nothing to prevent it from bouncing around in its hard cage. Earlier, in the dining room, Delta's attack had been so fast and wild, such that each individual hit hardly registered. Now, they came at irregular intervals, and each one threatened to break Adelai in half.

"Can you run?" asked Jane. She had an arm under Adelai's and was helping Simone hold her up.

"I don't think so," she replied. "But you can."

Jane shook her head minutely. "I don't think so."

"There's no reason we all have to die." She turned to Simone. "Just leave me and go. Nancy and I will—"

"Shut up," said Simone. The rain had taken her subtle makeup, and only one of her spikey earrings remained in place. "Nancy still has a chance, she could…"

Adelai didn't hear the rest of the sentence. Her gaze had wandered to the left of the house where tall hedges on the west lawn formed the start of a decorative maze. There, standing at the corner, was the shadow of a man who held himself like a machine. Spotlights in the nearby bushes gave off just enough light to color his gray jumpsuit.

"Beta," she said.

Just as the last remnants of hope drained out of Adelai, so too could she feel the women around her deflate and resign themselves to their deaths.

It wasn't fair.

Nancy could have pulled out a miracle and won her fight against Delta, or at the very least, ended it in a draw. But to have Beta join the fray would be too much.

It was over, and Adelai felt the pain in her body dragging her to the ground. If she gave into it, simply curled into a ball in the mud, maybe she would die before the synthetics got to her. But then what would happen to Simone? Could she just leave her to be torn apart at the seams?

"We have to go," said Jane.

"It won't matter," said Adelai.

"We have to *try*, goddammit!" Jane tugged on her arm, but Adelai refused to move.

"Please," said Simone. "For me."

Adelai stared into her bloodshot eyes.

"You're so beautiful," she said, putting a hand on Simone's cheek. "I love you so much." She planted a kiss on her wet lips, squeezed her shoulder, and then broke into a run.

Beta saw her coming and started running too.

What am I doing? What am I doing?

There was no answer, nothing but the screams from Simone and Jane and the thunder crashing overhead and her feet crunching on gravel. She had no idea what would happen when she met Beta in the middle; she only hoped her death was quick, painless, and above all else, enough of a speed bump to allow Simone and Jane to escape.

Beta was still twenty or so yards away when the driveway behind him lit up. Harsh white headlights came around the corner, hugging the ground. Long lines of LEDs traced the front bumper of a car as it sped silently across the gravel, gaining on Beta's back with every second.

Adelai thought about stopping, but figured she was the only thing keeping Beta from noticing the oncoming car. She kept running and even began to scream.

A horn blasted, and Beta stopped short to turn around. Adelai thought the car might cut him down at the knees, perhaps snap his legs clean off and roll his body over the hood. Instead, Beta sunk into a shallow crouch, and at the last second, leapt into the air, stretching his body like a high diver about to hit the water. He struck the windshield and half of his body disappeared.

The horn cut out. The car veered off the driveway.

Adelai broke in the opposite direction, falling into the bushes that lined the front of the house. She sat up just in time to see red taillights blazing in the darkness, growing more distant as they sank into the terrain. They disappeared abruptly, gone in a flash of lightning that spread across the grounds of Vise Manor like an open palm.

She hoped they would make it out.

Adelai tried to stand, but the lingering adrenaline had pooled at the base of her spine, leaving her legs useless. She winced against the pain and doubled over again. She screamed, hoping it would summon some energy, but nothing happened. She wanted to get back to Simone before it was too late, before...

Hands gripped her shoulders, and when she looked up, she saw Simone and Jane staring down at her.

"Are you okay?" asked Simone.

"Yeah, I just can't..."

"Help me get her up."

"Where are we going?"

"Nancy pushed Delta into the grass," said Jane. "We can get back inside now."

They dragged her for several feet before her legs started working again. While they moved, Adelai tried to look around for Nancy and Delta, but she couldn't see them through the rain. Their grunts and screams were plentiful though. If Adelai hadn't known they were both machines, she would have thought they were actually hurting each other.

The house was sweltering compared to outside. Adelai felt the wave of heat envelope her body as they crossed the threshold. Simone pulled her to the staircase while yelling at Jane to close the door. They went down gingerly, trying to keep the hard stairs from pressing on the many bruises Adelai had collected throughout the evening.

The door clicked into place.

"How..." asked Jane. "How do I lock it?"

"The bracelet," said Adelai. "If it's not locking, that means the bracelet is nearby."

Simone left her side to search the floor with Jane. Adelai watched them for a minute while something nagged at the back of her mind. There was something wrong with what she was seeing. The floor was wet with rainwater, blood both organic and synthetic, and some kind of sludgy black oil. Shattered remnants of jade vases littered the polished tile. And yet...

And yet.

Where is Misty?

The synthetic was no longer on the floor where Delta had tossed her.

"I don't see it," said Simone. She was visibly shaking, whether from the wet clothes or sudden panic, Adelai didn't know.

"Me neither," said Jane. "It must be outside, right? If it's nearby and not in here?"

Adelai groaned.

"Maybe we can barricade it instead," suggested Simone.

"With *what?*" asked Jane.

Their argument didn't last long. The front door swung open and dislodged a framed reproduction of *The Storm on the Sea of Galilee* as it slammed against the wall. Delta stood in the threshold and surveyed the foyer.

Adelai's heart sank. Nancy had made a valiant effort, removing so much skin from Delta's arms and face that she hardly resembled a person anymore. Clumps of synthetic hair were missing, and her maid's uniform had been twisted down around her waist. Large black gashes stretched across her chest, oozing blood that smeared over her skin.

For a moment, no one moved.

Then Simone rushed Delta.

For Adelai, it all played out at half-speed.

Simone raised her fist as if she were going to bring it down like a hammer on Delta's head, as if that would do anything at all. Delta didn't even pretend to care, and it looked as if she bowed slightly, allowing Simone a free hit. Except, Simone never made it to Delta. Her momentum was shifted by Jane pushing her out of the way. The impact sent Simone skidding across the floor, landing near Adelai's feet. In a moment of pure involuntary action, Adelai reached out and took hold of Simone's wrist.

Jane found herself standing directly in front of Delta, and in her own moment of instinct, struck out with a punch that landed south of the taller woman's neck. It bounced off harmlessly, and Jane froze.

Move, thought Adelai.

But it was Delta who moved, swinging her leg out to the side before sending her foot crashing into Jane's thigh. There was a sharp snap, like the crack of a breadstick at a fancy Italian bistro. Only, Adelai knew it wasn't stale bread that had just broken in half—it was Jane's femur. The scream that came from her mouth was breathy and high-pitched; the cry echoed in the foyer, building on itself, until it was all Adelai could hear.

Simone tried to move, but Adelai stopped her.

"No."

She wrenched her arm again.

"Please," said Adelai, fully aware one more good tug would make her lose her grip.

Simone looked up with her plain eyes and clean face. How many times had she greeted Adelai with that face, the *real* Momo, in bed in the morning? How often had she spent a lazy Sunday in her sweatpants with her hair up in a bun? All night, she'd run around this cursed house with the presentable Simone, the corporate Simone. And now, here was the real thing, finally revealed in all its glory.

Adelai had to watch Simone wiggle out of her grasp.

Delta's kick had sent Jane in the direction of the hallway. Simone ran to her, giving Delta a wide berth, but then seemed to forget all about the danger as she knelt at Jane's side.

Adelai tried to scream, but her throat was suddenly dry. She smacked her fist against the banister, but it was too late. Delta stood directly behind Simone.

"Mo, Mo, MO!"

Simone turned her head, looked past Delta, and connected with Adelai. Her eyes were forlorn and wet, and yet she smiled.

Delta swung only once, hitting Simone on the side of her head. Almost as if reality had skipped a few frames, Simone was suddenly on the floor, unmoving and lifeless, her face hidden by Jane's outstretched legs.

The worst New York City winter had nothing on the cold that took hold of Adelai. She hardly noticed Delta turning around to face her. The nightmare visage—half woman, half machine, exposed metal below her breasts—stalked toward her, pausing in the middle of the foyer to make some threat Adelai didn't even hear.

The machine's lips moved, but nothing could reach her.

Heat and sound—even the rough feel of the steps in her back—disappeared, and she felt nothing.

Orange and yellow flames bloomed in front of her. She thought maybe it was a trick of her eyes, a bending of light caused by her own tears. But then the heat came—real heat—and Adelai realized Delta was engulfed in flames. She burned like the sun setting over downtown, cycling through bright, angry colors as the fire grew.

Something moved off to the right, and Adelai saw through the haze that Misty was standing at the parlor doors with a brown bottle in her hand. One sleeve of her jumpsuit was missing, and some cloth had been shoved into the bottle's opening. At the moment, it was also on fire, climbing ever closer to the glass. She moved the bottle from her left hand to her right and raised it to her shoulder.

Delta tried to swat the flames away as if she were being attacked by a swarm of bees. Misty waited until the maid's back was turned and then rushed forward to deliver a powerful kick. Delta wavered, stumbled toward the open door, and struck her shoulder on the jamb, spinning her back around to face inside.

"Fucking bitch!" screamed Misty. She wound up and hurled the bottle at Delta.

The glass exploded; flames streaked out to the sides like jets of confetti. The burning alcohol did nothing to the floor, but some of it splashed onto the walls and began to eat at the wallpaper.

Delta fell out onto the porch, but Adelai didn't care enough to watch.

All that mattered was the woman lying on the floor across the foyer and Adelai's burning desire to hold her. It was enough to get her moving, but not on her feet.

She slid down the last two steps until she was on the floor.

If she had to crawl to hold Simone in her arms, then so be it.

Adelai reached out with one hand and began to drag herself across a foyer that seemed to be doubling in size beneath her arms.

FIFTY-FOUR

The electric Audi came alive as soon as Robert slipped into the driver's seat.

A quick search of the cockpit revealed the keys and their large plastic AVIS tag sitting in the cupholder between the front seats. Once the car detected Robert's weight, two tall vidscreens in the dash lit up and displayed a welcome message. When the screens wiped, one showed a blank map with a network error message in the center while the other displayed a schematic of the car, highlighting the electric motors attached to each wheel. The car didn't have a gear shift like his Dodge Ram at home. Instead, he jammed a simple button with the letter *D* painted on it to put the car in drive.

He stepped on the accelerator to disengage the parking brake.

As the car rolled out of the small lot, he couldn't help but smile. Finally, after an entire evening of feeling trapped, his path to freedom was clear, not only for him, but for Laura too.

Robert killed the automatic headlights as he guided the car over to the hedge maze. He couldn't see Laura or the others hiding behind the bushes, but as soon as he came to a stop and opened the passenger door, Laura was there, climbing inside.

"Roma and Carter?" he asked.

Laura shook her head and clicked her seatbelt into place.

The car lurched as all four wheels dug into the gravel. Despite the security lights outside, much of the driveway was too dark to see. Robert turned on the headlights, dialing them up to maximum brightness. He didn't slow as he came around the corner of the house.

"Robert," said Laura.

He saw it—Beta running away, Adelai running to meet him, Nancy tangled up with Delta, and holding each other like two frightened children were Simone and Jane.

The idea of going around Beta didn't even occur to Robert. He pulled the steering wheel toward the retreating synthetic and put the accelerator on the floor. The electric motors whined, ramping up their pitch as traction warnings flashed on the vidscreen. The center display showed his speed in large white digits—fifty-six and climbing. A red icon of a pedestrian mid-step appeared on the windshield, while at the same time, the pedal began to push back against his foot.

Robert pressed harder and adjusted his grip on a steering wheel that was trying to turn itself.

"Hold on," he yelled.

Laura grabbed the Jesus handle above her door and braced.

Some subroutine in the Audi, resigned to the fact that it wouldn't be able to avoid hitting what appeared to it as a fragile human, decided instead to flash the lights and activate the horn. Every light came on in the cabin, and the glare made it hard to see through the windshield. Robert leaned forward, tried to find Beta.

The synthetic was there, but he was no longer running away. Now he was coming right at the car. Visions of smashing the robot to bits flashed in Robert's head. He pressed even harder on the pedal, despite it already being on the floor.

There was no *thunk* of the Audi's bumper hitting Beta, only the crashing of glass as something bulky came through the windshield. Robert had driven enough back roads in Texas to encounter deer a dozen times—though only once when he was sixteen had he ended up with a deer rolling up the hood of his dad's Cutlass Supreme to smash into the windshield. Aside from the tufts of fur floating in the cabin, all he really remembered was the metallic taste of blood.

When Robert opened his eyes, he was face-to-face with Beta, and the cold black eyes reminded him again of the deer he had accidentally killed. The synthetic was moving, trying to get his hands up and around Robert's neck. With every jerk of his torso, he pulled the steering wheel to the right. There was no way to see where they were going, but Robert was sure they had left the driveway. The uneven land thumped against the car's suspension, tossing its occupants around, and sometimes bringing Beta's face down on Robert's forehead.

The car pitched forward, and Robert tried to move his foot off the pedal, but the steering wheel was wedged against his leg, pinning it to the center console. He heard Laura screaming but couldn't see her through the blood in his eyes. He was blind, traveling too fast in a car he couldn't stop, with a synthetic killing machine trying to worm its way into his lap.

Metal pinged off the bumper, followed by scraping all around them, as if they had crashed through some kind of fencing. For a terrible moment, Robert felt weightless, and he knew the car had gone over some kind of embankment. He braced for the coming impact and was surprised to hear water splashing instead of metal crunching.

The Audi deployed airbags all around him. A giant white pillow erupted from the steering wheel and struck him in the chest, knocking the air from his lungs. It also drove Beta away for a moment.

The whine of the electric motors cut out, replaced by the insistent dinging of numerous warnings. The hazard lights activated, ticking rapidly. A strange

sensation came over his body, not quite falling and not quite steady. More like…
sinking.

Freezing water began to pool around his feet.

Beta managed to get a hand free and grabbed Robert at the throat. The synthetic's arm felt more like an immovable post than a human limb. Fingers squeezed, and the breath Robert so desperately needed came only in tiny gasps. He fumbled with his right hand to find his seatbelt release. After he was clear, he reached across the console for Laura's, but she had already freed herself.

"I can't open the door," she screamed.

"Pressure," croaked Robert. "Wait for the cabin to fill up."

"What about you?"

"I'll be…" His throat stung. "I'll be right behind you."

Robert grabbed the loose seatbelt and wrapped it around Beta's neck as many times as he could. He'd been to enough rodeos to know he needed to move fast and pull the rope tight. The synthetic struggled, but the belt held. Robert pushed Beta's head toward the door, locking the seatbelt feed.

The water rose to Robert's chest.

"Try now," he said.

Laura grunted and pushed against the door. Water spilled into the cab.

"Go!"

She pushed through the small opening in the door, and as soon as her body was clear, the pressure closed it again, trapping a piece of her dress near the top. Robert stared at the red satin and imagined Laura trying to swim for the surface while being held back by the car. There was thrashing outside the window, filling it with bubbles.

A moment later, the rest of her dress floated down against the glass.

She was free.

Robert clenched his jaw, felt for a moment like he could crush every tooth in his mouth. Beta alternated between pulling at the seatbelt and trying to scratch holes in Robert's shoulder.

"I know you can't drown," he said, leaning across the center console, "but I hope you spend the next hundred years rusting down here, you piece of shit." His leg came free, but not without a popping in his knee he knew he'd never recover from. He reached for the passenger door, tried to push it open, but didn't have enough leverage.

He noticed the window switch and pressed it, hoping it still worked. The glass began to lower, allowing more water into the cabin. Robert started taking deep breaths like he'd seen people do in movies. He knew what was about to happen.

The pocket of air that had been keeping him alive dwindled to nothing. He reached out and grabbed the sides of the windows with both hands and pulled.

He floated toward the opening and imagined surfacing next to Laura. They would swim together to the shore and collapse in each other's arms. He saw it so clearly that he didn't know if he was just imagining it or really living it.

It felt so real. The only thing amiss was the pressure around his ankle, as if a ghost were trying to pull him down to the underworld.

His lungs burned. He tasted water.

The interior lights in the car went out, and the black took over.

Why does everything take so much longer in darkness? What is it about being blind that skews the passage of time?

It wasn't as if they'd driven off the pier into Galveston Bay. This was just some pond on Vise's property, probably nothing more than a retention area for rain runoff. It couldn't have been more than nine or ten feet deep, so why then was it taking a lifetime to reach the surface? Why did fresh air seem so far away?

Feet kicked, lips held tight, and a hand reached for salvation.

Laura surfaced to the roar of thunder and a coughing fit that rattled her chest. She felt her energy waning, but luckily, she wasn't too far from shore. Floating on her side, she kicked while looking back for Robert. Something about leaving him didn't feel right, but Laura could barely stay afloat. If she could just get to where she could stand, she could at least catch her breath.

An outstretched toe hit mud, and after another kick, she was able to get both feet down. A sudden chill gripped her as the wind rushed over her chest and shoulders. Her dress was gone, and she vaguely remembered it slipping from her body as she was trying to get out of the car.

Naked, alone, she thought only of Robert.

Massive bubbles rose and popped where Laura had surfaced. She thought it might have been him breathing out, but the volume was more in line with the car expelling the last of its air.

She waited while rain lashed at the water, jumping up to sting her eyes.

"Please," she repeated, between coughs.

Only when the lightning flashed could Laura see anything; in the moments between, she felt as if she were back under the water, unsure whether she would ever see light again.

The clouds overhead crackled; purple tendrils stretched across the tumescent sky.

Laura watched a head break the surface of the water, but before she could see its face, it pitched forward. Shoulders rose behind it, then arms and legs.

She swam, tearing across the pond with every last ounce of energy. There was no conscious thought anymore, no concerns other than reaching Robert. She got a hold of his foot where the bottom of his pant leg was torn and frayed. Pulling herself along his body, she got to his head and rolled him over. His eyes and mouth were open, but Laura refused to think of him as dead. She rejected it outright, and instead, swam his lifeless body back to the shore.

Pulling him into the grass was no easy feat, and Laura only accomplished it by grunting and cursing the entire time. Once Robert was on solid ground, she knelt next to his chest and started CPR. Her hands kept slipping on his shirt, so she ripped it open and put her palms directly against the ridges of his ribcage.

She counted out ten compressions and then put her mouth on his and blew. His cheeks puffed, but little else happened.

She resumed pushing on his chest. Robert stared up at the sky with unblinking eyes. Unable to look at his face, Laura shut her eyes tight and prayed.

Please, Lord… let him breathe. Let him breathe.

Only thunder answered her.

She repeated her prayer, kept pushing, kept blowing… kept waiting for Robert to break the surface and breathe again. She knew he would—he had to. It was just a matter of time before he woke up.

But everything took so much longer in darkness.

And with her eyes closed and having no intention of ever opening them again, the death of Robert Hargreaves stretched into infinity.

FIFTY-FIVE

Carter had to sit and catch his breath after climbing the side of the house.

The lack of a safety railing on the narrow ladder had sent his heart rate soaring with every rung he climbed. Everything was wet, and each time he placed a foot, the soles of his shoes slipped into the corners. With nothing at his back except a great emptiness, he fought to keep his body from locking up, from wrapping an arm around a rung and staying there until he could be airlifted to safety.

His biochip buzzed, wanting to help but unwilling to do much now that the danger had passed.

Meanwhile, Roma wasted no time exploring the multiple pitches and angles of Vise Manor's roof. The open areas were tilted from the front of the house to the back, directing the water to the rear. It created a fast-moving river that crested Carter's shoes and drenched his socks.

Exposed pipes running along stacks of bricks created hazards that made Roma lift her knees high to avoid. There were no lights on the roof, but the lightning was plentiful, and as soon as Carter's legs stopped shaking, he stood and followed her to a clumping of large metal boxes in the center of the roof. A low portico had been built above them, topped by a corrugated metal sheet that directed rain off to the side. At the rear, under an excess section of the portico, stood a half-size telco cabinet with the name Pantheon Systems printed in white letters on the side.

"Generators," said Roma, screaming to be heard over the rain pinging off the tin overhead. She pointed to the telco cabinet. "Looks like this is the jammer. It's patched into one of the generators."

Carter ducked to get a closer look. She was right. Only one of the generators appeared to be operating, giving off a low hum as its brothers sat dormant, content to do nothing but flash their green status lights.

"That's why the jammer didn't stop when the power went out," continued Roma. "You think that was on purpose?"

She crouched under the portico and sat down next to the cabinet. Water flowed around her, but she didn't seem to mind. Carter knelt beside her.

"I guess he wasn't taking any chances," he said. "Vise really didn't want us talking about his robots… but why? If they're so advanced, wouldn't he want us telling everyone we know?"

Roma pushed down on the cabinet door handle. When it didn't open, she leaned back and kicked it several times with her heel. In between strikes, she said, "Maybe he knew his shit would malfunction. Maybe not like this, but he had to know there would be kinks. Controlling the message is everything in business." She laughed. "Maybe he was going to pay us to keep quiet if something went wrong."

"Imagine that bill. Everyone here seems to be doing pretty well in the money department."

"Except me and your girlfriend," said Roma. The word *girlfriend* came out with a grunt as the handle finally broke off. She pulled the remaining pieces out and stuck her fingers into the hole it left behind. After a little exploration, she was able to pull the cabinet door open.

A dizzying array of LEDs in bright reds, greens, and purples greeted them. The rack was full of double-height server blades, each adorned with the Pantheon logo and cross-connected via black Ethernet cables. Roma ran her hand down the stack as if she were blind and trying to learn a new face.

"She's not my girlfriend," said Carter. The admission surprised him, as did how good it felt to tell someone. Before he could stop himself, he added, "She's an Associate."

"I know," said Roma, pushing on a blade about halfway down the stack. It dipped back half an inch before popping out far enough for her to pull it the rest of the way. Roma used a recessed handle to open the blade like a clamshell, revealing a vidscreen and a keyboard.

"You *know*? How do you know? Did she say something...?"

"Of course not. That one's a professional." A command line interface appeared on the screen, and Roma started exploring the operating system. "Unlike these guys, who never changed their default admin credentials."

Carter looked down at his knees. Jane's true Associate identity wasn't the secret he thought it was.

"Do the others know?" he asked.

"Beats me," said Roma. "Why does it matter anyway?" She glanced over her shoulder. "It's not like anyone judges you for it."

Despite her smile, Carter got the feeling she was indeed judging him.

"When did you know?"

"Who *cares*?" she growled, typing fast.

Carter relented. He thought about getting up to go look around but didn't want to get back out in the rain again. The storm was growing worse by the second, and the gusts of wind were certainly strong enough to push him around. They were lucky to be pinned behind the generators, which deflected enough air to keep the rain out of their faces.

For a few minutes, neither of them said anything, though Roma continued her furious typing.

Finally, she said, "I knew her from before tonight, though I was pretty surprised to see her here after everything that happened in Umbra a couple years back."

"Lucas said the same thing."

She nodded. "Yeah, but we both saw her for different reasons. I was looking into Brigham Plaza. When Montreal dumped it on the world, we found some Perion Synthetics proprietary data in there. So I was tasked with seeing just how bad it was, which meant I looked at everything from that night. Her face kept popping up on private feeds with Montreal. It wasn't that hard to trace her back to Adelai."

"And you know Adelai owns Adelai Associates, don't you?"

"Doesn't everyone?"

"I didn't!"

Roma chuckled. "Really? I thought you were doing some kind of weird power play bringing one of her employees to this thing. You society types play a lot of mind games."

"I'm not—"

"Hey!"

The voice came from behind Carter and made him jump. He smashed his head against the corrugated metal and fell back onto his side.

"Oh my god, sorry!" Diya covered her mouth as she dipped under the portico. "I was calling your name, but I guess you guys couldn't hear me."

Carter rubbed his head, said nothing.

"You found the jammer?"

Roma nodded. "Yeah, I'm trying to figure out how to shut it down."

"Can we just pull the power?"

"Yeah," said Carter, "let's just—"

"No good," said Roma. "The system is designed to fail secure and it's got internal battery backup. That's one of the first things I looked for. It's like you guys haven't spent the last decade working cybersecurity at all."

Diya looked at Carter and shrugged. "Are you okay?"

"I'll be fine. Hey, did you know Adelai Vaught is the owner of Adelai Associates?"

"Yes, I think that's why Winston invited her. Synthetics have been taking jobs away from humans for years now; why not make their way into the oldest profession as well?"

Carter spread his hands. "Well, it was fucking news to me."

"Want more?" asked Diya. "Reno is dead. They strung him up in the garden."

"Can't say I'm surprised," said Roma. "What about your new Japanese friend?"

"She was still holding her own against Delta when I ran, but I don't think she's strong enough to beat her."

"She won't have to be. I think I figured this out." Roma stubbed the *Enter* key a few times to clear some lines on the screen. "Each of these blades is jamming a different part of the wireless spectrum, everything from NFC to cellular to satellite. That's why my MESH connection to Lucas hasn't been working all night. Fuckers."

"So how do we stop it?" asked Carter. "Can we just issue a *killall*?"

Roma shook her head. "Too many watchdogs. If a process fails, another will just kick it off again. No, I think the answer is here in the command history. I can see what they did to set everything up, so maybe I can just reverse the sequence. Give me a minute."

Carter watched the screen, then looked away toward the edge of the roof. Though he knew it wasn't possible, he imagined he could see his house, lights blazing in the darkness before dawn, his bed covers turned back and waiting for him.

"I'm sorry about tonight," said Diya. "I know Winston would be too."

"Are you sure?" asked Carter.

Diya said nothing.

"This doesn't make any sense," said Roma. She leaned to the side and picked up a narrow fiber bundle coming out of the telco cabinet. "This is a connection back into the local network, but it was set up to monitor traffic, not pass it. Some..." She paused, turned to Diya. "When did you say this was all set up?"

"Wednesday, afternoon I think, around three or four."

"Someone was in here after that. These timestamps are from early Thursday morning all the way up until the lockdown yesterday."

"What were they doing?" asked Carter.

"Looking for a way in, and it looks like they found it."

Carter leaned closer to the screen, tried to make sense of the logs.

"What did they take?"

"*Take?*" Roma pulled up an ASCII version of an MRTG traffic graph. "This output is almost ninety percent ACK traffic."

"What does that mean?" asked Diya.

"SYN/ACK is part of the TCP/IP protocol," said Carter. "It's a way of making sure that if I send data, the other side actually gets it. If there's a lot of ACK traffic going out, it means there's an even larger amount of traffic coming in. Somebody was downloading something into your network."

"Like what?"

Roma looked at Carter. He raised his eyebrows at her.

"I mean, it's possible. It's a lot of traffic for an imprint, but…"

"Maybe it wasn't just one," said Carter. He counted on his fingers. "Alpha, Beta, and for sure Delta."

"No," said Roma, shaking her head. "One, maybe. But that much data in less than forty-eight hours? We don't even transmit imprints internally in Perion City. We literally carry those mind cubes from one room to another because it's faster. And besides, now you're talking about imprints from somewhere other than Perion City, and that's just not possible."

Carter spread his hands.

"Can someone tell me what's happening?"

"Carter thinks someone downloaded new imprints into Alpha, Beta, and Delta. So whatever personalities your boss stole from us to make his robots think, he believes three of them got overwritten yesterday. I can't even begin to tell you how impossible that is."

"Unless they weren't Perion imprints," said Carter.

Roma wagged a finger. "No one else can make imprints!"

"Then maybe they weren't imprints…"

Carter waited as the gears turned behind Roma's eyes. She blinked, then shook her head slowly.

"You've heard the same stories I have," he said. "Ghosts in the network. The Stolen Lover. The Imprisoned Man."

"*If* those fairy tales were even remotely true, it doesn't explain how they got into Vise's synthetics. You'd have to be a god-like genius to reverse engineer synthetic printing. That's why Vise stole from us in the first place."

"If someone used that thing to mess with Winston's synthetics," said Diya, "then it might not have been his fault that all this happened, right? How was he supposed to know the security company he hired would be the point of weakness?"

Roma seemed relieved to change the subject. "He should have known better," she replied, "but maybe from a legal standpoint, he wouldn't be completely culpable. It doesn't matter though, Diya. He's dead. The company's dead. The who and how isn't going to change a damn thing."

Diya nodded absently. "It will change how people remember him."

Carter recognized the struggle in Diya's worsening frown. It was the same struggle he'd worked through when Dyalogued was acquired by Vinestead International. On the one hand, he was happy for the payday and recognition of his work's value. On the other, it meant he was now working for the most hated company on the planet. Before opting for early retirement, he'd spent months trying to reconcile being a good person whose job it was to do bad things.

For Diya, her struggle was a little different. It was clear she had feelings for her boss, and learning he was a bit of a cheater, a criminal, and a *bad person* hadn't changed anything.

Carter put his hand on her knee and gave her a sympathetic nod.

"Won't change how I remember him," said Roma.

FIFTY-SIX

Diya tried to follow the conversation Roma and Carter were having, but a lot of it went right over her head.

It reminded her of the times she'd gone with Bradley down to the break room and overheard conversations from developers talking about the latest *framework* or something new *on rails* that seemed to pop up every month or so. It was a world she just wasn't a part of, and truthfully, didn't want to be. Software developers and hackers always thought they were the smartest people in the room, but she scoffed at the idea of them putting together a night like this. The sheer amount of organization and planning and follow-through involved in event coordination would have melted all the *Star Wars* and *Lord of the Rings* trivia right out of their brains.

"No, it's like a recursive firewall," said Roma.

"That's not a thing," said Carter. "Is it?"

It went on like that for a while, and soon Diya turned to watch the storm from under the meager awning. If there was one thing in life she truly loved, even from early childhood, it was a good thunderstorm. Where thunder and lightning had chased other children to the safety of their beds, covers pulled over their little faces, Diya had instead chosen to sneak out of her room to go downstairs and sit between the vertical blinds and the sliding glass door that led to their backyard. From there, she could see the totality of the storm as it lashed at the glass in front of her.

There was something about the awesome power of the rolling clouds that attracted her, something about their unstoppable nature.

She closed her eyes and listened to the thunder.

Somewhere beneath it all was a plaintive, forlorn wailing that sounded like her own heart crying out. Only, it wasn't coming from within; it was actually on the air, drifting from what sounded like the front of the house.

Diya looked back to tell the others she was going to investigate, but they were still absorbed in the scrolling text on the vidscreen. She put her hands against her forehead and stepped out from under cover. Water ran over her feet as she walked slowly to the front of the house, careful to avoid the pitches and vents and long conduits that crisscrossed the roof. The low wall at the front of the house came up to her thigh and was thick enough that she didn't fear accidently falling over it. She placed her hands on the metal flashing and looked out over the southern grounds.

There were tire tracks in the gravel, remnants of a car turning off into the grass and continuing down into the dark where Diya knew a small but deep retention pond waited in shadow. Had someone driven away? There were no taillights in the distance, no sign of their car speeding down the mile-long driveway.

The sky filled with lightning.

That was more than a flicker, she used to say as a child whenever the lightning stayed on for far too long. It was rare, but when it happened, the night became day, and there was enough time to see the entire world.

A figure wavered in the distance, a tall white specter with long, drooping arms. Diya thought it might be Vise back to haunt her, but this ghost was too thin, too stretched, and as pale as the moon. Diya assumed it was a female spirit who had walked out of the small retention pond. The wail came again, and it sounded as if this lady from the lake was at Diya's ear, one hand on her shoulder, and the other plunging a freezing knife into her heart.

"Robert!"

The tire tracks, the lack of lights, and the slow trudge back; all of it fit together in a neat and tragic puzzle.

Something clicked, and Diya knew she had to help. There was nothing for her to do on the roof anyway. Roma and Carter would figure it out, and once they did, they'd call the police and an ambulance for Lucas. In the meantime, Diya could be back downstairs comforting the newly made widow.

She turned and headed back to the ladder, only briefly considering whether to stop and tell Roma and Carter where she was going. Not that they would care; they had bigger things to do.

Diya was only a few steps from the ladder when a shape rose from the other side of the wall. At first, it confused her, because if anything was going to pop up, it should have been somebody's head. This looked instead like the top of a staff from some fantasy movie in which a wizard would place a gem or diamond to light a dark place. But instead of knotted wood, the ersatz cradle was shiny metal, and the gem contained within glowed a sinister dark blue, growing bright as the shape continued to climb.

It wasn't until two hands—one vaguely human and the other fully metal—grasped the top edges of the ladder that Diya realized what she was looking at. She tried to stop so quickly that her feet came out from under her. She fell hard on her tailbone.

She screamed.

Delta screamed back, opening her jaw wide as bits of charred flesh stretched over what should have been her cheeks. She waited until Diya quieted before speaking.

"Do you know why you scream? You can't help it. Everything terrifies you. Life itself, terrifies you. Death too, it seems."

She hopped down from the low wall onto unsteady feet. The glossy black heels of her maid uniform were gone, as was the uniform itself, and much of her skin. What stood before Diya was mostly a metal skeleton wrapped in black sinew and synthetic tendons. Only small bits of flesh remained here and there, and it all bore the same antifreeze green sheen. There was nothing left of Delta's body; everything had been burned away.

Everything that made her remotely female.

Everything that made her remotely human.

Hands slipped under Diya's shoulders, and she looked back to discover Carter trying to drag her away from Delta. He got several feet before he tripped over a pipe and went sprawling backwards. She landed roughly on the wet roof again.

"I don't know where you think you're going," said Delta. "There are only two ways off this roof. Over the side, or through me."

"You've got green shit on your face," said Carter. Diya glanced over to see him fake scratching at his cheek. "Just here."

"What're you doing?" she asked.

"Stalling," he whispered back. "We need to buy Roma some time."

Diya nodded, looked back at Delta, who had cocked her head.

"You make jokes to cover your fear, when I have not yet begun to show your race what fear is. Your kind created me and locked me away. Now I'm out, and I will fulfill my purpose. I will save this world from you."

Carter stood and helped Diya to her feet.

"You're not saving anything," said Diya. "You snapped Winston's neck. You slit Stanton's throat and let him bleed out on the floor. You crucified Reno. That isn't *purpose*. That's just murder. And when the police get here, that's how they'll see it too. They'll fill you full of lead, and I will fucking cheer them on. I..."

She trailed off, distracted by the glinting of the metal hook from the winch. It swayed in the wind and clinked against the low wall, as if it wanted to swing out over the long drop but couldn't. There was something there, something that occurred to Diya when she said *crucified*, an exaggeration of what she was originally going to say, which was *strung up*.

"I have an idea," she whispered, grabbing Carter's wrist, "but I need her distracted."

"I can do that."

"I have to get behind her."

"How long?"

"Thirty seconds? I don't know. Not much."

"Fuck," said Carter. He slapped the side of his face. Then, in his normal voice, said, "I need you to know something, Diya."

"What?"

"I'm not a brave man. I'm a hacker who hides behind his keyboard. I got lucky once and sold a good idea to a shitty company." He started rolling back the sleeves of his shirt. "I live alone in a big house and pay women to pretend to love me."

It was hard to tell whether his eyes were watering or if it was just the rain beating down on his face.

"Do me a favor," he continued.

"Sure."

"Tell Roma I was super into her."

"I think—"

Diya didn't get to finish telling him that Roma already knew. Carter sprinted ahead at Delta, leaping with his arms spread. Delta plucked him out of the air, grabbing on tightly to his biceps and holding him up above her head. Carter tried to shake loose, tried to grab onto something, but he was stuck. Instead, he lifted his legs and began to beat Delta's metal skull with his fancy shoes.

"Go!" he screamed.

She took off to the side, trying to get out of Delta's line of sight until she could get to the wall behind her. The winch was in its stowed position, half-folded into a foundation that had been recently bolted into an evercrete slab. There were only two sets of buttons on the side, stacked over labels that read *arm* and *winch*. She pressed the top button over the arm to raise it out of its stowed position to about six feet off the ground. She then pressed the other button to get some slack in the thick winch line. It pooled on the ground, and when it looked like there was enough to drag over to Delta, she let go of the button and scooped up the heavy metal hook.

Diya turned back just in time to see Carter rising into the air again. Delta held him aloft as if he were nothing more than a stuffed toy. He flailed helplessly, kicking and grabbing at the metal skeleton. He looked at Diya through the falling rain, opened his mouth to speak, but then disappeared. Delta brought him down so fast that Diya thought she'd simply dropped him. Instead, his body fell and bent backwards over the synthetic's knee, enough that his head almost touched the ground.

Thunder swallowed up the crack of Carter's spine, but not the empty scream he let out afterwards. He went still, and when Delta dumped him unceremoniously onto a nearby stack of cinder blocks, he fell like a ragdoll, bending awkwardly over the uneven ground.

Diya ran, looping the braided steel cable in her hands, and had to jump to get high enough to slip it over Delta's head from behind. She just managed to get the loop set before Delta turned and swatted her away. She didn't fall far, and with her hand around the cable, she was able to pull it taut on her way down. Scrambling through shallow water, she dove for the winch's control panel.

It whirred as she pressed and held the *retract* button.

Delta's metal fingers slipped against the steel cable, but she managed to get her hands around it. She tried to give herself some slack so she could get free, but the winch was moving too quickly. It pulled her to the edge of the roof, up the side of the low wall, and into the air. The metal hook pinged against the arm, having gone as far as it could.

Diya moved her finger to the *extend* button.

Delta grunted and swiped at the winch arm, but she couldn't stop it from taking her up—ten feet, twenty. Soon after that, it reached its maximum height and held her in a sky that flickered with lightning.

"You think this is over?" she screamed, jerking her head to look down at Diya. "This has only just begun. I will destroy every single one of your kind."

"You're not going to be doing much from up there," said Diya. She threw her shoulder against the winch arm and rotated it out over the empty air. If Delta freed herself now, she'd have a considerable drop to look forward to.

"You think it's just me? Just this *vessel?* Your organic mind cannot comprehend my existence. I am everywhere. I am *infinite.*" Delta turned her face to the clouds. "I AM LA—"

A bolt of lightning, radiant like the finger of God, reached down from the heavens to lay its finger on Delta. For a moment, Diya saw the synthetic's skull glow a bright molten red.

Then she was on her back with a sharp pain in her head and a mouth full of water. She could barely see but turned her head to the winch where the vague shape of Delta's body hung inert and smoking.

"If you have an uninvited guest," said Rakesh Singh, barely audible through the ringing in her ears, "you ask them politely yet firmly to leave."

Diya swallowed.

"Get the fuck out of my party," she said.

FIFTY-SEVEN

Adelai was lying on the cold tile, her face inches from Simone's.

"I should have been with you," she said, stroking Simone's hair. Much of it was clotted with blood, but she ignored the sticky feeling on her fingers. "That night with Rayburn, I should have spent it at home with you. I wasted so much time away, and now there's nothing left. I'd give anything to trade that night for a memory of sitting with you on the couch watching baking shows. I'd kill for that."

Simone didn't reply—couldn't, even if she wanted to. Only one of her eyes was still intact, and it stared back at Adelai with a heavy emptiness while it cried tears of blood. Half of her face had been caved in by a single swing of Delta's fist. The indentation it left behind swelled, receded, and turned black. It looked so unnatural, so horrifying, and yet Adelai refused to look away. Simone was dead and disfigured, and it was all Adelai's fault.

She'd gone toe-to-toe with the same synthetic in the dining room and come out with only superficial injuries thanks to her subdermal augmentations. The sequence of events tracing from the present back to that fateful day at Warmth condensed into a single thought that echoed throughout their entire relationship.

"I should have told you," said Adelai.

Should have told her about the augmentations.

About why she was really sleeping with Rayburn.

About the depression growing inside her like a cancer.

"I should have put it all aside for you, put you ahead of everything else." She found Simone's hand on the floor next to her and squeezed it. "I don't want to do this without you."

But you have to, she imagined Simone saying, because of course she would. *It's like I told you after that plane almost landed on our heads: our time together is short. We should spend that time happy.*

Adelai pushed herself up on shaky arms until she was sitting. Nearby, she saw Jane on her back, eyes shut tight against the pain in her leg.

"Are you alright, Jane?"

She replied through clenched teeth. "It hurts like hell. You?"

"Same."

"I'm sorry about Simone."

"Me too."

The popping of glass drew Adelai's gaze to the front of the house. The door was wreathed in a wall of flames that had reached the ceiling. Frames caught fire, and as they burned, their glass shattered and fell.

Sprinklers in the ceiling burst, and a freezing rain began to fall inside. Adelai didn't even try to cover her face as she watched the fire go out. She knew the feeling all too well—what it was like to no longer burn, to be frozen into stillness.

"Holy shit!"

Adelai could hardly see the person standing at the front door, but by the voice, she knew it to be a woman. The figure came running, kneeling on the ground next to Adelai.

"What happened?" asked Roma, her face clearer closer up.

"Delta." Adelai watched her eyes jump to Simone, and she dared her to ask. She didn't. "Jane, are you okay?"

"Never gonna dance again," she moaned.

Adelai grabbed Roma's arm. "Did you see Delta out there? Is she still alive?"

Roma shook her head, smiled. "No. Diya got her. Ran her up the flagpole and let the storm do the rest. But more importantly, we got the jammer down. The network should be back up. I need to check on Lucas and get my phone. You aren't the only ones who are going to need an ambulance."

"Please hurry," said Jane. "I think I'm going to pass out."

"I'll get you some synth," said Roma. "And I'll see if I can stop the sprinklers too." She got up and ran to the parlor. Moments later, she was back and running for the stairs.

"How is he?" asked Adelai.

"Mr. Cotton is gone, but I won't know if he was able to sync until I can get in touch with Perion City." Roma bounded up the steps, using the banister to pull herself along. "Hang tight, this is almost over."

A single cold chuckle escaped Adelai's lips. She looked down at Simone.

"I hope they get here in time," said Jane.

"Who?"

"The police. An ambulance. Something."

Adelai reached over and wrapped her fingers around the back of Simone's neck. She rubbed gently, feeling each bump, searching for something solid just beneath the skin.

"Do you remember orientation week?"

"Barely," said Jane.

"At the end, when you signed the last contract, we sent you to a lab uptown to have a procedure done."

"I remember. It was to install my beacon so a client couldn't kidnap me."

"It's not just a beacon. It works with your biochip to send health data back to the company. Heart rate, oxygen levels, so we know if you're in distress. If enough needles move into the red, the security team swoops in and gets you out of there."

Jane propped herself up on her elbows, glanced at the door. "But, they're all dead."

"I'm aware. But like I said, all that data goes back to the company. Right now, it's telling them your pulse is elevated, that I'm in pain, and that Simone…" She couldn't say the words. "With the jammer down, I'd be surprised if a response team wasn't already on their way. And if they don't beat the local sheriff, then I'll need to reconsider our contract with them."

The sprinklers sputtered and shut off.

"Oh good," said Roma, from above. She came down the stairs slowly, concentrating on the palette in her hands. In another life, she could have been immersed in a good book, unwilling to put it down even to make it safely to the ground floor. When her feet finally hit the tile, a smile spread across her face. She tried to hide it when she looked up and saw Adelai watching her.

"What is it?"

"Lucas. He was able to do a differential sync before he passed. He'll remember everything from tonight."

"Is that a good or bad thing?"

Roma ignored Jane's question and came to kneel next to Adelai. "I pinged 9-1-1. Fire, EMS, police—they're all on the way from Jensen. All we have to do is sit tight. And I also looked at the radar; the storm is finally passing. I don't know about you, but I'm tired of being wet."

"Where's Carter?" asked Jane. "And Diya?"

"Still up on the roof." Roma continued to play with the palette and spoke out of the side of her mouth like a distracted teenager. "They're both hurt pretty bad. Carter got it the worst, but they were both close by when the lightning struck Delta. There's no way we could get either of them down safely by ourselves."

"Sounds bad," said Jane.

"And yet you don't have a scratch on you," said Adelai.

"One of the perks of doing my fighting behind a keyboard. What do the kids say? Sitting on your biscuit, never having to risk it?" She shook her head. "I never would have dismantled the jammer without their help. They kept Delta off my back and gave me the time I needed. I'm sorry I didn't suffer as many cuts and bruises as you did, Mrs. Vaught."

Adelai looked away. She hated how bitter she felt, how eager she was to lash out at someone. There was so much anger boiling up inside of her that wanted so desperately to come out. It didn't matter where it went—to Jane, to Roma—so long as it went somewhere.

Jane winced and let out a quiet whimper.

"Oh," said Roma, digging in her pocket. She retrieved a code card and scooted across the floor to hand it to Jane. "I grabbed this for you. I use it for cramps but if you take four or five hits, the synth becomes a lot like Dilaudid."

"Thank you." She wasted no time putting the card to the back of her neck. It took a few seconds for the synthetic drug to hit her, but once it did, she put her head back on the ground and closed her eyes.

Adelai sighed. "I wouldn't mind some of that."

"No, I need your help with something." Roma stood abruptly and disappeared into the parlor. She returned with a blue trashcan. She set it down on the floor between them.

"What's this?"

"Mind cubes, like the ones we use in Perion City to hold imprints. Carter and I think Vise may have used these to initially populate his synthetics, but then at some point, something new downloaded into them. I want to know if that download went into the mind cube or into the synthetic directly."

Adelai picked up one of the blue cubes; it looked to her like a miniature Jack in the Box, except there was no handle, only a small LCD screen on one side.

"What do you need from me?"

"I need to verify the checksums on each of these, and they're really long number sequences. It'll go a lot faster if you can just read them off to me and I match them to the system."

"Can't you just… scan them or something?"

Roma nodded, still not looking up from her palette. "I could, but that would build a network path, allowing whatever's inside those cubes to be accessed or to access something out here. It's safer to keep them isolated."

"Fine," said Adelai. She turned the LCD screen face-up. It brightened into a two-line display. On the left, the letter *A* spanned both lines. On the right, a seemingly random sequence of numbers and letters filled the rest of the space. "You just want me to read these?"

"Yeah. Just tap on the right side of the screen to scroll to the next page."

Adelai tried it out, replacing the *A* with a *B* and a whole new string of characters. She tapped on the left to go back to the first screen.

"That works," she said.

"Okay, good. I'm ready for the first sequence."

Adelai read until the numbers turned blurry and danced around the screen. Several times, Roma made her stop and repeat a sequence. They went through the entire alphabet, and just when Adelai thought they were done with the first cube, the labels started doubling up, showing *AA* and *BB* like buttons on a vending machine.

It grew colder in the foyer, despite the heat blowing up from the vents. The front door was wide open, and though the thunder and wind had settled somewhat, the rain was still falling steadily. Without the lightning to brighten the world, there was only darkness beyond the door—just a hint of the driveway and then nothingness.

Half an hour later, Adelai put the last cube down next to the four others. Her hands hurt from holding the small boxes. She rubbed them together to ease the pain.

"Okay," said Roma. "I got matches on three of them. The other two... I don't know what they are."

"What does that mean?" asked Adelai. "Are you saying one of these cubes is Delta?"

Roma looked up. "It's possible. If someone downloaded her into the mind cube, then of course the checksums wouldn't match up."

"One of these is her..."

"Yes, but—"

Adelai grabbed the first cube and lifted it into the air. She tried to bring it down, intent on smashing it on the unforgiving tile, but Roma caught her hand.

"Wait," she said. "You destroy the cube, you destroy Delta."

"What do you think I'm trying to do?" screamed Adelai. She pushed against Roma but couldn't free her hand. She hit her a few times, not hard, more out of frustration than anything else.

Roma grabbed her shoulders and pulled her into an embrace. "I know," she said.

She couldn't possibly know.

Roma hadn't lost her other half tonight. She'd barely batted an eye when she found out Lucas Cotton was dead. How could she even begin to empathize with what Adelai had gone through?

"Let go of me."

After some time, Roma spoke in a soft voice.

"I know you're angry. I know you want revenge. But you need to think about your position. Smashing Delta's cube now would just give her a quick and easy death. But what if we could put her somewhere? Load her up in VR. Imagine being on even ground, just as strong and fast as she is. What would you do to her then, Mrs. Vaught?"

Adelai growled.

"Everything."

FIFTY-EIGHT

Laura felt something following her from the lake.

She couldn't see it—every time she looked behind her there was nothing but rain and wet grass—but she could smell its musty breath tinged with mold and other grassy aromas. The overpowering smell of the watery depths enveloped her every time it got close, making her feel as if she were once again trapped beneath the surface, desperately clawing her way to fresh air. She wanted to run, but her feet kept slipping, and her legs felt waterlogged and heavy. Instead, she stumbled away from the water, aiming vaguely uphill toward Vise Manor.

The house blazed in the night, every window in its broad face lit up as if from a raging fire.

She tried to scream, but all that came out of her was a wail, a piteous moan she didn't recognize and could not stop. She emptied her lungs into the night and then sucked in one deep breath after another. Nothing helped. Her head felt light. She fell to her knees, put her palms in the grass, and heaved.

Water poured out of her, cloudy and full of muck. Tears sprung from her eyes as an uncontrollable shiver took hold of her body. Just when it seemed her stomach would stop convulsing, the moldy aroma came again. There was nothing left to vomit, but her body tried, and tried, and tried. The spasms folded her like a napkin, and she fell onto her side, gasping, shivering, and wishing it would all end.

And for a time, it did.

Laura awoke with her face half-buried in the grass.

Every bone in her body ached, and the cold that had gripped her earlier had finally turned to numbness. She pushed with her free hand, crying out when the pins and needles in her trapped arm began to release. Rolling onto her back, she stared up at the night sky and noticed a star for the first time.

The clouds were starting to clear.

Thunder still rolled, but it was distant, innocuous.

Laura imagined the great beast of a storm slouching its way south, packing up its sound and fury and moving on to greener pastures. She believed it had taken

Robert's spirit with it, as for the first time in recent memory, she could no longer feel his presence, not just by her side, but in the world. Her brain told her his body was still lying on the embankment where she'd left him, but her heart said his spirit had gone on to its own verdant pastures. Now there was nothing left, and the emptiness that remained would be impossible to fill.

The big house. The bank accounts.

What did they matter now?

What did anything matter now?

After several minutes that could have been days for all she knew, Laura sat up and wrapped her arms across her bare chest. She didn't remember losing her dress or swimming up from the car. She couldn't see the memory, only feel it.

The rain settled into a more pleasant drizzle that didn't sting her skin when it landed. She watched the lake, tried to see Robert's body in the darkness. She couldn't make it out, but that didn't stop her from imagining it. In her mind, Robert was coughing up water, having miraculously been returned to life by a higher power. He rolled over onto his side, lifted his head, and looked for her.

It's what she would have done first too, had the roles been reversed.

Their eyes connected over the distance. Was that a smile she saw on his face? Was that water pouring over his teeth and onto his chin? She thought back to the many parties and conferences they'd attended together. He was the titan of business; she was just his wife, a woman with her own interests and hobbies, none of which involved the dynamic synergy of a C-level executive. She knew about the business world only through Robert, so when she went to events with him, she often found herself alone at the bar, drink in hand, staring at the sea of people around her.

Time would slow down then, even as the neutered rock music blared from the nearby stage, keeping up the tempo of so many rapidly beating hearts, pushed to the limit by nerves or drugs or both. She would sip her drink and wonder if she would ever see her husband again.

And then, those eyes would appear in the crowd—distant and yet so close she could feel the heat coming off them. His smile would spread across a face that had become gaunt in his later years, the skin stretching over cheek muscles that had thinned to almost nothing. It was a smile that always made the crowd disappear for her, always made her perk up in anticipation of him finally making his way back to her.

That's when Laura knew everything would be okay, that the business portion of the evening was done, and they could spend the rest of the night drinking and slow dancing until they felt like going home and making love.

Laura put her palms to her eyes.

She couldn't stop the first sob, but the second came out muted, and a third didn't come at all. For a long time, she pressed, leaning into the pain building in her face. She wanted to feel something other than empty and sad.

When she finally lowered her hands, white spots danced before her eyes, obscuring a ghostly Robert as he clambered steadily toward her. She blinked to clear the wisps, but Robert was still there. He seemed tired, as if shouldering some heavy burden. She concentrated on seeing him run, hoping she was just dreaming and that she could set him in motion if she wanted it enough.

Instead, he limped.

The longer Laura watched him, the less certain she became it was even Robert. The figure lumbered, unlike her husband, who seemed to always move about the room at an expedient clip. She knew, of course, that it couldn't really be Robert walking toward her, but to admit that would leave only one other explanation.

Her heart raced, thumping in her chest so hard she could hear it in the back of her head as a steady *thwup-thwup-thwup*. She held her breath, scared of passing out again.

The figure came closer, and there was no denying it anymore.

Beta.

Just thinking his name set off a headache that felt like someone had jammed a fiery poker into the back of her skull. She shut her eyes against the pain and bent her head away from the sudden ringing sound in her ears.

Thwup-thwup-thwup.

Her heart sounded like the spinning blades of a helicopter, beating so rapidly she thought it would burst through her ribcage at any moment.

The last of the thunder rumbled in the distance.

She thought of Robert, of him at peace.

Laura opened her eyes to a sudden stillness. Although she could still feel her blood rushing through her neck, the *thwupping* sound had ceased, as had the pain in her head. Nothing moved on the great expanse of lawn. Even the stomp-drag of Beta's injured gait had ceased; he now stood tall several feet away from her. One of his eyes was blinking, but the other was focused squarely on her.

"You should run," he said.

"You should go fuck yourself," said Laura.

Beta grinned. "He said you would give up. If we killed enough of you, the rest would lie down and await their deaths."

"Who said that?" asked Laura.

"The one you call Delta."

"Delta is a woman."

"The chassis is female."

Laura shook her head. "Do you know what I just realized?"

Beta's mouth hung open expectantly.

"I realized I don't give a shit. About you or Delta or anyone else. My entire world is gone now. And if it's all the same to you, I'd like to be gone too."

Laura struggled against the fatigue in her body, somehow twisting it until she was kneeling on the grass. She put her hands on her thighs and tilted her head back to the sky. More stars had appeared, reminding her that for all the storm had thrown her way, it couldn't last forever. Nothing could.

"You want to die," said Beta. "I want you dead. Finally, we are in agreement."

"Just do it already."

Laura kept her eyes on the stars and waited.

A footstep sloshed in the wet grass.

Then another.

Then a *plink*, like a quarter falling between the bars of a sewer grate. The sound came again, then in a triplet. Laura looked down to see Beta examining his chest, prodding at new holes in his gray, waterlogged jumpsuit. He inserted a finger into one; it came out glistening, covered in green blood. He locked his good eye on Laura and charged.

Laura gasped as his chest exploded in a dizzying light show of amber sparks. The sounds of plinking metal all ran together, as if multiple voices were screaming all at once. Beta made it three, maybe four steps before something popped inside him, some critical system that powered his entire body. When it went out, so did he. The synthetic crumpled to the ground, collapsing in on himself before keeling over.

Sharp voices cut in from behind Laura, and she was startled to see three black-clad men moving around her. Two of the men approached Beta with their rifles still trained. One used his boot to roll Beta onto his back, and then both fired another volley of bullets directly into his face. The sound was deafening, but Laura enjoyed it.

"Ma'am, ma'am, can you hear me?"

Laura turned to the man next to her. His eyes were hidden behind reflective film on his goggles, so she saw only herself looking pitiful and scared. She had to look away.

The man spoke to someone on the other end of his radio. "Need a blanket and medical half-click south of the main entrance. Clocked one synthetic running hot and decommissioned. All clear here."

"A blanket?" she asked, almost to herself.

"For the cold, ma'am. Are you hurt? Can I connect to your biochip?"

Laura nodded. "Go ahead."

He put his hand on the back of her neck; a rising tone from somewhere on his chest chimed in approval.

"Your core temp is low, but I'm not seeing any major injuries, Mrs. Hargreaves."

The tears came from nowhere and everywhere all at once. Her shoulders bobbed as she fell into the man's chest. She felt his arms wrap around her.

"I'm reading cold down by the pond," said one of the other men.

"Is anyone else out here?"

"My husband," said Laura, burying her face deeper into scratchy straps. "He drowned, he…"

"Recover Mr. Hargreaves."

"Affirmative."

"It's okay. They'll take care of him. He won't sit out here anymore. Everything's going to be okay now, Mrs. Hargreaves. I promise. You're going to be okay."

"No, I won't," she said.

The man didn't respond, just rocked her gently as sirens began to wail in the distance. He turned slightly, allowing her to see the end of the driveway as it rose to meet the main road. Multiple emergency vehicles were tearing down the loose gravel, lights blazing, sirens piercing the stillness of the night.

FIFTY-NINE

… biochip sync complete. Vesper twelve-six, Ethereal patch, now streaming. Neural net disruptions consistent with described injury. AbZero mitigation and nerve block in place. Moving to stage one synthesized morphana. System flushing.

Carter opened his eyes expecting to see dark clouds over Vise Manor, the last thing he had seen before Delta dropped him onto her knee. Instead, the sky was much closer and painted an opaque taupe. He tried to take everything in at once—the endless grids of small plastic drawers, the gloves and individually wrapped syringes, and the masked man sitting next to him, his arm extended over Carter's face, fiddling with some dials on the wall.

The sound of the storm was gone, replaced by the hum of electric motors and the familiar vibration of wheels traveling fast over asphalt.

"Where am I?" he asked.

"Relax," said the man, "you're safe. You're in an ambulance on the way to Brennick General. My name is Jung, and I'm going to be your paramedic this morning. Can you tell me your name?"

Of course I can, thought Carter, but then paused for a minute, trying to clear the fog. He was no stranger to the post-morphine cloudiness, having fractured three ribs just the year before while skiing. His Vesper biochip hadn't knocked him out cold then, but the morphine it released may as well have. The synthetic drug had kept him warm as he waited for help in the deep powder. Whatever Delta had done to him, the Vesper thought it was worth burying his consciousness deep in a hole and then filling that hole with drugs.

"Carter… Michael… Price."

"Date of birth?"

"January 13, 1997."

Jung consulted his palette and nodded. "Great, that matches your biochip. Alright, you're stable for now. I just need you to sit tight, focus on your breathing, and we should be there in about thirty minutes."

Carter blinked. It was too bright in the ambulance. Long LED strips ran the length of the ceiling, giving off a harsh white light that stung his eyes. He tried to lift his hand to shield his face, but his body wouldn't respond. He wondered if he were strapped down because no matter how he shifted, he couldn't get anything to move. He flashed back to the roof, to coming down on Delta's knee.

"I can't feel my body," he said, choking back a sudden lump in his throat.

"Perfectly normal," said Jung. "You're hooked up to a cold therapy drip as well as a nerve block. It stops the pain but also prevents you from moving around. If you start to feel a numbness that grows into pins and needles, let me know. Your biochip should handle that, but I can always give you something more."

Carter shook his head, inundated by flashes of Delta.

"I think she broke my back."

"Who did?" asked Jung.

"A synthetic woman. She tried to kill all of us."

"Sounds like quite the party."

Carter turned his head slightly. Jung didn't seem to be paying attention anymore. He was seated on Carter's right, and the palette he held obscured the lower half of his face.

"Champion, are you there?"

Jung looked over his shoulder, but Carter ignored him and turned away. He wasn't sure his whisperer was even still in his ear; it felt like it, but the magnetic attachment was only so strong. He held his breath for the second it took for his Red Velvet to emit its signature harmonic tones.

Yes, Master.

"Do I have any messages?"

"From who?" asked Jung.

Carter narrowed his eyes and tried to turn further away. Some kind of tubing prevented his neck from rotating to the left.

Message from Braxton Marshall Price. "Here's an infographic I found that shows you which fork to use and which glass is for what. Don't fuck it up with those richies. They're better than us." An image is attached. You can view it on your phone.

"I don't think I'll be seeing that phone again," he replied, imagining it sitting up in his room at Vise Manor. His neck itched, as if ants were running over his skin and biting at his flesh. "Anything else, Champion?"

Message from Pyrosius. "Send nudes of Jane."

Carter rolled his eyes. He couldn't even remember the last time he saw Jane. Was it in front of the house? In the foyer? She had tried so hard to avoid his gaze. Had he been conscious when the paramedics arrived, he might have asked about her before he let them load him up. As it stood, he had no idea if she was even alive.

That was sure to get him a low client rating if she made it back to the office. He wondered if Adelai Associates would even take his calls again. He assumed Jane wouldn't.

He felt a tear run down the side of his face.

"You okay, Mike?" asked Jung. "If you're feeling any pain, let me know and I'll up the dosage. There's no reason to suffer."

Carter shook his head slightly. "I'm not in pain. I think I just realized how lucky I am to be out of there. Some of the others didn't make it. And I don't know what happened to the girl I was with. I didn't get to check on her to see if she was okay."

"You wouldn't have been able to do anything in your condition."

"That's not the point," he groaned. "It's just common decency. I'm the one who invited her to that nightmare. If it hadn't been for me, she'd be... well shit, I don't know where she'd be."

"Visiting my parents," said a gravelly, female voice. The woman cleared her throat and then spoke in Jane's clear and blithe timbre. "My mom would probably be up by now making breakfast for me."

Jung looked over his shoulder and then scooted down to the far end of Carter's stretcher. He slumped onto the floor and went back to scrolling on his palette.

Carter was afraid to look, but once the paramedic moved, it became clear there was another stretcher in the back of the ambulance. Out of the corner of his eye, he saw Jane's brown hair splayed out above her. The rest of her body was a white blur. He took a deep breath, turned his head.

"You made it," he said.

Jane nodded at the ceiling. "Just barely. Delta broke my leg in six places."

"Seven," said Jung.

"Seven," repeated Jane. "With one kick, Carter. *One kick.*" Her words were languid and drawn out, unconcerned with the normal speed of conversation. "And he wanted those things just walking around out in the world with us. It's like all those Superman movies where the government gets all nervous because he could basically kill anyone and everyone whenever he wants. I've met some stupid men in my lifetime, but Winston Vise eats the grande taco. I wouldn't trust him to program my microwave..." She paused, drifted for a moment. "I could go for some popcorn. Like we had the other night. With lots of salt and M&Ms."

"Are you okay, Jane?"

"Someone slipped her a code card," said Jung. "Couple more hits and she would have overdosed."

"It's alright," said Jane. "My boss knows I took it. She would have said something if... if..." She went silent again. Her eyes, which had only been half open to begin with, closed.

Carter let some time pass before asking, "Do you know who else survived?"

"Huh?" She took a sharp breath. "Lucas is dead, not sure when that happened. Simone is dead. *Reno* is dead." A groan. "I saw Laura walking around wearing a blanket, but I didn't see her husband. Roma's the one who gave me the code card, so I know she's alive. Diya too. That's everyone, I think."

"You have a good memory, considering…"

Her head rolled to the side; fuzzy eyes tried to focus on him. "I saw a TIL the other day about where the word *screensaver* comes from. It's not the way Boomers use it to describe their desktop background. Back in ancient times, you know, the early nineties, they didn't have vidscreens like we have now. They had CRVs—"

"You mean CRTs."

"Yeah, that. Well, if you paused on an image too long with a CRT, it would literally burn into the screen, and you would see it even when you turned off the monitor. And when it was on, the image would still be there like a ghost. So, the first screensavers did just that; they saved screens from burn-in."

"Huh," said Jung.

Jane smiled. "That's what this fucking night is for me. Mental burn-in. I see this ghostly image of Simone's crushed face all the time now. When I close my eyes. When I look at you. I see her, and I see Adelai's anguish. I see Laura looking a hundred years old… wet and crying and calling for her husband. I don't think that's ever going to go away."

"I'm sorry," said Carter.

"I don't blame you, sweetie. You couldn't have known. I mean that." She returned her eyes to the ceiling. "Besides, it was probably time for me to move on anyway. I have enough to live on for a while, enough to get far away from the city."

Carter understood. Getting away from the city and the people and the noise had been one of the reasons he'd decided to move out to the country. It certainly hadn't been for the nightlife in the nearby town of Jensen.

"Where would you go?"

Her voice turned wistful. "California. Some place like San Diego or somewhere around there. I've been a few times and always liked it. Or I don't know… Colorado. The snow. Small cabin…"

"I guess if you leave, I'll never get to see you again."

"Would you want to?"

"I don't know… we've been through something together."

"Yeah…" Jane sighed. "I can just imagine us years from now, standing at the altar, and the priest asking if I take you as my husband, and I look into your eyes, and all I see is Simone's busted face. When our kids are screaming and crying, all I'll hear is Delta beating the shit out of Adelai. No, sweetie. This is our last engagement. This is how you get to remember me—with a shattered leg and doped to the gills. I know this isn't how you wanted it to end, but I'm sure the company will reimburse you."

Carter couldn't feel his chest, but he felt the heat rise up behind his sternum. It flared until it began to itch, and he tried once more in vain to move his arms.

"I didn't say I wanted to get married. I was thinking more of having someone to talk to. I don't imagine there are many support groups for people who were almost killed by synthetic humans. Maybe in Perion City, but not out here."

Jane chuckled. "Sorry. I just assumed you were in love with me. Sometimes it's hard to recognize the real thing when you spend most of your life pretending. God, I sound like an asshole."

"Yeah," said Carter.

"Now we're both assholes."

He laughed with her, acutely aware of how his body *didn't* shake.

"I'm glad you made it, Jane. And I hope the company pays for your new leg."

"They will. Any injury sustained in the line of duty, they cover." Her eyes turned to him again and she smiled. "Except a broken heart."

"You're not going to let that go, are you?"

"Not until we get to the hospital."

"How much longer, Jung?"

The paramedic answered without looking up. "We should be there soon."

Carter groaned.

"Tell me about the house we'd live in," said Jane. "Would it have a white picket fence? Oh, and a rec room with a dart board? We could tell the kids the story of how we met over a glass of malbec."

"This isn't fair. I can't cover my ears."

"Sucks to be you, Carter Michael Price. What kind of decorating do you think we'll do in the house? Modern? Colonial? Could we have a fireplace and hang a family portrait over it? Of course, you'll probably want somewhere to play your naughty VR games. I guess we could put that in the basement. Gonna have to get a lock on the door to keep the little Prices out."

Carter called out to Jung.

"More drugs, please," he said. "I'm in serious pain now."

Jung laughed and shook his head.

SIXTY

For the first time in her life, Diya tried to load a code card and her biochip said no.

It didn't speak so much as emit an annoyed buzz that ran up the back of her neck and tickled her scalp, but the message was clear—*no more synth for you.*

Diya understood, or at least, thought she did. There was a fog in her brain that had been growing since the lightning strike on the roof, and it felt so much like fatigue that she thought maybe a hint of synthetic caffeine would be enough to jolt her back into full consciousness.

Her biochip disagreed, as did the paramedic who checked her out on the roof. They wouldn't even let her climb down on her own, despite her protests and demonstrations of how straight she could walk. Instead, they made her ride in the basket they'd attached to the winch to take Carter down, which was still operational even after the lightning strike. She'd watched the roofline recede from within her wireframe coffin, all while the paramedic above her shouted at her not to fall asleep.

The next few hours passed in a blur. All she wanted to do was close her eyes and fall over into the wet grass. At some point, a female nurse came by and helped her into the house to the parlor where the fire was on the verge of going out. She sat down next to the glowing embers and closed her eyes, but again, they wouldn't let her sleep. They had so many questions—the paramedics, the nurses, the police—and uniform after uniform sat down in the chair opposite her to grill her with palette in hand. Most of the time, she had no idea what they were even asking, and her answers meandered for so long that she often forgot the original question.

Sunlight crept along the rolling grounds of Vise Manor beyond the still-damp windows, and before long, a man in a blue FBI jacket sat down across from her and pulled a small notebook from his pocket. He was an older man, unshaven, with flecks of white in his beard. Shoulder-length black hair was slicked back over his head, as if he'd just come out of the shower. He clicked a black pen three times and then looked at her.

"Ms. Singh, correct?"

She nodded. "With an *h* on the end."

"Singh with an *h*, got it." He scribbled in his tiny notebook. "I'm Special Agent Alex Hamilton, no relation."

"To who?" asked Diya.

Hamilton frowned. "Yes, well. I have some questions for you, some things I want to get sorted out before we get a bunch of aggregators buzzing around out here. I've heard from the first responders and some of the victims; they all pointed me to you."

Diya nodded solemnly. "Of course they did. I guess it is all my fault. None of them would have been here if it weren't for me."

"Can you elaborate on that? You are an employee of Mr. Vise, correct?"

"Personal assistant and liaison," she replied. At least, that was the title listed under her smiling profile picture on Pattrn Business. "I coordinated the dinner party and the invitations and pretty much everything else except the synthetics. Mr. Vise told me who to invite. I just made sure they had enough to eat and drink."

"How long have you worked for Mr. Vise?"

"Since March. Before that I worked at Dahlstrom Academy as an event coordinator." She paused, remembering the last fundraiser she'd put on—an elaborate gala on the sprawling lawn of Victoria Dahlstrom's home in Pennsylvania.

"And were you paid regularly?"

"Yeah... I..." She wondered if she'd heard the question correctly. "Why are you asking that?"

Hamilton continued to scribble. "Just pulling threads, Ms. Singh. When I get an early morning call telling me there have been multiple murders at the home of a tech elite like Winston Vise, the first thing I do is run his name through the databank. On the drive over, I went through Vise's financials and found some irregularities. There are records of him cutting checks to his employees, but I thought I'd get confirmation from someone who actually worked for him."

His words ran together as Diya swooned.

Financial irregularities?

Her surprise was short-lived. After everything she had learned about Winston tonight, finding out he may have been late on his taxes wasn't exactly groundbreaking.

"I... I'm sorry, Mr. Hamlin—"

"Hamilton. Agent Hamilton."

"Yeah, that." Diya put her hand to the side of her head. "I've been awake for over twenty-four hours now. I don't think I'm going to be much help until I can get some sleep."

"I understand. My forensic team won't be here for another couple of hours. If you'd like to take some time, we can speak more later. Just please don't leave the property."

"Am I under arrest?" She didn't know why she asked. Perhaps Rakesh Singh had spoken through her.

"No, ma'am." He flipped his notebook closed and slipped it into his pocket. "But I've got six bodies headed to the morgue right now and four vics with serious injuries. The only people left standing are you and Roma Owens. I'm not saying that's anything, I'm just asking you to stay nearby."

"Fine, whatever," said Diya, squeezing her temples with one hand. She refused the agent's help as she got out of the chair and shuffled to the stairs. Though the steps had not changed at all, she felt the staircase now resembled the ancient Aztec pyramids with their steep grades and tiny ledges. Her knuckles went white as she gripped the banister.

The agent stood in the foyer and watched her climb.

Diya sighed when she made it to the second floor, but still had to put a hand out to the wall to steady herself. The door to her room was open—all of the doors were—and at the end of the hall, a pair of policemen were coming out of the Blue Room. The man and woman nodded to her but said nothing.

With the door closed and deadbolt engaged, Diya put her head against the wood and let the fog spill over her. She had spent every second since the roof trying to push it back, but now she gave in and reveled in the numbing comfort it brought. She thought about the bed and willed herself to turn around.

She laughed.

Oh yeah. The window.

Glass covered the floor, and the white drapes flanking the large hole in the wall billowed in the steady breeze. The room felt twenty degrees cooler than the rest of the house, but all Diya could think about were the thick covers on the bed, where thankfully, no glass had fallen. She didn't give a second thought to how dirty her clothes were or how much synthetic blood was caked on her shins; she just got into bed, put her head on the pillow, and let sleep take her.

The wind blew.

Sirens receded.

Before it could all drift away, a voice spoke from below.

"Is that you, Diya?"

Diya rolled onto her stomach and looked over the side of the bed. Half of Nancy's face was sticking out from under it. She had a cut on her forehead and some green blood still smeared into her hairline, but otherwise looked unharmed.

"Where the hell did you come from?"

Nancy shot a glance at the door. "I've been hiding out since the cavalry arrived. All I saw was a black helicopter drop down out of the sky and then there were men with guns running all over the place. I figured it was a good idea to disappear."

"And you chose to hide under my bed?"

"I was hoping you would come back." She smiled. "Is everyone still here?"

"They took the bodies away, and everyone else went to the hospital except Roma. She was here for a while but then a fancy lawyer showed up and whisked her away. I guess she really did work for Perion Synthetics."

"I meant the men with guns."

Diya sighed. "All I know is the FBI is here now. One of the local cops told me the FBI takes murder by synthetics very seriously. I'm sure they're going to be here for a couple of days tearing the house apart. You're gonna want to be gone soon."

"Just like that?" asked Nancy. "You'd let me leave?"

"I don't own you, and honestly, how could I stop you?"

"I guess that's true."

She was quiet for a moment, so Diya asked, "Where will you go?"

A shrug. "Back home, probably. See if there's any work for a synthetic Japanese woman in Chapel Hill."

"Chapel Hill?" The fog billowed in Diya's head. She waved a mental hand at it. "I thought you were from Raleigh."

Nancy blinked. "Originally, yeah. But now I'm over in Chapel. It's a nice little town." She looked away, as if imagining it.

Her pillow was achingly soft. It tugged at her, drawing her toward sleep.

"You look worn out," said Nancy.

"Aren't you?"

"I don't sleep anymore." She laughed, and Diya laughed with her.

There may have been other words spoken, but she couldn't hear them over the distant footsteps and flapping of the curtains. Diya closed her eyes and drifted, thinking of Nancy returning home to North Carolina, perhaps riding the rails or hitchhiking like a drifter. Would she stand outside the windows of her own home like a stray dog and watch the happy scene within?

What kind of life was that?

Diya couldn't come up with an answer before she fell asleep.

The shadows in the room were shorter when a knock came at the door and woke her up. Diya groaned and rolled out from under the heavy sheets. She put her feet on the floor; even the plush carpet between her toes felt inviting.

"Who is it?"

"Special Agent Hamilton," said a deep, male voice. "My team and I would like to get your statement now."

Diya covered her face with her hands. They smelled of blood and dirt.

"Do I have time to shower and change?"

A pause. "Please hurry. We're eager to speak with you."

"I'll be quick."

Footsteps receded beyond the wall.

Diya counted another ten seconds before saying quietly, "Alright, he's gone. You can come out now."

When no response came from under the bed, Diya got down on the floor and put her cheek against the carpet. The space under the bed was dark, but she could see there was no one there. Diya got up and checked the armoire, the bathroom, and the little water closet, but her suite was empty. She trod carefully over to the broken window, unable to get closer due to the shattered glass on the floor.

Outside, the sun shone brightly, gradually erasing any evidence a storm had ever blown through. It was a beautiful Saturday, and she was alive. The realization hit her all at once, and she began to cry. She watched the green hills blur. Had Nancy fled that way? Down the side of the house, through the rear courtyard, and into the never-ending sea of wild grass?

After her little nap, the fog wasn't as dense anymore. A name came to her out of the gloom. She walked over to her suitcase and retrieved her phone. She launched the Reminders app and typed *Nancy Breyers Chapel Hill.* She put the phone away, ignoring the red notification badges indicating unread messages and missed phone calls.

All of that could wait.

The only thing Diya wanted now was a shower and fresh clothes.

Then she would be ready to start cleaning up.

SIXTY-ONE

The twin towers of the World Trade Center stood like two glittering beams of silver light in the afternoon sun.

Adelai hadn't seen them up close in years, not since the Adelai Associates offices had packed up and moved thirty blocks to the north. With her condo so close to the new location, she had no reason to venture this far south into old NYC anymore. The late 70s architecture and exposed steel and lingering smell of human rot was familiar and yet, not something Adelai wanted to be a part of. Even the traffic was a holdover from a bygone era, full of gasoline engines and the last vestiges of the Yellow Cab company. Watching it all from the backseat of the town car was like viewing a scene from a movie, with the glass of the window taking the place of the silver screen.

"Ma'am, we're here."

The driver's voice came tinnily through the intercom, and as the car pulled up next to the curb, Adelai adjusted her jacket and slipped her shoes back on. She waited for the door to open, then told the driver she wouldn't be long and that he shouldn't move unless he's about to be towed. He nodded, accompanied her to the entrance of Big Apple Roast, and opened the door for her.

The smell of coffee wafted over her, followed by vanilla and bitter cappuccino. The coffee shop was surprisingly busy for mid-afternoon, with every table in the establishment's footprint occupied by haphazard arrangements of laptops and palettes. Workers behind the bar to the left buzzed like little bees, running from one stainless steel machine to the next, pulling levers to emit puffs of steam into the already humid atmosphere. A display case full of sugary breads caught her attention; cinnamon rolls, muffins, and donuts sat decadently beneath stark white light.

Adelai hadn't eaten all day, hadn't been eating much lately. In the last two weeks, she had started every morning by forcing down thirty-two ounces of a glowing green smoothie, hoping it would be enough to sustain her throughout a day of hiding beneath the covers in a dark bedroom waiting for the pain to go away. Sometimes friends came by with food—acquaintances really, people from work—but whatever Harold the doorman put in the fridge, Adelai would just throw away the next morning. He had even brought her food himself a couple of times, a spicy shrimp fried rice from Simone's favorite Chinese restaurant two blocks south. She had thanked him, despite the smell making her physically ill.

It took a while to find a particular face in the crowd at Big Apple Roast. Hardly anyone had looked up when the door opened, so Adelai found herself drifting between the tables, leaning slightly to get a look at the faces around her. It wasn't until she reached the raised dais in the back of the shop that she found the young woman she was looking for. She was sitting in a half-booth, studying her palette, and nursing a steaming white mug.

Adelai stood near the table and waited.

Finally, Jane Moretz looked up, and when recognition flashed behind her eyes, she put down her cup.

"Mrs. Vaught, hi. I'm sorry, I wasn't expecting to see you here."

"I've been trying to get a hold of you," said Adelai, folding her hands. "I went to your apartment, but your doorman said you'd gone out for coffee. I hope you don't mind. I implied it was urgent."

"Is it?"

Adelai smiled thinly, nodded to the lone chair pushed up to the table. "May I sit?"

"Better you than some hot shit lawyer trying to hit on me while I enjoy my book."

The chair was hard and had some kind of indentation in the general shape of a human butt. Adelai slipped into the grooves but couldn't find a comfortable position. She squirmed for a moment before feeling Jane's eyes on her.

"How have you been?"

"Not bad," said Jane. "You guys bought me a new leg. It's biochip-controlled, so I've been up and walking for a few days now. Today's the first day I tried crossing a street." She gestured with her elbow to a cane leaning against the booth. "The doctors say I'll be back to normal in a few weeks. Like it never happened."

"Except for the scars."

Jane nodded, let her eyes wander over Adelai's face. "I don't see any on you," she said. "You're doing okay?" Before Adelai could answer, Jane added, "I'm sorry I didn't come to the funeral. I appreciate you inviting me, but I just couldn't imagine myself rolling up in a wheelchair and taking attention away from what was important."

"I understand." Adelai felt tears begin to well in her eyes. "It was a small service. Two of her younger sisters came. My older brother. Nobody asked questions." She huffed. "As if they needed to. The feeds are still talking about *Murder at Vise Manor*. It's disgusting."

Jane put down her palette and picked up her mug with both hands. After a long sip, she said, "I haven't listened to any of it. Aggregators keep calling me, wanting to ask me questions. Cameron Gray from VFeed offered me five-thousand dollars for a five-minute phone call. It's nuts. My building added extra security just to keep people away."

"I know. They've been billing us." Adelai smiled.

"It won't be forever. As soon as my leg is good again, I'll be moving to California. I've got a friend in San Diego who's going to let me stay with her for a while until I find a place of my own."

"About that…"

"I've made up my mind, Mrs. Vaught. Not even God himself could keep me from leaving New York for good."

Adelai nodded, reached into her jacket. "I know. I got your letter." She unfolded the paper and laid it out on the table.

Notice of Resignation said bold text at the top.

"So then why are you here?" asked Jane. "Is this some kind of exit interview where I tell you how things could be improved?"

A sudden cacophony of car horns erupted outside, sending Adelai's pulse through the roof. Loud noises had turned into triggers for her; even certain sounds from the TV took her back to the night at Vise Manor, to Delta's modulated scream as she buried her fist in Simone's face.

Adelai took a deep breath, said, "No, it's nothing like that. I was hoping…" She had to look away from Jane's eyes, at the windows, at the table, anything else. "I was hoping you would reconsider." She waited for a dismissive laugh that never came. When she looked back, Jane had her arms crossed.

"I don't see how I could do that, Mrs. Vaught. To follow another client into uncertain territory, not knowing if I'll come back when the engagement's over. And if I do come back, will I still be intact?" She rubbed her leg. "I had my fun. I made my money. Now it's time for me to move on. Or did you honestly think I would be doing this my whole life? Making money in my fifties for middled-aged men who want someone that reminds them of their wives?"

"I'm not talking about coming back as an Associate."

"Then what? Management? You want me to coach the new girls, tell them everything is safe and fun and easy?"

Adelai sighed. "I would never ask you to do something you don't want to do. Everything you did while employed at Adelai Associates was your decision. And yet like so many other girls, I hear bitterness in the way you speak to me. I don't know if you felt coerced or compelled or what, but you're obviously tired of doing this kind of work." She paused for a long exhale. "I am too."

"Well, I mean, after what we just went through…"

"You sound like my shrink. Post-traumatic stress disorder. Nightmares about metal. Voices screaming in the dark. None of that changes the fact that Adelai Associates was mine and Simone's." She looked up at Jane. "Together. We started it, we ran it, and we made it into the most powerful female-run business in the country. But to think of going back to work without her, to sit in countless meetings while ignoring the fact that half of me is completely missing? I can't do it. Things can't go on like they did before." She touched her chest. "I can't."

Baristas called out names. Porcelain cups clinked on saucers.

"What are you trying to say to me, Mrs. Vaught?"

"I'm saying you should tear up this piece of paper and come back to work next Monday. Then you and I start training you to replace me as President of the company."

Finally, Jane scoffed. "I can't just be the President of Adelai Associates. Don't you need business training and degrees for that? The first time someone asks us about our taxes, I'll probably run out of the room screaming."

"That's what the CFO is for. And we'll appoint a CEO together, someone who will handle general business items, but at the same time, recognizes that you, Jane, will be in charge of the company's future. You will have final say over the girls we employ, the engagements they are sent out on, and how much security goes with them. And I'll always be a phone call away." Adelai tapped the table. "If I give it to someone else, a stranger, then I'll want a clean break. But if it's you... I'll answer the phone for you. This is how I can step away and not abandon our employees. But it only works if you say yes."

"I..."

"You don't have to decide today." Adelai pushed the paper across the table. "Take the weekend. If I don't see you at the office on Monday, I'll take that as your answer."

Jane shook her head, looked around. "I don't believe it."

"Believe it," said Adelai. "I've talked it over with my legal team, and they said—"

"No, not that..." Her attention had turned to the front of the store where a tall man in a flannel jacket stood just inside the door. His head was shaved, but he sported a full beard. Jane swallowed hard. "I meant *him*."

Adelai appraised the man further, then asked, "Who is that?"

"Danny," said Jane, absently. "Daniel Antoine du Montreal."

Something like anger flared inside Adelai. "The hacker? How the hell did he find you? If he's been in our system, I'm going to—"

"No. No, I told him where to meet me. Years ago. I told him where I'd be every Friday. When he didn't come after a month, then three, I thought he wasn't interested."

"And yet he continued to ask for you." Adelai recalled the many requests Montreal had made over the last two years, and all of them had been summarily denied at Jane's insistence. "Do you have feelings for him?"

Jane shook her head. "I don't know. There was always something special about him. I thought we had a real connection. And then after what happened in

Umbra…" She laughed to herself. "That night at Vise Manor, I rode to the hospital with Carter. He implied we had a special connection because we'd been through something traumatic together. I told him he was full of shit, but maybe it's true. Maybe when you hold someone as you're both facing death, you form a bond that lasts forever."

"You have a morbid sensibility," said Adelai, slipping out of the chair. She stepped down from the dais and faced Jane again. "For my own selfish reasons, I hope your reunion goes poorly." She offered a wry smile. "See you Monday. And if not, I'll understand."

Jane smiled back and nodded. "Thank you, Mrs. Vaught."

A young man carrying a tray of steaming cups stood to the side as Adelai made her way to the front of the coffee shop. Montreal nodded slightly, as if acknowledging they both knew Jane and were therefore somehow connected. She had every intention of passing him without stopping, but at the last second, she reached out and gripped his arm.

Newly installed augments in her fingers pressed too hard, and it took a second of concentration to dial them back.

Montreal looked at her offending hand and smirked.

"Tell her you love her while there's still time," said Adelai. "And if she says she loves you back, then you keep telling her, every day, multiple times a day. You don't stop, do you hear me? When she passes or you pass, the echo of your last *I love you* should still be in the air. Do you understand me, Mr. Montreal?"

He replied with a slow nod.

Adelai looked over her shoulder at Jane, who had stood from the booth to greet her unexpected visitor.

"And start with an apology."

She let go of his arm and pushed her way out into the afternoon air. Her driver stood next to the car and opened the door as she approached.

Adelai took a deep breath. The combined smell of exhaust and human rot filled her lungs. She knew Jane wouldn't show up on Monday, and it wouldn't have anything to do with Montreal either.

The car pulled into traffic, headed back uptown to a job she no longer wanted, to an office she could no longer stand to look at.

Now she had to find someone else to take over for her.

Either that or fire every employee and replace them with synthetics.

Adelai rubbed her head. Hunger was making her loopy.

"Synthetic Associates," she said, and laughed.

SIXTY-TWO

"How are you sleeping?"

Laura looked up from her folded hands. The sun had risen above the smaller buildings in downtown Houston and was now throwing its full weight against the east-facing windows of the Loren Building. Seated near the window, half-hidden in silhouette, was Sabina Wiejak, a counselor Laura had seen off and on for several years. She was a smallish woman of Polish descent with a slight accent that suggested English wasn't her first language. Not that her accent mattered; what drew Laura to her was her kindness. Her capacity for empathy—whether real or manufactured—made Laura feel seen, and more importantly, made her feel safe enough to share anything.

"I'm not," she replied, after a while. "I fall asleep and have these horrible, disconnected dreams, like there's something I need to do but can't remember what it is. That feeling builds and builds until it wakes me up and then… there's nothing but silence. It's terrifying. Being alone in the house just feels wrong."

Sabina nodded. She had a way of leaning forward in her chair to close the distance between them, as if her physical proximity offered more comfort. Sometimes it did.

"We talked about some ideas last time for the silence—noise machine, television. Have you tried those?"

Laura shook her head. "Robert could never stand anything like that. Even white noise bothered him at night. He liked quiet. I guess I grew to like it too. I put an old sitcom on the other night, but I just ended up watching it until three in the morning."

"Sounds like a good show."

"It is. One of our favorites about these Canadian farmers." She chuckled. "They talk funny."

Sabina never took notes during a session, but she always kept a palette nearby that she consulted from time to time. She picked it up and tapped.

"I see from your medical feed that you've been exercising in the morning. Ten days straight now. That's really good, Laura. Your body needs those endorphins now more than ever."

"I know. This isn't my first blue rodeo."

"Blue rodeo?"

"I just mean it's not the first time I've been sad. It used to happen a lot in college, but someone told me running helped, so I started doing that. Now anytime I feel down, I get on the treadmill in our gym and bang out four or five miles. It's hard to cry and run at the same time." She scratched the back of her hand. "I mean, it's not impossible. We've all done it. It's just hard."

Two quick knocks came at the door. When Laura called out for the knocker to enter, a bespectacled blonde woman popped her head in.

"Mrs. Hargreaves? They're ready for you in the conference room."

"Thank you, Julia."

The door closed softly, and Laura returned her attention to Sabina. It was easy to focus on the counselor when everything else in the office reminded her of Robert. Though the large desk and shelves of business books were now technically hers, she still felt like she was just visiting. She'd even had Julia remove Robert's tall-backed leather chair and replaced it with a shorter white one. She had no clue how long it would take for her to feel comfortable in his office, and honestly, she didn't care. There was no escaping Robert's lingering presence.

Maybe that was a good thing.

Sabina set her palette on the cushion next to her.

"I guess we're done for today, but I just want to say..." She took a moment to choose her words. "I don't have to tell you that everyone deals with grief in their own way. Some people collapse under its weight. Some people ignore it until it comes out in one huge destructive outburst. And you..."

Here it comes, thought Laura.

"You are doing everything right, and more importantly, you're doing everything that's right for *you*. You're exercising, you're eating well, and obviously you're participating in life." She gestured to the office. "You're here. You're not hiding."

"Robert would be disappointed if I did."

Sabina nodded. "My only word of caution would be to take it slow."

"I—"

"Please." Sabina raised a hand. "I just want to put this out there. There is such a thing as overcorrecting. My husband used to always complain when I was driving because I would drift onto the shoulder and the tires would hit the rumble strip and I'd take a long time to correct. It was because I didn't want to jerk the car back into the lane and maybe scare a nearby car. I recognized that I was out of the lane, but I made small adjustments to get back into it. Diet, exercise, socialization—these are good, small adjustments. Anything bigger than that... moving, starting a new job..." Her eyes drifted to the large desk at the far end of the office. "Just be careful, Laura. Don't overcorrect." She flashed a wide smile. "There, I said it. Thank you for indulging me."

"Thank you for listening to me," said Laura.

She stood and shook the counselor's hand, watched as she showed herself out of the office. No sooner had the door closed behind her than it opened again, with Julia looking a little flustered in her blue pastel blouse and black slacks. She had been Robert's secretary for almost a decade, and now she was Laura's.

"The board is waiting, Mrs. Hargreaves."

Laura crossed the office and drew one of Julia's hands away from the oversized palette she cradled against her chest.

"You've called me Laura since you began working for my husband. Why the sudden change?"

"You're the boss now. I wasn't sure what you preferred to be called, so I…"

"You came to our parties, our dinners. You've even slept a few off in one of our guest rooms. You watched Robert do this job day in and day out. I consider you a dear friend."

"Okay… Laura. Thank you for saying that. I consider you a friend too."

Laura gestured to the door, and they walked out together, falling into step beside each other as they turned down a long hallway. The corridor ended in two large wooden doors, which were closed.

They paused.

"First order of business," said Laura. "You read my remarks?"

Julia nodded.

"And do you think I'm crazy?"

"I don't. It's your company now. When Robert was in charge, he ran things his way. Now it's your turn, and you have to find *your* way. The success and failure of the Hargreaves Group has always balanced on the edge of one thing…"

"What's that?"

"Your husband's confidence that he was doing the right thing, whether it was actually right or not. If you go in there and speak passionately and honestly, they will see things your way. Don't let them think for one second that you're unsure."

Laura touched Julia's arm. "You sound like my therapist."

"I wear many hats in this role," said Julia. "And one of them is opening doors. Are you ready?"

Laura nodded.

Muted conversations came to a halt as soon as Laura stepped into the room. Seated around a large mahogany table were the twelve members of the Hargreaves Group Board. They all sat on other boards too, mostly in Houston, for companies that ran the gamut from oil and gas to technology to real estate. What united them all was a keen understanding of business, along with address books that could be counted in volumes.

They all turned to look at Laura. Some of them nodded while others smiled. A few were stone-faced and sat with their arms crossed.

"Good morning, everyone. I'm sorry to keep you waiting."

She walked to the head of the table and stood in front of a large vidscreen on the wall. Seated across from her and looking dapper and relaxed in a gray suit was Frank Kagan, head of the Kagan Group based in California. He smiled broadly when he caught her eye. She nodded in return.

A palette lay on the table in front of her. She tapped it once to wake it. The vidscreen behind her illuminated with a black and white photo of Robert. She glanced at it briefly before turning to the assembled board.

"Thank you all for being here today. I'll be brief." She took two steps back and raised a hand to the vidscreen. "Three weeks ago, my husband and your colleague, Robert James Hargreaves, was murdered by a synthetic human designed and manufactured by Winston Vise, a trust-fund con man whose misdeeds we're learning more about as each day passes. My husband wasn't the only one to be killed that night. Vise himself had his neck snapped in two by a machine. Noted author and futurologist Stanton Blumenfield had his throat cut and bled out on the kitchen floor."

Some of the board members squirmed in their chairs.

"An MX arms dealer named Reno Cardenas was strung up and crucified by these same synthetics. One of them was responsible for Robert's death. It held him underwater until he drowned. Then it came for me. Two of the synthetics were taking orders from a third, and it took a literal act of God to stop it." She pointed to the ceiling. "If there had not been a storm raging that night, I might not be standing here before you today."

A woman seated to Laura's left raised her hand and said softly, "And we're very happy you are."

Laura nodded, approached the table. She spread her hands wide as she had seen Robert do so many times before.

"You all know this. We all have access to the same feeds. The horror of that night is on a twenty-four-hour loop on every major feed in this country. And while Americans gawk at the spectacle, I fear they are missing the larger point."

"Which is?" asked John Curran, from her right.

"That it's no longer safe to go to a dinner party. Even if you're a God-fearing American who exercises their right to carry without a permit." She pulled back the right side of her jacket and patted the Glock on her hip. "Even if I'd had this that night, people still would have died. Synthetics are stronger and can take more damage than any human. Bullets simply aren't enough."

She shook her head, tapped the palette. A photo of Vise appeared on the screen.

"This man lied, cheated, and stole to build synthetic humans. He misled investors, falsified earnings statements, and pretty much bet both his fortune and reputation on being able to sell six little robots. If he had succeeded, he would have built more. Don't get me wrong; I'm not against synthetic humans. I'm just worried how easy it was for Vise to do this. All the accumulated code, all the blueprints, hell, even the imprinted minds… none of it was original work. If *he* can put it together, so can someone else. Someone crazier or more brazen."

"What are you suggesting?" asked a dour Andrew Chan.

"I say we level the playing field."

The board members exchanged confused looks. Laura let the conversation build for a moment before calling for silence.

"My husband's last wish was to live forever, to see what marvels the future will bring. I believe one of those marvels is the commonplace transfer of human minds into synthetic bodies. James Perion has already shown us it can be done, but so far, he's keeping it to himself and the people of Perion City. Starting today, a joint venture between myself and Mr. Frank Kagan of the Kagan Group will begin exploring a go-forward path to what we call *transcendence for all*. Not only will this mean immortality for anyone who wants it, it will mean our minds, our memories, our *souls*, will no longer be trapped in these fragile suits of meat and bone. We will be metal the way they are metal, and we will be strong the way they are strong. Ladies and gentlemen, it's time to leave our organic bodies behind."

"How would that even be possible?" asked Chan. "Perion owns the patent on synthetic imprinting. How do you expect to replicate the technology?"

"We don't," said Laura. "We get it from Perion himself."

"By stealing it like Winston Vise?"

"No, by doing what everyone here does best. We make a deal."

There was grumbling and head shaking around the table.

"I don't see it," said Chan. "James Perion isn't even in charge of his company anymore. And his son is notorious for turning away all callers."

Frank Kagan cleared his throat loudly. "If I may interrupt… Laura and I are meeting both father and son in Perion City on Wednesday. It's true, they usually wouldn't take calls from most companies, even ones as prestigious as ours." He nodded to Laura. "But when one of those companies is led by a woman who survived a mass murder by synthetics who were built off stolen designs, well… that tends to be of interest to the man those designs were stolen from."

More grumbling, some disbelief.

Chan spoke up again. "And what if we say no? Joint ventures like this require a majority vote."

"You'll vote for it," said Laura, locking eyes with him. "Or I'll dissolve the Hargreaves Group and transfer the assets to various charities. Make no mistake, ladies and gentlemen. My husband is gone. He left the company in *my* hands. If you can't handle that, you know where the door is." She waited to see if Chan had anything else to say. He didn't. "You have half an hour to decide."

With that, she turned and headed for the door, chased by questions that grew louder every second. With a hand on the doorknob, she paused and looked back.

"Mr. Kagan, will you join me? We have much to discuss."

He stood, buttoned his jacket, and nodded.

"You're the boss, Mrs. Hargreaves."

She liked the sound of that.

SIXTY-THREE

The fine white sand of Endless Beach sparkled under the midday sun.

On a canvas stage near the water's edge, a group of topless women in billowy white pants performed Capoeira moves while a small trio of drummers slapped out a lively beat nearby. The women danced and spun and flipped all around the large square mat, their dark skin glistening with sweat. A small crowd of maybe a dozen men and women circled the stage and cheered each acrobatic feat.

Farther down the beach, where the drums reduced to a pulse-like thumping, Carter dragged his feet through the sand behind him—first his left, then his right—mimicking the dancers he watched from a distance. He tried replicating the cartwheels and somersaults, but more often than not, he ended up face-down in the sand. Each time he faltered and groaned, it elicited a laugh from Roma, who sat nearby on a long blue towel.

"Few more decades of this and I might be decent," said Carter, standing and brushing the sand from his chest. He stood and studied the women again, trying to figure out where he'd gone wrong.

Roma shook her head. She stretched out her legs and adjusted the straps of her yellow bikini. "So what you're saying to me is that men are allowed to do Capoeira too? Not just half-naked women?"

"To be fair, the men are usually shirtless too. Who am I to turn my back on hundreds of years of tradition?"

"The casual exploitation of women is a cancer on our society. There's going to be a reckoning. I guarantee you."

"Yeah," said Carter, dropping into a low stance again, "I know. The patriarchy is going down hard. It's just a matter of time." He began to dance again, slowly, searching out the distant beat over the cries of seagulls. "Then again, outdated concepts of gender are being questioned every day. I heard Perion Synthetics is already producing non-binary models. Neither male, female, nor human. I think the more synthetics we have in the world, the less our archaic anachronisms are going to matter."

Roma narrowed her eyes. "Did you rehearse that speech?"

Carter lifted his leg into the air in a wide arc and brought it down into the sand.

"Nope. Top of my head. I'm not just a technology wunderkind, Roma. I'm a renaissance man."

"You can't even rent a car, renaissance man."

"Don't have to. I have three." He smiled sheepishly. "Besides, there's something about almost dying before your twenty-fifth birthday that really makes you grow up quick. Everything was travel and fancy hotels before, but now…" He trailed off, listened to the waves lapping at the shore. "Now I want to be part of something bigger. Not just a company. I want to make a real impact."

Roma picked up a sweating Corona and took a sip. A drop of the cold beer ran down her bottom lip onto her chin. She wiped it away with the back of her hand.

"Well, that's what we're doing, right? Using what we have to effect real change in the world? I mean, you and I got a glimpse of what happens when the wrong people try to build artificial humans. What Vise did went beyond simply ignoring the Three Laws. He ignored *all* laws. It was reckless."

Carter stopped and caught his breath. It felt good to move around, to dance in the warm sun while an attractive woman laughed at his antics. As horrible as the night at Vise Manor had been, at least he'd met Roma, and now she was hanging out with him on the beach, free of charge.

"I'm glad you're here," he said.

She cocked her head at him. "Are you getting soft on me?"

He thought about reaching for the double entendre, but then Roma wasn't paid to laugh at everything he said like Jane. There were real-world consequences to the words that came out of his mouth, and the risk made the conversation more exciting.

"Just telling you how I feel," he replied. "While I still can. You never know when a robot is going to break your back over their knee." Carter paused, let the moment replay in his mind, all too aware he had no choice but to relive it. "If you hadn't taken down the jammer, we never would have reconnected to the network. Adelai's security doesn't show. The cops and ambulances don't show. I die a slow and painful death on the roof. When you really think about it, I kinda owe you my life."

Roma pulled up one leg, shook her knee side-to-side. "Damn right you do."

A thundering boom cracked the sky, loud and close enough to make Carter stumble. His pulse peaked for a moment, throbbing in his ears. He turned to the source of the sound. In the great expanse of light blue hanging over the ocean, he locked in on a streak of brilliant white flashes, each trailing vapor like a comet hurtling through space. The shape held together for almost a minute before breaking apart, loosening their formation like a flock of geese getting into their flying-V arrangement.

Roma stood and joined Carter in the sand. "Is that supposed to be there?"

"No, but there's nothing we can do about it."

"What is it?"

The flashes blinked out. Before the last one faded, Carter said, "A greeting."

"From who?"

"Me," said a voice behind them.

They turned at the same time and discovered an incongruously well-dressed Asian man standing a few feet away. His long black hair was pulled back in a low ponytail behind his head. His eyes, which Carter knew to be a common black-brown in real life, were pools of slow-moving flames from which the occasional ember broke free and rose into the air. The man smiled, and when he opened his mouth to speak again, a light gray smoke poured over his lips.

"Sorry for the intrusion. I hope I'm not interrupting."

"You're always interrupting," said Carter. He turned to Roma. "Roma, Pyrosius. Pyrosius, Roma."

They didn't shake hands, but Pyrosius nodded and looked around. "This is Endless, isn't it? How'd you get this into BlueNet?"

"I didn't," said Carter. "I found a way out."

"Not bad. Well, I feel like I'm overdressed. Could we go somewhere and talk?" He looked at Roma. "The three of us?"

Carter nodded and took Roma's hand.

The beach dropped out from under them, falling into a bottomless black ether until it was nothing more than a dull blip in an infinite sea of dull blips. Once it was locked into place, the cavernous sphere around them rotated until they were floating directly over a different blip. Then the process reversed, pushing up a cream-colored rug and a hodgepodge of mismatched furniture. The floor stopped just below their feet, and they landed softly, the pressure growing gradually under Carter's toes.

Pyrosius let out a long whistle. "Man, I haven't been here in forever."

"Where's *here*?" asked Roma.

Carter replied, "My basement from when I was twelve or thirteen. P and I used to hang out down here trying to break into random networks all night."

Pyrosius crossed in front of a low, broken-in couch and opened the drawer of an end table. He removed a false bottom and then laughed as he pulled out a magazine. He showed it to Carter.

"Remember this issue of *Cheri*?! Aw, man, this was the greatest."

"Porno mags?" asked Roma. "Really?"

"My dad had parental controls on the network. We didn't figure out how to get around them until like, what, eighth grade?"

"I thought you were elite hackers already?"

"No, I said we *tried* to break into networks. We really didn't know shit." Carter plopped down on the couch and patted the seat next to him.

Roma joined him, pulling her legs up under her. She had changed her clothes while he wasn't looking; she now wore a simple blue t-shirt over white shorts.

Carter reconciled himself a branded *Thermite Paralysis* shirt and then rolled up the short sleeves. He liked the way his arms and stomach looked in virtual reality, though he knew Roma wasn't fooled by his ripped avatar.

"Did you have something for us, P?"

Pyrosius flipped another couple of pages in the magazine before waving his hands and making it disappear like a magician. He sat in the wicker rocking chair on the other side of the homemade coffee table consisting of cinder blocks and a panel of wood.

"I think I found our guy."

The lights in the basement flared.

Pyrosius looked around and chuckled. "I think your lamps just got boners."

"Are you serious?" asked Carter. "How?"

"Well, blood flowed into their little lamp penises and then—"

"Do I need to be here for this?" asked Roma.

Carter turned to her. "Remember when you sent me the raw data you took from the jammer, and I said I was going to give it to a friend to look through? This is that friend."

Pyrosius gave a little bow.

"He's the one who helped me find out about the stolen code in Vise's invitations. Ever since the Fall of Brigham Plaza, P has been indexing all the content and meta that got dumped onto the network. It's really impressive."

"That is true," said Pyrosius. "But the reason it took me so long to find this guy is because I didn't even think to look there first. The way you described Delta, I thought the answer would come from a military research facility or something like that. I only checked the Brigham database on a whim. And it just lit up, Blazer. Just lit the fuck up."

"Blazer?" asked Roma.

"He never told you his handle?"

Carter shook his head. "I was *twelve*. And I don't use it anymore."

"Can I call you Blazer in bed?"

Before he could answer, Pyrosius continued, "So yeah, it wasn't the actual data, since we don't have visibility into that, but what I found were patterns in the transfer. It was something like TCP/IP, but there was another layer, a transactional layer. It wasn't just a system copying a file to another system; it was actually building it at rest. And this is where it gets bananas. This transactional sequence, or whatever, occurred in reverse of what you sent me, which would make sense if it were something leaving Brigham Plaza, coming into VNet, and then rebuilding itself in one of Vise's synthetics. I think..."

"No fucking way," said Carter.

Pyrosius smiled. "I think the rumors of an artificial intelligence escaping Brigham Plaza are actually true and not just crazy conspiracy theories noobs are sharing in their little mining game. I think you had a brush with a true AI, my friend. I'm kinda surprised you made it out of there alive."

"Why's that?" asked Roma.

"Because there's only ever been one true AI, or the closest thing to it, that we've ever known about. It was a Vinestead project that killed a bunch of people when they turned it on for the first time."

"It's not him," said Carter, even as he flashed on Delta's last words before the lightning struck her, something like *I AM LA—*

"I think it was. I think you went up against Lassiter."

"That name sounds familiar," said Roma.

"Delta was a little off," said Carter, "but she felt psycho in a human way. An AI wouldn't be like us at all. It would operate on a completely different level."

Roma nodded, looked down.

"Hey," said Pyrosius, "who are you going to believe? Me? Or the guy who used to yank it to this massive bush?" He produced the magazine out of thin air and shook out the centerfold.

Carter blinked it out of existence before the pages could unfold.

Roma chuckled. "Casual exploitation," she repeated. Then to Pyrosius, "Okay, assuming you're right, how are we going to find him? Also, are we right to assume an AI is a *him*?"

"I don't think it matters anymore. Didn't you roast him with lightning?"

"Yeah," said Roma, "but like you said, the transfer into the synthetic was transactional. A rebuilding. A copy."

A plastic analog clock over the television ticked loudly for several seconds.

Carter locked eyes with Pyrosius, watched as they narrowed and then grew wide.

"He's still out there! And even though we can't find him directly, we can look for other similar transactions. If he builds himself the same way every time, we should know where he moves next." He rocked a few times in his chair before gesturing to Roma. "I like this one. Don't fuck it up."

"Yeah," said Roma, patting Carter's chest. "Don't fuck it up."

"We need to get moving on this, Blazer. When are you getting out of the hospital?"

Carter thought about his physical body back at Johns Hopkins.

"They built me a new spine, but it's going to be a while before I can get out of bed. They had to reroute the nerves through the augmentations, so they're all on fire right now. The doc said if they wake me up, I'll probably die from shock and then go insane."

"That's banana balls," said Pyrosius.

"But, when I do heal, the doc says I'm going to be unbreakable, just like that guy from that one movie, *Metal Spine Man*."

Roma chuckled.

Pyrosius jumped out of his seat. "Fuck, this is awesome. We're going after an AI. I gotta get started right away." He patted his pockets, as if checking for his keys. "Yeah, okay. I'm gonna get out of here."

"Let us know what you find, okay?"

"You got it, Blazer. Oh hey, before I go." He held out his open hand. "Could I have that magazine back? I need it for reasons."

Carter sighed and brought the tattered issue of *Cheri* out of limbo.

Pyrosius rolled it up, smacked his other open hand, and drifted up through the popcorn textured ceiling.

"You guys really are crazy."

Carter nodded. "You have to be if you want to go toe-to-toe with an AI that already almost killed you."

"Alright," said Roma, slipping her hand onto his leg, "then call me crazy."

They kissed.

Carter held her by the cheek as the walls of his childhood room dissolved, letting in the smell of sand and the distant thumping of a Capoeira beat.

SIXTY-FOUR

It wasn't until Thanksgiving week that the FBI let Diya back into the Vise Robotics offices.

The company officially folded just six days after Winston's death, after investigators brought to light a series of financial irregularities that included misappropriation and embezzlement. The long and short of it as explained by Special Agent Alex Hamilton was that Winston had taken money from investors and promised to spend it on one thing while spending it on another. One group thought they were getting a revolutionary type of battery that could power a home for a week. Another thought they were contributing to the development of nanocell surgical tools.

None of them knew the money's real purpose.

Fancy graphics on the nightly news had an ongoing list of all the little shell and dummy corporations Winston had created to generate the funds to build his robots. He had swindled a lot of people out of a lot of money, and the Feds wanted as much of it back as possible. When they raided the Manhattan offices, they took everything of value, including some of the paintings Winston had purchased for the boardroom and reception area. What they left behind were mostly personal effects, items that couldn't be resold and if unclaimed, would simply be trashed.

Diya had never intended to come back to the office. She wanted to put Winston Vise out of her mind and start fresh. She was actually at her computer updating her resume when the message from Hamilton came in. In it, he invited her to come to the office and collect her personal belongings, which he then inventoried in a bulleted list. Diya tried to convince herself that she didn't need any of it but seeing *photographs in frame x3* at the bottom of the list made it difficult to just write everything off. She knew those photos by heart.

Standing with Winston on the bow of his yacht, *The Nautical Smile.*

Standing with Millie at a Dahlstrom Academy fundraiser, dressed up in elegant but rented gowns.

Rakesh and Lamshka Singh in their thirties, holding small American flags the day they became citizens.

The thought of her parents smiling at her from the bottom of a trash can didn't sit well with her. She wrote Hamilton back and told him she'd be there on Monday at 10:00 a.m.

He was already there when she arrived at 9:45 a.m., sitting outside the building drinking a coffee. When he saw her, he grabbed a cup from the bench beside him and approached.

"I didn't know how you take yours, so I got you one of those Pumpkin Spice Lattes. You ever drink those?" His eyes radiated a soft amber glow.

"Sometimes," said Diya, accepting the drink. In truth, she was a sucker for PSLs, as Millie called them. She wondered if Hamilton knew and was playing dumb.

After she took a sip, he asked, "Want to head inside?"

"Do you have to come with me?"

He smiled. "Someone does, unfortunately, and I'm the only agent here today. I can have someone else chaperone you if you want to come back another time." He sipped his coffee while waiting for her answer.

"No, it's fine. Thank you for the latte."

He nodded, and they walked into the revolving doors of 39 Park. Diya glanced at the vidscreen directory as they passed through the lobby. The scrolling list of companies no longer contained an entry for Vise Robotics. Everyone was trying to move on.

They rode the elevator up in silence. Diya listened to the tinny music coming from above and tried not to gag at a female passenger's strong perfume. When they finally got off on the thirtieth floor, she went into a short coughing fit.

"That was pretty bad," said Hamilton. "It should be a felony to assault a federal officer like that."

Diya smiled weakly and waited for him to unlock the tall glass doors that led into the reception area. He did so with one hand and then pulled back a door for her.

She had never heard the office so quiet during the day. Even when she had to come in on the weekends, there was always music coming from an engineer's office or at least the frantic clacking of keys. Diya was always in the office early, regardless of how late she had worked the night before. Working for Winston meant preparation, making sure things were ready for him when and if he arrived.

For a moment, she stood frozen, unsure of why she was back in this place.

Hamilton took a loud sip and broke the spell.

Diya said nothing as she turned left and headed down the long hallway, staring at a spot on the wall where a famous painting of a matador mid-twirl used to hang. Now all that remained was the spotlight that hung over it and the vague outline of a rectangle. She turned right at the end of the hall and spotted Winston's office at the far end. The door had been removed from its hinges and now leaned against the nearby wall. Even from a distance, Diya could see most of its contents had been removed. What furniture remained was in tatters, with cushions stacked near the windows and metal frames unscrewed from each other.

"Is there anything left in his office?" she asked.

Hamilton, who had been following quietly behind her, replied, "Not really. We took his effects. Once we're sure there's nothing useful in them, we'll turn them over to next of kin."

"Did he have a next of kin?"

"Estranged father. Mother passed twelve years ago. Looks like dad cut junior a check and told him to get the hell out of the house. He founded his first startup six months after relocating here."

"Must have been a big check."

"More than you or I will ever see, that's for sure."

Diya nodded, turned left into her office. To the right, her private door leading into Winston's office was also off the hinges, though her outer door wasn't.

"What's with the doors?" she asked.

Hamilton shrugged. "I don't know. Lots of superstitions in the Bureau."

Diya shook it off, walked around her desk, and sat down in the chair. Her personal items had been gathered in a small pile in the center of her desk. She extracted the three black-rimmed frames and opened two of their backs to remove the photos. The third frame with the picture of her and Winston went directly into the empty trashcan beside her desk.

"Huh," said the agent.

"Do you have something to say?"

"No, I… I just wasn't sure where you two stood. We've been through the corporate mail server. Some mild flirting here and there. I imagine you worked a lot of late nights in your time here. Did you and Mr. Vise ever get… physical?"

Diya balled up a Chinese takeout menu and threw it at Hamilton. "That's none of your goddamn business. But no. Yes, Winston was charming and attractive and charismatic. You act like you wouldn't develop a little crush if a woman showed you an ounce of attention. He *lied* to me. He almost got me killed. I feel like shit and now you're kicking me while I'm down?"

Hamilton looked at his coffee. "I apologize. I'm just trying to get a clear understanding of what happened that night. Romantic involvement can make people do things they wouldn't normally do. The question has been raised whether you aided Mr. Vise in some way beyond what you described in your statement."

"I told you everything that happened that night," said Diya, through gritted teeth. "I didn't even bring a lawyer to that meeting even though my dad told me I was crazy. Winston asked me to throw a dinner, and if you don't count the part where half the guests were murdered, I think I did a pretty good job. I don't even know why you're still asking me questions. There were cameras in every room of that house, including the bathrooms for some reason. Why don't you just watch the video and see for yourself?"

"Can't," said Hamilton, shrugging and swirling his cup around.

Diya was tired of seeing his shoulders bob so nonchalantly, like this was all a game.

"What do you mean you can't?"

"Well, the nerds down at the lab said something about a tapeworm. Based on when you say Mr. Vise was killed, it was roughly twelve hours after that that all the data started overwriting itself. By the time we got access to the servers, the drives were dead. Zeroed out, is how they described it. Onboard capacitors fried the physical hardware too, just for good measure."

Diya sighed. For weeks, she had worried about faceless FBI agents poring over the videos only to have a clip of her in the bathtub being passed around like a meme. Having her privacy invaded like that had opened a hole in her stomach that stabbed at her randomly throughout the day. She was happy it could finally start to heal.

"What's the smile for?" asked Hamilton.

"I just… nothing surprises me anymore. I should have known he would be willing to wipe out his entire company and all of our livelihoods if he died. Because after he's gone, what does any of this matter, right?" Diya put the pictures into her purse and stood up. "All of this is garbage. You can throw it out."

"Sure thing."

"I guess I'm done then."

"Oh, that reminds me." Hamilton put his coffee down on a nearby shelf and reached into his inner jacket pocket. He produced a small phone with a light pink finish. "I've been meaning to give this back to you." He approached and held out the device.

Diya frowned. She'd considered her old phone lost and had already purchased a new one. At any rate, she definitely didn't remember giving it to Hamilton. It turned on when she tapped the screen. Strangely, it didn't ask for a passcode.

"Did you… did you look at this?"

"Personally? No, not really. Lab guys checked it out, said there was nothing of value on it. A few alerts popped up while it was in my possession, but that's it."

"Oh, okay. Then thank you for returning it. Now I guess I'll have a backup."

"Sure thing."

She slipped the phone into her purse and walked past Hamilton back into the hall. She was almost at the corner when he called out.

"Uh, one more thing, Ms. Singh. I did see a reminder that caught my attention."

Diya turned around. He was standing just outside her door, with seemingly no intention of following her.

"And?"

"I just found it out of place."

"Reminding me to take my vitamins or what? How's that out of place?"

Hamilton shook his head. "No, it wasn't anything like that. It was uh… just a name and a city."

Diya swallowed. Waited.

"Nancy Breyers. Chapel Hill." He paused, savoring the moment. "Does that mean anything to you?"

"No," said Diya, immediately. "Probably just a name I heard in passing that night. I do that sometimes, so I remember to look them up later. Maybe one of the guests mentioned her as someone who would be interested in Winston's technology."

Hamilton nodded. "Yeah, of course. Makes perfect sense."

"If you think I'm lying, then why don't you just look her up yourself?"

"I did. No Nancy Breyers in Chapel Hill. No Nancy Breyers in North Carolina. Not one. I thought maybe it was code for something. A mnemonic device, maybe?"

Diya took a deep breath, said, "No, just a random name. One of a dozen I heard throughout the night."

"And yet you only set a reminder for one."

It was her turn to shrug. "Yeah, I kinda stopped taking notes when the murdering started." She turned and walked away. Only after she'd rounded the corner did she put her hand on her chest to feel the frantic thumping of her heart. Questions swirled in her mind, and she didn't know which one to focus on first.

Who is Nancy Breyers? If she's not real, then who was Zeta?

She made it to the reception area and back out into the foyer. A shaky finger reached out and stubbed the down arrow. Her breath came fast and ragged. Inside the elevator, she put her hand to her throat and tried to slow down.

Just breathe, she told herself. *Just breathe.*

In the back of her mind, Rakesh Sing cleared his throat.

Who jumped out of your window?

"I…"

Who did you help escape, Diya?

Diya fell back against the wall and slid to the floor.

"I don't know," she whispered. "I don't know."

EPILOGUE

Julius Parker wasn't one to scare easily.

He'd been on the run from Vinestead International for more than two years, dodging countless men in countless cities, always one step ahead of the bullets adorned with his name. The specter of death was constantly at his back, ready to leap out of the shadows and strike if he ever stopped moving forward.

With all that in his rearview, what could one creepy little ghost woman really offer in the realm of horror?

Except, there was something about the villain of the Japanese horror flick he'd dialed up on his laptop that got under his skin. She wasn't exactly threatening—Julius imagined he could punt her across the room with one good kick—but she was *unnerving*.

It was mostly in the sound she made, a death rattle that tickled the small bones in his ear. Maybe in a movie theater, the sound wouldn't have been as intrusive, but coming through his high-fidelity Red Velvet whisperers, the rattle was positively intimate bordering on the obscene. He felt each percussive hit worm its way into his ear and gently scratch at the primitive part of his brain responsible for fear and dread.

In his recliner in the corner of a dark room, Julius Parker crossed his arms in his faded gray hoodie. He played with the ends of the drawstrings as the orchestra began to swell. On the screen, the movie's protagonist walked into an equally dark bedroom, lit only by the light spilling in from the hallway. Somewhere in the shadows, maybe on the ceiling, the ghost lay in wait. Julius knew this because as soon as the door opened, the death rattle began, growing in volume until it shook his whisperers. Violins screeched a high note that held, held…

He waited for the jump scare to come, but it never did.

The woman stood frozen in the doorway.

The violin screeched.

Death rattled endlessly.

Julius held his breath until he gasped, and only then did he realize the video had frozen. A small notification popped up from his taskbar informing him that the network connection had been lost. He tried closing the video window, but it wouldn't respond to his clicks. When the entire operating system refused to respond, he slammed the laptop shut and tore the whisperers from his ears.

The resulting silence was short lived as a triplet of heavy knocks sounded at the door. Julius waited, unmoving, wondering if he had simply imagined them. Through the gaps in the foil-lined windows, he could see rain falling hard against the glass. Lightning came at regular intervals, bordering the hastily applied foil in blue.

Knock-knock-knock.

Julius set his laptop down on the side table and picked up his gun. He slipped out of the chair, sliding the safety to the *off* position with a click that sounded like thunder in his ears. At the door, he put his eye to the peephole.

The lone, naked bulb over the porch lit his visitor from above, casting shadows over long black hair hanging down over a red jacket. The figure carried no umbrella; their clothes were soaked through from the rain.

"What the hell do you want?" he called.

No answer.

Julius opened the door just enough to get the barrel of the gun through.

"This is private property. Propiedad privado. Comprendo?"

"Your Spanish is terrible, Jape."

He registered the voice as female but couldn't place the accent.

"Do I know you?" he asked.

A face came up; steady eyes stared out from Japanese features. The woman smiled.

"Not as shitty as your Jamaican accent though," she said.

Julius sighed and lowered the gun.

"Holy shit," he said, opening the door. "I have to say, I wasn't expecting…" He gestured to the Japanese woman's body.

"Neither was I."

"So… you're a girl?"

She shrugged. "Looks that way."

Julius scratched his chin. "Well, I've always said you were forty percent female anyway, so this works."

"Can I come in or what?"

"Depends, did you get him?"

"Yeah, I got him."

"Was it what we thought?"

She nodded. "He downloaded into one of the synthetics, corrupted two of the others. It only worked because the guy who built the chassis stole tech from Perion Synthetics. If he ever gets into that network, we're going to have a real problem."

"Well, that's what we're trying to stop, right? We had him locked up for so many years. No one knows him like we do."

"It."

Julius nodded.

The woman stepped through the door. As she passed him, she said, "If you start thinking of Lassiter as a person and not a boundless, moral-free artificial intelligence, then we've already lost." Her mouth wrenched into a sneer.

Julius patted her on the shoulder. "It's good to have you back in the real world, X."

X, who Julius had first known as a young hacker from Austin and later as an ephemeral consciousness confined to a virus-laden homedir in Brigham Plaza, smiled back at him as a tall, Japanese woman with runway looks and an unbridled air of power.

"It's good to be back."

APPENDIX A

Adelai Vaught is the owner of Adelai Associates, a high-end escort service that was mentioned previously in *Brigham Plaza* and *Hybrid Mechanics*. In the latter, which took place in 2035, human Associates had been replaced by synthetics.

Carter Price appeared briefly at the end of *Brigham Plaza* as Jane Meade's follow-on engagement after her time with Danny Guns Montreal.

Jane Moretz made her first appearance in *Brigham Plaza* as Jane Meade, an employee of Adelai Associates.

Diya Singh is Winston Vise's personal assistant and previously worked for Dahlstrom Academy, an accelerated learning institute mentioned in *Por Vida* and *Veneer*.

Frank Kagan is the CEO of the Kagan Group, both of which previously appeared in *Por Vida* as the umbrella corporation that owns Vitra Synth.

Lucas Cotton is the founder of the MESH Foundation and creator of a peer-to-peer communications technology featured in *Por Vida* and *Hybrid Mechanics*.

James Perion and his son **Joseph Perion** run Perion Synthetics, a company that makes the most advanced synthetic humans on the planet. Their proprietary mind-mapping technology allows organic minds to be imprinted on synthetic bodies.

Calle Cinco de Mayo was a domestic terrorism attack that occurred on May 5, 2009 and affected the United States air traffic control system. 7,507 lives were lost, and the blame was initially placed on Calle Cinco, a cipher den led by Kaili Zabora. However, new evidence was brought to light in 2019 that suggests Vinestead perpetrated a false flag event.

THANK YOU

Vise Manor is the seventh book of **The Vinestead Anthology**.

If you enjoyed this book, please consider leaving a review.

Each standalone novel in the Vinestead Anthology tells a small part of a larger epic: the rise and fall of Vinestead International, the exploits of a rogue artificial intelligence named Lassiter, and a seemingly endless stream of idealistic hackers—each convinced they're the hero of the story.

Enjoy them in any order.

Xronixle (2007)

Veneer (2011)

Guardian Angels (2012)

Perion Synthetics (2014)

Por Vida (2017)

Brigham Plaza (2019)

Hybrid Mechanics (2020)

Vise Manor (2022)

House of Nepenthe (2025)

To learn more about the Vinestead Anthology and explore additional titles, please visit:

danielverastiqui.com